There was a bestial h
curb and the soldier
there lunged. The
squarely in the chest
not halt the creature's momentum. The body
into Stiles full force and knocked him right off his feet. One of the shotguns slid away across the pavement. He wrestled the cadaver aside, killed it, and went for Danner again, but by now there were others there to protect him, four of them at least, with more on the way. Stiles caught the next one coming in with another chest shot, side-stepping the hurtling body this time. A female caught him from behind and immediately began clawing and scrabbling for his throat. The shotgun flew backwards into her ribs with crushing force, over and over, and once the hold was loosened he turned and dealt with her permanently.

More of the creatures started to gather . . .

T. CHRIS MARTINDALE

Nightblood

ORBIT

An *Orbit* Book

First published in Great Britain in 1991 by Orbit Books
a Division of Macdonald & Co (Publishers) Ltd
London & Sydney

*All characters in this publication are fictitious
and any resemblance to real persons, living or dead,
is purely coincidental.*

Printed and bound in Great Britain by
BPCC Hazell Books
Aylesbury, Bucks, England
Member of BPCC Ltd.

ISBN 0 7088 4923 7

Orbit Books
A Division of
Macdonald & Co (Publishers) Ltd
Orbit House
1 New Fetter Lane
London EC4A 1AR

A member of Maxwell Macmillan Pergamon Publishing Corporation

To the memory of my father, Ted F. Martindale

Acknowledgment

Thanks to my brothers Ted and Kevin for their suggestions; to Ron, for technical advice and a talent for mayhem; to Rick, for the editing lessons; and most of all, to Mom, whose sharp ear and unending patience are a writer's best friend.

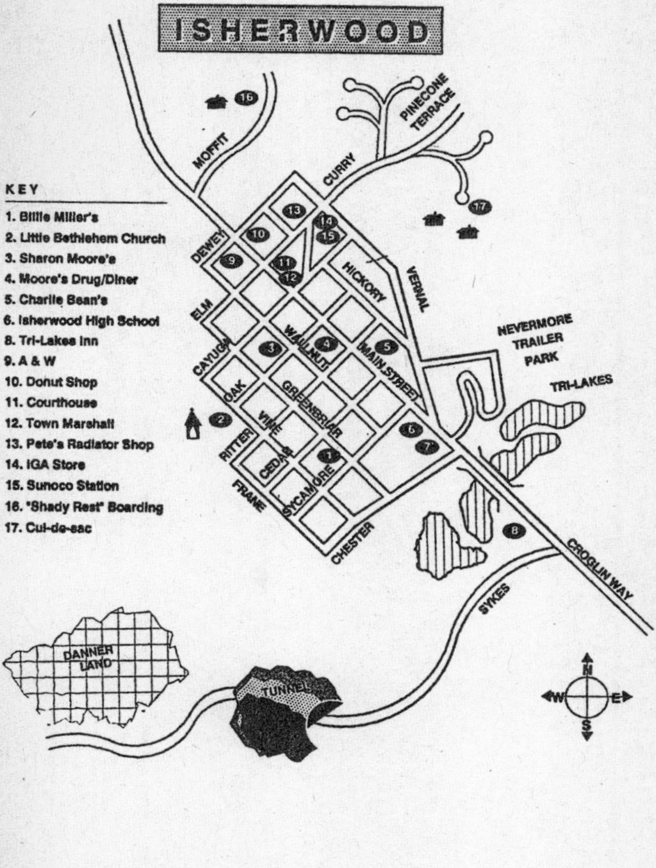
ISHERWOOD
KEY
1. Billie Miller's
2. Little Bethlehem Church
3. Sharon Moore's
4. Moore's Drug/Diner
5. Charlie Bean's
6. Isherwood High School
8. Tri-Lakes Inn
9. A & W
10. Donut Shop
11. Courthouse
12. Town Marshall
13. Pete's Radiator Shop
14. IGA Store
15. Sunoco Station
16. "Shady Rest" Boarding
17. Cul-de-sac
MOFFIT
CURRY
PINECONE TERRACE
DEWEY
ELM
CAYUGA
OAK
RITTER
FRANE
VINE
CEDAR
SYCAMORE
WALNUT
GREENBRIAR
MAIN STREET
HICKORY
VERNAL
NEVERMORE TRAILER PARK
TRI-LAKES
CHESTER
CROGLIN WAY
SYKES
DANNER LAND
TUNNEL
N
W
E
S

Introduction

Stiles lay flat on his back in bed with his eyes shut. And he listened.

The old television in the corner popped and hummed like a live wire, decidedly livelier than the rehashed *Tonight Show* monologue it played. Now and then the walls creaked, either from settling or the wind. And things scampered incessantly across the low roof. Too big for mice. Squirrels maybe, more likely rats. He'd shot one last week. The fields were full of them.

Outside the shack's single window the night was alive with sound. The breeze sawing through the tall, dry grass. The chirping of crickets. The light patter of kamikaze insects pummeling themselves against the screen door. In the distance a dog barked, and even farther away, an engine revved, then faded.

As he listened, he knew there was someone in the room with him.

He wasn't sure just how he knew. There had been no specific sound to alert him. The screen door hadn't creaked, and no one had jiggled the knob. The window had not rattled. There had been no heavy footfall, no spoken word, not even a cleared throat. No breathing.

Still, there was someone there. He could feel it. And he knew who it would be.

He raised himself up on an elbow, scratched his whiskered

chin, and looked around the dingy little one-room building he'd called home for the past three weeks. It was mostly dark, which was just as well since he'd grown to despise it in that short length of time. The solitary light in the room was the flickering glare of the old black-and-white Motorola in the corner, which due to age and a failing picture tube was fading in and out with annoying regularity, but receiving the audio undisturbed. He grunted with indifference. *Best of Carson* anyway.

The strobic flash of the TV was a distraction, but soon his eyes adjusted and he was able to look past it, to search the darkened fringes of the room where shadows gathered like strands of cobweb. There was the wobbly dining table where his gear was laid out, the matching stool, the Peg-Board on the wall where hoes and rakes had hung, back when this was a toolshed and not the caretaker's quarters. Next to the basin was a wooden counter, its top stained black by peat moss and potting soil, these days a home for his hot plate and toaster. His eyes shifted across the rest of the room. Past the Motorola and Karnac the Magnificent was a tall but leaning bookshelf that held nary a book, just some Beanee Weenees and a can of tomato soup and what little else he could afford from the Village Pantry near town. Beyond the bookshelf and hidden from the TV's luminescence was a La-Z-Boy from the early Mesozoic. Its time-frozen gears were locked somewhere between upright and recline, and its scaly, torn vinyl had been disguised with a throw cover.

And that was it. The entire room, the entire building in fact, and he'd found nothing out of order. Damn.

A movement caught his eye. It was very smooth, very subtle, and would have gone unnoticed had he not been looking for it. A shadow seemed to step away from the side of the bookcase. It took form and substance, glided laterally, and sat down in the La-Z-Boy and crossed its legs. A low whispery voice sounded, barely audible over the clamor of the studio audience. "You're getting dull, Hoss," it said. "If I'd been a robber I could've killed you."

Stiles's expression remained unchanged. "If you'd been a robber," he said, raising his arm and letting the sheet slip away to reveal the Smith & Wesson 9mm in his hand, "you could've tried." Across the room the shadowy figure gave a weak laugh in reply.

At least it sounded like a laugh. Chris Stiles could never be sure where his brother was concerned.

"It's been a while, hasn't it, Alex?" He lowered the stubby pistol and laid it on the orange-crate nightstand next to his Maalox and his reading glasses and a dog-eared Harlequin Romance.

Alex "laughed" again. "I don't know. Has it?"

Stiles remained humorless. "Only three years. S'funny, I was beginning to think you weren't coming back."

"You mean hoping, don't you?"

"I didn't say that."

The man in the shadows kept his same dull tone. "You didn't have to, Hoss."

Stiles frowned and shrugged off the other's words. "Do me a favor, Alex. Don't be screwin' with my mind tonight. I'm not in the mood." He swung his legs over the edge of the bed and groaned, stretching his stocky frame and wincing at the chorus of creaks and pops that greeted his ears. His muscular physique was still solid and impressive, but the years had been hard and the wear was beginning to show. He was constantly reminded of this by the roadmap of scars across his bare torso and thighs. Some he'd carried out of the jungles of Southeast Asia. Most he had acquired since.

"So . . ." Alex sighed. "How are you doing these days?"

In the relative silence of the caretaker's shack, Stiles never expected to hear his own laughter. But the absurdity of the question, especially in light of the shithole they were sitting in . . . Apparently his sense of humor had warped a bit in the last few years. "Look around you, Slick," he spread his arms. "Can't you see I'm in the proverbial lap of luxury?" He turned away just long enough to scoop up the Harlequin paperback and splatter a roach on the wall above the bed. "Paradise it ain't. You ever tried to get a job in Indiana? They're few and far between to say the least. I finally met this one old guy who was willing to give me a chance. He runs a manufacturing company in the basement of that house across the way. I've been working there for a few weeks now. Repackaging silicone—I take it out of here and put it in there, from barrels to caulking tubes. Sounds fun, huh? After a couple of hours with that stuff, your head is just roaring from the fumes and you can't get it out of your clothes, but what the hell, it's money, right? I get a whole two-fifty an hour in cash, that and this place to bunk in, and I've got to be damn grateful for that. So much for the American dream, eh?" He nodded toward the table. "The money would only stretch so far this time. I barely had enough for the ammo, let alone any groceries. So here I am, Alex. Somewhere in the boonies with less than ten bucks to my name. You tell me, how am I doing?"

Alex was quiet for a moment. "Don't whine, Hoss," he said. "At least you're still alive."

At that Chris Stiles went rigid. His weathered face tightened and his eyes flared. He stood slowly, stalked across the room, stared into the shadows at his brother and hissed, "Don't you lay that guilt shit on me. Don't you dare! I've given up everything for you. I've laid my ass on the line time after time. I've paid you back for 'Nam and more, so don't you ever start that shit. Alive, you say. Am I? Really?" He walked to the table, picked up his cigarettes, and lit one with a shaking hand. "I thought so for a while, when you didn't show up again. I had a job in Louisville. The money wasn't bad and I had friends. There was even a girl there. But then I get this feeling, this gnawing at the back of my neck. 'Go to Indiana,' it says, 'Alex is waiting,' and I drop everything just like that, just like before. I dropped my life for you. So don't ever get in my face like that again! You hear me?" He ground the Vantage into the ashtray after just a few puffs and sat down at the dining table, turning his attention to the reloading press there, his back to his brother.

For a while there was silence, save for Carson on the jittery tube. "Our first guest is someone I'm sure you're all familiar with. . . ."

Alex coughed, then cleared his throat. "Kind of edgy, aren't you, Hoss?" he managed weakly, but humorous quips weren't going to help him now. He saw that and fell silent for a moment, fidgeting uncomfortably in the old recliner. "I'm sorry, Chris. Really. It's just . . ." He paused, inviting the silence back while he sought the words. "It's hard for me, sometimes. All these years without rest . . . I'm tired, Chris. And scared. I'm afraid this is never going to end, that we're never gonna win. I guess it gets to me sometimes."

"It gets to me, too," Stiles said over his shoulder. His voice retained its bitterness but was now softer, more controlled than before. "I know it's not easy for you. And I'm still trying to help. I came, didn't I?"

Back in the shadows Alex smiled, or at least gave a semblance of a smile. The closest he could manage. "Yeah, you did, Hoss. That you did."

Charles Nelson Reilly began telling a story to Johnny and Ed. The picture had faded for the moment, but he could still be heard, rambling madly.

Stiles lifted the Uzi pistol off the table and worked the bolt on the compact submachine gun. "So, what is it this time?" he wondered aloud. "The boogeyman?"

Alex shrugged. "Who knows? I can never be sure. I just feel a tingle, like a Geiger counter. I know it's there, somewhere. It's real evil this time, and I mean hard-core evil. It's strong, and it's getting stronger."

Stiles reached for another cigarette. "You're not making me feel any better," he muttered around the butt. "You think it might be the Enemy?"

Alex's voice changed slightly. "It could be. It's damn thick this time, almost smothering. Just like that night." For a moment he seemed lost in thought, in a sudden surge of memory. After a moment he grimaced and shook it off and returned to the present. "Are you ready?" he asked.

Stiles turned to the table where the tools of his trade were laid out and asked himself that same question. *Are you ready?*

The Heckler & Koch carbine lay stripped and cleaned before him; originally a civilian Model 94 semi-automatic, it had been converted to full auto and an integral suppressor had been installed on the barrel. The laser sighting system had been mounted as well and was fully functional. He put the Mini-Uzi down beside it and checked his second Smith & Wesson 669, this one still nestled in its Cordura shoulder rig. Loaded and ready.

The center of the table was monopolized by ammunition: thousands of rounds of 9mm hollow points he'd loaded on the press over the last several days. There were also packages of factory ammo, all of a certain make. He preferred the Glaser Safety Slug, a particularly destructive round. On impact its copper jacket would simply peel away, allowing the number-12 shot within to expand and chew up the intended target. A Glaser round did maximum damage, and that was just why he used them, though they were too expensive for the wasteful autofire of the SMGs. So he saved them exclusively for his pistols.

He picked up his Alice pack and combat vest from the floor and inspected the pouches and pockets where his munitions were tucked away. In all, there were enough arms and armaments before him now to wage a highly effective one-man war. Which is just what he did for a living. If you could call it that.

Would it be enough? The doubts were always there, like splinters beneath the skin. "Ready as I've ever been," he finally reported. "Where do we fight this time?"

"Not far from here," Alex told him. "Just east of Bedford. A little town called Isherwood. And this time you've got something to go on. The word Danner. Whether that's a name of a street or a store, I don't know. Just Danner." With that the dark figure stood and stretched mechanically. "Will you start soon?"

"First thing in the morning."

"Fine." Alex stepped away from the La-Z-Boy and stood in front of the television. When the picture abruptly came back to life, his shadow was not visible on the walls. "I'll be with you if I can. If they let me."

Chris watched his brother and Johnny Carson at the same time, for his view was unhindered. He simply looked through Alex's torso, which was becoming more and more transparent as he watched. "Alex," he whispered, "what's it like to be dead?"

Alex "laughed." "You always ask me that, Hoss."

"Yeah. And you never answer."

Alex stopped laughing and faded from view.

Part I

THE HUNT

Chapter One

➢

It was midautumn in Indiana, and the countryside showed it. The trees clung to their garments of red and gold and copper and refused to let even one leaf flutter away without a fight. Still, some leaves did fall when the wind picked up, only to be blown across fields and pastures and swept into backyard drifts for children to dive into. The air was crisp and clean and carried the scent of woodsmoke. It was chilly out, but not too bad for late October—what the locals called sweatshirt weather, the perfect time for a pickup game at the church field or a ritual get-together, with steaks and dogs sacrificed on the patio gas grill.

But, strangely, few people took advantage of the day—few even paused to acknowledge those attributes. A pall of sorts had settled over them and the rest of the Midwest, and with its approach the fall no longer seemed so bright or beautiful. Now, all the people could see were the shapes of things to come, the naked trees and gray, shaded skies, the stark shadows, the white isolation of winter. "Enjoy this while you can," was the downcast phrase of the day. "It won't last long. You can feel it."

Of course, this creeping melancholy was not new to the region. It returned each year at about this time, and most people took the dismal nature of the season in stride or dismissed it entirely. But this year it seemed somehow different—more imminent, more . . . threatening? Perhaps, this year, there was something in the air after all.

A long-bed Dodge van wheezed along Highway 50, headed east. It was an older model, '76, and showed its age; it wore each ding and dent and scratch like a battle scar, and its fenders were losing the war to an angry creep of rust. The engine ran rough and would probably need a tune-up soon, if there was enough money. The driver's window was down, letting cool air spill in and music back out. The cassette was a worn copy of John Prine's best, turned up nearly all the way to drown out the whine of tire rubber on pavement.

Stiles wrapped what remained of the Egg McMuffin he'd picked up in Bedford and dumped it back into the paper sack that had spawned it. It hadn't been a pleasant eating experience, certainly nothing that would qualify as "breakfast," but it had put something in his stomach and calmed the tremors of hunger, and that was all it was supposed to do. It had also further depleted the already paltry sum in his pocket. Five dollars left, he reminded himself. Spend it wisely.

He let his mind wander as he tried to enjoy the scenic beauty along the roadway and the wry-witted music of Prine, and a casual glance in the rearview mirror almost caught him smiling. Despite the dreary winter herald in the air and the croupy engine and the lack of funds in his pocket, Stiles was in a comparatively good mood. Certainly better than he had been of late. And that surprised him. He'd been slowly drowning for weeks now, waiting, killing time as best he could, feeling the minutes inch by and the bitterness build within him and fill his throat. Waiting was always the worst. Too much time for worry and regrets and resentment. Too much time, period. Now the hunt was on again; at least he had something to do. He wasn't quite sure what it was or how to do it or what he'd be doing it to, but it had to be better than sitting idle.

The hunt is on again. Deep down, the thought gave him a tingle of anticipation, almost excitement. But he didn't acknowledge it. He never would.

He still felt guilty for yelling at Alex the night before, though he wasn't sure just why. Hell, he had a lot of gall just popping in like that after three whole years, no hello, no how's my favorite brother. Just smart-ass remarks and self-pity and here's your assignment, Mr. Phelps. Nothing personal. Just business.

He sighed to himself. *But what did you expect? An enthusiastic thank you, a pat on the back? An apology for not getting around to see you, maybe a promise to take in a ball game or go fishing like brothers really should? Get serious,* he snapped to himself—*this is Alex you're talking about. You couldn't expect things like that when he was alive, let alone now. Still distant, still impersonal. Always had been. Always will be.*

He didn't like ragging his brother like that. There had been a time when things weren't so bad between them. But he tried not to think about 'Nam these days. There were too many conflicting emotions interwoven with the memories, and he'd never been good at sorting the two out. The heat, the rains, the nag of impending death or dismemberment waiting just along the trail . . . He still had nightmares after all these years. But there had been good times as well. Hell, he'd be the first to admit it—he had thrived there. He had been alive. He'd had his skills, his men. And his brother. It was there that he'd finally gotten to know Alex, something the previous nineteen years had failed to accomplish. He had depended on Alex then, counted on him. They were finally getting closer. Or so he thought. He didn't learn until much later just how self-serving Alex's motives were. He got what he wanted, didn't he: an expertly trained killer to follow his lead like an obedient puppy, bound by a leash of family loyalty.

Too bad Alex didn't recognize the same bonds, he thought ruefully. Three years without a visit, without a sign or postcard, without knowing if he was hurt or happy or . . . At times Chris wished he had his brother's sense of loyalty. Maybe then he could walk out on this hunt and not look back. Maybe then he could start a life of his own.

His mood was darkening, and he was determined not to let that happen. He pushed Alex out of his mind. There were other things to think about.

A sign rose up on the right and swept by the passenger window. It was small for a roadsign, and his eye almost missed it. ISHERWOOD, 2 MILES, it read.

Stiles reached for a cigarette and patted down the many pockets in his down vest before remembering that he'd thrown them out somewhere south of Bedford. It was time to stop smoking, he'd decided. Maybe it was good that the hunt was back on; he'd been lax over the last few years, let his discipline slacken and his senses dull, and as soon as there was an opening his old habit had reasserted itself. It would be hard to stop again, but he'd do it. He couldn't allow his wind to be cut or his reflexes hampered. In his "business" the slightest slip could have decidedly unpleasant consequences. Like death. Or worse.

It was incentive enough. He settled for a fossilized piece of Wrigley's he dug from the van console. It tasted like cardboard but he chewed it anyway.

Up ahead another sign rose into view. It flanked the highway on the right, immediately opposite the merge of a secondary road, one which cut from Highway 50 at a sharp angle and snaked over a rise and disappeared. Stiles pulled the van onto the shoulder directly in front of the sign. It was really two sheet-metal placards on one pole, both light green and peppered with buckshot and 22s. The uppermost marked the new road as Croglin Way. The other sign simply read ISHERWOOD in modest letters and pointed down that same pike.

Alex's words echoed in his ears as he pulled onto that side road. *Real evil this time*. His hand strayed beneath his vest and touched the butt of a pistol for reassurance.

Croglin Way was a typical country road, well traveled but rarely cared for. The pavement was pocked and pitted and it played hell with the van's suspension. The road's edges were crumbling away, and the abundance of tire gouges in the mud beyond testified to its narrow width. It was lined on one side by near-naked shade trees that left a stuttering tattoo of sunlight on the windshield, and on the other by a jigsaw of farms and open fields. Rusty strings of barbed wire edged the latter, grown over with cotton-haired milkweed and withering stalks of sunflowers, and completely fallen down in some places. Leaves swirled everywhere when the wind picked up, through the fields and onto the road like brown snow, a constant reminder of winter's approach.

For those enamored with country life, this setting would have evoked a certain rustic charm. But not to Stiles. His reactions were guarded; he was always wary and watching, trying to see beyond the placid images before him. Because, in his experience, the essence of evil always seemed to permeate rurality. It was not a hard and fast rule—even the Enemy, whatever it really was, had killed Alex in one of the biggest cities in the country. But such incidents were generally isolated. The majority of the evil he had encountered over the years, no matter what form it took, had at least one foot planted in the countryside.

The reason had always seemed self-evident. Rural areas had changed the least over time and still had many ties to the past, especially concerning myths and superstitions. Nowhere else were they upheld and revered as they were in the country. Most were transplanted long ago from the Old Country and elsewhere, but the origin mattered little in the end. Folktales were well-loved traditions in these parts, a glimpse back into time, a heritage to be savored, even if a few of those old stories did raise the hairs on the back of one's neck. Hellhounds, haunted houses, boogeymen—they all existed out here, not consciously but down deeper, on a primal level. They fed a fear that still resurfaced from time to time when the lights went out and the sounds of the night closed in.

The stories fed the fear. And maybe it was that fear that attracted the evil.

What the hell, he shrugged. It was logical. Fear could indeed be a lure, a sort of spinner bait for the supernatural. But that gave rise to a counterargument: if it is tradition that binds these primal fears to the country, wouldn't that self-same tradition lend rurality its ultimate strength? In this age of city corruption and forgotten ideals, wasn't the country the last vestige of "goodness" in the world, the anchor of traditional values, the stronghold of steely, don't-tread-on-me, Bible-thumping faith? How could evil thrive in the very shadow of God?

Stiles had heard such sentiments before, so many times over the years that the inherent smugness made his jaws ache. It was usually given voice by a stark-eyed pastor whose piety refused to let him see the horrors that threatened him or his flock. No, it can't happen here, they would always say. There can't be a ghoul or zombie or whatever it is at our doorstep, no, not here. We are a God-fearing people, and we've supported charities and had pancake suppers and yard sales in the name of the Lord, and the collection plate is fuller than ever, and we're adding a prayer room next year, so evil cannot harm us.

Of course, not all the people he'd met were playing at faith or hiding behind it. There were those here and there who had it, true and unflinching, and some were of the church. But the rest were simply factory workers and teachers and farmers who relied on the Lord as often as their watch or their Chevy or the "AG-Day" report. Whether their vigilance ever brought them reward was anyone's guess, but he did know that they were good and kind people and therefore the perfect targets. How could evil thrive in the shadow of the Lord? Simple. If there was a shadow to thrive in, evil would be there, just as it had always been, moving like a wolf through a flock, searching for the weakest. For that would be the ultimate prize, wouldn't it? To get one of the good ones, to lure or cajole or steal or destroy just one. One would do.

He laughed to himself at how far he'd let his mind wander down Philosophy Road. Good versus Evil. God and the Devil. Heady stuff for a college dropout with no job and an Egg McMuffin ossifying in his gut. In the long run it didn't matter why evil was a country boy at heart. The only important thing was that it worked to his advantage. The country was a perfect hunting ground: not as many civilians or cops or places to hide. Here in the heartland he could roll into town like a wandering gunfighter, call the villain out, get the job done, and move on down the road. He could play the game his way.

And that was the only way to play.

His mind came back to the road. He was leaving the heart of cow country; the sprawling pastures were thinning out and more houses dotted the landscape now, not farmhouses but more staid, residential homes. He topped the next hill, and it gave him a sweeping view of the land. Croglin Way stretched out before him, down the side of the hill and across a relatively flat section of earth. Then it skirted the base of another lazy slope and disappeared behind it. But it was that flat place that caught his attention. For there, squatting on that very same road like a clump of birds on a power line, was the town of Isherwood.

Unconsciously, he patted his vest for a smoke.

It was a small town, barely a dot on most maps and on some

not there at all. Reaching its suburbs was no harder than turning off the main road. But its size was not due to youth. In fact, its founding predated that of its much larger neighbor, Bedford, by almost ten years. Rather, its size, from the start, had been a matter of choice. While the other towns had invited industry and commerce and loosened their belts with the resultant expansion, Isherwood was content to watch from the sidelines. It was still doing that to this day; it wasn't so long ago that the city council decried "fast food," but finally bowed to pressure and allowed an A & W stand to be set up. Still, there was some carefully measured growth these days, but all of a residential nature. Land and housing were cheaper here than the rest of Lawrence County, but still close enough to Bedford to allow a leisurely commute to the foundry or the quarries. Those moving to Isherwood offset those leaving, whether they be graduating high-schoolers or out-of-work families or simply people tired of the slow-as-molasses pace of small-town life. The population wavered at times, but on a good day it reached almost eight hundred.

Stiles passed the "Welcome to Isherwood" sign and the so-called Tri-Lakes that flanked the road just beyond—actually three overlarge ponds suffering from natural erosion. The adjacent motel, naturally called the Tri-Lakes Inn, was a small cluster of cabins and an empty parking lot with a perennial "Vacancy" sign out front. He noted that for future reference. On past the elementary school and the equally small junior high, he came to the four-block stretch of brick buildings that marked the center of town. He eased his van into the first empty space he found, got out, stretched, rubbed the tired eyes behind his sunglasses, and made a sweeping inspection of the town. He was parked in front of the Isherwood Barbershop, and it was flanked in turn by Isherwood Hardware and the Isherwood Coin-Op Laundry. At least they were imaginative, he mused. In the next block was a Woolworth's and a clothing store and Ed's Automotive, and in the block past that the signs pointed out the courthouse and the town marshall's office and, across the way, the local fire department. One engine, no doubt. There were a lot of empty shops and office space on either side of the street, one on the corner where Dante's Pizzeria had moved out, another across the way between the *Isherwood Herald*'s office and Moore's Drug and Diner. There were a few people on the street, just enough to cancel the first impression of a contempory ghost town. Most were older men, retired to the benches that lined the fronts of the shops, content to watch the days slowly pass them by. Their faces all looked alike to him after a while; wherever he went they were the same small towns, the same old men. A hundred Isherwoods over the years had jaded him.

He sniffed the air wishfully, as if his quarry might have some telltale scent he could follow. If only it were that easy. But there was nothing, only the aroma of fresh coffee drifting over from the diner. His stomach groaned. He could use something to wash down that damned Egg McMuffin.

"Pardon me, bud," someone said from behind him in a slow drawl, "you wouldn't have a spare nickle, would you?"

Stiles turned, half-expecting some down-on-his-luck derelict scrounging for Ripple money. What he didn't expect was a uniform.

The deputy was standing by the Pepsi machine outside the barbershop, counting out a handful of change he'd quarried from his pocket. He was really wearing only an officer's coat and cap; the rest of his uniform, a plaid shirt and Levi's and a worn pair of Converse tennis shoes, were not very businesslike, but somehow fit the rest of the town. He wasn't even wearing a gun. He was at least ten years older than Stiles and a few inches taller, and the snug fit of his clothes suggested that he ate better and a bit more often.

"Sure," Stiles managed, digging into his pocket but keeping his arms close to the body to hide any bulge from his shoulder holsters. He pulled out a coin and flipped it to the deputy, received a nod and an appreciative horsegrin in return.

Gears were turning in Stiles's head. He'd dealt with the law before, more times than he cared to remember. And something on a purely gut level told him that this man wasn't what he appeared to be. This one was sharp. He'd have to be careful.

The officer punched the button for Mountain Dew (appropriate for the surroundings) and pulled a hair-flecked towelette from his collar. "Thanks again, Russell!" he yelled back into the shop, running a hand over his close-cropped hair. The man inside with the broom nodded and waved.

He turned and ambled slowly toward the van like a big, lanky bear, extending a gibbonous right hand. "The name's Bean.

Charlie Bean. Either one'll do. I don't think we've seen you 'round here before, have we?"

"My first time," Stiles said with a smile accepting the greeting. The handshake was a real knucklepopper, one of those manly rights of passage that some individuals never seem able to surrender. Stiles just winced a little and endured. One thing he'd learned over the years was to avoid attracting attention, especially the law's, and matching the deputy strength-wise might tend to make him stick in mind a little longer than necessary. "Chris Stiles. It's good to meet you." He sighed (mostly from getting his hand back) and looked around him. "You've got a pretty nice little town here."

Bean laughed, probably at the familiarity of the line. "We like it," he nodded. "It ain't nothing big, you know, but it's comfortable. You got relations around here, Mr. Stiles? Coming to visit, or . . ." He left the line open deliberately. Stiles smiled to himself. The deputy was baiting him already.

"No, no relatives. Just passing through, I guess. It's kind of a working holiday."

"Oh?" Deputy Bean seemed genuinely interested, but Stiles caught his roving eye and saw his interest was mainly in the van. He drifted past Stiles's shoulder in a casual, unsuspicious movement. "What kind of work do you do?" He glanced through the side window, raising a hand to cut the glare on the glass. His gaze fell immediately on the rack of power tools Stiles had taken pains to situate in plain view. It always diverted prying eyes, and Charlie Bean was no exception. "A handyman, eh?" the deputy grunted, moving on to the fine paneling and cabinetry and the hardwood bunk built across the back. "You fix this up yourself?" He nodded appreciatively—"That's mighty fine work there, mighty fine"—and continued to peer through the window, searching.

Stiles grew a little anxious at the officer's curiosity. "Is there something I can show you, Deputy?" he finally said.

"Nah, that's okay," Bean shrugged, turning from the van with a bit of a guilty chuckle. "But I was just thinking, Mr. St—. . . Chris, right? I was just thinking, Chris, if you're looking to pick up some change, we've got a desk up at the office that could use some minor repairs. You interested?"

"I might be."

"Well, good," Bean's perpetual smile widened. "You want to go look it over now?"

Stiles shook his head. "Maybe later. I was thinking about taking my van somewhere to get the transmission looked at." He motioned toward the diner across the way. "And I have been looking forward to a good cup of coffee. Can I get you one?"

The deputy held up the still half-full Mountain Dew. "Thanks, but I'd best be getting back. You might try the gas station 'round the block, over by the IGA. They do pretty good work. Tell 'em I sent ya."

"I'll do that."

"And whenever you want to look at that desk, you just stop by, okay?" He started his slow and measured stride up the sidewalk, and Stiles saw for the first time that he was indeed wearing a gun. It was a Ruger .357, holstered way back on his hip, the combat grips mostly hidden by the tail of his jacket. He stopped abruptly and turned. "Oh, Mr. Stiles. I mean Chris. One more thing." There was a measured pause, then an equally measured grin. "You enjoy your stay in Isherwood. You hear?"

The soldier laughed himself and waved and finally let his jaws unclench. That was too close, he reminded himself. This deputy was sharp, a lot more so than the folksy exterior would suggest. A suspicious lawman could complicate things. "You're not making this easy, are you, Alex?" he whispered as he locked the van and headed for the drugstore across the street.

A cowbell clanked overhead, triggered by his opening the door, and it made Stiles wince. He didn't like attracting attention, but that was just what it did. All four people in the store looked in his direction. There was a girl behind the register and another behind the lunch counter along the north wall and a couple of locals sitting in the dining area nearby. Stiles tried to ignore them. The smell of fresh coffee was stronger in here, enticing, and mingled with it was what, hot apple pie? He started picking his way through the aisles and displays.

A placard caught his eye. It was white poster board on which someone had scrawled *Bargain Basket* in Magic Marker. It leaned against an oversized laundry basket full of damaged goods and underselling merchandise. There was an abused He-Man doll, some kitchen utensils, lotions, dishtowels, a fire truck missing one wheel, and several Harlequin Romances.

Treasure! He rescued one of the paperbacks. *Love at Sunset*. Had he read that one? It didn't sound familiar. Neither did *Train to Istanbul* or *Under a Pale Moon*. And there were others, not in the greatest condition but still readable. He checked the price . . . three for a dollar! He dug the sole five-dollar bill from his pocket and looked it over and tried to talk himself out of it, then stacked six of the books and took them to the register. The young girl behind the counter snapped her gum and smirked at seeing the covers but didn't say anything.

She didn't give him a sack either.

He took his bounty to the lunch counter and chose a stool away from a spindly old woman in a scarf and sunglasses with too much makeup and a match between her teeth. He sat the books on the counter and made sure the receipt was in plain view, then picked up the menu and glanced over it, careful not to let the jelly stains rub off on him.

"Hey, you read those too?" the woman behind the counter said in a husky voice, soft but with an appealing, gravelly edge to it. "Or are they for your wife?" The voice brought his eyes up from the menu card. Two things about her caught his attention. First, her face. She was lightly freckled and wore no makeup, at least none that he could see. Her features were strong but feminine and had that ageless quality that could have been twenty or forty, though he placed her somewhere a bit younger than himself. Her dark hair was almost shoulder length and curled about her face and contrasted the light of her smile. No raving beauty, but nice. What Charlie Bean had said about Isherwood. Comfortable.

The second thing he caught was a bit of plastic pinned to the ample busom of her turtleneck sweater. It bore a happy face and said, "HI, MY NAME IS" with *Billie* written below. Billie, huh? The name fit the voice, and the voice fit the face.

Comfortable.

"Yours or your wife's?" she repeated, blushing a bit, and he finally realized he was staring at her.

"I'm not married," he managed.

"So, in other words, they're yours," she said, teasing. "Hey, don't be ashamed of that. A good read's a good read, you know?" She plucked the top book off the stack and flipped through it. "Now this one's pretty good." She leaned a little closer, and whispered, "I guess I'm the reason they're on sale. I read when it gets slow here, and I guess I kinda bend the covers." She worked as she talked, wiping the counter and setting a cup and saucer in front of him. "But, no harm done, right? I mean, so much the better for you, right? You did want coffee, right?"

"How did you know?"

She gave a mock salute. "It's my job, sir. In case you didn't see this god-awful tag, my name's Billie. I've never been much for wearing the stupid thing seeing as how I know most everyone in town, well, at least the ones that come in here. But you never know when strangers might come through, and here you are. That is what you are, isn't it? A stranger?"

He laughed. "I think I might qualify, yes. My name's Chris." He offered a hand over the counter and was relieved to find her grip a little less relentless than Charlie Bean's.

"I guess you got the third degree from Charlie already." She motioned toward the window. "I couldn't help but notice. I hope it didn't bother you too much. He doesn't mean anything by it, you know, he's just doing his job."

Stiles nodded. "He was nice enough about it. Even offered to give me some work."

"Oh? What do you do?"

"Woodworking mostly," he said, blowing the steam from his coffee. "But it's just to pay the bills. I'm really a writer. At least at heart."

"Oh, really?" Her eyes lit up and she leaned further over the counter as if they were sharing some fascinating secret. Her closeness surprised Stiles. She smelled like Dial soap. Something in him growled, and he knew it wasn't the Egg McMuffin this time. "Have I read any of your stuff?" she asked.

Writing was a popular cover with him because it fit with his traveling and afforded him at least a modicum of respect—something the handyman story seldom garnered. But it was always tricky, especially around well-read people. That's why he stuck to "Small presses, anthologies, that kind of thing. Nothing major. Yet." He caught her eye drifting back to the Harlequins. "Oh, no, that's just to read. I don't have the flair for that kind of story. I write horror for the most part."

"Oh," she said, still interested but a little disappointed that he wasn't some handsome, romantic scribe come to sweep her off her feet. "Is there any money in that scary stuff?"

He laughed into his coffee. "I haven't seen any of it. But you never know. Maybe there's a best seller somewhere down the road. In a way that's why I'm here."

The old woman with the match in her teeth cocked her neck sideways like a wizened old dinosaur and squeaked, "Billie honey, could you get me another Coky-Cola?"

"Be right there," she called back. "Are you writing a book about Isherwood or something?"

"Depends on whether I find one worth writing." He fixed an eye on her and prepared to catch even a slight response with his next question. "You wouldn't know anything about the name Danner, would you?"

Billie rolled her eyes and nodded her understanding. "I should've put that much together," she laughed. "You must've heard about that anniversary stuff, huh? Seventy-five years later, or something like that? There was something about it in the morning paper, if I can remember where I put it. . . ."

From down the counter came, "Billie honey . . ."

"Okay, okay." She found the folded paper over by the stove and dropped it in front of him. "That should get you started, if you haven't seen it already. I'll be right back, so don't you go anywhere."

"I'll be here," he said, watching her walk away. Then he turned to the newspaper on the counter. She'd been referring to a small local-interest column to one side of the day's headlines. The title immediately caught his eye. DANNER "MURDERS": REAL STORY BEHIND LOCAL LEGEND. There was even an old, grainy photograph there, the small portrait of a stern-faced young man whom the caption identified as, SEBASTIAN DANNER: MURDERER? Stiles silently studied the face for a long time, then reached behind the counter for the coffee pot, refilled his cup, and made himself at home. He was going to be here for a while.

Chapter Two

➢

Charlie Bean eased the squad car away from the doughnut shop and made another patrol through town, cursing Rusty Sanders every inch of the way.

It was just like that little sonuvabitch to call in sick at the last minute, making Bean pull a double shift on a Friday night. *Fever, my ass*, he fumed. The only thing fevered about Rusty was the head of his dick. Twenty bucks said he was across town at the Nevermore Trailer Park right now, in his "sick bed" with that big-titted bimbo Georgetta Stovall and a quart of Wesson Oil.

What a waste of good oil.

Jesus, had Susie hit the ceiling when he told her he had to work! Bean had hated to even call her—not that she had any kind of hold on him. Certainly not. They just lived together, and shared the rent and utilities, and a bed. It wasn't really what he'd call a relationship, but whatever it was, it worked and he had no qualms in admitting that she was the best thing to happen to him in years. He really hated to disappoint her like this. He knew she'd had plans for tonight: there was a new Chuck Norris movie at the theater in Bedford, and they were going to catch the early show, then splurge on steaks and salad at the Golden Corral before taking a drive up to Lake Monroe. It was a chilly night out, but he was going to pack his heavy sleeping bag into the back of the station wagon along with a coolerful of Bud for him and Little Kings for her and shit, would they have been set!

There would be no lovin' tonight, he realized. Susie'd still be on her high horse when he got home, and he guessed she had a right to be. He was on duty for the next couple of nights, and next week she had the second shift at the Woolworth, so no night out then either, and by the time they finally got around to it the movie would probably be gone and some damn Meryl

Streep film in its place. Oh well, no sense complaining, he decided. If she bitches, she bitches. Nothing he could do. It was, after all, his job. They couldn't just get someone else to fill in for Sanders—they were the only two deputies on Isherwood's paltry three-man force. Okay, technically he could have backed out, could have simply patched the lines in to county authorities as they did every night when the last shift was over. But dammit, he needed the money. What with the bills, and child support to his ex, and that new Ruger P85 semi-auto on the market. If only they hadn't waved overtime under his nose.

Rusty Sanders, you little shit. . . .

It was no way to run a law enforcement agency. How many times had he said that over the years? No matter, it was never as obvious as now. He wished he could be rid of incompetents like Sanders or even Larson for that matter. But Isherwood was small, and public office had less to do with actual skill than popularity. Dutch Larson was a community name and property holder, not a lawman, but it was all the qualification he needed for town marshall. And Rusty Sanders—shit, Bean could remember when that punk was pushing kids on the playground and smoking dope in the bathroom. But he was Asa Sanders's boy, and Old Asa and Old Dutch were butt buddies from way back. It was all who you know or who you blow, same as it was everywhere, and Bean had no taste for it. The only reason he held a position at all was to cover Larson's ass: there had to be someone responsible around, just in case something big ever did go down around here.

Not that there was much of a threat of that happening. He couldn't remember a major crime around Isherwood in the last seven years, not since he'd put on the uniform and gun. Armed robbery? Well, little Ethan Stooly took five bucks out of Mrs. Moore's register once. Assault? The occasional drunken brawl, a fight at the playground. Murder? Now that was a laugh. Isherwood hadn't seen a murder or close to it for as long as he or anyone else could remember. Just the Danner story, he thought with a chuckle, and that morning's *Herald* had said that it was all bunk, just a local legend after all.

Murder. Now that was wishful thinking. If only they'd have one now and then. Nothing big, mind you.

He made a sweep of the downtown area, especially Morty's

Pub, where a few of the locals sometimes got rowdy and ended up wrestling and puking on each other in the parking lot. This time it was empty. Must be a slow night. He went across the street and reached the IGA just about closing time and stuck around until all of the cashiers had made it to their cars and waved him on. Then he went across the lot to the Sunoco station which had closed an hour earlier, and pulled up in front to check the doors and buy a can of Mountain Dew.

There was a van sitting to one side, off-white with pitted fenders and a rash of rust on the lower panels. So, Mr. Stiles had taken his advice after all, he thought. Then he realized that this was a short-bed and the handyman's had been a maxi. He looked around the rest of the lot but there were no other Dodges present.

He hadn't seen Stiles all day, not since they talked on the street earlier that morning. Last he'd seen, the "handyman" was headed toward the diner for a cup of coffee and was still there well past noon. Bean had spied him twice through the window. He was keeping Billie preoccupied, that was for sure. She was fawning over him and rolling her eyes and laughing and damn near crawling over the counter onto his lap, for Christ's sake. It wasn't that Bean was jealous or anything—he'd only taken Billie out a few times in all the years he'd known her and hell, he was tied up with Susie these days. She just shouldn't have been acting that way toward a stranger, that's all.

Stiles must have had that kind of effect on people, he figured. Instant likability. He was not an unpleasant-looking man, he supposed, and he was soft-spoken and friendly, the kind of person you take to right off like a long-lost fishing buddy or high-school chum. But Bean refused to buy it. He had trained himself to look beyond a person's veneer, to probe beneath the skin so to speak. There was something hidden behind that young man's lean, bearded face, behind those intense eyes. There were secrets there. And that bothered him.

Bean may have had Stiles pegged in his own mind, but he still hadn't decided what to do about him. On the one hand he was a nice enough guy and had threatened no one and done nothing wrong that he knew of. And until he did so, he had every right to be where he was. On the other hand, he was a question mark, a random element that gave the deputy a case of the mental itchies, and he would've slept a lot easier with Stiles on his way. And yet, Bean was curious. Part of him wanted to sit back and wait, and watch, and see what kind of trouble Stiles might want to stir up.

Murder. That was wishful thinking. . . .

One last pass by Moore's Diner. The lights were still on—on weekends they were open till almost 2 A.M. for the late-night crowd—but Stiles's van was no longer across the street and hadn't been since late afternoon. He knew it was gone, but not where, and that was like an itch he couldn't scratch. He sort of hoped Stiles might come back, just so he could keep tabs on him. Billie was working a double shift herself tonight, and that was incentive enough. But no such luck. He headed for the Tri-Lakes Inn, the only motel in town. But the parking lot was still empty. No van there either.

Maybe he's gone, he figured with a mixture of relief and disappointment. *Maybe I scared him off this morning.*

Nah. Not very likely.

He glanced at his watch and started the last leg of the patrol.

Sykes Road split from Croglin Way before it reached Isherwood, directly across from the "Welcome" sign, and cut to the west. It rolled through farm and field for the first mile and forest for the second. But it was the next stretch that was popular. Especially at night.

They called it the Tunnel. It was almost a mile of poplar and dogwood and oak and elm that crept right to the edge of the ill-maintained pavement and reached out over it with groping limbs. Those limbs in turn formed a canopy so dense that even in losing their leaves they still held the light at bay and kept the roadway in a perpetual gloom. Daylight there was spooky enough; riding into the Tunnel was like entering some nether realm, haunted and surreal. Children were fond of riding their bikes out there. It was a test, actually, to see who could stay there the longest before their imaginations went too wild. Before the wind became a man's voice, crying for help, before the looming trees took on human form and began to uproot themselves to give chase. Bicycles left the Tunnel much faster than they entered, but their pale riders would conquer their fears long before they reached town and already begin planning their next trip out there.

Bean mounted the next rise and the Tunnel came into view,

at least what he could see of it. In the dark it was amorphous, an amoebic void blacker than the night around it. It swallowed Sykes Road whole and refused to spit it out. As he drove toward its gaping maw his mind conjured images of a great cave or, worse yet, a monstrous serpent, and then he was past the jaws and into its throat, leaving the starlight behind. It was in that instant before his eyes had time to adjust to the gloom, when his headlights were the only lights in the whole world, that he felt a communal twang of panic. Afraid of the dark. He could never be completely free of it. No one could.

This was the real Tunnel, he observed, the after-dark Tunnel. Pitch black, or as close as you'd want to get. Quieter. Scarier. More fun. At night it was a carnival funhouse for the bigger kids, the ones with cars and a girl to impress. The softening asphalt had become badly rutted after years of nocturnal traffic, and the tire-worn grass just off the road and between the trees had completely given up and refused to grow. There were other places in Isherwood to hang out like the IGA parking lot and Dante's "new" pizza place and the video arcade, but as long as the weather held out the Tunnel was *the* place. It was a warped kind of tunnel of love, a make-out lane where Vincent Price or Rod Serling would feel at home amid the twisted trunks and heart-carved bark. Once the motor was turned off, the silence would close in, and wind would sift through the trees like a whispery voice, and the arthritic limbs overhead would sway and send the dimmest of shadows to dance on the ground around them, and that was where the stories always began. The escaped psychopath with a hook for a hand. The vanishing hitchhiker in the mud-spattered prom dress. The rapist glimpsed hunkered in the backseat of a woman's car. Each would tell a story more horrific than the last until the girl jumped into her young man's arms, or vice versa. And the rest. . . .

He could pick out the individual cars now as he cruised slowly by: most had pulled far enough off the road so as to be obscured by weeds and trees, but a few were in plain view. There was a glimpse of bobbing heads and bare legs here and there, and one couple was clinched on the hood of a Mustang, seemingly oblivious to the nip in the air. But most were hidden behind well-steamed windows.

Bean was always amazed when he patrolled the Tunnel at just

how loose kids were today. Not that he was a prude. He'd had his share of sexual escapades over the years and was more than happy to discuss them in detail with anyone who cared to listen. But these were high-school kids. Hell, when he was in high school, copping a feel was a week's worth of bragging. Nowadays . . .

There was nothing here, at least nothing he should be concerned with. No brawls with jealous boyfriends, no out-of-town punks looking to cause trouble, no unwelcome advances from overamorous suitors. It was a comparatively quiet night. How boring. Might as well cut it short and call it a night.

Normally he would've U-turned in the middle of Sykes Road and gone back to the office to tie in the lines and go home, and he was never more anxious to do so than tonight. He had a lot of apologizing to do, and a lot of arguing and probably a fair amount of begging as well. But something kept the squad car pointed straight ahead, out of the Tunnel and on into the night. Maybe it was the old curiosity. He saw the Danner place often enough: they patrolled the Tunnel and the rest of Sykes regularly even though it was outside city limits, mostly as a favor to the county boys. But he usually had the day shift, and it was different then. Certainly different than he remembered it.

Like most kids from Isherwood, he had gone out to the Danner place once, at night, to see if the stories were true. He hadn't seen anything—to his knowledge no one ever did—but there had been a certain feeling.

He shrugged off the recollection, dismissing it as the product of a childish imagination. *We'll see*, he told himself. *We'll see.*

The road past the Tunnel was traveled less frequently. Indeed, this entire area was less developed, less populated, and the Danner legend played an important role in that. The land out there was tainted, some said, and no matter how much evidence you showed to the contrary you could not convince them otherwise. But, ironically, the same superstition which had stagnated suburban growth on this side of town appeared to be the prime reason for future development. Local lack of interest in the land had driven prices way down, and it was those prices that were attracting attention from Bedford and elsewhere. Out-of-towners didn't give a damn about local horror stories, not when the bottom line was a good per-acre value. It wouldn't be long, he reckoned, till Sykes Road would be lined with driveways, the Tunnel would be no more, and the "spreading evil" of the Danner estate would be a housing division with two-car garages and cable TV. There was even talk of rezoning the town and pushing the boundaries out to encompass more. Our town is growing, the mayor and his cronies were fond of saying, a little overoptimistically, Bean thought. But most of the "residents" did live outside the present limits and perhaps it was time for a change.

The Danner land was an actual part of Isherwood. He wished he could be a mouse in the council chamber when that came on the agenda. There was sure to be fireworks.

The gloom and spookiness had lifted once he'd cleared the Tunnel and now it was just another chilly, star-flecked night. It was still decidedly unspooky when he rounded a bend and came to the big iron gate of the Danner place.

There was a car parked in front.

It was a Ford Torino, red with a white stripe along the side like the car Starsky and Hutch used to drive. He had a good idea whose it was—how many like that could there be around town—but to be cautious he flicked his lights to high-beam and eased in behind the Ford and just waited.

Two figures moved inside, silhouetted by his headlights, and then the driver's door swung open and a stocky figure stepped out brandishing a Louisville Slugger and squinting against the brightness. Bean sighed and hit the dimmer switch and let Ted Cooper's eyes adjust so he could see the bubble-gum machines on top of the cruiser. Recognition set in gradually; the young man broke into a relieved grin and relaxed his grip on the bat and came sauntering back to the cruiser. He leaned in the window. "Hiya, Charlie," Ted said in his deep, older-than-seventeen tone. "What's the poop?"

"What're you 'uns up to, Teddy?" Bean asked in his usual soft drawl. He reserved his policeman's clipped severity for speeders and drunks and general assholes.

Cooper shrugged. "Just looking. Doreen hadn't been out here before. I told her you can't see anything from the road, but—" He just shook his head, the old "you-know-women" gesture.

"Well, lookee here," Bean advised. "I'd appreciate it if you and puss would go back to the Tunnel or on home or someplace else. That place is pretty run-down. I want to make sure no one goes running around in there and getting themselves bunged up."

Ted looked hurt. "We weren't gonna go inside, Charlie."

"I know you weren't, Teddy, but I'd appreciate it if you move on anyway. Okay?"

Cooper thought a moment and then bobbed his head compliantly. "Whatever you say, Charlie. Doreen was starting to get scared anyway." He strolled back to his car, dragging his bat and yelling, "How about some fishing 'fore it gets too bad" over his shoulder. The deputy waved a reply as the young man gunned the Ford and swung it out onto Sykes Road and back toward town.

Charlie Bean sat there for a moment and stared at the gate. He turned off the lights and the motor and just sat, letting the silence of night flood in around him. He didn't know what he expected to happen, but whatever it was, it didn't.

He stepped out of the car and walked over to the gate, retracing steps he took as a boy. The gate had looked so big then, so imposing, as if it held back all the demons of hell. But now . . . well, now it was just an antique, corroded by time and the pollution-tainted elements. He peered through the bars at the shadowy woods beyond as Papaw's words came back to him and Pa's voice after that, repeating the same litany as they sat around the fireplace. *Don't go near it, Charlie. The land is astink with evil. It's in the soil, in the roots, and the groundwater. He planted it there, he did, Sebastian Danner. And it's his ghost that'll reap its unholy harvest for all of eternity.*

But there was no harvest evident through the gate, except for the milkweed and poison ivy that had grown wild and uninhibited through the years. It was just woods. A little gloomy, but that's all.

He looked at the bars, then at his own moist palms, remembering smaller hands that had shook at the prospect of touching them. This time he didn't hesitate. He reached out and grabbed the bars. And gasped. But because they were cold, nothing more. There was no squirming evil inherent in the metal, no malignant charge of energy to course through his palms and along his spine.

Nothing.

He walked back to the car, satisfied that he had finally outgrown childhood fears and superstitions, and yet somehow disappointed. He had always given the stories a sort of reverence, no matter how much he scoffed, because they were tradition. His mother and father had believed, and their parents before them. Now, standing there in front of the gate and feeling not even an inkling of fear, he realized he'd just proven them all fools.

He climbed into the cruiser and drove back toward town, wishing he hadn't even gone out there in the first place.

As soon as the deputy's car was out of sight, a pair of headlights flashed to life back in the underbrush across the road from the Danner gate.

Chapter Three

The T-Bird eased out of hiding and parked in front of the gate where the Torino had sat minutes before. Tommy Whitten cut the engine and sent a stream of tobacco juice through the gap in his teeth. "Jeez, thought they'd never leave," he sneered, tipping his dad's flask to his lips. He leaned across the other two teens sandwiched into the front seat and peered out the passenger side. "So that's the Danner place, huh? I don't know, Miller. Looks pretty spooky to me."

The other two nodded in agreement. One of them, Doug Baugh, sat bolt upright and craned his neck to look around the car. "What was that?" he whispered, waggling the cigarette cemented to his rubbery lower lip. "You guys heard it too, didn't you?"

"I did," whined "Fat Larry" Hovi, trembling a little too fearfully. His acting wasn't up to par and he couldn't keep the giggle out of his voice. "Sounds like something back in the trees . . . coming closer. . . ." The giggle began to win out.

In the backseat, Bart Miller turned to look at his younger brother Del, and the boy replied with a grin of reassurance. "You weinies can cut it out now," Bart reported to the front seat. "I already told you, he just doesn't scare easy."

Del, age eleven, beamed in the glow of his brother's praise, but his own estimation of his courage was considerably less. He was acting, pure and simple: he only wished he was as stout-hearted as Bart bragged. Sure, he'd seen all the splatter flicks, the Living Dead movies. Sure he'd accumulated a collection of *Fangoria* despite Mom's protests, and devoured every blood-soaked page without a tremor of uneasiness or disgust. But there was a difference between a strong stomach and a strong back-bone.

He looked out the window at the gate. It was large and looming, bigger than when they first drove up, a tremendous thing of wrought iron and rusted hinges. The lock must have failed with age; it was now secured at the center bars by a log chain and Master Lock from the hardware store. That made it even worse, Del thought. It reinforced the warning that the gate itself implied: DO NOT ENTER. IN GOD'S NAME, DO NOT ENTER.

Stars pierced the night, he noticed, everywhere but beyond the gate. The trees there were creating the shade, he knew, but the effect was still the same. A land of complete darkness, of ever-night, a realm of evil, the gate to . . .

Don't enter. In God's name . . .

He lowered his eyes. *Don't think about it. You're going and that's it.*

He wouldn't do this for anyone else, not for a million bucks, not even for the fifty they were betting. Hell, who gave a shit what these stupid grits from Seymour thought of Isherwood and them? But a dare was a dare. Besides, he and Bart would show 'em that "Woodies" weren't scared of no ghost stories, and they'd win some pocket money to boot.

He glanced back out the window. The gate was even larger than before, each bar as thick as his arm, and there were shadows moving in the woods beyond.

"Del, did you hear me?"

The boy turned with a start at his older brother's voice. Half brother, actually. Their mother had been married, and widowed, twice. That's why they looked so little alike. Bart was tall for sixteen and wiry like a runner, and his flame-red hair went in every direction. Del, on the other hand, was small and stocky and wore his dark hair short and parted on the side like Mom wanted. He looked like his father that way, she insisted. Back before the cancer.

"This is your last chance, Cap," Bart repeated, ignoring the snickers and ghost sounds from the front seat. "You don't have to do this if you don't want to. We can take you on home."

"Hey," Baugh muttered, "that wasn't part of the bet."

"Screw the bet," snapped Bart without looking at them. "It's up to you, Cap. You can pull out if you want."

A sigh of relief almost escaped the boy's lips but he held it in check. Bart was giving him an out—he did know Del was scared. Was it that obvious? No, probably not. Bart was just being Bart, covering all the bases. But which was he doing, trying to save him from the bet or trying to get rid of him, to get this scared little kid out from under his feet?

Easy out, said his conscience or his common sense or whatever that little voice was that always turned pussy and pragmatic at the first sign of trouble. *Have them take you home. You're a little kid, you don't have to prove anything. Not to these jokers, certainly not to Bart. He won't think any less of you.*

Will he?

"C'mon, let's take the baby home," Hovi sneered, "it's probably time for his bottle."

"Shut up, lard-ass," Bart said in a soft but steel-edged voice. Despite Hovi's being a year older at seventeen and half-again Bart's weight, the taunting stopped.

Del's temper flared as well, making his decision for him. "I'm sticking," he snapped, flipping Hovi the bird. Bart grinned.

"Get your stuff, Cap. It's time to go."

Everyone piled out of the T-Bird, with Tommy opening the trunk to extract their supplies. Bart took their sleeping bags and tossed them over the wrought iron fence, then strapped a knapsack across his back and secured a Mag-Lite to one of the shoulder straps. Del zipped his down jacket and hugged the warmth of a thermos bottle close to his body. *It's the cold that's making you shiver*, he told himself. *Yeah, that's it. The cold.*

"Just remember, Miller," Baugh harped from his perch on

the car fender. "You stay in the house—not on the grounds, not in the woods, not even on the stoop. And you bring something out with you to prove it, or the bet's off."

"You just have the money on you in the morning," Bart said over his shoulder as he clambered up the ivy-covered fence to the right of the gate. The creeping vegetation gave purchase to his hands and feet and in just a few movements he was at the top and leaning over into darkness. He dropped to his feet on the other side with hardly a sound. "Your turn, Delbert."

The boy leaned his face between the bars. "I don't know if I can make it over, Bart."

"Oh, come on," the older Miller scoffed. "I've seen you go up trees like a squirrel."

"It's kinda high—"

"Look, you little shit," Bart growled, barely keeping his voice to a whisper. "I gave you a chance to cut out but you said no, so get your ass over the fence. Or go home."

Del started to pout but caught himself. Mom wasn't here to give in, and Bart would only get angrier and the others would taunt him and call him a little baby. *Straighten up*, he cautioned himself, turning his anger inward. He went to the wall without another word and scrambled up the vines like a monkey, then over the top and into the trees. Bart halfway caught him as he tumbled to the other side.

Tommy ran up to the gate and pressed his face against the bars and in a deep voice said, "Good night . . . boys," and gave them a gibbering, maniacal laugh. Doug and Larry joined in, as the three piled back into the Thunderbird and gunned the engine. It lurched forward with a spray of dirt and gravel, and the Miller boys watched after them, until even their taillights blinked out of sight.

Del listened to the quiet for a moment. "How come I've suddenly got this feeling we're in deep shit?"

"We're gonna be fine."

"Are you serious?" He looked at the shadowy woods around them and whispered, "You know the Danner stories—"

"Forward and backward," Bart finished, "and that's just what they are. Stories. And if you'd read more of the paper than the funnies you'd know that already. It was on the front page this morning, with tonight supposed to be the anniversary of the murders. The *Herald* did some research and found out it's all a bunch of hogshit. Sebastian Danner never chopped up his wife and brother—least there's no proof of it. No police report. No investigation, no search of the grounds. Nothing. The article said the Danners probably just moved to Europe or outta state."

"Doesn't mean it didn't happen," Del said skeptically, "just that nobody ever found out about it."

"You beat everything, you know that? You'd almost think you were trying to scare yourself."

"I wouldn't have to work at that," the boy replied with an involuntary shudder.

"Look, there's nothing in these woods, least nothing that ain't alive—a dog, something like that. And if it's alive, I can knock its goddamn head off." He reached under his jacket and pulled the nunchaku free with a flourish, spinning it in a figure eight and over his shoulder and back under where he trapped it in his armpit. He'd been practicing with the chucks since he was ten and saw his first Bruce Lee movie. Del felt safer at the sight of them; it was the next best thing to having a gun. The redhead replaced the sticks in his belt and unhooked the Mag-Lite from his shoulder strap. It was one of those official police flashlights, a gift from Charlie Bean when he'd dated their mother. "Now," he sighed, picking up his sleeping bag. "Can we get going?"

He flicked the little rubberized switch on the flashlight and adjusted it to wide beam. It illuminated a cobblestone drive that over the decades had been reclaimed by the forest, conquered by an army of crabgrass and wildweed and creeping brambles. With the heavy foliage and the stones well hidden beneath it, the only suggestion that a drive had ever existed lay in the relatively tree-clear path that wound through the otherwise dense woods. Sometimes even that appeared to be in transition; young saplings were bursting through the drive a little further along, growing tall and strong with flat stones still embedded in their exposed roots.

Del found some good-sized sticks nearby, just like he did when Mom took them mushroom hunting years back, and they used these to brush aside the stickers as they walked and to prod the bushes for late-in-the-year snakes. The cobblestones underfoot were a good guide. Whenever their tennis shoes sank into soft mud they knew they were off the track, and had only to seek solid footing once again.

Del looked back over his shoulder two or three times, and each glance showed the gate, their doorway back to the real world, getting smaller and smaller. *Deep shit*, he repeated to himself. *We're in deep shit*.

"Okay so far?" Bart asked.

"No problem," he lied.

A few more minutes of walking and Del had already grown to hate the flashlight. It showed the way but that was all it showed. The beam's radius only reached so far on either side of the trail, and the rest of the woods seemed darker because of it. Trees were looming shapes in the blackness, arthritic scarecrows that might not have been trees at all, that might move at any minute. And if something touched his foot in the tall grass or tugged at his pantleg, he wouldn't kick at it or even look to see what it was. He would only quicken his pace and hurry on.

There were sounds around them.

It's nothing. Just normal forest sounds. You've heard them every time you've gone camping. See, Bart isn't scared. Why should you be? He wagered himself: he should be able to identify any sounds they heard out there. He was a country boy, after all. If he just concentrated, and listened . . . There. That was the slap-slap of dewdrops falling from the trees to the fat leaves below. And the groan of an old tree limb. And that call in the distance may have sounded like a woman screaming, but he knew an owl when he heard one. There was the swish-swish of Bart's corduroys rubbing as he walked, and the light clatter of things in his pack, and the sound of still-dry leaves crunching underfoot.

He reached out for Bart's back pocket and pulled him to a stop. He motioned for him to be quiet and put his hand to his ear. *Listen*.

The patter of falling dew. Creaking trees. Birds in the distance.

Bart had humored him long enough. "What the hell am I listening for?"

"I heard footsteps in the leaves."

The older boy just shook his head. "We're walking in leaves, Cap."

"No, it wasn't us. It was out there." He pointed away into the dark.

Bart swung the flashlight around and swept the area in question. Nothing. "Did you ever think of animals, Delbert? They've been known to hang out in wooded areas, you know."

"Very funny. What I heard wasn't an animal."

"You're that sure," Bart sighed. Impatience had edged into his voice. "Now, if you don't mind, can we get on with this?" He headed back up the drive, towing the boy behind him with a hand still locked on his back pocket.

Putz. Pansy. That was probably what Bart thought of him by now. *Quit acting like a baby. What do you want him to do, hold your hand or something? Grow up. It's just . . .*

A voice giggled in the dark.

. . . your imagination. That's all.

Someone whispered behind him.

Imagination.

A high, tittering laugh.

Gulp.

His throat was suddenly too dry to swallow. No voices, he said to himself, over and over so it filled his ears and drowned out the sounds around him. He could see movement from the corner of his eyes, dark figures with capering white faces, peeking from behind the trees that lined the path.

There's no one there, no one . . .

He closed his eyes and lowered his head and trudged along behind his brother, waiting in dread for the whistle of Sebastian Danner's descending ax or the cackle of the mad and the dead. And waiting. And still waiting.

Bart pulled to a stop. "Hey, Cap," he said, "we're almost there. Look."

Del peeked past him and saw the trees ahead thinning, becoming an overgrown thicket. Past that the drive swung to the right as far as they could tell and circled around a front lawn nearly an acre in size that hadn't seen a mower in years. And beyond the waist-high grass they could make out Danner house, framed by wisps of groundfog that all but glowed in the moonlight. Bart trotted on through the thicket for a better look, breaking the boy's grip on his pocket and leaving him temporarily behind.

Del stared at the house in the distance and actually felt his spirits sag. It wasn't nearly as foreboding as he'd been led to believe; too many Vincent Price movies had colored his image of haunted houses. Everyone knew they had to be built on a craggy bluff or a steep hill, with a small base and at least four or five floors like the Bates Motel or the House on Haunted Hill. Plenty of upper floor windows were mandatory for figures to dance in or lights to flash from, as well as a spiderweb of winding stairs that creaked when you stepped on them and sometimes when you didn't. But this—this was just a big sprawling old house, and not even the eeriest fog could help it. What a dog!

With his disappointment, all the sounds of the forest disappeared; the screams, the moans, the specters of Sebastian Danner he'd expected, almost wanted to see. Legends die hard, it seemed. Bart had been right. Just a house. Just a crummy . . .

There was movement off to the right. He caught it from the corner of his eye; not a leaf swaying or a stray beam of moonlight through the trees. Something else.

A figure was moving through the bushes ten or fifteen yards away, but it wasn't the leering ghost he'd expected a few minutes before. This was a man, very old, bent by the years till he leaned on a stick for support. His silvery white hair and beard and his pasty complexion made him look like a negative image against the pitch black of the woods. He wore dungarees and a tattered coat with the collar up, and stopped every few steps to catch his breath and lean heavily on his stick.

No ghosts, Del assured himself. *Just some old hobo.*

The old man went suddenly rigid, as if the boy's thoughts had been spoken aloud. He turned and looked directly at Del and the boy froze.

His eyes . . .

There was something in that gaze, an intensity that couldn't be readily identified or described. Fear. Or hatred.

Or madness.

The old man stared at the boy and his mouth moved as if he were trying to speak. Then he started to move crookedly through the brush toward him, forgoing the support of his stick, which he shifted to a two-hand carry.

Except it really wasn't a stick at all. Now Del could see that he'd been leaning on a thick handle, and at the far end, by now caked with soil (and blood?) was the slim, funny-looking head of an ax.

The thermos and sleeping bag slipped from numb fingers and were forgotten. Del backpedaled, fell once, scrambled to his feet, and ran full out through the thicket.

Bart was just coming back to get him when they collided. He caught a meaty shoulder in the gut as the younger boy's momentum spilled them over in a tangle of arms and legs and camping supplies. Bart wrestled his brother aside and immediately slipped his pack off and began sifting through its contents, muttering, "I'll bet that mashed the sandwiches just surer'n shit. What the hell's wrong with you, anyway?!"

"There's a man!" Del whispered urgently, his voice shrill and choked with fright. "An old man, after me! Back there!"

Bart's brow furrowed. He looked from his brother to the woods and back, and there wasn't any doubt in his eyes. He set his jaw and slipped off his jacket and pulled the nunchaku from his belt. "Stay here," he said as he stalked back into the darkened forest.

"Be careful, Bart."

There was a long silence, save for the crickets. Del began to fidget and thought about going back after him but then leaves crunched underfoot, approaching, and a familiar red head peeked out of the shadows. Bart's sticks were back in his belt and he was carrying Del's discarded sleeping bag and thermos, unscrewing the latter to make sure the seal wasn't broken. Del was incredulous. "Didn't you see him?"

"Nope," he answered, securing the thermos into his already bulging backpack. "Are you sure you saw something, Cap?"

"Yes, I saw something Cap," the boy spat defensively. "It was an old man with a long beard, kinda bent over, and he carried this skinny, funny looking ax, and . . ."

He didn't have to go on. At the mention of the ax his brother sighed and rolled his eyes behind closed lids just like Mom. "So it was old Danner chasing you through the woods," he muttered, shaking his head. "Why did I let you come along? I should have my head examined."

"I'll go home now," whispered the boy. "Let's just call it off. Okay, Bart? Okay? I don't like it out here."

"Well, that's just tough," Bart snapped, waving a finger in his face. "You had your chance. Now get moving toward that house or I'll kick your butt all the way there!" He threw the boy's bag in his face, then shouldered his own pack and waited. Hesitantly Del moved out, slowly at first, but faster once he realized that at least he'd be leaving those damned woods behind. He waded into the hip deep grass of the front lawn, and his brother followed close behind.

Even from the field they could see that Danner House was still in good shape despite the years, a mute testament to the construction materials and craftsmanship of the late nineteenth century. In the pale moonlight one could readily imagine the opulence this place must have enjoyed. It looked like some misplaced southern plantation house; two floors of red brick and elaborate wood trimming, a frontal parapet with four massive limestone columns, all elaborately carved on closer inspection. Unfortunately, a closer look showed the scars of time as well. The stone was splotched and discolored from years of acidic rainfall. Paint was peeling from the wood in large chips and showing termite infestation beneath. But the most insidious damage had been planned, for ghost stories had not deterred everyone. The mark of the vandal was emblazoned everywhere in red spray paint, on the columns and across the limestone porch and all along the facade. This was no urban artistry, just squiggles and serpents and crudely drawn pictures with grossly inaccurate anatomies. On one column, *Perry loves Tracy* was encased in a heart, while another declared, *Ozzie Osbourne is king*. Some imaginative soul had scrawled *Helter Skelter* on one of the large double doors, while the other read, *Toby Morton is a fag and a half*. There were more names written in paint and ink along the bleached stone and upon the flaking white of the doorjamb and trim, some even readable in the dim cast of the moon or with the help of the Mag-Lite, but neither Del nor Bart recognized any of them. Probably out-of-towners. Few Woodies ever came out here. The Danner legend was still viable locally, but that didn't stop the inquisitive and the daring from as far off as Bedford and Seymour and even Bloomington. If anything, the stories attracted them. The Danner legend was a novelty, something to check out instead of cruising the square or bumming beer off someone's older brother.

The relentlessly thick crabgrass gave way a bit nearer to the porch where the cobblestone drive circled back in front of them and around the side of the house. There were beer cans to be found amid the weeds and a few on the front steps, some old ones bleached almost white by the sun, others of the lite variety that could have been dropped bare minutes before they arrived. Bart stooped near the porch and picked one up and held it before him like a crystal ball, stroking it to detect sweat or a lingering chill. He retrieved his lockback hunting knife and used it to pierce the thin aluminum skin and peel it aside. "It's not wet," he said, dropping the can. "These've been here for a while. C'mon." He climbed the steps while Del lagged behind, craning his neck to look at the upper floor windows. Like the lower ones, some were patched with plywood while others held only slivers of glass like solitary teeth in dark yawning mouths. No ghosts danced there. No phantom lights. No old men. Just windows. Just a house after all.

Still, he fought off a sudden chill before hurrying up the steps.

Bart was jimmying the lock with his knife when the right-hand door simply swung open on nagging hinges. The boys exchanged looks out of an Abbott and Costello movie. "It's not what you think, Cap," the older cautioned. He kneeled to inspect the locking mechanism along the door edge and found it not only antiquated but heavily scarred from prying. "Look at this. The bolt's worn down. No wonder it came open so easy. Just jiggle the damn thing and that bolt'll slip out every time."

"Yeah," Del doubted out loud. "Except when we try to get out. Then the damn thing will work just fine."

Bart scowled. "You're a lot of fun, you know that?" He went back to the steps for a beer can and crushed it underfoot, then wedged the lump of aluminum into the door's hinge space. He then tried to move it but it wouldn't budge. "Satisfied?"

Del nodded. It did make him feel a lot better having an open escape route. And he suspected that Bart hadn't done it entirely for him.

The doors opened onto a foyer and that in turn onto an entry hall that, to Del, looked like a hotel lobby. It was a big, airy place with an open, vaulted ceiling that looked bare without a chandelier. A magnificent wooden staircase started to their right and wound lazily around the room to the second floor landing like a great banistered millipede. Most of the rails were missing, the carpet on the stairs was old and torn, and the tile floor was strewn with leaves. But despite a delapidated condition, it was still an impressive place, summoning images to mind of . . .

"Collinwood," Bart sighed.

"Huh?"

"Collinwood. From *Dark Shadows*. You know, that old soap?"

The boy shook his head. "A little before my time."

"Mine too, but I saw the movie version on channel thirteen a while back." He looked about the open chamber. A set of sliding mahogany doors were ajar on the right, their beauty marred only by the "Smoke a joint" slogan smeared across one panel. To their left an ornate arch led into what appeared to have been a sitting room back when there was something to sit on, and straight ahead a narrow service hall led deeper into the house. "Well? Where do we camp out?"

"Over here." Del was pointing to an alcove just off the foyer. "It's a great big closet. This way we're close to the door, but out of sight if any of those beerheads come along. Neat, huh?"

They stepped into the closet and flashed the Mag-Lite about. No furnishing. Just cobwebs and coatpegs and a shelf for hats. "Home sweet home," Bart sighed.

It took nearly half an hour to square away the cloakroom to their satisfaction. Bart tore the cobwebs away as Del swept aside the dust in one corner so they could lay down their bags. Once they were settled in, they broke out the thermos of hot chocolate and a few peanut butter and jelly sandwiches, mashed flat but still edible.

"I want to check this place out before we turn in," Bart said between mouthfuls. Del stopped chewing and gaped at him as if he'd eaten a bug.

"What the hell for?"

"Well." He thought a moment. "How would you like it if there was some old hobos and sterno-drinkers camped out in the back of the house, and while we were sleeping they snuck into this closet and cut your throat?"

The boy swallowed. "I don't think I'd like that at all."

"Okay then. Besides . . . I'm curious." He downed a capful of hot chocolate before climbing to his feet and returning the nunchaku to his belt. "I'm taking the flashlight," he said casually, "so you can either sit here in the dark or come along. What's it gonna—"

The youngest Miller had poked his mouth full and was already heading out the door.

They started in the parlor, turning their collars up to the breeze that whistled through the broken windows. There was little to see in the big empty room, just a few pieces of furniture too decrepid to be stolen. The same was true for the study, with its sliding doors and empty bookshelves floor to ceiling, and likewise every other room on the first floor. The only thing to set them apart was the varying degree of ruination each was in, from warped baseboards and rain damage to vandalized gouges in the walls themselves that revealed skeletal frame boards and the house's outer skin of brick.

Just off the dining room they found a set of French doors that still retained many of the original glass panes. Through it was a small limestone courtyard that jutted just beyond the protective overhang of a balcony above, with steps leading down into a once-elaborate garden. Though overgrown as was all the Danner property, they could still make out cobbled walkways snaking through the grass, leading out to where the familiar, less vegetated drive met them and formed a circular turnaround. Beyond that was the dark mass of forest that surrounded the property.

Bart pointed up toward the balcony above the porch. "Master bedroom?" he wondered. "That must be where the heinous crime took place, nyah ah ah." He hunched his shoulders and dragged one foot. "Shall we look for bloodthtains, mathta?"

"Cut it out, dork."

"You ain't still scared, are you?"

"No."

Bart laughed. "Yes you are. Wuss. C'mon."

They went back to the entry hall and checked their gear before starting up the delapidated staircase, with each step making the requisite groan and quickening their ascent. They found the landing less windblown than below and the carpet in somewhat better shape. They checked each room as they went but found nothing, just drawerless bureaus and fallen shelves and bedframes too massive to be looted. Soon they were at the closed door of the master bedroom.

"You sure you're ready for this?" Bart teased as he gave the door a gentle shove. It swung open, revealing a flurry of dark commotion inside. Del sucked wind and was halfway down the hall before Bart's yells brought him to a stop. "It's okay, Cap. It's just birds! Get back here!"

Del returned sheepishly, eyes still bulging, and peeked inside. Most of the birds had vacated by that time, vanishing through the glassless balcony doors, but a few starlings and swallows were still on the floor or roosting on the mantle. Bart walked into the center of the room, forcing a few irate blackbirds from his path, and held out his arms. "See? No ghosts. Just birdies."

"I wasn't scared."

"I know."

"I wasn't, Bart. I was just . . . surprised, that's all."

"Whatever you say, Cap." He looked about the room. There was the obligatory bedframe, this one even larger than the others and discolored by bird droppings. There was no other furniture, just an empty fireplace and lots of nests and excrement. "No bloodstains," he observed. "You'd think there would be if old Danner had chopped up his wife and brother in here. There'd be lakes of it, if you ask me."

"Would you shut up?"

"What is there to be scared of, Cap? There were no murders. We came, we saw, we discovered the truth. End of story. I proclaim this house ghost-free." He blinked his eyes which were by now reddened from fatigue and too much dust. "I think we can turn in now."

"To sleep?"

The tall redhead nudged him back into the hallway with the flashlight. "I doubt it. But what else are we going to do, watch TV? You can take first watch."

On the way back down the creaking old stairs, Del paused. He took the Mag-Lite from his brother's hand and shined it back under the stairway. "There's someplace we haven't checked," he said, sending a beam of light into the darkened service corridor where the shadows overcame it.

Bart shrugged. "Nobody's back there."

"I want to be sure."

Another shrug. "Go for it then. I'm going to bed."

Del started to give in but thought better of it and decided to call his bluff. "Fine. But I'm taking the flashlight." He descended the stairs and crept toward the narrow hallway, and was almost through the arch before his brother fell in behind him. "Make it quick," Bart warned.

The hall was not very long. It led to three rooms, side by side, each not much bigger than the cloakroom they were calling home, and a slim passage across from the rooms led to the kitchen, which they hadn't noticed earlier. The rooms must have been servants' quarters, Bart guessed from the size of the cots, and the lack of windows.

There was one other door, at the end of the hallway. It was heavy and old and sported a closed bolt latch instead of a true knob. It was not locked; Bart gave it a solid yank and swung it open, hinges creaking just as every other part of Danner House creaked. They found themselves staring into complete darkness, and Del felt his heart skip a beat. The smell was dank and old, like a grave, and before his mind had time to conjure any more colorful analogies he swung up the Mag and sprayed light into the cellar. Steep wooden stairs, irregularly cut and not so sturdy looking, led down into the inky blackness of the cellar where the beam couldn't reach.

Del swallowed. "I'm not too hot on going down there."

Bart gulped as well. "Well, if you don't want to go, Cap, we won't do it. We can—" He furrowed his brow, shielded his eyes against the glare of the Mag-Lite, and peered deeper into the cellar. "Shut that off," he whispered.

"What? Are you—"

"Shut the light off!" he hissed, grabbing it and flicking the switch himself. The darkness, like peat-stained water, flooded back immediately, and for a moment Del feared he would drown. He clung to Bart's jacket sleeve like a dying man and kept telling himself, *There's nothing wrong, nothing wrong, your eyes will adjust . . .*

"There!" his brother whispered. "Do you see it? Dammit, Del, look!" He put his hands on the boy's head and forced him to look into the cellar.

As his pupils dilated he realized that it was not pitch black as he had believed. There was a soft glow in the cellar, splashed across the wall at the foot of the stairs before them. It was dim, like the light of a television left playing.

Del clamped a hand over his own mouth but couldn't contain the childlike whimper that sounded deep in his throat. "Someone's down there!"

"Looks like it," Bart replied. Holding the flashlight but leaving it off, he put his foot down on the first step and waited for it to creak, and when it didn't, he tested another. Del grabbed his arm.

"Are you crazy?" he squeaked nervously. "Let's go!"

"I want to see who it is," the older boy said calmly.

"What?!"

"Look, by now he knows we're here. It's only fair we know who he is. I won't be long, I just want a look. You stay up here—"

"Bullshit," Del snapped, starting down the steps after him. "I'm sticking to you like glue. And keep those damned chucks ready."

They eased quietly down the steps, Bart in the lead with the unlit torch, testing each step with a tennis shoe before committing his weight. Halfway down, one slat of wood changed its mind and let out an arthritic groan that made both of them wince. But no one came running. After a very long half-minute they continued their descent.

It had been cold upstairs, with the midnight breeze drifting unhampered through the shattered windows, but in the cellar it was damn near freezing. It was dank and musty and had that clammy feel of an underground room. The drip-drip of seeping groundwater could be heard, and water sloshed underfoot when they stepped off the staircase, soaking their tennis shoes clear through.

"Look back there," Del whispered.

The soft glow was coming from the far end of the cellar, almost the length of the house. Its source was obscured by boxes and refuse heaped there decades ago.

"Did you see anyone?"

Del shook his head. "Just the light. Now let's get out of here, okay?"

"Sshh. C'mon."

Straddling the puddle, they found to their surprise a floor not of packed earth, but hewn stone. Still, this was no contemporary basement, not like any Del had ever seen. There were no windows. There was no paneling, no washing machine or ping pong table or cardboard boxes marked *Toys* or *Junk* or *X-Mas Tree Decorations*. In fact, in the pale glow of whatever lay ahead, it didn't look so much like a cellar as a cavern.

Something small brushed past Del's leg and skittered away. He wished he were carrying the flashlight. *Don't panic*, he tried to rationalize. *It was just a stray cat. Yeah. Sure it was.*

As they grew closer to the light they could pick out small details of the cellar around them. The walls segued from uneven stone to large, squared brick where additions had been built onto the original house. There were racks along one wall with a few small kegs still in place and a row of shelves along the other that might have held canned goods or homemade preserves long ago. They could also see that the cobwebs were thick and hung all around them like mosquito netting, undisturbed except along the path they were following.

They reached the ridge of garbage and, with much trepidation, peeked past it.

There was no one there. The weakening light was from a Coleman lantern in the farthest corner of the cellar, on the floor amid a collection of mallets and chisels and other tools, as well as a pile of chipped rock and powdered mortar. The wall that it best illuminated had been partially disassembled. Old-style bricks measuring nearly six inches wide had been pried from their places and discarded on the cellar floor, leaving a foot-wide gap in the wall there.

Bart ambled out into the light and began to survey the equipment and the damage. Del followed close behind. "Who's stuff is this, do you think?" whispered the younger boy.

Bart picked up the lantern and turned it around in his hands, then did the same with each tool. "No engraved names. But I think I know what they're up to." He motioned toward the wall.

"Vandals?"

"Treasure hunters," he nodded. "There's always been stories about mad old Sebastian's ghost, guarding a pile of hidden dough. It looks like someone's been taking them seriously."

Del looked around at the chisels and crowbar and powdered stone at his feet, and his mouth dropped open with sudden recognition. The old man in the woods . . . his ax . . .

A pick ax?

"Hold on," Bart was peering into the hole in the wall. He stuck his hand in and felt about. "You know, there's two walls here, two entirely different walls." His knuckles knocked against something solid. "Strike that. Three walls. The third hasn't been broken yet."

"So what? Let's get outta here before whoever it is comes back."

"Hang on a minute, Delbert. Don't you know what this means? Our treasure hunter might be onto something. What would you wall up, three times, unless it was valuable?" Delbert muttered something about a dead boy or two, but Bart ignored him. "Wouldn't it be something if there was money behind there? I'll tell you, I'd—" He looked around warily. "Did you hear something?"

Del's breath caught. "Oh, goddamn it, don't do that," he complained, clutching his heart. "What did it sound like?"

"Scratching."

The boy breathed a sigh of relief. "Is that all? It's just rats. I think one brushed my leg back there somewhere." He motioned into the darkness. "C'mon, let's get out of here."

"Okay, okay," Bart sighed, still peering into the hole. "Jeez, I wish I knew what was back there." He reached in and rapped that third wall once again. Only this time the stone wasn't in place. His fist encountered empty air and kept going, and his arm sank through the opening up to the elbow. He lost his balance and fell against the wall and said, "Shit."

He said it even louder when something grabbed his wrist.

It was clammy and cold, nearly freezing. His crotch shrank at the mere touch. And it was strong. It jerked his arm further into the hole, shoulder deep, banging his face against the wall and shaking the flashlight from his grasp. His neck was bent at an angle against the brick till he could barely breath or cry out, and still the pressure grew. All he could manage was a gasp.

Then the last of the Coleman's fuel burned up and the lamp winked out.

Chapter Four

➢

Del couldn't be sure how long he stood there. Nor could he tell which direction the stairs were in or the walls or even Bart for that matter. He was lost in the blackness. It disoriented him, tilted the floor and turned the world on its side and made him fight to stay on his feet. "C'mon, Bart, this ain't funny. Where are you? Bart?"

There was an uncharacteristic whimper in reply. "Oh, shit, something's got me, oh shit, oh shit. . . ."

"Hang on, Bart. Just hang on. Dammit, where's the flashlight?!" He flailed his fists helplessly at the claustrophobic darkness as if it were a tangible thing. There was a whimper rising in his own throat but he forced it down. *Not now. You can't be scared now.* He dropped onto his hands and knees and crawled along the rough stone floor, fighting his tears back. "Where's the flashlight!" His knees were bruised from the rubble, and something ragged cut his palm and made him cry out in pain. But he wouldn't stop. Don't stop! Keep looking! He was starting to cry when his hand finally closed around something long and thin and smooth. But the rat connected to it hissed not a foot from his face and he slung it away with a shriek. "I can't find it," he sobbed. "Bart, I can't find it!"

"Goddamn it, Del," came a pained voice, gasping and full of tears, "gimme a fuckin' hand!"

"I'm trying!" He scrambled across the floor on his knees, feeling about in earnest, this time determined to strangle any rat that crossed his path. He brushed against Bart's tennis shoe, then felt along his trouser leg. It's got to be right around here somewhere, this is where he dropped it just before the lights . . .

"Oh, shit, Del . . ."

His hand found cool metal.

"Got it!" He thumb-stabbed the rubber switch and sprayed the walls with a flash of lightning, then hit it again and this time the bulb stayed on.

Bart was in the same position as before, jammed up against the hole in the wall, his face pressed to the stone and distorted by fear. He tried pulling his arm free but he was too off balance and panic had sapped his strength. Tears were streaming through the dust on his face.

Del looped his arms around his brother's chest and pulled as hard as he could but the older boy wouldn't budge. "C'mon, Bart," he urged, "pull your arm out. You can do it." He tugged again. Bart groaned. "Bart! Pull your arm out!"

"I can't, you little dumb-ass! Something's got me!"

"Bullshit." The boy moved around to where he could look into his brother's face. "C'mon, you pussy. You can do better than that. I ain't carrying you." There was a spark of anger in Bart's reddened eyes. A sneer curled his lip. "That's it," Del taunted. "Get mad! Pull!"

With a growl Bart lurched backward, gaining only scant inches of freedom but enough to bring up a foot and brace it against the stone. With like effort he raised the other leg and planted it as well, till he was bent double and clung to the wall like an imprisoned insect. "Del," he wheezed, "grab hold." The boy did as instructed, locking his arms around his brother's middle. "On three. One. Two. Three!"

It was like surging against a steel cable. Neither of them budged; trembling with strain was the only evidence of their efforts. Eyes bulged. Sweat broke and slid down their faces. Teeth grated. Leg muscles quivered, almost spasming. Something popped.

"Oh, God . . ."

"Bart, what . . ."

"Don't stop!" There was pain in his voice, mingled with the fear. "Del, don't stop! It's coming!" He wrapped his free arm around his shoulder as if to hold it in the socket and the tug-of-war continued.

"It gave!" Bart grunted. "It gave! Pull harder!"

Del worked until he could squeeze a shoulder between Bart and the wall and then locked his own legs against it and pushed. He could feel the give long before he heard about it. "It's coming," Bart reported. "My shoulder's out. Keep going. Now my elbow—harder, Del!" The boy gritted his teeth and strained. "Here it comes . . . oh, Jesus . . ." His voice drained. Del turned, keeping a shoulder planted in his brother's ribs to hold him, and looked at Bart's arm.

It had cleared the hole. But it had brought something with it.

Reaching from the darkness of the hole, still clutching Bart's wrist, was a hand or something that had resembled one once. It was thin and bony, the knuckles and joints protruding, nearly tearing the sallow skin that enclosed them, and it looked incapable of the strength that held Bart in check. Its nails were ragged and long, but some had been torn to the quick from scratching away mortar and digging at the stone of the third wall. The flesh around the fingertips was brittle and split. There was no blood.

Bart's legs began to quiver with revulsion. "Get it off me!" he yelled. "Get it off me!"

"Lock your knees!" Del ordered, slapping Bart's legs until he obeyed. Then he slipped the nunchaku sticks from his brother's belt and started to twirl them in the limited space, just as Bart had taught him. "Hold still," he warned, as he brought the sticks down like an ax, striking the hand just behind the knuckles. *Whack!* The sound echoed through the cellar. The flesh there dimpled like a thumbprint in soft wax. But the hand did not let go.

"Again!" Bart was frantic. "Hit it! Hit it!"

Del dropped the Mag-Lite and swung the sticks with both hands, over and over, and the air was filled with the slap of wood meeting flesh and the crackle of metacarpals breaking. Del could feel them give even through the sticks. But the hand refused to loosen. The fourth blow split the flesh over the knuckles; calcium whiteness peaked through, but there was still no blood, still no sign of release. Bart was being pulled inexorably closer to the wall. "Give, you bastard!" Del swung again, this time for the wrist, and the bone there shattered with a satisfying pop. The hand opened and Bart tumbled backward to the floor, moaning, cradling his injured arm.

Del backed away warily, watching the hand flop and claw at the air and send monstrous shadows across the wall. Seeing it move like that reminded the boy to be scared; this wasn't an old bear trap Bart had stumbled into. This was alive, or something like it. And its owner was just beyond those walls. Something. Moving.

The talon receded into the hole slowly, like a pale moray eel returning to its den. It disappeared into the darkness there.

Bart lurched to his feet and picked up the Mag-Lite and shined it into the hole. "C'mon! Show me your face, you sonuvabitch! C'mon!"

There was only silence.

Del strained to see into the hole as well but didn't want to get too close. "What can you see?"

The older boy wiped his eyes against the cloud of dust that glittered in his light. "Nothing. I don't see nothing but another wall . . . no, wait." He stepped nearer. Del had to stop him from getting too close. "Jesus, Del, there's a room back there. No bigger than a closet, but—" His eyes widened. His mouth was working but nothing came out.

Del edged his brother aside and looked directly into the hole. And the face there looked back.

It was only there a second, staring, gaping at them, before vanishing back into the darkness. But its image remained before his eyes like phosphor burned into a TV screen. Waxen, dead skin, stretched taut over bones too large for it. Eyes bulging from cavernous sockets. Sunken cheeks, one with a ragged, black scar. Thin, almost translucent lips, barely concealing the abundant teeth behind them.

Had it been an old man? Despite the shrunken, withered countenance, the tangle of greasy hair had been too dark for that. And the eyes . . . He began to wonder if it could have been a man at all. The eyes had been dull and empty, devoid of any spark that would remotely suggest life. And yet . . . in the glare of the flashlight they had shone silver.

Bart was the first to stammer, "What the hell was that?"

Before Del could answer, the face reappeared. The atrophied muscles along the edges of its mouth jerked and constricted. Whether it was a smile or a grimace was hard to tell, but it accomplished the same end. It showed them its teeth.

"Oh, lordy, this can't be right. A vampire."

"There ain't no such thing, Del."

"Then you tell me what the hell it is!"

Bart fumbled for logic but he must have left it upstairs with his knapsack because nothing would come. He could only stare at the horrific thing and rub its taint from his wrist. "Move, Del. Now." They began to back away slowly, keeping the flashlight trained on the hole. In its trembling light they saw the hand emerge again, clawing at the air, reaching for them. They could hear its owner grunting, straining against the walls, and it spurred them on. Neither breathed until they were halfway across the cellar and out of its sight.

A voice called out from behind them. "Boys." It was hoarse and croaking, like audible sandpaper. A voice that grated from lack of use. "Boys. Come . . . back . . ."

"Keep moving," Bart whispered, pushing Del ahead of him.

"BOYS!"

The tone was frenzied and rising like a banshee's wail, and it froze them in their tracks. Even after it had died the echoes carried it on, all around them. That's why they didn't hear the other sounds right away. The ratlike scraping of its nails on stone. The trickle of dislodged mortar. The thud of a falling brick. Two. And that frantic, sandpaper voice, muttering to itself, "Boys . . . mine . . . mine . . ."

Oh, God, it's getting loose.

Del couldn't will his legs to move. They simply wouldn't obey, not until Bart shoved him from behind and that was all the incentive he needed. He splashed through the puddles and clambered up the darkened cellar steps on all fours to keep from falling, and would've been on down the hall if the darkness at the top hadn't been so tangible. Instead he waited at the cellar door, panting, until Bart and the flashlight could catch up. The older boy cleared the doorway a few steps behind him, gasping as well, still cradling his arm, and was barely through before Del slammed the door shut and jerked the bolt home.

"You think this'll hold him?" he asked fearfully.

The answer was obvious. They both bolted down the hallway and out the front door.

Del was already wheezing with effort when they cleared the porch and plunged into the tall grass. The front yard seemed so much longer now, like two football fields, end to end. He began to fall behind about halfway across. "Can you make it, Cap?" Bart called back.

"Don't worry about me," the boy wheezed, "I'll be—" But Bart was no longer there to listen. He was running the other way and pulling Del after him. "Another one!" he was yelling. "Another one! The woods!" Del looked there immediately. There was something moving near the tree line. He caught a glimpse of milky whiteness. Two silver specks of reflected moonlight, staring back. Then he was running again, back toward the house and even faster than before.

The banshee wail rose behind them. "No! Nooo!" Del felt his innards twist at the sound. It was coming. He passed his brother like he was standing still. By the time Bart reached the house Del was already at the door, digging at the wedge so he could close it. "You freakin' idiot!" he cursed as his brother came across the porch, "why'd you jam it in there so tight?!"

The redhead's only response was to grab the boy by the collar and virtually walk him through the door and up the winding staircase like an oversized puppet. They collapsed on the second floor landing and flicked off the flashlight just as a shadow spread through the open doorway like running oil.

Del pressed his face to the mouldy carpet and clamped a hand over his own mouth to muffle his wheezing. He wanted to hide his eyes but the voice inside his head said, *No, keep it in sight, or it'll be on you in a minute. If you lose it, you're dead.*

He looked over at his brother. Bart must have had the same thought, for with an agonizing slowness they both raised their heads enough to peer beneath the bottom rail of the banister.

It stood in the doorway below, dark and featureless, a stickman dripping his shadow across the dusty tile. It had fallen silent upon entering and now looked around the room like a preying mantis, craning its neck mechanically, sniffing the air. Enough moonlight spilled through the doorway that, when it turned, they could make out individual features. The face had that same withered, skeletal appearance as the thing in the cellar, the same dark greasy hair, the same prominent brow and aquiline nose, now grown stark with the shrinking of its countenance.

The same. Del looked at its wrist. Sure enough, it hung limp and crooked, and a shard of bone gaped through the flesh. *But how? How did it get out ahead of us?*

The thing wore remnants of an old-style frock coat around its gaunt shoulders, and its vest and trousers were likewise threadbare and nearly rotted through. Its tall riding boots had given out near the sole, allowing long toenails to peek through the rift.

Del watched the creature stalk about the entry hall, its walk a stuttering caricature of walking and yet almost casual in nature. Like a man on a stroll. It looked at the bare walls and muttered under its breath. It sneered at the graffiti on the study doors and wiped at it with its sleeve. And, for the moment, it did not seem to be looking for the two boys. It was as if something had overridden its hunger. But what? Del wondered. Nostalgia? Maybe that was it. Maybe it just hadn't seen its house in that condition before.

Its house? Of course! "Sebastian Danner," Del whispered unconsciously, realizing a split second too late how even a whisper would be amplified in the silence. Realizing that he had just given them away.

The vampire turned slowly, looked up at them and smiled, showing yellowed dog teeth. "Good going, dickhead," Bart snapped at his brother. He triggered the flashlight, and the vampire flinched at the sudden brightness in its eyes. "Get out of here!" the older boy demanded. "Leave us alone!"

It cleared its throat and laughed again. "Come," it motioned with a toothpick arm as it came to the foot of the stairs. "Come. Boys."

"Go fuck yourself."

More laughter. It cleared the first step.

Bart looked around the landing, then ran to a small table there. Despite its size, it was constructed of stout oak and heavier than he expected. They tried to lift it, but Bart howled and grabbed his shoulder. The table didn't budge.

Boot soles landed on the sixth step. A third of the way up.

"Drag it," Del ordered, pulling the table toward the stairs, his shoes scrounging for traction and tearing holes in the timeworn carpet. Bart put his weight behind it and pushed. The table crept forward.

Halfway up.

A little further, a few more inches. Then Bart motioned Del aside and put a foot to it. The table tipped toward the staircase and fell with a thud upon the top step. Two legs snapped off. And that's where it hung.

Two-thirds of the way. Still coming.

Del cursed, gave it a kick of his own. This time gravity took hold. The heavy tabletop slid off that step and onto the next, then caught and flipped and began tumbling chaotically. The vampire tried to evade the impromptu missile but its reflexes were as atrophied as its muscles. A corner of the spinning table caught it square in the crotch and threw it backward, bouncing it off the wall like a rag doll before both fiend and furniture crashed through the banister to the floor below.

"That won't stop him," Bart cursed, grabbing his brother by the coat sleeve and pulling him toward the hallway. But Del shook his grasp just long enough to tuck the nunchaku into his belt and retrieve one of the broken table legs at the head of the stairs. The end was jagged and sharp. Then he grabbed Bart's back pocket and followed close behind as they headed down the hall. He looked back once—*Keep it in sight or it'll get you*—but there was nothing on the stairs yet and then he was jerked through a doorway. Bart slammed the door behind them.

Starlings fluttered and squawked about the master bedroom like disturbed spirits before finding their way through the empty frames of the balcony doors. Bart wasn't far behind them. "C'mon, Cap," he stepped through and out onto the balcony that overlooked the garden. "We don't have much time."

"What about the door?"

"Fuck the door. It wouldn't hold him anyway. C'mon." Bart swung a leg over the balcony rail, chanced a look down, then kicked over and dropped out of sight.

"Bart!"

Del squeezed through one of the door frames, ran to the rail, and peered over. His brother was sitting on his butt on the discolored limestone below, rubbing one cheek tenderly. "C'mon, Cap. It's not that far."

"Are you kidding? It's at least ten feet."

"So what?"

"So I could break my neck, that's what."

"You little dick. If you don't hurry, that sonuvabitch is gonna do it for you. Now move!"

Del groaned his disapproval but there wasn't any arguing about it. There couldn't be, not if he wanted to live. He climbed over the rail and stood on the bare ledge. "Catch me if I fall, okay?"

"Delbert—"

"Okay, okay." He closed his eyes and stuck one foot into space. *C'mon, putz, you can do this, nothing to it, just drop for Chri'sake.* His hand left the rail. "Here goes nothing."

The doors made a calamitous sound as they shattered, filling the air with splinters of wood and the Christmasy jingle of broken glass. Del almost toppled from his perch from the shock. He made a desperate grab for the rail and held up the stake in futile defense against an attack that would overtake him in a split second.

Except . . .

It didn't.

He opened one eye and peered beneath his upraised arm. The balcony doors were intact and undamaged. For that matter so was the bedroom door. It was still closed. The room was empty.

Then what . . .

He looked down. What was left of the French doors that led to the garden now littered the porching below. The remaining panes of glass had shattered as well, littering the limestone with crystal fragments of reflected moonlight. There was no sign of his brother.

"Bart?" he whispered. There was nothing at first. "Bart?"

A grunt then, from nearby. A gasp.

Two figures sprawled from under the balcony and into the moonlight, struggling, growling. The taller, gaunter of the two was on the attack and forcing the other to his knees. One fractured forearm was pressed atop the youth's shoulder, holding him down, while the other had tangled in his red hair and pulled it mercilessly aside to bare his wildly pulsing throat. The teenager was fighting like a madman, pummeling that hideous countenance that loomed over him, but his blows had little effect. He couldn't keep that face from descending, or that cold mouth from fastening to his throat. All he could do was scream.

Del jumped without hesitation, aiming for the figures below, and he swung the wooden stake with all he could muster. The point struck home between jutting shoulder blades and sank deep, forcing a gust of abscessed air from the vampire's lungs and freeing Bart from its grasp. It staggered and fell to the porch, mouthing silent curses as it groped for the shaft that transfixed its back.

Del scrambled to his brother's side, found Bart wide-eyed and clutching his throat. "It bit me," he stammered, over and over. "It bit me, it—"

"Get up, dammit!" Delbert cursed, pulling him toward the garden steps. "We've gotta move now, while it's down, we've gotta—" Then he saw Bart's eyes grow wider still, staring past his shoulder. Oh, Jesus . . . He swallowed hard, forced himself to turn and look.

Their pursuer was getting to its feet, standing, facing them. And for the first time Del noticed that he'd driven the stake clear through his target—the point even tented the front of its shabby coat. But then the glowering vampire jerked the coat open, and the boys saw with horror that the wooden shaft did not sprout from its breast as they'd hoped. Instead it jutted from the pasty flesh just below the pectoral muscle, missing the heart completely. "Good . . . try," the thing said icily, taking hold of the stake's point and pulling it the rest of the way through with a guttural growl. Then it held the table leg out, pointed it at Del. "You first," it whispered, coming across the porch.

"Run, Cap!" Bart yelled, throwing himself between the two of them. But the stickman was too focused on the younger boy to pay him any heed. It simply batted him aside with the table leg, caught him just below the ear, and snapped his head around until his body had to follow. He spun across the porch and toppled down the garden steps.

Del went after him dizzily, nearly falling down the steps himself, fighting the tears from his eyes. He found Bart crumpled in the weeds like a much-abused doll. His arms and legs were akimbo. Blood flowed from his nostrils and lip. Del was frantic. *Oh, jeez, what if he's dead or hurt bad and I don't remember how to check for a pulse even and Oh, God what am I gonna do? How did they do it on TV?* He put a hand along his brother's carotid. *Oh, Lord, no . . . wait, there it is. Weak, but . . .*

"Not dead," came a hoarse voice. "Yet."

The skeletal figure on the porch tossed the stake aside and began to descend the steps to the garden. Its stark features were twisted and feral, but there was no emotion at all in those empty, dead eyes. It pointed to him. "You," it croaked as it came forward, and its tongue lolled obscenely. "You first."

Del stood on numb, shaking legs and drew Bart's chucks from

his belt. He swung the sticks in a lethal figure eight. "Come and get me, asshole."

A toothy smile. "Yes."

It took a step. The nunchaku snapped outward like a striking cobra and crushed the bridge of its nose, leaving a divot two fingers deep. The vampire recoiled, not so much from pain as surprise. When it came forward again, Del feinted to the head and went for one bony knee, cracked it soundly, then back to the face to reform the waxy flesh over its cheekbone. Anger flashed for an instant in those empty silver eyes. It attacked again and received the same treatment, but this time it did not retreat. Del hit it and kept hitting it, three and four times running, but each blow had less effect. They dimpled the flesh and split it and cracked the bones underneath, but pain did not register in those eyes. Only emptiness. The boy was straddling Bart's unconscious form now and could retreat no further. But still the enemy advanced. He swung out of desperation now and split the flesh over its cheekbone, separating the scar there, rupturing it so that it no longer resembled . . .

A cross?

Of course! Why didn't he think of it before? He brought the nunchaku around to a two-handed grip and crossed them, relieved that the chain was long enough. And finally he got a reaction. The undead thing reeled away from him, wide-eyed, gasping as if scalded. Its arms rose to shield its eyes. And then . . .

Then it did something to freeze his blood.

It laughed.

It peeked from under its arms and looked at him, directly at his mighty, improvised cross, and it laughed. Madly, hysterically. "Tsk, tsk," its dry voice grated. "Ye . . . of . . . little faith." It continued to cackle as it grabbed the boy by the jacket collar and lifted him off the ground.

And then the laughter suddenly faded.

It lowered Del back to the ground, for the moment ignoring him. It was looking away, over his shoulder, across the gardens and drive. Toward the woods.

The boy twisted around to follow its gaze.

There was a figure standing there in the moonlight, in swirls of midnight fog. Watching. The man was still some distance away, so his features were no more than a charcoal smudge. He was stoic and silent, a shadow in a long coat and floppy brimmed hat. Unmoving.

The vampire grinned at the prospect of a larger meal, but the expression became uncertain. "Who . . ." it cleared its raspy throat. "Who are you?"

The shadow man did not move nor answer.

The ghoul appeared unnerved, if any emotion at all could be read from such a face. Del's thoughts echoed its own. An enemy? Competition, perhaps? It must have decided on the latter, for it hoisted the boy aloft once more, feet dangling in the air, and pronounced, "Mine! Mine!"

Still no response.

"Who are you!"

The stranger finally moved. His right arm, hidden until now by the angle of his stance, brushed aside the flap of his coat and raised a stubby rifle. Del heard the bolt slam forward. He also heard a faint click, and saw a small red eye blink to life just above the barrel.

Del knew a laser sight when he saw one.

The fog illuminated the pencil-thin beam of redness as it lanced across the drive and gardens and over Del's shoulder, widening imperceptively as it went. The boy looked back to see a nickel-sized red dot dancing between the vampire's silver eyes.

There was a muffled burping sound from across the yard, short and stuttering.

Del heard the bullets whir past his ear like a swarm of angry bees and then the smack as they hit home. The vampire stumbled backward. Del fell to the ground beside his brother and stayed there, well out of the line of fire. He looked back as the vampire stumbled about near the garden steps, disoriented. A large section of its brow and left eye socket were now gone. There was no blood. The only redness there was that of the dancing dot, still zigzagging across a face that the creature was too stunned to cover up.

"Shoot!" Del cried. "Blow its fuckin' head off!!"

The machine gun burped again, and the vampire's face all but ceased to exist.

Each round slammed home with deadly efficiency, jolting the thing backward a step or two, sending bone shards and tissue spinning into the air like confetti. Its left cheekbone and eye disappeared completely and part of the jaw with them before the dot strayed to the other side of its face and spread the destruction there as well. There was still no blood; it was like shooting animated clay. It stumbled on the garden steps and fell and the laser followed, ignoring the hands that tried to fend it off. Another burst tore through its raised right talon and continued the devastation on the face beyond. "Who are you!" it cried again before its lips were torn away and its sharp, yellow teeth scattered across the steps. It wailed and gagged on pieces of itself as it tried to escape, fumbling and feeling its way out of the gardens and then along the side of the house.

The gunman had crossed the drive turnaround and was now standing at the edge of the garden, still firing at the fleeing figure. The red dot danced along its right leg and the accompanying burst ripped open the calf muscle and destroyed the knee joint above it, spilling the vampire onto its face but still not stopping it. It just scrabbled onward on all fours, a crab in the crabgrass, moving blindly toward the sanctuary of the woods.

The stocky man in the long coat paused there to pull the jungle clip from his rifle and flip it to the charged end. He then detached a plastic box from the ejection port and dumped the spent brass into his coat pocket. His eyes never left the escaping target. "Go after it," Del snapped. "Go after it, for God's sake!"

The bearded stranger barely granted him a glance. "I've already taken care of him," he said, then whispered over his shoulder, "It wasn't him, was it?"

Another voice sounded, deeper, huskier, but Del couldn't tell from where. "Not the Enemy," it said anxiously. "Hurry, check the house." The stranger nodded and stepped past Del, and for an instant the boy thought he had left his shadow behind on the tramped down grass. But then a cloud crossed the moon and the shadow was gone.

The man knelt beside Bart and checked his pulse, then inspected the puncture wounds on his neck. "Missed the artery," he observed, wiping the trickle of blood from the bite. "He'll be all right." He motioned for Del to come closer. "Are you okay?"

"I . . . I think so."

"Have you ever shot a rifle?"

"Just a twenty-two."

"Good enough." He worked the bolt and laid the machine gun in the boy's hands. "If you see anyone but me, put that light in the middle of their face. If they don't stop, just squeeze the trigger. Okay?" He brushed back his coat and drew two pistols, each a stainless steel semi-auto sporting an extended twenty-shot magazine and a miniature flashlight mounted to the frame. "Stay here," he warned. "Don't go near the house."

Like a gunman from the Old West with duster billowing and six-shooters at the ready, the stranger stalked onto the porch and through the ruined French doors, into the shadowy bowels of Danner House.

Del stood silently in the garden with his brother, cradling a machine gun in his arms and wanting to ask, who was that masked man?

Stiles stood in the cellar before the ruined wall and its exposed cell, pistols at his sides, and he wept. Not for the cell's prisoner, the thing he'd blown the shit out of in the gardens above. It deserved whatever it got.

Instead, he wept *because* of the cell. Because it was too small, too shallow. Because there was only enough room for one person inside, only one set of broken shackles. One entity, one evil. And it hadn't been the Enemy.

Again.

He slumped against the wall and slid onto his butt, feeling the fatigue wash over him and the tears burning his cheeks. He swept the cellar with his flashlight, but was no longer looking for monsters. Now he would've settled for a familiar shadow, the grumble of an accustomed voice, even an insincere "You tried, Hoss." But he already knew he was alone. His brother had gone, and an air of bitterness was all he'd left behind.

Chapter Five

Stiles retrieved the boys' gear from the cloakroom and stalked back through Danner House with a quick, determined stride. But his movements were no longer as cautious or focused as before. The hunt was over once again: still no Enemy. So the adrenaline rush that drove him, that kept him on a razor's edge, was fading, leaving him weary and disgusted and haunted by thoughts of Alex. He rationalized that it wasn't his fault, just as he'd always done in the past. *Alex led you here. It was Alex's job to find the evil. It's his failure, not yours.* But none of the excuses could assuage his guilt or make the hurt go away.

His mind was still preoccupied with his brother as he stepped through the doorway to the garden, so he didn't notice the quivering red dot that suddenly appeared on his chest. It was only a split second later, when the laser touched a wisp of fog between the porch and garden and became visible, that the realization jolted him. He barely had time to drop his burden and dive back through the doorway as the H & K's sputtering report rolled across the clearing like muffled thunder. Three rounds tore into the doorjamb just above Stiles's head, while the rest of the volley sizzled past him and stitched a ragged pattern on the nearest wall. "Whoa, kid, waitaminute," he called. "It's me!"

"Oh, lordy. I'm sorry," came an adolescent voice, cracking with fear. Stiles dared to peek around the doorjamb and found the two boys still in the garden where he'd left them. The older one had regained consciousness and was propped on an elbow, feeling at the wound in his neck, while the younger kneeled beside him and still held the machine gun at his shoulder. When he saw Stiles's face he gave a nervous smile and finally lowered the muzzle. "I, uh, didn't know, you know, that it was you, and I, uh . . . sorry."

"Never mind," Stiles sighed as he stepped back onto the porch. "You only did what I told you to. I should have yelled first." He picked up the sleeping bags and backpacks, carried them down, and piled them at the foot of the garden steps. Then he took the machine gun from the boy's trembling hands, flipped the safety, and slung the weapon over his shoulder on a nylon strap.

"Why'd you let that fucker get away, huh?" Del wanted to know. "What was so important about getting into the house?"

Stiles knew better than to try explaining. "Nothing. Just being careful."

"I coulda told you there weren't any other vampires in there. At least we didn't see any. Just that one. Hell, you shouldn't'a even bothered with the house. You should've just nailed that sonuvabitch when you had the chance."

Stiles almost snapped at the boy—he didn't need reminding of his own impatience—but he caught himself. Del was just letting his fear talk; it was either that or give in to the tears that he was barely holding back. "You're right, kid," Stiles admitted, though his casualness, his lack of alarm seemed to calm the boy somewhat. "I should have destroyed him when I had the chance. But I did tear him up pretty good, and that's the next best thing. I don't think he'll be bothering anyone again."

Del was still apprehensive. "How can you be so sure?"

"Trust me," Stiles said and managed a slight smile. "I've been in this situation before. Now, what's your name?"

"I'm Del," the boy told him, "and that's Bart."

"Nice to meet you," Stiles said. Then he turned his attention to the red-haired teen, who was not only conscious but had finally managed to sit up straight. Bart's jaw was already dark and starting to swell where he'd been struck, and he kept a hand clamped over his throat. "How're you doing?" the soldier asked him.

"I've been bit, that's how I'm doing," Bart snapped irritably. His voice was anxious, almost panicked. "Jeez, what's gonna happen to me now, huh? I mean, how bad is it, or—"

"Just calm down," said the soldier, prying the boy's hand

away from his throat to reveal the bite mark. Bart tensed; he expected a gasp of horror, maybe a sigh of futility. "Like I said before," Stiles shrugged. "It's not too deep, and he missed the artery. You'll be fine."

"But what about aftereffects? Dammit, what's gonna happen to me!"

"Don't worry about it," Stiles said, shaking his head. "Take my word for it, you're gonna be okay. Right now, let's concentrate on getting you two out of here." He pulled the young man to his feet. "You think you can walk?"

Bart forced a weak grin. "Don't worry about me, Rambo. I can run if I have to."

"Good. My van's parked not far from here, about a mile past the front gate, around the bend in the road. You two stay close to me and—"

"You mean through the woods?" Del interrupted. His eyes were wide and incredulous. "But . . . but that's where the thing went. It crawled into the woods."

"Not in the same place," Stiles assured him. "Besides, he's in no condition to give us any trouble. Just stay close to me and you'll be all right."

"Nuh uh, no way. I ain't going nowhere near there. No way."

"Suit yourself," the soldier shrugged. Then he turned and walked away.

Bart and Del exchanged looks. Then the older boy grabbed up their bags, pushed one into Del's hands, seized him by the collar, and started walking him across the garden. "Hey, Rambo," he called, "Wait up, will ya?"

Stiles slowed enough for them to fall in behind him. The younger boy was silent, obviously terrified. "Just stay close," Stiles whispered. "You'll be fine. I promise."

The boy nodded but said nothing. He just took a good hold on Bart's back pocket, and Bart in turn grabbed the tail of Stiles's long coat. "You don't mind, do you, Rambo?"

The soldier pulled a flashlight from his belt. "What I do mind is that name," he said softly. "It's Stiles. Chris if you have to. Screw it up again and you'll get four C-cells up your ass. Got it?" The teenager managed a feeble grin and said nothing. Stiles flicked on the light, unslung the H & K and towed his charges toward the woods.

A lump started to form in the back of the soldier's throat as they neared the leafy wall of shadows. It had the familiar bitter taste of fear, and he couldn't understand its presence. *There's nothing to worry about*, he told himself. *The vampire is helpless now; it hasn't any eyes to see with or mouth to bite with or even a knee joint to support it. It's slithering around out there like a slug in the dirt, more interested in a place to hide than any victims it might crawl across. It's helpless.* But it was no use. All the rationalizing in the world couldn't ease the tension in his muscles or the knot of apprehension in his gut. Perhaps it was for the better. Being afraid put him back on guard again. It brought back that rush of adrenaline, chased away the fatigue, focused his concentration, sharpened his senses. It also brought back memories. For a minute, it was like old times again, walking point, back in the jungle.

Almost.

"Wait a minute. I heard something."

"You always hear something, Cap. I'll tell you, Ram . . . er, Mr. Stiles, you should've heard him on the way in here—"

"No, I did hear something. Footsteps. It sounded like footsteps in the leaves."

The soldier showed no alarm. "I blew its knee off, Del," he said without turning. "It can't walk, remember?"

The boy was silent a moment, considering. "It might have healed itself or grew another one or something," he decided. "You never know about these vampires. They're dead. They're all messed up."

"Oh, get real, you little dick."

"Screw you, Bart. I'd rather be a dick than an asshole."

"Hey, squirt, how about I stomp a mudhole in your ass here and now?"

Stiles stopped and shined his light back on the tall redhead and the short dark-haired child. "You're brothers, right?"

"How did you know?"

He shook his head. "A lucky guess. C'mon."

It was even darker in that stretch of the woods than along the drive where the boys had come in; the trees were dense, maze-like, and they couldn't take three steps in any direction without fighting off the grope of low limbs. More than once Del shrieked, only to find in the glare of Bart's Mag-Lite that he'd been snagged by a particularly unterrifying sticker bush. Stiles slipped through it all with quick, sure steps, as if the path had been burned into his memory on the way in. But to the boys it was bewildering —for all they knew they were going in circles. The tendrils of fog became opaque in the glare of the flashlights, not only obscuring their path but closing in behind them, hemming them in. "How much further?" Del kept asking anxiously.

"We're here," Stiles said, leading them under the bough of a leaning dogwood. They found themselves facing a seemingly impenetrable obstruction of weeds and vine. A dead end. Del started to hyperventilate but then the soldier reached out with his gun barrel and pulled aside some of the creepers to reveal brick beneath. A wall . . . the privacy wall that surrounded the Danner estate. The boys sighed heavily as Stiles threw their gear over the top, then held out a gloved hand at waist level while keeping the machine gun ready with the other. "Step up, Del. You're first."

He had to lean down to get the boy's shoe in his hand but, once in place, Del locked his legs and was boosted to the top of the wall. From there he could see the man's van, rusted fenders and all, parked just off the road in the underbrush and concealed by it. He dropped to the other side just as Bart stepped up. Despite Bart's larger size, Stiles lifted him to the top as well. Then he handed up his rifle, took a few steps back and vaulted to the crest himself. From there, they dropped to the ground next to Del.

"Now what?" the boy wanted to know.

Stiles walked to the van with them still in tow. At least they'd let go of his coat. "First I put something on Bart's wounds."

"And then?"

"Then I take you home."

"And then?"

Stiles turned and looked at them squarely. "Just what are you getting at, kid?"

Del was incredulous. "Aren't you gonna do something about that . . . that thing?"

Stiles offered the machine gun. "You want to go in after it?" The boy begged off. "I didn't think so. Look, kid, I'm not stupid. That thing may be crippled, but it's still dangerous, especially in the close quarter of the woods. Why take the chance tracking it now when we can just wait it out? It's already as good as dead."

"Oh yeah? And how can you be so sure?"

"Experience," the soldier replied. "I'm a hunter. I've stalked a lot of strange things over the years. And a few of them were like your friend out there." He opened the side door of the van and ushered the boys inside, then followed after them. "Sit down here," he motioned to Bart. "I want to put something on that bite."

Bart looked to Del fearfully. "What are we talking here? Holy water?"

Stiles laughed. "Not quite." He took a first-aid kit from one of the cabinets, and from that retrieved a bottle of Bactine antiseptic. "This might sting a little," he warned, tilting the boy's head so he could spray the wound.

"That's it?"

"You watch too much TV. This isn't any different than a dog bite. It only counts when they drain you completely."

"What you said 'while ago," Del asked the soldier, "about hunting other things. What kinds of things?"

"It's a long story," Stiles replied. "But there were a few vampires. Let me see . . . there was one in New Orleans, and one in California. And in Maine . . . hell, when I was in Maine, they were running like cockroaches. So, yeah, I guess that makes me an expert on the subject, and this expert is telling you that most of your movies and TV are full of shit." He finished bandaging Bart's neck, then reached into the cooler between the seats where the ice had all but melted and handed him a Coke to hold against his swelling jaw. "There. I think you'll live, but you'd better see a doctor just to be safe."

Bart groaned. "Mom's gonna hit the roof."

"She should," said Stiles. "What the hell were you doing in there?"

The redhead shrugged, embarrassed. "A bet. A stupid bet, and it almost got us killed. What were you doing in there, Mr. Stiles?"

Stiles took off his coat, then his holsters, then his combat vest. "Like I said. I'm a hunter, of sorts." He touched a button on the van's built-in cot. A latch clicked and the front panel fell open, revealing the strapped-in Uzi pistol and magazines and the empty recess where he quickly mounted the H & K rifle. "You didn't see this," he cautioned the boys after shutting the panel. "Is that clear?"

"Yes, sir."

Del moved to the window and stared outside, into a darkness his eyes could not possibly penetrate. "It's still out there," he said, shivering. "I can feel it."

Stiles put a hand on his shoulder. "Let me tell you about vampires. We're not talking about Dracula here. There's nothing romantic or seductive about them. They're just like you saw tonight: dead bodies who refuse to die, who have to feast on the blood of the living to survive. Aside from that, it's hard to tell where the legends stop and the bullshit starts. There's no black capes or hypnotic gazes. They can't change into bats or rats or fog—"

"Then how did he get out of the cellar ahead of us?" Del interrupted. "An outside door?"

"No," Stiles told him. "The outer door was still padlocked and nailed shut."

"Then how?"

He gave it some thought, then shrugged. "How the hell should I know? But there has to be some other way, 'cause he didn't turn into smoke." The boy looked skeptical. "Okay, smart-ass, answer this. If he could turn into a wisp of fog, how come he didn't do it while I was blasting the living shit out of him?" Del pondered that long and hard, exchanged looks with Bart, and finally settled for a shrug of his own. "Boys, if they could change, I'd have seen one do it by now."

"How much of the other stories are true?" Bart asked. "How do you stop them?"

Stiles sat down in the pilot's seat and swiveled it around so he could talk to them. "Some of the traditional ways hold up —wooden stake, sunlight, fire, the cross—"

"No, I tried that one," Del made a face. "The asshole just laughed at me."

Stiles nodded. "I know, I saw you. But the cross does work, the same as holy water and wafer and the Star of David and any other religious symbol. There's just a catch to it. Their power is only proportionate to the faith of the wielder. If you don't believe, it doesn't work."

"Now hang on. I go to church every Sunday—"

"And sleep through the sermon," said Bart. "Admit it, Cap. We both go because Mom makes us." He looked back to Stiles. "What about decapitation?"

"Sure. And that's where it gets interesting. If decapitation works, why not dismemberment? Hell, they're flesh and blood, or flesh at least. They should obey the same basic physical rules as everyone else."

"Physical rules?"

"Simple body mechanics," Stiles explained. "If I cut off your legs, you can't walk, right? The same goes for a vampire. Blind it, it can't see. Destroy its mouth, it can't bite, its knees, it can't get around. It won't die, but it won't heal either. It's dead flesh; there's no regeneration. Whatever condition you leave them in, that's the way they'll stay."

He motioned toward the window. "Take our friend out there. He's blind, faceless, crawling around in the dirt and the leaves. He won't find prey. He won't get off that estate, not with these walls to hold him. He'll wallow around, searching for someplace to hide, a hollow tree or a shallow cave, and if he's lucky he might find it. But sooner or later the sun will catch up to him, and when it does, Poof! Dustball. So there's nothing to worry about, Del. It's as good as dead."

The boy nodded his understanding. But he still kept his vigil at the window.

Stiles finished putting his gear away, then started the van, and steered it out onto Sykes Road, heading back toward town. Bart climbed into the passenger seat while Del curled up on the cot in the back, pulled his coat over him, and fell silent. He felt a semblance of safety laying there atop the soldier's cache of weapons. The sheer firepower granted him some solace. But when they passed the Danner gate even that wasn't enough. He hid his head and kept it hidden most of the way to town.

The boys were silent, and that worried Stiles. Del could've been asleep for all the rearview mirror told him but Bart was wide-eyed and staring. He tried to talk to the boy but received only monosyllables in reply. The shock was just now setting in, Stiles could tell; they were finally realizing that it hadn't been a dream after all, nice and neat and set apart from the rest of the world. It was real, and it existed right alongside the Tunnel and the town and everything else they knew intimately. The sight of things familiar along the roadway was bringing the horror home.

He wondered if they'd come through it okay.

He had. But that was a whole different circumstance. He was battle-hardened by the time he had his first confrontation with the supernatural, and it had still left him numb and shaken for days. He'd gotten used to it, of course, but only because he had to; he had Alex's mission to complete, an Enemy to hunt. But these boys . . .

They neared the perpetual dark of the Tunnel and Bart tensed, squeezing the edge of his seat frantically. But his eyes adjusted quickly once inside and his grip loosened. He looked at the cars parked just off the roadway and surprised himself with an ironic chuckle. "If they knew what was running around just down the road," he said, "what do you bet they'd shit their pants for sure?" He took the Coke can away from his jaw, popped the tab, took a big swig, and grimaced. "I hate Coke. Got any Mountain Dew?"

Del roused in the back. "Did someone say Mountain Dew?"

Stiles grinned. They were going to be just fine.

They drove into Isherwood and turned off into the suburbs, passing streets with names like Chester and Walnut and Sycamore. Two houses past the corner of Greenbriar Avenue, the van eased to a stop before a small brick two-story with the proverbial white picket fence. Along the side of the mailbox MILLER was emblazoned in red letters. Stiles stared at it. Wasn't that Billie's last name, the girl at the diner? Nah. He shrugged. It was a common name—probably three or four even in a town that small.

Bart pointed toward the empty driveway. "The car's not here." He sounded puzzled. "Mom worked s'afternoon . . . wonder where she is now?"

"Take your gear inside," Stiles said. "Maybe there's a note."

"I doubt it," the boy shook his head but complied anyway. "She wasn't expecting us home. We're supposed to be spending the night with a friend." He loaded both bags over his shoulders and trudged up the walk a bit dizzily. He paused at the door to fish a key from his pocket, then went inside. Within a few minutes he returned. "She's working an extra shift at the diner tonight," he reported, "till two. Could you give us a ride over there, Mr. Stiles? I'd just as soon you were there when the shit hits the fan."

The diner, huh? "Sure," he smiled. "I could use a cup of coffee about now."

Billie Miller didn't realize her eyes had strayed to the front door of the diner until Frank Sipes's voice chided her: "Billie old gal, I think I'd just as soon have my coffee in a cup, if it ain't too much trouble."

She looked down, uncomprehending, to see a river of Sanka on the countertop and not a drop of it in the salesman's cup. "Damn!" she cursed, with a few shits and hells thrown in under her breath for good measure, as she grabbed for a roll of paper towels. "Where is my mind tonight?"

"If you ask me," he continued, taking pains not to slur his speech, "I'd say you're kinda expecting someone. Eh?" He gave her an exaggerated wink and guffawed loudly.

Billie lined up his cup and hit it dead center this time. "Drink your coffee, Frank," she ordered, ignoring his comments. "The quicker you sober up, the quicker your wife will let you in."

"To hell with Irene," he sneered, throwing up his arms dramatically. Just as quickly his features softened again and he grinned and patted Billie's hand on the countertop. "There are other places in town to spend the night. Eh?"

That brought a raucous laugh from the older woman working the grill behind Billie. Sharon Lou Moore, the store's owner, glared over her bifocals at the drunken salesman and warned, "Peddle your wares somewhere else, Frank. She's waiting on someone, remember?"

The salesman blinked at them numbly as if hit, but slowly his grin returned, minus its bravado, and he just shrugged and stared into his coffee.

Oh great, Billie sighed. *Now his feelings are hurt. What a day this has turned out to be!*

But it had started off so well. She'd met this guy from out of town, a writer, and they'd hit it off from the start. There was something about him . . . It could've been because he was articulate, or funny, or simply because they could maintain a conversation beyond the weather-and-what's-on-the-menu stage.

And then again, maybe it was his looks. She wasn't above the attraction of rocky muscle and rugged features. Even a beard. But whatever it was, it gave her the chills, and Lord knew she hadn't felt those for a while. Hell, Gordon never gave her chills, not once, and she married him! This man Chris Stiles, he had something special. It had to be to make a grown woman feel like a giggling teenager, and even more so to make her act like one. Which is just what she was doing.

Admit it. That's why you volunteered for late shift. Not the money, though it was certainly incentive. You thought he might come back in. He didn't say he would, but since the diner was open late tonight . . .

"Snap out of it, Bill," Sharon Lou interrupted, sliding two burger-and-fry platters along the counter. "Table three's up."

The diner section of the store was relatively busy at close to one in the morning. There was Frank Sipes, of course, perched on his sobriety stool just like every weekend. Ted Cooper was also there, sitting at table three with his perennial sweetheart, Doreen Moody, ogling each other dreamily, holding hands and playing with each other's fingers as they waited for their food. The only other customer, a tall, gaunt figure in dark clothes, sat at the farthest table along the wall. At first Billie didn't recognize him; George Bailey seldom ventured down from the boarding-house-cum-nursing home on the hill, and the few times she had seen him he was always bearded and unkempt. But this man was newly shaven and had slicked down white hair and a well-pressed suit, if a bit out of style. He looked clean, like a wet cat. She'd never realized how skinny he was, how frail and old, at least in his nineties. Billie felt sorry for him. A forgotten old man, alone, getting dressed up only to sit by himself and stare into his coffee. She shivered. At least she had her boys.

The cowbell over the front door clanked, louder than during the day or at least it seemed that way. Billie looked up and smiled, but the man coming through the door didn't return her greeting. Charlie Bean was in no mood to smile.

He came around the front along the chain cordon that separated the diner area from the drugstore. He wasn't in uniform, just a white T-shirt and jeans, though the bulge of a pistol grip was evident beneath his shirttail. Everyone said hello or waved. But Bean was silent, and for him that just wasn't natural.

"Trouble on patrol?" Billie asked as he sat down at the counter.

"At home," he corrected, lighting a cigarette to replace the butt he'd flicked away outside the door. Lou was already moving, setting an ashtray and a bowl of chili in front of him before he could think to ask. "Thank you, Kreskin," he nodded. "What about something to drink?"

Billie sat his coffee in front of him. "What did Susie throw you out for now?"

"She didn't throw me out," he said defensively, then softer, "She just won't let me in."

"Here, here!" Frank Sipes cheered a kindred soul. Everyone ignored him.

"What for this time, Chuck?"

He sighed dramatically. "Because we had plans, and I had to cancel to take late shift. What is it with women? Don't they realize that working pays the bills and puts the food on the table? What the hell are they thinking of?"

Billie leaned against the counter, tired and annoyed. "That's right, Charlie. Us women don't appreciate how hard the world is. We're too busy out buying minks and diamonds and making life hell for you men."

Bean grinned. "That's what I thought."

"I've just had a brainstorm, Chuck," Lou said. "Why don't you use your keys to get in? Did it ever occur to you?"

"Yes it occurred to me, wise-ass." He leaned closer and cleared his throat to cover his words. "She's got chairs jammed under the knobs."

"Here, here!" This time Bean stared Frank back into his coffee cup.

"Just give her time," Billie counseled. "She'll simmer down. She always does."

"Yeah, but until then I'm sleeping at the jail." He looked around him, then into the darkened drugstore. He snapped his fingers. "A gift! I'll take her a gift. You got something around here she'd like? Something cheap?"

Billie shook her head and chuckled. "You're a real romantic, you know that?"

He brushed her off with a sly grin. "Oh, it's romance you women like, huh? Like that character I saw you fawnin' over this morning?'' She feigned ignorance. ''Oh come off it, Billie. I saw you batting your eyes at him and giggling like a schoolgirl''—her face blushed at her own analogy—''and him being a stranger and all. Hell, you don't know a thing about him.''

''Says you.''

''Oh, you do? Such as?''

She reached across the counter as if to punch him. ''The cops on TV do that a whole lot better. If you want information on the guy, why don't you run a check on him.''

He finished savoring a mouthful of soup and saltines. ''I already did. I want to know what he told you.'' She made no move to answer. ''You're really after this guy, aren't you?

''I'm not after anybody.''

''Okay, let's trade. Yours for mine.''

She considered that and agreed. ''His name is Chris,'' she said, calling up information that hadn't strayed far from her mind all day long. ''He's a writer—''

''But he told me—''

''—who does handyman work to get by and would you please not interrupt. He heard the ghost stories about the Danner place and thought there might be a book there. He's staying at the Tri-Lakes Inn for a few days. Maybe longer.'' She held back from saying, ''if I have anything to do with it.''

The slack look on Bean's face told her it was nothing new. ''A writer, huh? Well, I've never heard of him.''

''Well, coming from a man who can't finish a *TV Guide*, that doesn't surprise me. Now cough up, Charlie. He checked out clean, didn't he?''

The deputy bowed his head in defeat. ''Nothing good,'' changed to, ''Nothing major.'' He looked her straight in the eye. ''You really are smitten, aren't you?''

She blushed and took a swipe at him with a menu. ''Would you stop? I just think he's . . . interesting, that's all. Stop making more of it than there is.'' She looked back toward the door expectantly. ''Hell, it's academic anyhow. He's probably heard all about the Black Widow of Isherwood by now, an' how she marries 'em and buries 'em.''

Bean winced at that and almost gagged on his coffee. ''Aw c'mon, Billie. No one thinks of you that way,'' he assured her, hoping he wasn't blushing too badly. Her "Black Widow" moniker was, after all, his invention—a drunken remark made years ago during a game of darts at the tavern. He'd never meant for it to get back to her, and had been regretting it ever since. "You're still a damn fine . . . well, you know what I mean."

"Here, here!"

"Drink your coffee, Frank."

Ted Cooper pulled his eyes away from his date just then as a sudden chill swept the diner. "Damn," he said, reaching for his jacket, "I feel a draft." He looked across the store. "Hey, dude. Close the door, okay?"

Billie looked up. The bell hadn't sounded but the door stood open nonetheless. Chris Stiles held it propped with his foot. Everyone turned to stare at the mystery man, silhouetted in the doorway by the street lamps outside. Billie started to wave hello but hesitated, her anxiousness giving way to apprehension. Why hadn't the bell rung?

"Hi," he said. "Is that chili I smell?"

"Of course," Lou snapped, "so get in here and shut the door. You're letting the warm air out."

"I'll buy that," he nodded, "but do you have enough for three?" He motioned outside. Two figures shuffled along the display window and stepped past him. Stiles closed the door behind them, and this time the bell sounded.

Billie's mouth went slack as Del and Bart managed a weak "Hi, Mom." There was no argument: they looked awful. Both wore jackets smeared with dirt and leaking wispy down from half a dozen rips. The bandages on Bart's neck had absorbed a spot of blood, and that single spot seemed to magnify the severity of the wound fives times at least. He just gave them a lopsided grin and tried not to move his swollen, discolored jaw any more than he had to.

"How're you all doin'?" Del said to break the silence. Then everyone came rushing over to see to them, or almost everyone. Frank Sipes looked concerned but didn't stray from his stool. George Bailey didn't move a muscle, not even to turn and look.

Billie ushered the boys to the nearest table, ignoring their assurances that it wasn't as bad as it looked. Everyone hovered around them. Sharon Lou brought a first-aid kit from under the counter, though their wounds appeared already well tended. Ted offered to take his Slugger to the perpetrators, several times if necessary. Charlie Bean just stood nearby, listening, watching Stiles. "Are you all right?" Billie asked, touching their bandages and flinching for them.

"We're fine, Mom."

"Are you sure? Maybe we should call Dr. Collins. . . ."

"I said we're okay, Mom! Jeez, don't make such a federal case out of it!"

Stiles spoke up. "I think they're all right, Billie."

"Oh?" Bean raised an eyebrow. "You done much doctoring, Mr. Stiles?"

"Just the battlefield variety. Vietnam." Bean nodded and fell silent once again. "Billie, I'd feel better if you get them a checkup in the morning."

The pretty young mother suddenly turned stern and grabbed her youngest son by the shoulders. "All right, young man," she demanded. "What the hell happened?!"

"Yeah," echoed Frank, "what the hell happened?!"

"We got into a fight."

"That's obvious. With who?"

"I don't know. Can I have something to eat?"

"The whole story this time. Did Jay Simpson have something to do with this? I knew that kid was trouble—"

"Cut it out, Mom." Bart was defensive. "Jay had nothing to do with it. We didn't even stay at his house. His mom didn't know anything about his inviting us over, so we just went out jackin' around."

"Jacking around?"

"We went out to the Tunnel," Del said, glancing at Stiles for support, "to play a practical joke. And then these guys jumped us, beat Bart up pretty good. Pretty straightforward if you ask me. What about that chili?"

"A fight at the Tunnel?" Ted stomped his foot, disgusted. "We were just out there a little while ago. Damn, I miss everything!"

"We didn't recognize them, Charlie," Bart said. "Probably out-of-town guys. We didn't even get a good look at their car, the Tunnel was so dark. It's just a good thing Mr. Stiles came along when he did."

"Did you get a look at the car?" Bean asked Stiles. The latter shook his head.

"I was more concerned with these two, to tell you the truth. Sorry. I guess I should've been a little more observant."

"I'm just glad you were there when you were," Billie took his hand, then leaned over and kissed his cheek. The boys exchanged bemused expressions. Charlie Bean just looked bored.

"I didn't know you 'uns knew each other," Bart grinned, still lopsided. Billie suddenly became aware of the eyes on her and drew away from Stiles, busying herself with the boys instead. "How about something to eat?"

"It's about time," Del sighed.

Sharon started for the counter ahead of Billie. "Three bowls of chili, on the house." Stiles smiled at that, and so did his empty pockets.

The furor over the boys' condition finally subsided as the three of them sat down to their late meal. Ted and Doreen left; knowing Ted, probably to cruise the Tunnel with his bat close at hand. Frank quieted down as he sobered up. Mr. Bailey just sat.

Billie perched herself between Stiles and the boys and gravitated between casting him smiles and continuously rechecking Bart's wounds or scolding Delbert. Charlie Bean sat astraddle a chair at the next table, finishing his coffee and watching the boys. "You sure you're all right?" he finally asked. They nodded, for the fourteenth time. "Well, it sure is lucky you came along, Mr. Stiles."

"Chris, please."

"Oh, that's right. Tell me, just what were you doing out there?"

Stiles gave him an open, innocent expression. "Ghost-hunting. I went out to look at the Danner House. But you can't see it from the road, and the gate's chained shut. So, I came back toward town and that's when I spotted these guys. You think you'll catch the ones that did this?"

Del and Bart exchanged glances.

"With no description of them or the car?" Bean snorted. "Not likely. Like a needle in a haystack, that's what it'd be. I'd just consider it a lesson learned the hard way and forget about it. You boys are going to stay away from the Tunnel from now on, aren't you?"

Billie was shocked. "That's it? A lesson learned? What kind of police force is this?"

"Goddamn it, Billie, what do you want me to do?"

"Calm down, Mom," Bart shushed her, embarrassed. "He's already said there's nothing he can do. Leave it alone." He looked around the diner. "Hey, has anyone seen the paper today?" He went over to George Bailey's table and asked for the folded *Herald* on the chair beside him. The old man slapped the paper into the boy's middle without looking up. Bart returned to their table, whispering, "What's up that old guy's ass?"

"He's just old, honey," Billie said, looking at the stick-thin man with sympathy. "He lives up on the hill. I don't think he has anyone." The thought made her impulsively hug Del, much to the boy's embarrassment.

"Well," Bean said with a raucous sigh as if to announce something important, "I'm going home." He ground his ninth butt into the ashtray and laid a bill beside it. "If she doesn't open up this time, I'll kick the door down."

"You mean you'll sleep at the jail?"

He broke into his patented shit-eating grin. "More than likely. Boys, you take care of yourselves." He turned to Stiles. "Still interested in that work?"

"I'll be over first thing in the morning."

"Well, I won't. Late shift again tomorrow night. But I told the marshall you'd be by sooner or later. Well, g'night, all." As he went out, he opened and closed the door several times but couldn't keep the bell from clanking. He finally gave up and left, shaking his head.

"I'd better get back to work," Billie said. "We'll be closing pretty soon. Chris, how'd you like to come by for a drink after I get off?" She realized immediately how serious she'd sounded and thought to add, "Wouldn't we like that, boys?"

He shook his head. "It's getting kinda late. . . ."

Del reached over and touched his hand. "Please, Mr. Stiles?" The fear was still there in his eyes.

He smiled. "Sure, why not?" Billie beamed radiantly and, straightening her apron, went back to the counter where Frank Sipes had fallen sleep on folded arms.

Del looked over at his silent brother. "Hey, Bart," Del wondered, "what are you working on?"

The older boy had spread the front page of the Friday paper on the table and was doctoring the photo on it with an ink pen. He finished and offered it to Stiles. "Look familiar?"

The face in the grainy photograph had been withered with blue ink, the cheeks hollowed and a scar added, the brows darkened, the hair grown long and wild. In fact, the photo no longer looked like Sebastian Danner at all. It looked like something altogether different, something monstrous. Something from beyond the grave . . . or beyond a cellar wall.

Chapter Six

At a little past two in the morning, the Tunnel wasn't nearly as busy as it had been earlier. Only a few cars remained, their drivers either those too drunk to make it home, or waiting each other out to see just how scary the Tunnel could be in the wee hours of the morn. Most were parked near the Isherwood end.

Headlights appeared in the mouth of the Tunnel and moved slowly past them. Most dismissed it as Charlie Bean on patrol again. A few noticed the yellow T-Bird, didn't recognize it, and prepared themselves for some out-of-town trouble. But the car didn't stop. It drove on into the blackness of the Tunnel, until it was swallowed up.

Only when it reached the far end did it cut its lights and ease itself into the brush alongside the road. The motor grumbled and went silent.

"Well, fuck me!" Fat Larry wheezed, looking around as he took another drag off the joint Doug Baugh had just passed him. "What the hell are we doing back out here?" He shivered. "I don't like it. It's goddamn spooky's what it is."

Tommy climbed out from behind the wheel and crawled atop the car's hood, reclining against the windshield with his hands behind his head. "I don't know, I kinda like it out here. Any reason why I shouldn't? Huh?" In the front Doug just shrugged stupidly, drained his beer can, and crushed it against his forehead. "What about you, Fatso?"

Larry climbed out the back window and staggered threateningly around the side of the car. "Don't call me fatso," he warned.

"That's right, Tommy," Doug corrected, lighting another joint and grafting it to his lower lip. "He doesn't like fatso. Now lard-ass, that he doesn't mind, but fatso . . ."

"I don't like that either."

"Then why did you let Miller get away with it?"

"Well, I . . ." The fat kid mulled it over and kicked at the grass, then caught their questioning glares. "What, you think I'm scared of him? Bart Miller? Hell, that redheaded fart, I could feed him his ass for breakfast if I wanted to."

"You just didn't want to, is that it?"

Larry grated his teeth and looked as if smoke might puff from his ears. "Why don't you get out of the goddamn car, Baugh, and I'll show you how scared I am."

"No, I don't think so," Doug smiled between hits on the joint as he put his feet up on the dash. "I'll just stay in here. Thanks anyway."

"Chickenshit."

"I think I know why Larry held off," Tommy decided. "He didn't want to screw Miller up and make them chicken out of the bet. Isn't that right, Larry?"

"Uh . . . yeah."

"After all, fifty bucks is fifty bucks, right? Who knows, we may have enough left over to pay your brother back for the beer. Maybe."

"Hey, Tommy," Doug wheezed through another drag. "What makes you think we'll win the bet?"

Tommy gave them a gap-toothed grin. "Old son, I'd just about say that money is in the bag."

"Uh oh," Doug said, climbing out of the car and suddenly interested, "I'd say the boy's got something up his sleeve."

Tommy opened his jacket sleeve and peered inside. "I don't see anything. . . ."

"Quit jackin', Tommy. What've you got in mind?"

The oily grin spread even further. He slid off the hood and

sauntered to the back of the car, taking his time until the others followed behind. Then he popped the trunk open. "Who's for big fun?" he asked, swinging it wide.

Doug reached into the box of Halloween supplies there and pulled out a ghoulish rubber mask with one bloodshot eyeball bobbling loose over the cheek. "What the hell is this all about?"

Tommy cocked the brim of his Daiwa cap and beamed. "They say that old Danner place is haunted. I just want to make sure, you know?"

Larry stared blankly. "No, I don't know."

"We're gonna scare the shit out of the Millers, Goodyear," he snapped, irritated. "Anybody ever confuse you two with nuclear scientists? Never mind. Help me get this stuff out."

The box contained a little bit of everything: plastic glow-in-the-dark fangs, Vampire Blood, fluorescent makeup, rubber masks, and rubber hands and some rubbers that didn't belong there at all and were quickly pocketed. There was an ax too. "That's my coup de gracie," Tommy said, hefting the "Red Chopper" camp hatchet with one hand. "They see me in my outfit with this thing and they'll shit in their skivvies."

"This is gonna be great," Larry agreed after claiming a pitted and bloody hockey mask for his own. "I just got one question. Why did we park all the way back here? Why didn't we just park near the gate?"

"Yeah, Tommy, how come?"

"Didn't you two see all the cars parked back there? If that deputy should come back on patrol, he's not gonna ask any questions about one more car, is he? Besides, if we go over the wall just up the road we can come up on the house from a different angle than they did, so they won't see us coming."

Fat Larry looked down the dark road and shook his head. "I don't know, Tommy. Looks like a pretty good distance."

"What's a matter," Doug laughed, "afraid you'll walk off a few pounds?"

Tommy shot the heavy boy a withering glare. "You could always stay with the car. Is that what you want?"

"Hell no," he ruffled. "I was just thinkin'. . . ." but he trailed off and finally let the notion die. "Screw it," he shrugged, dismissing the chill at the back of his neck. "Let's go get those bastards. Nobody calls me Lard-ass."

Each of them stuffed a few Halloween goodies into their jackets; then they shut the trunk and fished the last few beers from the cooler in the backseat and started down Sykes Road on foot. Within fifty yards the T-Bird was gone, swallowed by the darkness behind them.

Larry walked a few steps behind the others, unable to keep up with them or keep his eyes off the overgrowth all around them. The moon was a spotlight in the sky, so bright and clear he could almost see Jackie Gleason's face in it, but a bank of clouds kept upstaging it and limiting their visibility to just the road before them. The fog seemed denser as well, and glowing.

He buttoned his jacket up around his neck and kept walking.

Tommy and Doug seemed caught up in their own worlds. Tommy was talking incessantly about a big-titted checkout girl at the IGA who'd had an eye on him earlier, while Doug matched him word for word with talk of carbs and headers and how it wouldn't be long before his Ramblin' Rambler was "street lethal." Neither one of them seemed to notice the silence. But Larry did. There was not a cricket chirping anywhere. Not a frog, not a buzzing insect. Nothing. *It's just too late in the year*, he tried to rationalize, *too cold already for insects and reptiles*. But he'd heard such sounds just hours before, when they dropped the Millers at the Danner gate.

"Hey, you guys? Maybe I really should wait at the car. My stomach . . ."

They both stopped and looked back at him. In the limited light Larry couldn't tell whether Tommy was smiling or sneering. Tommy reached into his jacket, pulled out his mask, and slipped it over his head. It was a rubber face of Tor Johnson, the star of vintage grade-B horror movies: squat, bald as a bullfrog, the mouth agape, and the eyes rolled back as in his most memorable film roles. There, in the middle of a country road, at night, the dead actor's blank countenance with a Daiwa cap perched atop it was curiously more unsettling than any of the other ghoulish masks from Tommy's box. "Too late to back out, Larry," Tommy said in a muffled voice. "We're all in this."

"Oh, let him go," Doug shrugged. "He just—" Tommy cut him off with the wave of an arm.

"Don't screw with my fifty bucks, Larry," Tor Johnson said. "Now, c'mon." He started back up the road, still wearing his mask. Doug followed obediently, and then Larry. This time there was no small talk of tits and hot rods. Tommy dictated silence, and the others obliged. Larry's queasy feeling remained. *This is just a joke. We're just playing a joke. That's all.*

"Lighten up, Tommy," Doug was saying up ahead. "This is getting to be a drag. If you're gonna start acting like a shithead, I'm outta here."

"You forget," the one in the mask pointed out, "I'm driving." He motioned them off to the right. "Here's where we go over." When the moon next peeked out of hiding, they saw glimpses of brick through the underbrush.

Using the Red Chopper, Tommy cleared some of the weeds and tanglevine away from the wall, being careful to leave enough to aid in climbing. The wall itself was nearly eight feet tall. They would need all the handholds they could get.

"Dougie, you're first," Tommy decided.

"Why me?"

"Because I said so." Tommy puffed out his chest and threatened with the ax. Whether he meant it or not was hard to tell with Tor Johnson covering his face. "Just climb the wall and tell us what you can see. Now, is that so hard? Or are you the chickenshit Larry said you were 'while ago?"

Doug stood and glared at him, and Larry would've sworn he was going to punch Tommy, who was smaller. He'd seen him do it to other guys and for a lot less—unlike Larry, Doug Baugh wasn't one to bluster and stomp and cuss when he got pissed. He just hit someone. And he had that same look on his face right now. *Go ahead*, Larry silently urged, *knock him on his ass so we can get out of here*. But in time Doug just grinned and lit another cigarette and, once it was pasted to his bottom lip, started clambering up the wall. "Damn stickers," was all he grunted before swinging over the top and vanishing to the other side.

"What do you see, Doug?" Larry called. "Doug?"

There was silence. No insects. No frogs. No Doug.

"Something's wrong," Larry fretted. "I knew this idea sucked. . . ."

"Quit screwing around, Baugh," Tommy snapped, lighting up a cigarette that protruded through Tor's grimacing lips. Smoke came out the open rubber nostrils. "Baugh?" He motioned to Larry. "Go see what's keeping him, Fatso."

"You gonna give me a boost? Bend over so I can step on your—"

"Oh, fuck it," fumed Tommy, flipping away his smoke and handing the ax to Larry. "You want something done, goddamn it . . ." He tested the vines with a boot and started up, struggling as much as climbing, the mask doing more to hinder him than anything, and even catching on the stickers near the top. "Baugh," he panted through rubber, "if you're jackin' with me, your ass is grass."

He cleared the top of the wall and had to readjust his eyeholes to see. Only then did his gaze fall on the ghost pale, glowing face, floating there in the air not a few inches from his own, eyes wide and fangs gnashing. Tommy sucked air so hard the mask collapsed inward and his efforts to backpedal sent him tumbling back to the ground. Larry, having seen Tommy's terrified reaction, was already in motion, ass to the wall and nose toward the road.

The apparition sat down on top of the wall, gagging with laughter, the tears washing the glow-in-the-dark paint from his face. Doug spat the plastic fangs into his hand and gloated, "Who's the chickenshit, Tommy?" He bugged his eyes and trembled in imitation, then laughed all the harder. "Man, you better check your shorts."

Larry was coming back from the road, saying "Baugh, you sonuvabitch, that wasn't funny," when Tommy grabbed Doug's foot and yanked him off the wall. Doug dropped clumsily to the ground and was just as quickly hauled up by the lapels and slammed back into the brick. Tommy Whitten, the smallest, thinnest of the three, held him at bay and Doug made no move to retaliate.

He couldn't. Not with a gun barrel stuck in his eye.

"Jesus, Tommy!" Larry gasped, stepping forward and then retreating just as quickly, unsure of what to do. "He didn't mean it, man. Let him go."

"Hey, Tommy," Doug was trying to smile, "hey, what's the gun for, you know? I mean, shit, it was just a joke. Just a joke, goddamn it! C'mon, man, put the gun down. We're supposed to be friends." The paint was coming off in streams as sweat beaded on his forehead and lip at the sight of the small but threatening revolver bore. "Calm down, dude. I take it back, okay? Okay?"

Tor Johnson stared at him blankly, unspeaking, and Larry began to wonder if Tommy Whitten was still in there. Finally Tommy lifted the mask. He was smiling. "Had you going, didn't I?" He lowered the short-barreled gun and stuck it back into his jacket pocket.

"That wasn't real, was it?"

"The gun?" Tommy shrugged. "Sure."

Doug wiped his brow, staining his coatsleeve in the process, and quickly lit a cigarette with shaking hands. "What the hell did you bring it for?"

The grin came back to his face, just before he lowered his mask again. "What else? Snakes." The other two traded worried glances. "Don't worry, you guys. We're gonna have fun. C'mon, over the wall. You two first."

"Why us first?"

Tommy sighed with exasperation. His hand slipped back into his pocket. "Are we gonna go through that again?"

Doug bent and gave Larry a foothold, then, straining, boosted him to the top of the wall. He followed next. Tor was not far behind them. He dropped into the pitch blackness on the other side a few feet from them.

"I don't like this," Larry muttered.

The woods were dense and shadowy. What few shafts of moonlight sifted through the canopy overhead served only to backlight the swirling fog that lapped at the tree trunks like milky water. Tommy fished a small disposable flashlight from his jacket pocket but the diminutive beam was impotent in these surroundings.

"Nobody chickens out," he told them. Standing apart from them, he was little more than a vague shadow with a bulbous head and a hand in his pocket. "Nobody."

"Tommy?" Doug half-whispered. "What if the Millers don't scare, not even with this stuff? What then?"

"Yeah," Larry said softly. "What then?"

"Then . . . we think of something else." He chuckled. "Know what I mean? I think the house is in this direction." He started off into the fog.

Doug leaned over to Larry. "I always knew he was an asshole," he whispered, "but I didn't know he was nuts. Let's—"

"Why whisper?" Tommy asked, suddenly right beside them. "We're not anywhere near the house yet. There's no one out here to hear you. Right?" He held out an arm to show the way. The two grudgingly started in that direction, walking deeper into the primal wood.

And as they walked, the darkness waited for them and listened with its one good ear.

To the north of Isherwood the main road skirted the base of a hill before it left the town altogether, and it was on that bend that a second, less-traveled lane branched away from it. The sign identified it as Moffit Trail, and it climbed that gentle bosom of earth in a long, languid spiral. A taxi, one of Isherwood's three, turned onto that side road in the wee hours of the morning and followed the gradual incline. Its potential destinations were limited; there were few houses on the hill, and most of them less than halfway up. But it passed them by. It drove almost to the crest, where an old two-story boardinghouse stood, and that was where it eased onto the shoulder and parked near the mailbox, right near the walkway and the gate in the fence. And it waited there with the motor running.

George Bailey sat in the back of the taxi and made no move to get out. He was peering out the window, watching the house, the surrounding grounds. "Damn," he sighed, squinting. His eyes weren't what they used to be. And that security lamp on the telephone pole at the side of the road wasn't much help either. It lit the open front yard just fine, and the fence too and the rock gardens beyond it and most of the walk. But not the porch. The old elm tree up close to the house cast the last few feet of the walkway in midnight shade, and the wall of shrubs beyond completed the effect: he could not even see the front door from the road. Too dark, he thought. Too many shadows.

He checked his watch. Two-thirty. Almost four hours till dawn.

"You need some help getting out, Pops?" asked the gum-popping cabbie, who was at least sixty years Bailey's junior. The old man was short with him.

"No, *sonny*. I think I can make it."

"Okay, okay. Just thought I'd ask."

He looked out the window again. Too many shadows . . .

"Look . . . the meter's still running, you know. . . ."

Disgusted, Bailey dug a coin purse from his pocket and threw a few crumpled bills in the front seat. "There's your money, you little shit. Now go on, get out of here." He pushed the door open quickly, before he could think about it, and with the help of his cane climbed out.

Immediately, the chill touched him—was it that cold a few minutes ago?—and the night became personal again. The dark was that much closer. He could feel its presence, its palpability. The distance to the front door had doubled. He swallowed hard, forcing down a lump that was half fear and half pride, and leaned back into the taxi. His tone was less gruff now. "Um . . . could you do me a small favor? Would you wait here until I get to the doorway? I've always been a bit . . . afraid of the dark."

"The dark? You've got that light right out there."

"Please. Here—there's an extra dollar in it for you."

The driver's face went slack. "A dollar? A whole dollar, just for me?" Then he saw the pitiful look in the old man's eyes. "No, you keep your money, Pops. I'll stick around."

Bailey nodded a curt thank you, then straightened with the help of his cane and closed the car door. He walked stiffly to the fence gate and reached over to unlatch it, easing it open carefully lest it creak. No creaking. He couldn't have taken that. He stepped through and eased it shut with the same care. He was still in the pale wash of the security light. But the shadows waited just ahead. *Straighten up, you old fool*, he cursed himself. *You've lasted this long. Don't go to pieces just because of the dark.*

He started up the walk. His cane pecked a solitary cadence.

He had stayed with people as long as he could. He knew his fellow housemates would be in bed early—they invariably were—and the idea of whiling away the night in his room with only his imagination for company was unacceptable. So as soon as he'd gotten home that night he'd cleaned up and went right back out, ending up at the diner for the last few hours. He seldom went there and could barely identify anyone present, but at least they were there. That was important. He felt safer with people.

But now the diner was closed.

A branch swayed overhead. He heard it just as he stepped under the tree. He put a hand over his heart to keep it from bursting from his chest. It subsided only after the squirrel chittered down at him, apologizing for the disturbance. *Calm down, old man*, he thought. Slow and steady. But not too slow.

He made it to the steps and felt for them in the gloom with his cane before daring them with his fragile weight. *Creak*. He flinched but kept going, wringing equal racket from each step until he was at the top. He groped in his pocket and found his keys and had them ready when he stepped up onto the porch. He could make out the shape of the door now.

Made it. You've made it.

The cab driver barely tapped his horn, and Bailey jumped as if shot. The keys slipped from his hand and clattered to the planks underfoot. He looked back to see the driver wave and pull back onto the road. Leaving him alone. *No . . . I dropped the keys, don't . . .* But the words wouldn't come. He stood there silent and shivering, watching the taillights shrink down the hill and disappear. The night quickly settled around him.

Find the keys. Find the keys!

He bent to the porch despite the groan in his lower back and swept long, thin hands across the wood, hissing when they found splinters and peeling paint but not stopping, knowing better than to stop. It was too quiet; the silence was total and awesome and surrounding him and waiting, just waiting to be shattered by a —there, the keys! He scooped them up but couldn't see them, felt blindly along their profiles and damned his fingers for their numbness. *The round one, the round head, that one! Now, get it in the door . . .* His hands were shaking violently now as he grabbed for the knob and stabbed at the keyhole three times before it sank home and turned and the lock clicked. The old man shouldered the door open, lurched inside, and immediately slammed it behind him, locking and bolting and security-chaining it in a few frantic moves. Then he slumped against the door for support and waited for his breath to catch up. And he listened.

Nothing. He sighed. *There's nothing out there. It was all your imagination.*

Wasn't it?

Leaning heavily on his cane, he moved away from the front door and crossed the entry hall as quickly as he could manage.

He was almost to the staircase when he noticed the bar of light beneath the parlor doors to his left. He hadn't seen the light from outside—the drapes must have been drawn. Who would be up at this time of night?

He slid open the double doors to find the television playing and three of his fellow boarders cast in its flickering glow. "Uncle Jim" Taggart's wheelchair was parked at one end of the couch, his head thrown back and his pinched, half-moon face flexed from the efforts of snoring. At the other end sat Hubert Ranall, the only black roomie in the house and one of the few in all of Isherwood. He was the youngest of the residents, a mere baby at seventy-eight, and age had yet to shrink his solid frame. A big, amiable bear of a man with a fringe of frosted hair and a neon smile, he was scribbling away in his notebook as usual, adding yet another chapter to the memoirs of a decorated veteran in the Pacific.

Ida Fleming was there as well, wrapped in her shroudlike housecoat and hairnet, sunk deep into her recliner near the TV. The diminutive woman, with her granny glasses and basset-hound jowls, did not look well; her heart condition had worsened over the past few years, leaving her wilted and fragile. Still, come hell or high water, she made it to the television every day. For while Hubert had his Good-War memories to fill the hours of the day, she had her televangelists, and she followed their antics with great fervor. From Falwell to Swaggart to Tilton, she watched them all with a steely resolve and her leatherette Bible spread upon her lap.

Now, in the wee hours, she had to settle for the Reverend Zachary Farnam, one of the Lord's gaudier prophets, complete with snow-white hair and a hackneyed Elmer Gantry delivery. She hung on every word of it and didn't even notice Bailey's entrance, nor did Ranall. It was shrunken old Jim Taggart who suddenly roused, his rheumy eyes clouded with senility. "Gawdammit," he grumbled in his heavy Hoosier drawl. "Ah told y'uns to play outside now. Dinner won't be ready fer a while yet."

"Look again, Uncle Jim," Hubert said. "It's just George." He looked Bailey up and down. "Well, lookee here. You shaved your beard off. All dressed up too . . . you got a little chippy in town?"

"Never you mind," Bailey said in his normal gruff tone. "Is that all you people have to do, stay up late so you can razz me?"

"Hardly. We just can't seem to sleep's all." He glanced at Uncle Jim, whose head had already rolled back. He started to snore again. "Well, me and Ida, at least. So, did you have a nice night?"

Bailey shrugged, lowered himself into a swivel chair. He was frowning; small talk never came easy for him. Rather than try, he found himself staring blankly at the television set. Hubert finally shrugged as he always did and returned to his writing.

Mrs. Fleming perked imperceptively and eased forward in her seat. Hubert noticed it, and even Bailey paid a bit closer attention to the program, though they already knew from her response that Reverend Farnam had "commenced to healin'."

"The Lord is working through me now, praise Jezuuz," said the minister as he squeezed his eyes shut, deep in prayer. His hand moved up to clutch at his breast and, unconsciously, Ida did the same. "There's a pain . . . right here. That heart . . . that poor heart's done worked itself unto death, hasn't it? But there's a spark there, yes, a spark and you know what? I can feel it growing. God's fanning that spark, fanning it into a flame. Give that heart unto him and it will be reworked, don't you see?" He smiled, sighed. "That's it. That pressure, it's easing, isn't it? And that pain? It's gone too. Hallelujah—you've got you a new heart, that's what you've got. Praise God for that, friends. C'mon, praise him now. Say it with me. Thank you Jezuuz . . ."

Farnam went on to heal two cataracts and a bum kidney, but no one was listening to the television anymore. Not even Ida. The two men were watching her, knowing precisely what her reaction would be. She let go of her heart and opened her downcast eyes, and the smile she wore was thin and defeated. She stroked the cover of her book with a trembling hand. Then she looked up, acknowledging their presence for the first time since Bailey came in. "Well, it's getting awfully late," she said softly.

Hubert yawned on cue. "Yes, I was just about to go to bed myself. Can I give you a hand, Ida?"

"So soon?" Bailey stammered. "I mean, we could sit up for a while . . . you know. Talk?"

Hubert was helping Ida to her walker. "George, we're old

men,'' he said. ''Time's all we've got. Tomorrow, the next day, next week. But right now it's late.'' He left the room with Ida, returning only after the electric hum of the elevator seat marked her ascent of the staircase. Then he kneeled beside Uncle Jim's chair and nudged his shoulder. ''Jim? You need some help to bed?''

The barely tufted head raised and craned toward him, blinking with uncertainty. He cleared the thick sleep from his throat and muttered ''You ain't mah nephew.''

''Not hardly. C'mon, I'll help you to bed.'' But the senile old man's perpetually glazed eyes were already closing, his tortoise-like head angling onto his shoulder. Hubert grabbed a pillow off the couch and wedged it in there before the two came together. Then he took a blanket from the cedar chest in the corner and draped it around Taggart's boney shoulders. ''Well,'' Hubert said, stretching his lanky frame, ''it's been a long day.'' He scooped up his notebook, saying, ''I'll leave the hall light on for you,'' and trudged upstairs.

George Bailey sat there for several minutes, listening to the silence that settled around him despite Reverend Farnam's incessant requests for ''tax-deductible gifts for Jezuuz.'' Then he turned off the TV and the lights, left Uncle Jim in the dark, and climbed the stairs himself. He went very quickly to his room and locked the door behind him.

He turned on every light available and checked the windows, reaching behind the drapes to make sure they were locked, but not daring to look. Only when he was satisfied did he move to the bed which dominated the room and lay back, trying to calm his heart. But even bathed in light, he trembled. He could still feel the darkness, the night, waiting out there, pressed against his window, looking for him. The fear that had festered in the pit of his stomach for most of his life was growing worse. It had made him young again; not the youth he craved, not the vitality and strength of it, but the uncertainty. It was the superstitious, smothering fear of every child when the world turns black and closes in. When he is alone. Afraid.

Nothing in the dark can hurt you, dear. God protects his children.

His mother's words had rung true in the past. But what about now? He had led a cynical adulthood. There had been little of late to bolster his faith—these days even the town minister was rumored to visit porno shops in Bedford. Was there enough belief left in crusty old George Bailey? Was he still one of His children? Or had the Lord forgotten another elderly man, just as society and the world seemed to do? He couldn't help but think of poor Ida Fleming sitting before that television and praying her hardest and waiting, waiting for something to happen. Had she been forgotten too? Had they all?

He knew how Ida would have answered that. She would have said that her disappointments were her own fault, that she expected too much, that her own faith was not strong enough, not yet at least. And she would be right back there tomorrow, in front of that television set, quoting scripture and making out checks for their crusades and ministries and holy amusement parks and praying that maybe tonight it would be enough.

He lay there on the bed without undressing, and he prayed for the rest of the night. He spoke in a soft voice that only God could have heard and he asked for strength never granted and courage never fulfilled. And he prayed for dawn. Hours later when that last prayer was answered he finally relaxed and let himself sink deeper into his pillow, exhausted. And he clutched to his chest the ornament he'd carried since he came into the room, the one he had taken from the nail on the wall.

The big rosewood crucifix had been an heirloom from his wife's family. When he slept, he dreamed of her.

Part II

THE RECKONING

Chapter Seven

"Isn't it great like this?" Billie said, inhaling deeply the crisp morning air, letting it sting her lungs. She was perched atop the porch railing, hugging herself to fight the autumn chill since her sweater was not enough. "It's so clean and peaceful out this early. No screaming kids, no Big Wheels, no neighbors fighting. The world's kind of relaxed this early, you know? At peace. It's like the sun is cleansing the earth. God, I really love the morning. Gordon used to love it too." She grew pensive at the recollection, but not melancholy. A smile lingered on her face. "He used to love the sunlight, warming his skin. Even after he got sick I used to wheel him out here onto the porch and we'd have breakfast and watch the sun come up. He always liked that." She looked at the man on the porch swing across from her and blushed. "I'm sorry. I didn't mean to ramble."

"It's okay," Stiles said, sipping his coffee. "You still miss him. I understand."

She shrugged. "It doesn't hurt as much these days, but before . . . You know, sometimes I wonder if there's a masochist hiding inside of me. I mean, first there was Mike, Bart's dad. His death really got to me. We hadn't been married all that long—the whole thing threw me for a loop. So when I finally get my act together again what do I do, first thing? I fall for Gordon and he gets cancer and the whole thing starts over again." She shook her head in bewilderment. "Not that I wouldn't do it again, mind you. I would. I really did love him. Both of them. But something about losing people, I don't know, the hurt goes so deep you think, I'll never do that again. Once makes you gun-shy, but twice, that gets you downright scared. I can't say I've been close to anyone since Gordon. I mean really close."

"I find that hard to believe."

She bristled. "Meaning?"

"You're an attractive woman. I can't believe you haven't had any offers."

She blushed again and forced a laugh. "Who needs the grief? Besides, I'm kinda used to my independence now. It's okay, really. I've got my kids and my work. And I've got me. There's nothing wrong with being alone."

"Nope. Only with being lonely."

Billie nodded in agreement but couldn't decide whether he was referring to her or to himself. At times, sitting there with his vest collar turned up to the cold and cradling his coffee cup in both hands, he could look gruff yet quite vulnerable, like a lost child, searching for something. Then he would look up and smile, as he did just then, and the impression would fade. She cursed herself for a gabbing ass. They had sat and talked all night long, but she had done most of it, making up for times when there was no one else to talk to but the kids. She told him about them and their fathers, and about her family in nearby Ellettsville and her life in Isherwood. And she told him about herself. Not just trivial things, surface details like where did she go to school or her favorite color, but deep-down things. Her successes. Her failures. Her dreams. She couldn't believe it herself, even as the words came pouring out of her like water from a spigot she couldn't turn off. And finally she quit trying to understand. It felt good to get things off her chest after so long. To finally confide in someone. She hadn't done that since Gordon was alive. Somehow this stranger had touched something in her. It was beyond just physical attraction, she was sure of that. He listened. He cared. He knew how to draw her out of herself. But at the same time he gave very little in return. Chris Stiles was still as much an enigma as when he walked into the diner yesterday morning.

She went over to the swing and scrunched into the seat beside him. Every mystery must be unraveled sooner or later, she decided. Especially this one. "You know, this really isn't fair."

"What isn't?"

"Your letting me do all the talking. You know nearly everything about me but I don't know nothing about you. Tell me about the real Chris Stiles."

He gave a slight chuckle. "There isn't that much to tell."

"Let me be the judge. C'mon, Chris, play right. Tell me about, let's see . . . how about your family?"

Where her own remembrances a moment ago had brought a sentimental expression to her face, she noticed just the opposite in him. It was as if the stirring of memories raised a faint, unpleasant odor. She reached out and took his hand. His expression softened somewhat.

"My mother's name was Mary," he said hesitantly. "Mary and Griffin Stiles. Just your average parents, you know, struggling to get by, raise a family. Pop worked in a tire factory during the day and pumped gas at night. Mom took in sewing to help us out. We weren't rich, but we weren't hurting. They were good providers. Of most things."

He stared into his coffee cup. "I never got a whipping when I was little. Can you imagine that? Not one spanking. Neither of them ever laid a hand on me. Oh, they did Alex, my older brother. They really laid into him at times. But never me. Hey, I thought, this is all right. For a while. Then I realized it was because they just didn't care. It was as simple as that, really. Alex was their pick. I wasn't. Not that I didn't try to get their attention. Especially Pop's. I played football and baseball, ran track, wrestled. I excelled in everything. But it was never enough. So I tried to get his attention in other ways. I excelled in trouble. I ran with the wrong crowd, I stole, you know, that whole sob story. Still nothing from Pop. Well, finally, after Mom had died, I was grabbed for some pretty serious stuff, assault and a few other things. So here comes Pop down to the station and I was never so glad to see him because I think, hey, he's finally looking at me, right, and he's going to bail me out. Well, he looked at me, all right, eye to eye. And he says to me, 'You can rot in there. You're no son of mine.' Not exactly what you want to hear from your pop, you know?" Billie was silent. "Mom died when I was what, fourteen or so. Pop, he might still be alive. I don't know. I haven't heard anything to the contrary. Hell, I think he's too ornery to die. Alex keeps saying I ought to look for him and get all of this off my chest but . . ." He shook his head. "After all this time I guess I don't really give a shit."

"How do you get along with your brother?"

"Not very well," he sighed and drained his cup. "He's been dead for a while now."

Billie was shaken. "Oh, Chris, I'm sorry. I didn't mean to . . . it's just that you said . . ."

"It's okay," he squeezed her hand. "He was killed while I was in Vietnam."

"Killed? Was it an accident, or . . ."

"He was murdered."

She pondered that a minute, then fought off a sudden chill. "Lordy. I don't think I've ever known anyone who was murdered. It kinda gives you the creeps." She trembled again and he put an arm around her shoulders. "That's one good thing about a town like Isherwood. No one ever gets murdered around here. Bored, maybe, but never murdered." She waited for him to continue but he didn't. "Is that all?"

"You want me to make something up?"

"It's an idea. What about marriage?"

"Billie, we just met. . . ."

"You know what I mean, wise guy. Were you ever married?"

He thought for a moment. "Not that I can recollect."

"Chris, I'm serious."

"Okay, seriously. No, I haven't." She glared at him. "More? Hmm. I've been close once. Twice. No, just once, that one didn't count. And the other . . . I guess she just wasn't my kind of woman."

One slender eyebrow arched with exaggerated curiosity. "And what, pray tell, is your kind of woman?"

He grinned mischievously. She couldn't tell whether it was a fleeting memory or he saw through her paper-thin questioning. "That's a hard one," he sighed. "I suppose the usual stuff; you know, bright, beautiful, able to leap tall buildings in a single bound . . ."

"You don't want much."

He reached out, took her face in his hand, and turned it toward him, and she could see from the look in his eyes that he wasn't kidding anymore. The sincerity shone through. "I'd settle for someone I could talk to," he told her. She started to laugh and make some flippant remark about his tight-lipped manner, and how she must not be the one because you can't listen when there aren't any words, no matter how willing you are. But looking into those dark, piercing eyes, she realized it wasn't what he'd told her already. It was what he was going to tell her. About his family, his brother. About Vietnam. About himself.

He pulled her closer then and kissed her, and she was surprised. Not by the kiss—she'd been hoping for that and planning on it, and at that moment would have initiated it herself had he not moved when he did. But it was the kind of kiss that caught her off guard. In the years since Gordon's death she had dated and become used to passionate, kneading, probing embraces with little behind them beyond the physical need of the moment. That was how Stiles had struck her at first; rugged and appealing, good for a few nights, and then he'd be on his way again and out of her life. But this was entirely different. His kiss barely brushed her lips, but the sensations from it, the tenderness, sent out shock waves she hadn't felt since . . . she'd never felt, period.

He drew back slowly, still touching her cheek. His smile was hesitant as he searched her face for a response. It wasn't long in coming. This time she went to him, straddling his lap in the shallow swing and wrapping her arms about his neck. "I'm listening," she whispered.

A door banged inside. Bare feet sounded on the stairs, louder than an entire squad of combat boots as they slapped against the hardwood and then the kitchen tile. "Mom! Where's the cereal?"

Billie drew away, a bemused smile cracking the frustration on her face. "Did you ever feel like killing a kid?" She yelled through the screen door, "Try the counter where you left it!" She slid off his lap, but not before a last, lingering kiss. "Don't lose our place."

The screen door swung open and Bart stumbled out onto the porch in long thermal underwear with a tear over one bony knee. His red locks were more disheveled than ever and his eyes were still glazed with sleep. His jaw looked worse this morning, if that were possible. It was not only swollen but had turned a deep shade of blue and was well on its way to black. It looked sore; that probably had something to do with his bypassing any kind of solid breakfast in favor of a glass of Nestle's Quik. He sat down in a lawn chair with bad webbing at the other end of the porch and sipped his chocolate milk and waited for his brain to catch up with his body. He looked at them. Nothing registered, or if it did he had not thought of a way to respond. "You're still here," he said to Stiles.

"Yes, he is," Billie said, suddenly self-conscious in front of her son. She got up from the swing. "We've been talking all night. How's your jaw?"

"It hurts," he snapped, then rubbed his eyes and softened his tone. "It's fine, Mom. It'll just take some time. Don't worry about it."

"Well, I do worry, young man. I think you're going to the doctor today. The both of you."

"On a Saturday?" Del said coming through the screen door. He was still in his pajamas and carrying a bowl of his nick-namesake, Cap'n Crunch. "Couldn't we wait till Monday to go, so we can miss some school?"

"Sorry, sport. But that's the way it is."

Del went to sit by Stiles on the swing. "I thought you'd still be here," he grinned, then gave his mother a thumbs-up sign behind his back. "Did you two have a good time?"

"Delbert!"

"It's okay, Billie. Yes, Del, we had a good time last night. Talking."

"I'll bet you did," Bart muttered under his breath.

"So," Del was trying to sound casual, "will you be staying around for very long, Mr. Stiles?" There was an unspoken question in there somewhere, and it didn't take a code book to decipher it. *Danner's on the loose*. Stiles picked it up with a subtle nod.

"Yes, I'd like to know that myself," Billie said, for an altogether different reason. "Will you be staying long? In Isherwood, I mean?"

"That depends." He looked first to Billie, then met Del's still-nervous gaze. "I do have a few commitments around here." Both of them translated that in their own way and were apparently satisfied. "But for now," he stood up and stretched, "I've got to get going."

Billie stood with him, her disappointment evident. "So soon? We haven't even had breakfast."

"I'm sorry, but I've got a few things to do, like that desk at the marshall's office." He patted his pockets. "I could use the money. As for breakfast . . ." He stole Del's spoonful of cereal, tasted it, and went back for seconds. "Not bad," he winked, much to the boy's delight.

"Chris," said Billie, conscious of Bart's suspicious stares but simply ignoring them, "do you have any plans for tonight? I was just thinking we might go out and eat, maybe take in a movie. Boys, how about it? There's that Chuck Norris flick in Bedford you were wanting to see."

"Bart's already seen it," Del was quick to report, "and I, uh, I don't really feel up to it. Why don't you two just go without us?"

Billie looked at him with motherly concern. "No, maybe I should stay here tonight. If you're not feeling good . . ."

"I think they'll both be okay," Stiles assured her. "And I have nothing planned. It might be fun."

She seemed uncertain, at least until Del gave her a wink and a grin. She returned the latter. "Sure. C'mon, I'll walk you to your van."

He put an arm around her as they stepped off the porch and strolled down the walk. Bart stood, holding his chair to his butt, and scooted it closer to the swing. "What the hell was that all about? I haven't seen that movie."

The younger boy gaped at him. "You like being a third wheel?" Then he saw the defensive look on his brother's face. "You don't like him, do you?"

"Sure I like him. Just not for our mother. He's not right for her."

"And who is?"

Bart scowled. "How about someone with a steady job. I mean, what if Mom gets serious about this guy?"

Del grinned. "Wouldn't that be great?"

"Jeez, what if she decides to marry him or something?"

The grin widened. "Wouldn't THAT be great!"

"Cut it out, Cap. We don't know anything about him."

"I know he saved our asses last night."

"So what?" Bart was animated now, getting up to pace the porch, barely controlling his voice so as not to attract their attention out by the street. "That doesn't mean I want him for a dad. I can just hear it now. 'Oh, what does my father do for a living? He hunts monsters. No, I don't think it pays too awfully well, but there's always Mom's income. . . ."

Del stalked toward him and threatened him with a milky spoon. "All I know is this, Bart. I had a nightmare after I went to bed last night, about that thing we found. I woke up sweating and crying. You couldn't help me. Mom couldn't. Then I looked out my window and there was his van out on the street, and somehow I wasn't scared anymore. I felt safe. That's the only way I got back to sleep last night. So if Mom likes this guy and wants to keep him around, I'm all for it. Hell, I'd almost marry him myself."

Bart was icy. "That's the only person you're thinking about, Cap. Yourself."

Del took hold of his brother's face in both hands and turned it toward the road. Stiles and their mother were there by the door of the van, in each other's arms, oblivious to their stares. "Tell me, Bart. Just who are you thinking about?" He took his cereal bowl back into the house and left his brother on the porch.

Stiles drove out to the Danner estate and parked off the road not far from the big wrought iron gate. It was six-forty in the morning when he settled in to wait for the three boys from Seymour to return for Del and Bart. And as he sat there, his mind started to wander.

How long's it been since you were in love, my friend? He kept denying the question. *I can't be, I'm not some dreamy-eyed high-schooler anymore and besides, it'll only complicate things and someone will end up hurt.* But it kept hovering in front of his eyes, refusing to go away until he at least recognized the legitimacy of it. How long had it been? Months? Years? Had he ever been in love, really? Maybe not, because he couldn't remember feeling this way before. He knew he had it, and bad; he'd told her about his family. Hell, he hadn't talked about them to anyone before. Not even Marion, the girl he had in Louisville, and he thought that was serious!

His family wasn't exactly a secret; there was no reason for it to be. He just didn't like talking about them, the same way an intelligent man keeps from pounding his hand with a ball peen hammer. It was just that, whenever he brought up his parents and Alex and his childhood, the bitterness he thought was well stored in the back of his mind would come flooding back as well, tainting his mood, fouling it. That's what was so strange this time. When he told Billie, somehow it was okay. It was the past, finally. It was behind him, it didn't bother him. Of course, it may have been that he was simply too preoccupied to notice. He could have been concentrating too much on Billie, on her face, and the caring expression he found there, on the closeness of her next to him in the swing, on the gravelly, sultry tone of her voice, a perfect bedroom voice . . .

Down, boy. Save it for tonight.

He'd have to pace himself today. He had a lot of things to get done before picking her up for their date (yes, it was a date so he might as well call it that). Once done here—if ever, he grumbled to himself and looked down the road impatiently—he would stop at the motel and catch a few winks, get cleaned up, then go to the marshall's office and see about that desk Bean had told him about. It shouldn't take long, probably an uneven leg or a rough drawer channel, something he could fix in an hour or so. If it were an old desk and anything worse was wrong with it, they would probably have to shit-can it. But he hoped that wouldn't be the case. He could use the pocket money tonight. Having never been swayed to the feminist cause, he was not one to easily accept a woman's paying his way.

He grumbled and glanced at his watch, then returned his eyes to Sykes Road for the umpteenth time. Almost nine o'clock. He'd been there nearly two and a half hours and still no sign of the T-Bird. Bart had said they were supposed to meet around seven—that was the predetermined time—but it was becoming readily apparent that the Millers' three "friends" had welshed on the bet and were not coming back. A practical joke. Just as well, Stiles thought. Three less things to worry about.

So much for phase one. Get on to phase two. A little hide-and-seek with Sebastian Danner.

That had been all Del could think about the night before. Every time Billie turned her back or went into the kitchen the boy was at the window, peering into the night, making sure his own personal boogeyman wasn't loitering on the back porch or picking the lock. He didn't sleep much either. Stiles could hear him padding around upstairs in his room, pacing, returning to the window over and over. Then, this morning, even though his spirits seemed to have improved, there was still that look in his eyes. At this rate he would worry himself into an ulcer, and eleven-year-olds shouldn't have ulcers. So Stiles was back today, ready to go into the woods if for no other reason than to ease the boy's mind.

Should he take his pistols? It would be dark in those woods even in daylight, perhaps even dark enough in places for Danner to still be moving about. Just because it was daytime didn't mean the creature would automatically be sleeping; that was a lesson he'd learned the hard way. Vampires, like the people they used to be, fluctuated in their need for rest. Some took the full twelve hours to hibernate, while others could get by on three or less and, if their lairs were dark enough, could be wide awake and active. That's why he wanted to head off the boys in the T-Bird this morning, to stop them from going to look for Del and Bart. It wasn't always safe in the daytime. Something could be waiting.

To hell with it, he decided. He left the guns hidden. *You're turning into a pussy, Stiles, a worrying old woman. Danner's already fucked up. Just stay in the light and everything'll be okay.*

He found a big stick by the side of the road, or was it a "stake?", then slipped over the wall of the estate.

The density of the woods did indeed limit the intrusion of sunlight. It left the grounds subdued, gloomy, with only occasional beams of liquid gold, like linear rainbows, stabbing through the trees. Faint shadows danced across his face and chest, dappled leaf stencils that moved with the breeze and distracted the eye. *Sharpen up. You don't have the time to waste.*

He worked his way to the house and started his search there, retracing last night's battle and even digging a few errant 9mms from the siding—he didn't like leaving loose ends behind. Then he followed in the footprints and, later, the crawlprints of the vampire as it had scrambled for the sanctuary of the woods. The trail wasn't hard to follow. Danner had flopped and thrashed like a landed trout, leaving nail furrows and a snake-belly impression clearly visible through the blanket of leaves and in the dirt underneath.

He followed it for almost fifteen minutes, under logs and through dense underbrush, losing it here and picking it up there, until finally it vanished altogether. He looked around, perplexed. There were no tree hollows nearby, no exposed roots Danner could have squeezed under. It was as if he had simply . . . disappeared.

No. No rats, no bats. No turning into fog.

There had to be an explanation. He poked at the earth with his stick, then stooped and sifted some of the soil between his fingers. Could this be Danner? There was sunlight here, faint but warming the back of his neck. And the vampire did die some time ago, around seventy years according to the boys. That would've made Danner a dustpile just waiting to happen. Like he had told the boys last night, a single beam of sunlight and poof! No more danger.

Then why was . . .

He cut the line of thought at its root. This was the only logical assumption. It would satisfy the boy, allow him to sleep at night. No, it didn't satisfy Stiles himself. Not altogether. But he was prepared to stick around Isherwood and see it through, to make sure that Danner was really dead.

No telling how long that could take.

He thought of Billie and smiled. Yeah. No telling.

A last cursory inspection of the immediate grounds, and then he went back to the van. His watch read almost nine-thirty.

Danner was reduced to a nagging inconsistency in the back of Stiles's mind as he returned to town. His thoughts shifted from the details of the hunt to the more mundane matters of the day, like rest. He went to his room at the Tri-Lakes Inn and sacked out on the bed till almost two-thirty, then showered and slipped into some fresh clothes. Then he headed into town to check up on his potential employment. He parked the van in the next block up from the diner and walked the rest of the way to the town marshall's.

From the outside the office looked like it was straight out of Mayberry, and even more so once he stepped through the door.

There was one main room, complete with low courtroom gate and cordons to separate the two deputies' desks. File cabinets and gun cabinets lined one wall; another was reserved for community citations and departmental awards and, more prominently, mug shots of the bass and catfish arrested at the last Lake Monroe raid. Across the room was a large bulletin board for wanted posters and notices and "DON'T DRIVE DRUNK" placards. On either side of the board was a doorway: to the left, a shallow corridor that led to what appeared to be holding cells on the one side and, further along, a supply room and restroom and extra bunk; to the right, the office of Town Marshall P. Thomas Larson. It said it right there on the frosted glass of the closed door.

The young man at the first desk with his feet up and a copy of *True Detective* in his lap stopped trimming his nails just long enough to fix the stranger in the doorway with a suspicious glare. Then he looked back to his magazine. "Whaddasay?" Rusty Sanders sighed, though it was a greeting devoid of civility. It was more a rote welcome, and could just as easily have meant "What the hell do you want?"

"My name is Stiles. I came for work."

The deputy muffled a snicker. "You wanna be a cop, huh? Well sorry, but we ain't got no openings." His nose went even deeper into the magazine. Sanders was a lanky boy with bony features and hair that was too long, and the beginnings of a beer belly gave him the appearance of a snake digesting a meal. His uniform was badly pressed and looked strange without a tie; he could have been a furnace repairman or a plumber, for all Stiles could tell. The soldier's eyes went automatically to the deputy's gun and judged him accordingly. It was a Smith & Wesson Magnum and was in poor shape. The bluing was bad and the metal wasn't just scratched but gouged. The wooden grips sported deep divots where it had been used to hammer nails. Stiles winced, wondering if Deputy Sanders carried his bullets in the gun or his shirt pocket.

"I'm here about a desk," Stiles told him. "Charlie Bean said you might need some work done on one."

Another sigh. Sanders pointed across from him without looking up. "That one. I think the top drawer drops out or something like that. It's probably nothing. You know how Charlie is."

"No, I don't," Stiles said, stepping through the gate to inspect the desk. "I just met him yesterday."

"Oh. Well, I'll tell you. Charlie's a good old boy and all, but he's a bit gung ho at times, if you know what I mean. Thinks he's Elliot Ness or something. Sometimes I just wanna say, 'Goddamn it, Bean, just sit down and shut up for a while,' you know?" Stiles nodded; he could see right through the boy's bravado, and knew those words would never be spoken to Charlie Bean's face. "I guess you'll be wanting to talk to Dutch, huh?" The young man made no move to rise; he just cupped his hands around his mouth and shouted, "Hey, Dutch! C'mere!"

The frost-paned door to the rear opened a crack, just enough for a squat, rounded head to poke through. Tommy "Dutch" Larson must have been in his late fifties, but he dyed what hair he had jet black and Brylcreemed it into a 1950's perpetual wave. "What is it, Rusty?" he barked around a mouthful of lunch, spitting crumbs in the process.

Sanders was back in his magazine. "Some guy's here about Charlie's desk."

"Oh." The door closed for a moment, and then the town marshall finally stepped out of his office. The pants beneath Larson's considerable stomach were newly snapped and his fingers licked clean of ketchup. He had slipped on his aviator shades, the reflective state trooper kind, despite the fact that the blinds were drawn. He rubbed his hands together, big meaty things without knuckles, and didn't offer one in greeting. "So you're the writer-slash-handyman, huh?" he said in a tone that made it sound like a punishable offense.

"Boy, word gets around."

Larson continued to eye him suspiciously through reflective plastic. "I don't know how to tell you this, mister," he drawled, "but I'm afraid there ain't no work for you here. Bean didn't really have the authority to offer it to you in the first place and, frankly, I've already promised the work to my brother-in-law."

"Then why hasn't he fixed it before n—" Sanders started before the marshall cut him off.

"Like I say, I'm real sorry. Maybe there's some other work around town. Better yet, maybe you should try Bedford. More people, more repairs."

Stiles recognized the pig-squint behind the marshall's sunglasses. It was the look of a property owner, the one reserved for trespassers. This guy's paranoia made Charlie Bean a piker by comparison. "Aren't you going to ask me my price? Maybe I can undercut your brother-in-law."

Larson actually smiled at that. "I'm sorry but—"

"Ten dollars . . ." Larson's eyebrows raised in unison. ". . . besides the cost of any new materials."

The marshall turned to examine the desk, walking around it and kicking the legs as if pricing a used car. He pulled the top drawer and it clattered to the floor. Luckily Charlie kept it empty for that reason. "Hell, I never liked my brother-in-law anyway. But if I don't like the work, you don't get a cent. Them's my rules, take 'em or leave 'em."

Stiles wanted to tell the haggling old fart to stick his rules up his ass, but there was tonight to think about, and Billie. "You've got a deal." He held out his hand, convinced that the fat man wouldn't take it. Larson regarded it like some alien gesture, then, to his surprise, shook it. Stiles wished he hadn't; despite his size, it was a limp handshake, all fingers, like a cloying politician's. With that the marshall turned on one heel and went back into his office, back to his hamburgers and his newspaper. He didn't wait till the door was closed before unbuttoning his pants to ease the strain on his belly.

"Real friendly, isn't he?" Stiles muttered, then realized Sanders wasn't listening to him either. He decided he had new respect for Charlie Bean. Anyone who could work with those two without killing them must have had tremendous self-control.

The phone on the deputy's desk rang, not once but four times. But Sanders made no move to answer. Stiles was just about to reach for it himself when the kid motioned toward Larson's office. "He'll get it." Then the phone stopped ringing. "See what I mean?" He went back to his *True Detective*, at least until the marshall's bassoon of a voice rattled the closed office door.

"Rusty!" he called. "Someone saw an abandoned car out by the Tunnel. Go check it out."

Stiles's blood went cold. The Tunnel.

"Aw, shit," Sanders muttered, dropping the magazine onto his lap. "Hey, Dutch," he yelled back, "somebody probably just went home with someone else, you know? They leave 'em there all the time. Why don't we wait till—"

"Goddamn it, Rusty, do I have to come out there! What the hell do I pay you for? Now get your goddamn nose out of that goddamn magazine and don't let the door hit you in the ass!"

"Yeah, yeah, yeah," Rusty sniped under his breath. He stood with an exaggerated sigh, as if it were the hardest thing he had done all day (and it may well have been), then picked a jacket and cap from the coat rack by the door. Last came his own reflective sunglasses, completing the "uniform." It all must have given him a false sense of authority; he turned and noticed Stiles still standing there, and he actually muttered, "What are you looking at?"

The soldier barely controlled his laughter. "Nothing, friend. I was just about to get my tools."

Sanders smirked. He started out the door, then went back and snatched the magazine from his desk before leaving.

An abandoned car? Near Danner land? It had to be a coincidence, Stiles thought. Didn't it? He had to be sure. So he followed the deputy outside and started for the van even as he watched him climb into the squad car at the curb. But when he looked back he realized he needn't hurry. Sanders had his *True Detective* propped against the steering wheel and was still reading.

Stiles sat in the van for nearly ten minutes, waiting impatiently, wondering if he should go on to the Tunnel and risk the deputy finding him there later. But then the squad car finally started. "About time," he muttered as it edged into the empty street and U-turned, headed back past him. Stiles pulled out as well, following at a discreet distance, confident that they would finally make it to Sykes Road this time. But that was underestimating Rusty Sanders. Before they got as far as the Tri-Lakes, the deputy pulled off the road and into the Nevermore Trailer Park. "What now!" Stiles sighed with disgust as he eased onto the shoulder, where he had an unhindered view of the park's main drive. Sanders drove all the way to the rear of the park, past the rows of Hollyparks and Westbrooks with their redwood decks and seamless skirting, and it looked as if he might turn the corner there and disappear onto the next drive. But he pulled in next to the last trailer in the row and stopped. Stiles fished through the van console for his field binoculars, and they brought the scene much closer. It was an older Windsor mobile home and it wasn't in the best condition; the siding was separating at the seams and showed signs of rust, and the window nearest the door was broken and patched with cardboard from the inside. Rusty Sanders climbed from the patrol car trying to look professional, cap on and clipboard under one arm, as he approached the door and knocked. He had to do so three times before it finally opened.

The woman who greeted him there may have been in her early thirties but looked older, at least in the face. Her hair hung straight and bodiless and her eyes, even at that distance, had a glazed tired look, which could have been sleep or something stronger. A cigarette dangled from her large lips. She was wearing an open bathrobe and underneath it a satin teddy, the kind from Frederick's of Hollywood, cut low in the front and high up on the hips so a little pubic hair is always in view. The kind that invariably looks better in the catalogs. Not that Georgetta Stovall had a bad figure; her bustline was an impressive sight to be sure and had been all but a landmark in Isherwood for some time. But the skimpy lingerie, while emphasizing those breasts, also showed a bit too much of a growing belly and the creep of cellulite that was beginning to threaten her thighs and hips. Neither of which seemed to affect Rusty Sanders. He looked around secretively to see if they were being watched, then said something to the woman. She flipped her cigarette into the yard and answered him with a curt, bored nod of her own, then reached out for his jacket collar and pulled him through the door.

Stiles shook his head with wonder. Not that he was against someone getting his pipes cleaned now and then, but while on duty? Well, at least it worked to the soldier's advantage. "Take your time, punk," he muttered as he wheeled back onto the road and headed for Sykes and the Tunnel.

It took him longer to find the yellow T-Bird than he'd expected. While not exactly hidden, it was parked at the far end, just around the edge of the tree line where a passing glance would miss it. It was only when backtracking that Stiles noticed it at all. He left the van running as he checked it out. Empty, and strewn with beer cans and burger wrappers. The registration sheet from above the sun visor read Lawrence Whitten, Seymour, Indiana. It didn't match the three first names Bart and Del had given him, but the city was right.

There was no doubt in his mind where the boys had gone. He looked up the road. The Danner land started not much further along.

He drove down the road a short distance, till the van was out of sight of the Tunnel, and then he parked on the weed-covered shoulder and continued on foot. He moved in earnest, crouched, close to the ground like a bloodhound, searching for marks or prints, any sign at all that the three boys were there. It didn't take him long to locate the cleared section of the boundary wall, where creepers and tanglevine had been slashed aside. Thorns near the top still clung to ravels of colored cloth. He swallowed hard. They definitely went over. But when? This morning? Last night?

He instinctively reached for a pistol before remembering them to be back in the van. You won't need them, he assured himself as he climbed the wall. But once atop it, upon looking into the perpetual gloom of the other side, his hand strayed to his belt and drew the bali-song from its nylon cocoon. A flick of the wrist opened the nine-inch butterfly knife. He reversed the grip, holding the blade back, flush with his forearm, then jumped down into the forest and began his search.

He careened through the woods urgently, much faster than before but missing very little. His eyes scoured the ground like mine sweepers, picking through the weeds and leaves, searching out the smallest details. Trampled grass. Footprints. Obscure impressions in the dirt. The greenish-yellow smear of fluorescent paint on the roots of a tree . . .

His toe struck something in the weeds.

He thrust a hand into the underbrush and brought out a dense clod of dirt. With vigorous brushing it became a revolver, a Harrington & Richardson .32, to be precise. He dropped the cylinder and poured the empty casings into his hand. Every shot fired.

Oh shit.

He established a perimeter around the spot where he found the gun and began to comb every inch of it, upturning rocks, sifting through leaves. On the northern edge he found a footprint. Another perimeter was marked off, another search conducted. Another find, this time a tennis shoe to match the footprint, and beside that a handprint. Complete with inch-long nails. Another footprint further on, this one a boot, set deeper in the soil and accompanied by scuff marks alongside it as if its creator had rested its weight on one leg and had . . . dragged the other. Stiles swallowed and picked up his pace, heading in the general direction the clues pointed in. Toward the house.

There was something lying in the trail up ahead. The Red Chopper had broken just below the ax head and the handle was nowhere to be seen. He picked up the head and ran a finger along its blade. It came away smeared not with blood but a milky white film, like thin gauze, dry and tough.

Skin.

He started to run. The clues were that numerous and that obvious. A hockey mask here, a pair of plastic fangs there, a half empty pack of Winstons. The trail was veering away from the house and cutting a wildly erratic course through the woods. Stiles cut back on himself several times and tried to imagine the terror that had spurred such flight. He finally slowed at the foot of a tall birch. The tree was bleeding. A huge gout of blood had splattered the trunk, running in crimson rivulets, absorbing into the veins of the bark. Stiles pursed his lips and stared. It didn't look real. He'd seen enough blood in his life and this just wasn't right. He touched it, sniffed his fingers. A syrupy, almost plastic smell. What is this, a joke? He stopped to look around the base of the tree and quickly located the empty tube of Vampire Blood. It had been flung against the bough. But on purpose? Who was setting him up?

As he moved, the soil underfoot belched wetly and the mud sucked at his boot before letting go. The sole came away stained red. "What the . . ." He stepped down again in the same spot. Shallow crimson rose around his boot, bubbling as if it were still in a human body. *My God.* He dipped a finger and sniffed. This time it was real. And it was all around him.

The trail was just that now, a congealing trail of blood that soaked into the soil, and it led him onward and stoked his anger. Much of his fury was directed inward; he blamed himself for allowing this to happen, for not stopping the vampire when he could. But he reserved a special hatred for Sebastian Danner. He had lost hope of saving the three boys, not with that much blood gone. But their trail might lead him to the vampire. He might find it, whiling away the daylight in hiding, still draped in the gore of its feast and bloated like a fat tick. And then the boys would be avenged . . .

He slid to a halt as the trail suddenly veered to the left through a briar patch and led straight to the boundary wall itself. The blood, now little more than a trickle, went to the wall and up it, smearing the stone and discoloring the autumn brown of the ivy there. Stiles wiped a finger along the top of the wall. It came away red. They made it, he sighed. At least one of them. And Danner couldn't have followed him over.

Now, if only he could find whoever got away.

Stiles picked his way through the stickers and vines and climbed to the top of the wall. He was almost a mile down Sykes Road from where he'd left the van, nearly halfway to the main gate of the Danner estate. The roadway on the other side was deserted. A shallow stream, nearly dried up, ran along the shoulder and beneath the road through a concrete culvert. There was no sign of the boys.

He dropped to his feet, shielding his eyes from the sudden rush of sunlight, and started looking for the blood trail. There was no sign of it . . . no, wait. There was a droplet, on a rock along the stream. Another, further along. A smear on the concrete. He looked at the culvert tube. There was no water coming through it.

If only he'd brought his flashlight. He patted himself down and thanked God he hadn't thrown out his lighter with his cigarettes. He tested the flint, then, brandishing it in one hand and the bali-song in the other, he bent and peered into the culvert.

There was an obstruction in the cramped darkness of the concrete tube, an amorphous shape blacker than the rest of the blackness. Except for one spot. That stood out, even to his unadjusted eyes. Almost glowing.

It was a face—he didn't need light to see that—but one strangely disproportionate. Larger than normal. The eyes and nose were too close together, and the mouth too low and too wide and grinning madly from ear to ear. And it didn't move. Hesitantly, he reached in as close as he dared and thumbed the lighter in front of it. The flame danced and reflected red in a dead man's eyes. Doug Baugh's paint-stained face stared back at him, but it was not larger than normal as he'd thought at first glance. The boy's mouth was not even open; his lips were still tightly pursed in an agonized grimace. It was his throat that grinned. The flesh there gaped raggedly, like the teeth of a smiling jack-o'-lantern. It had been torn from one jaw hinge to the other. There was no more blood; the flesh looked like bread dough. There was a bouquet of arms framing that face, his and others, twisted and warped at horrid angles, ever reaching, but not far enough.

There was barely enough room in the culvert for a child to crawl through. It must have taken some ingenuity, and not a little strength, to stuff three bodies into it at once.

Rusty Sanders finally made it to the Tunnel an hour after he started. But the deputy didn't take the T-Bird's presence as seriously as had Stiles; it was just one more abandoned car to him, and he'd checked out too many there in the past. He wrote down the license number and the name from the registration, and then he left.

Back at the office, Dutch pushed him to check further, and he finally phoned Lawrence Whitten in Seymour. But the man didn't seem particularly concerned; in fact, he sounded rather disinterested. His son was driving the car, and Tommy was a rambunctious youth. It wasn't unusual for him to be gone for days at a time, especially on the weekends. The boy would turn up soon, his father predicted, and the deputy tended to agree. The "investigation" was over before it began.

Late in the afternoon, Marshall Larson came out of his office and noticed that the handyman was still nowhere to be seen. He asked Sanders about it, but the deputy just shrugged. He didn't even look up from his magazine.

Billie hung up the phone slowly, giving away its message. Bart looked up from *The Brady Brunch* with concern. "Mom? What's wrong?"

"Oh, nothing," she said, forcing a smile. "Chris won't be able to make it tonight after all. He said he has something else to do." She brushed self-consciously at the new slacks and her favorite print blouse she wore, and touched the hair she'd spent most of the day setting so it would look just right. "I guess I'd better change my clothes. Wouldn't want to get this stuff dirty." She went toward her bedroom.

"I told you," Bart grumbled, throwing the *TV Guide* across the room. "I knew him and her wouldn't work, I knew it! I hope you're satisfied, Cap." He looked around. "I said I hope you're satisfied, Delbert."

But Del wasn't listening to him. He didn't hear Mike and Carol and the kids either, though he was staring straight at the TV show. His face had gone chalk white. "Don't you get it?" he whispered.

Chris Stiles wouldn't be able to make it tonight. And Del could guess why.

Chapter Eight

It was getting late. The movie's last showing would be letting out just about now. The doors would open and the crowds would filter from the theater to find shops closed for the night and the square virtually empty save for the occasional carload of teenagers roaming the night like the Flying Dutchman for something to do. The crowds, still laughing or grumbling depending on how the movie was, would dissipate as they reached the string of cars parked along the street.

Two of them would pause there arm in arm beneath the dimming marquee and wait until the rest of the people were gone and they more or less had the square to themselves. Then they would turn their collars up to the evening chill and, huddling close, they would stroll along the empty sidewalks, laughing and talking and window-shopping in darkened displays. If they were lucky they would find a diner open late, and she would relish being served for a change instead of doing the serving. They would sit there alone and stare at each other through the swirls of coffee steam and talk; about the movie at first and the weather and other inconsequential things, but slowly, as he opened up, the conversation would turn soft and serious. She would listen patiently to things he wanted to say, things he had to, even things she could not possibly understand or approve of. And when he was finished she would simply smile and reach across the table to take his hand, and nothing more would need to be said. And then . . .

And then?

Then they'd live happily ever after, Stiles grimaced, embarrassed at the sophomorism of his own mental fantasies. *Jeez, grow up! You're starting to sound like those damn Harlequins!* He picked an open paperback from the dash, bent down the page, and tossed it to the back of the van. Too dark to read anyway. *Tomorrow, old son, you change your reading tastes for awhile. Maybe something a bit more fitting*—a *little Bram Stoker perhaps. That should put you in the mood.*

He looked into the night around him and shivered. *Yeah, tell me about it.*

He fished a handful of pretzel sticks from the bag on the console and grumbled under his breath. The fantasy may have been strained, he granted, but there was always a remote possibility that it might have happened. If he'd really gone to the movies, that is. But what was he doing instead? Sitting in his van, in the cold, in the dark, watching and waiting and cursing his brother for getting him into this in the first place. "I hope you're happy, Alex," he said aloud, not really expecting a response. He didn't get one.

Billie's voice still lingered along the edges of his mind. Even through the muffled phone line he'd had no trouble picking up on the disappointment in her voice. But hell, what else could he do—tell her where he was really going? Oh well. There was always tomorrow night . . . that is, if something would just happen tonight.

C'mon, dammit! Let's get this over with!

He reached for more pretzels and grumbled again and wished for a cigarette to soothe his jangled nerves. There was no need for impatience; it wouldn't get him anywhere. It never did. But he just couldn't seem to beat it this time out. Too much time between stakeouts, he supposed, but that focused, waiting state of mind he'd developed in 'Nam and honed over the years seemed for some reason just beyond his grasp tonight. *You're concentrating too hard. Just relax. Let it happen.*

He exhaled slowly three times. Cleared his mind. Then he raised the pistol-gripped Starlight scope and peered through the trees that concealed him. His view of the culvert was unfettered.

The night vision system captured the moonlight and magnified it to a field of green, robbing the shadows of their substance, nullifying them. He sought his visual marker and found it. The hand still hung from the mouth of the culvert, blooming from the darkness like a pale and rigored lily, its petals curled and frozen. He watched it for several minutes, waiting for it to move and dreading it, but praying for it as well. It did not.

The eyes of any other would have seen the hand and merely from its shape expected motion, but not Stiles. At dusk he'd returned with his van and, after reconnoitering the area, had pried the bodies from the concrete tube. He didn't actually expect to find their killer hiding in there among them, but it had been worth a try and it did give him a chance to examine the bodies. Seeing Larry Hovi's deflated beach ball of a corpse up close, with sagging, sallow flesh the texture of butcher paper and a broadly laughing throat, was enough to strike from Stiles's mind any residue of lingering humanity. This was no longer a body, an arm, a hand. It was a cold thing, inanimate and unfeeling, and a sane man would no more expect movement from it than he would a T-bone in the Kroger meat display. That's what made the wait all the more unnerving—waiting for something to happen that shouldn't be happening at all.

He sat back with a sigh of exasperation and caught himself trying to light a pretzel stick with the dashboard lighter. The tremors were slight but there nonetheless. *So that's it. Damn smokes've got a better grip on you than you thought.* He kept his hands up and concentrated until the withdrawals subsided and the trembling eased. *That's it, once and for all. You stop this time and you don't start again.*

He smiled to himself and took a long deep drag on a pretzel stick. *Yeah, that's what you always say.*

He sat there for what seemed an hour instead of the fifteen minutes it actually was and tried to make some sense of what had happened. In less than twenty-four hours a fairly routine search-and-destroy had become a total fucking nightmare. The result? Dead civilians. What went wrong? What the fuck went wrong?

The little voice in the back of his head answered. *You did, asshole. You went wrong. You made the one fatal mistake that any cherry recruit worth his juice would've avoided. You underestimated the enemy.*

It had to be Danner. He'd killed the boys—the clues were too obvious. Another vampire would simply have bitten their throats, not ripped them out with his nails. Only a fiend hampered by a pulpy, fangless mouth would have gone to the trouble of opening his victims like pop-top cans. But how? How does a blind, faceless vampire find his prey, much less kill it? And how does he scale walls with a shot-up kneecap that wouldn't even support his skeletal weight? Unless . . . He slapped the wheel. *C'mon, Stiles. Goddammit, we've been over this. For the last time, no changing into bats or rats or wolves or fog. They never have in the past and they don't now. A person cannot change shape, living or dead.*

That cynical voice in his head laughed. *Yeah, sure. Dead bodies can't walk, either, but Danner sure bosanovas with the best of 'em, doesn't he?*

Stiles sighed with frustration. What happened to the rules? There had always been a game plan before. Vampires were just bodies and bodies cannot walk if you screw with their legs and they cannot eat if you screw with their mouths and they can't do a damn thing if you cut them in half with a little autofire. But this one . . .

He caught himself starting to shiver and stifled it. *You're out of practice. That's all. Your mind-set's gone bad, you're letting the superstitions get to you instead of analyzing the situation. C'mon, dissect it. Hold it up to the light of cold human reason. The rules are still in place. Only the circumstances have changed.*

Danner was lucky, that was all. The boys had come through the woods with their Halloween gear, doubtless intent on scaring Del and Bart, and the groping creature had merely happened upon them or vice versa. Once one was dead, the others probably panicked and became lost in the dense woods. It would have been easy enough to follow the sounds of their frantic cries and given them new reasons to scream.

Stiles fought his anger. Cool rational thought. *What about the wall?*

Danner could have found a tumbledown section to cross, or squeezed through a break in the stone. Maybe he burrowed under it, which would have been easy enough considering the length of his nails, or . . . A picture popped into his mind, one of a frantic young man careening through the woods with a hellish stick figure riding his shoulders like the old man of the sea. Its face was gone, shot away, but the bared gullet that remained was suctioned to the boy's torn throat like a leech. That was it, he decided. Danner rode over the wall. Carried to freedom even as he drained the life from his mount.

The mental image disgusted Stiles; he discarded it, but the damage had been done. He was angry again, and that was the one thing he didn't need. He was still itching for a fight; another dose of righteous indignation would have him spraying the bushes at the next strange sound.

Calm down. You've still got a wait on your hands.

Yes, the voice retorted, *but for how long*? It mimicked his own doubts. He was, after all, playing a hunch; there was no guarantee those bodies would resuscitate. There had been no actual bite—would that matter? How was this affliction or disease or curse or whatever the hell it was transmitted, anyway? Was it by supernatural means, as in the bite, the actual occult ritual of biting? Or was it some alien bacillus that reanimated a dead body with omnipotent hunger pangs? And how would such a supernatural germ get passed along—the mucous, the saliva? The vision of the dying child and his murderous burden came back like a shot. The wound could have been, must have been tainted by Danner's own spore. Which could mean . . . Stiles shrugged. Whatever it meant, he wouldn't take any chances. That was why he couldn't let Bean or Sanders or anyone else in on his find. Murders bring investigations and they bring the county coroner and the bodies are inevitably bagged and taken away. It just wouldn't do to have the three come back in the middle of their own autopsies, in a morgue where Stiles couldn't put them back to sleep.

Logic was another reason to wait. It made perfect sense for the boys to come back and for Danner to make an appearance. The latter had been lucky last night; it isn't every day one's supper comes to him so conveniently. He would not be so lucky again. Blind and crippled, Danner could flounder in the countryside for weeks, months, unless . . . unless he had three servants to search for him, to corral his meals, and watch over him and make sure he was hidden before daylight.

And besides that, logic aside, Stiles had a gut feeling. Most would have called it paranoia and dismissed it, but Stiles had been at this for too long. He knew when to ignore a hunch and when to play one. Danner would be back, he knew. He felt the anger rise again and tried forcing it down. He should have been cold, calculating. But he just couldn't seem to grasp the assassin's attitude this time out. Maybe because this time he wasn't just the gunman riding into town with no stake in the game. This time he was involved, because, like it or not, it was his fault. He should've cut Danner in two when he first laid eyes on him, but he was too intent on getting into that house, on finding the Enemy. For Alex.

"You got me into this, Slick," he said aloud. "Again. Why can't you ever get me out?"

There was no answer. There never was. Over the years, Alex had gotten to be as precise and predictable as clockwork. Ferret out some evil, lead Chris to it, and when the Enemy didn't show, immediately start looking elsewhere, leaving his brother to hold the bag no matter what form it took. It was an unspoken arrangement between the two—Chris was repaying a debt—but these days the debt seemed overpayed already and the deal completely one-sided. But that was Alex, and that was to be expected. He'd always been that way.

Well, not always.

Stiles's mind wandered back, away from Sykes Road and the culvert and Sebastian Danner, and as it did so he finally achieved that waiting state of mind. It was like riding a bicycle; once he stopped trying it came naturally, like second nature. His mind strayed while his senses did not; they stayed alert, watching the culvert, waiting.

Mechanically, he raised the scope and swept it across the roadway.

Nothing. He swiveled this way and that, straining to see through the rain-smeared lens, focusing his eye alternately on the red sighting dot and the lush jungle around him. Fronds hung limp and flapped heavily when the wind picked up, and the elephant grass, shoulder high in the open, waved like flexible sword blades. Little else moved in the face of the squall. No Charlie. No nothing. Damn.

He lowered the Aimpoint away from his eye and sat back against the exposed roots of a tree, where the downpour seemed a little less severe and laid his rifle across his lap. He was numb, and the pounding rain wasn't helping. He got that way when he walked, and they'd sure as hell done enough of that today, up one hill and down another and up a thousand more. His body just seemed to go on autopilot for a while, letting his mind wander but not so far that his senses couldn't call him back if necessary. Boredom must have triggered it, or monotony, or exhaustion. The trouble was, those three things were what this tour of duty, this country, was all about. Waiting for Charlie, walking,-waiting some more, always waiting. He was numb most of the time, as stuporous as any drug addict. He was like a grain of sand in an hourglass, slipping slowly, inevitably toward the middle, away from the World, further and further. . . .

He tilted back his helmet and let the wind lash needles of water across his face. *Jesus*, he thought, rubbing and slapping his cheeks. *I can barely feel anything. Better straighten up. Think about the men. They're depending on you.*

He looked behind him. They were a hundred or so feet away but already obscured by the rain, little more than shadows in the grayness. They waited there, resting.

If only he could find Charlie. Yeah, some 'Cong would do the trick. A sniper or two, or a small patrol. Hell, he'd take a whole fucking platoon if he had to. He was ready for them, waiting, all but hoping for those few minutes of life that combat granted. That was when the tension and the fear and the frustration melted away like poison sweated from the body. That was when his senses came alive—he could hear even beyond the gunfire, could smell a thousand scents and feel and taste—even C rations were a banquet then. For those few minutes he was really alive.

But doesn't that mean you like to kill?

He thought about it long and hard, then took off a glove and held his hand against the squall. The rain barely tingled.

I have to.

A poor-man's bird whistle sounded through the flooded gloom. The lieutenant was ready to move.

He acknowledged the ghostly shapes to the rear with a wave, then gave a like signal to the second point. Some fifty feet away in a banyan grove that flanked the designated trail (the one they were blazing, anyway) there was movement. A patch of sodden weeds tilted and raised as the helmet beneath it peeked out, followed by a chopped-down shotgun and crossed bandolier of shells. Pruett came into view looking like a soaked cat, his poncho plastered to his lean, lanky frame. He waved the pump gun in reply and waited for Stiles to move.

The tall, thin kid from Indiana was one of the better point men in the troop. He was quiet despite his size and could defoliate a patch of land with that scattergun before most could cycle a round. But he still deferred to Stiles in the field. They all did. It wasn't rank; Stiles was a faceless grunt, just like the rest. Nor was it age or appearance—they were all fresh-faced and innocent, or had been once. But still, something made him stand out. Something about him garnered complete reverence and even a little fear. What was it?

Reputation. And not just because he was deadly up on point.

He was also a psycho.

Stiles had heard the rumors and did nothing to refute them. A case of loose hinges had its benefits in the field. No one bothered him, not even the officers. Especially the officers. The threat of being fragged by one's own men was omnipresent these days, so an obvious loon was handled with kid gloves. For that reason he was never reprimanded and never given the shit jobs, except for point, which he didn't consider a shit job and most often asked for. The latter only added to his mystique. He always had a place to sit at mess, always a smoke when he was in the mood, friends when he wanted them, and solitude when he didn't. Besides, maybe he was a little nuts—what other kind of man would show off by going into the bush after Charlie with just his Ka-Bar knife? He was like a big cat, following the enemy slowly, methodically, his senses suddenly alive to the chase, his veins pulsing with adrenaline. And when he found them, whether it be two or ten, he'd take them out, one by one, striking like a . . .

Whisper?

He spun around to the rainy gloom, his rifle at the hip and swiveling there to cover the field of sight. But there was nothing within view, only the landscape, lush and green and bent to the fury of the storm. But there had been a voice, a whisper . . . hadn't there?

You're cracking up, Chris my boy.

He signaled back to the others. *Stay still. Stay low. Something's not right.* Then he waved to Pruett to start forward into the dense jungle ahead, to keep within visual contact, but Pruett wasn't even there to reply. He peered long and hard at the other flank, thinking the younger man had just blended back into the vegetation, but the other point had already moved on. *What a hot dog*, he thought with anger. *Now who's showing off?*

He moved along his own path into the vibrant green darkness ahead. Out of the sight of his men.

The tall grass fell under his boot and, with a twist of the ankle, stayed flat for whoever would follow. He knew better than to brush it aside by hand; the edges were like razors. After his first field mission he spent the next several days squeezing pus from his swollen, infected fists. He'd been sure to wear gloves ever since.

What a country. Even the fucking grass hates us.

The rain slackened as he entered the densest part of the forest, its fury lost on the canopy of tree branches overhead. Though it was drier there, it was also hotter. It was as if the heat had been waiting for him, a familiar enemy, just as thick and choking and oppressive as before the rains. The mosquitoes were back too, swarms of them hanging in the air like cobwebs, not even bothering to pounce, content to let him walk into them. He brushed them aside indifferently, ignoring their bites. There were worse things to think about.

The gloom was hard to penetrate. There were no hard edges to the shadows. The rain diffused what little light pierced the leafy canopy, leaving only varying shades of gray to overlap the black. In fact it looked more like some sort of fantasy world, where dreams and reality blended, making trees and bamboo shoots into shadowy creatures and waving fronds into groping limbs. He ignored it all. He knew that in this Never-Never Land, Captain Hook was his own age and had slanted eyes and carried

Russian rifles and left booby-trapped C ration cans all along the trail. His practiced eye scanned the animal run he was following through the brush and searched for his real enemy; the tripwires, the stolen claymores, the camoflauged pits whose gullets were lined with shit-stained pungi sticks. Those were the real dangers. Charlie was a comparative phantom. . . .

"Hoss."

Stiles froze. His rifle turreted at the hip, swinging left and right, all the way around as his mind refused to accept what he'd heard. There was no voice. There hadn't been a voice! And even if there had, it certainly wouldn't have whispered a name that nobody'd called him in years, not since his big brother had moved out and never came back.

"Hoss."

He crouched down in the grass and leaves, his eyes frantically searching the millions of vantage points that the rain forest afforded. So it had been a voice, okay, but it hadn't said that name, it only sounded like that name. . . .

Lightning flashed out there, beyond the jungle, and its momentary brilliance broke through like a thousand thin spotlights that barely reached the ground. But they did silhouette the figure standing only a few meters away. The man was perfectly rigid, his back to Stiles and his neck at an angle as if listening.

Stiles brought up his rifle and peered through the stubby scope he'd electrical-taped to the handle. The luminescent dot fell dead center of the shadowy figure's back, but he didn't squeeze the trigger. The man did not seem to be looking his way, nor did he seem concerned by the point man's presence. Could he not know Stiles was there? It seemed an impossibility given his less than stealthy approach but . . . Stiles's mind was racing, his heart pounding, flooding his veins with adrenaline and his senses with life. He could see the man's outline clearly now, the pained angle of the neck, the matted hair, the torn coat. He could not smell him yet nor hear his breathing but the rain was probably masking those. It didn't matter. He had his target.

He slung the rifle over one shoulder, slowly and quietly, then slipped his hand beneath the poncho and brought out his Ka-Bar. *Don't kill him yet*, he cautioned himself. *Silence him first —there may be others like this Hoss character he must have been speaking to. Don't go horseshit and start killing right and left, just recon and report back. Think of the men.*

He glided silently through the damp compost of the forest floor, so slowly that the mud didn't squelch around his boots to give him away. Up close he could make out little more of the man. He slid up behind him and stepped in between his legs to cut his balance, then looped an arm around his mouth and face and fell backward to drag his assailant to the ground.

But his arm didn't find any resistance. He tumbled back into the weeds alone, knowing that the man now stood directly over him. The knife was forgotten as he fumbled frantically for his machine gun, praying that he could at least take the sonuvabitch with him.

"I'd be ashamed, Hoss," said the voice, its deep timbre amplified in the silence. "All that training and you're still clumsy as ever."

Stiles gulped and gagged and for a moment thought he'd swallowed his tongue. His eyes crawled up the dark form before him, now silhouetted against the dim light that peeked through the lattice overhead. No, it couldn't be. . . . "Hoss?" he stammered. "Only one person ever called me Hoss."

The figure held out its arms. "Ta-da!".

"But you can't be my brother . . . he's back in the states. . . ."

"*Was* back in the states."

The voice. It had taken a few moments for its familiarity to sink in, to convince him. "Alex?" He rose hesitantly. "Is it really you?" He reached out to the shadowy figure, only to have it back away. "What is it? What's wrong?"

"Just stay back, Chris."

Stiles wiped his eyes. "C'mon, Alex. Let me get a good look at you. Did you join up, or—"

The figure stepped back, further into the shadows. "Goddamn it, Chris, I said stay back."

"I just want to see you—"

"Well you can't. You can't see me and you can't touch me."

"Why not?"

"'Cause I'm dead, that's why. There, good enough reason?"

Stiles just stood there, too confused to move. "Don't bullshit me, Alex. You mean you think you're gonna be killed, is that it?"

"I *was* killed. Tonight. Back home."

"And then you flew all the way here. Boy, I'll bet your arms are tired."

"Funny guy. I can see you need proof." He held out a hand that slipped from the shadow and into a column of daylight. The flesh was pale and bore a web of scars. Some were still open, though they did not bleed. "C'mon, little brother. Take my hand."

Hesitating, but thinking, *Why are you hesitating*?, he reached out and clasped it, and then he shivered. There was a hint of contact at first, a frosty chill that seemed to permeate his glove. And then the contact ebbed until Chris's hand passed completely through his brother's. Only the chill remained. "Jesus!" he stammered, tearing off his glove to rub at his hand, to erase the taint that lingered there. "Jesus H. Christ! You're dead!"

"Surprise. And you will be too if you don't listen. Are you listening, Hoss?" The ghost stepped before Stiles and peered into his face. The shadows seemed to prevent Stiles from peering back. "Are you listening? 'Cause they're all around you."

"Ghosts?"

"Vietcong. You're walking right through an ambush."

Stiles searched the jungle. "I haven't seen anyone."

"Then it wouldn't be an ambush, would it, stupid. They're waiting for you to pass and lead the men in here."

"Then I've got to warn them," he started, but Alex's words held him back.

"You move to the rear and you're dead before you take a step."

"Then what do I do?"

"You take them out yourself."

"You're nuts."

"No, I'm a ghost," Alex retorted, "and that is your ace in the hole." He pointed to Stiles's rifle. "Any good with that thing?"

"Sure."

"Good. So here's what you do. Wherever you see me next, you fire. Aim right for my breastbone. I'll be your pointer."

"I don't know—"

"Just do it, Chris. You don't want to be dead. It's no fun. Take my word for it." Then the apparition was gone.

Chris Stiles stood there in the mud and the leaves and stared into the gloom around him and felt his sanity slip away. That's what it had to be. There was nothing there. No Alex, no 'Cong, no nothing. *Jeez, you really went this time. Forget about numbness and daydreaming. Now you've gone completely wackadoo. Brothers you haven't seen in years suddenly pop up, casually dressed in shadows and doing a Casper routine. That's it, you're out of here. It's Section Eight time, back to the World and a padded room with a great view of the shock-treatment ward . . .*

"Quit dreaming, asshole," yelled a voice, too loud to be concerned with being heard. By anyone but him, that is.

He scanned the trees, from one identical trunk to the next, until a waving arm caught his attention. Alex was straddling a branch about forty feet up, waving and pointing at himself, at the center of his chest. Chris shrugged. What else could he do? He shouldered the rifle, switched it to semi-auto, centered the Aimpoint, and squeezed one off. The shot echoed through the jungle, giving flight to the monkeys and flushing birds from their roosts. Then the silence returned.

He lowered the scope from his eye. Alex wasn't there. The tree was empty. "Well?" he said under his breath. "I wonder if I hit anything."

"Absolutely," came his brother's voice now from behind him and about twenty feet away. Stiles stared into the darkness, knowing it impossible to find a shadow among shadows, but somehow a faint figure became apparent to him as if wrapped in an amber glow. "Pick up the pace now," Alex counseled. "They don't know that you're onto them yet. Go to automatic, too." He danced back and forth. "There's a bunch of 'em here."

Stiles opened up on the figure with three shot bursts, following it wherever it moved. One scream rang out, strangled and eerie in its solitude. Then the jungle seemed to come alive with gunfire.

He dove for cover even as a volley sizzled overhead and shredded the smooth bole beside him. He responded not to the attacks but to the figure that still pranced out there in the open, vanishing here and popping up there, giving Chris barely enough time to fire before moving on to the next target. Each of his shots was apparently dead-on. The barrage of incoming rounds was decreasing.

He scrambled for better cover and that was when he was hit. One round tore cleanly through his left shoulder while the rest stitched his rib cage like red-hot needles. But he felt only the initial jolt; the rest was extinguished beneath a pounding wave of adrenaline. He fought for his balance, twisting sideways on unstable legs as another volley passed hotly by his cheek, their buzzing barely louder than the mosquitoes around them. His eyes, by instinct, pinpointed the patch of grayness out there where the muzzle had flashed. One handed, he trained his rifle on that spot and emptied his magazine into it before his brother had even arrived there.

Chris fell back on his butt, instinctively fumbling with the jungle clip on his rifle despite the cessation of enemy fire. It was several moments until the silence finally registered. He looked around him, found Alex still standing over the last kill, inspecting his handiwork. "You got 'em all, Hoss," the ghost laughed, if a bit lifelessly. "I'll give you credit. You're better than I expected. Yessir, this might just work out after all."

Chris squinted at his brother. "What? What might work?"

Alex turned and started toward him, his feet walking a good six inches above the mud, and as he grew closer he also began to fade. "Your men are coming," he said as if from far off. "You'll be okay." Then he was gone.

If he had really been there at all.

Stiles blinked. What the hell had just happened? The pain from his shoulder and side was only now beginning to slip his defenses, an all-too-uncomfortable reality that made what had happened before it seem dreamlike. Alex hadn't really been there, had he? He couldn't have been, he was still back home in the states somewhere. There was no ghost. He'd just stumbled across a squad of 'Cong and time had slowed down like it does in battle sometimes and he'd just dreamed Alex up. Yeah, he'd just dreamed him. And once he got back home he'd look Alex up and they'd have a pretty good laugh over it.

But there was no laughing now. The pain was blinding. He climbed to his feet but staggered and collapsed and wasn't even aware that someone had caught him until he heard Lieutenant

Wilkerson's voice, sounding far-off and hollow as if yelling across a public restroom. "Stiles? Can you hear me? You men, secure the area! You, get that corpsman up here!" He saw Briscoe and Osteen and Shelton fan out from behind the CO, as Turner stood watch with his necklace of belted brass and his M60 leveled at the hip.

Stiles's eyes were so tired, too tired to keep open. Instead he just listened to the voices, distinct but distant, like a radio playing just in the background.

"How's he doing?"

"Is the area clear?"

"It's clear, sir, and you ain't gonna believe it. There's bodies everywhere. . . ."

"Where's that fucking—Corpsman! Get up here now!"

". . . must be at least ten of 'em. He got 'em all!"

"Has anybody seen Pruett?"

He felt hands on his shoulders, ripping at his shirt, blotting away the blood that ran warm down his chest and arm.

"Somebody's coming, sir."

"Identify yourself!"

"Hey, it's Pruett. Look, it's Pruett!"

The name snapped Stiles alert. He shoved past the medic and stood dizzily, leaning on his rifle to stand beside the lieutenant and peer into the gloom of the rain forest. It was true. Jimmy Lee Pruett was picking his way through the dense overgrowth, a drab shadow set apart from the jungle by the crisscrossing bandoliers across his ponchoed chest. He waved with his shotgun as he approached. The other man waved too.

Stiles struggled to clear his throat. "Who's that other guy with him?"

Everyone stared at him. "What other guy? Ain't nobody there but Pruett."

Oh, Lord. Oh, no.

"Shoot!" Alex yelled from in front of Pruett. "Shoot, dammit!"

"I—"

"SHOOT!"

He brushed drunkenly past the others and they didn't see his raised M16 until he started to fire in controlled three-shot bursts as before. Pruett jerked up onto his toes. His dance lasted only a second or so but its twitching choreography was sickening to watch. But watch they did, in stunned silence until the rifle went dead and Stiles began to fumble for a second clip.

Someone hit him from behind then, just below the ear, and the forest seemed to burst into flourescent color before his eyes. The weight of his attacker pressed him down into the mud as blow after blow rained down until he could no longer feel them. "You psycho sonuvabitch!" Briscoe cursed him, over and over. "He's one of us! He's one of us!"

It took three to wrestle him off, though Stiles couldn't have known. There was just a whirlpool of voices around him, and even the pain began to subside as he slipped further and further into unconsciousness. But there was suddenly something dragging him back, a voice saying his name, a familiar voice. The lieutenant.

He looked up painfully to find he was sitting up now, propped against a treetrunk. He was surrounded by a wall of men, each wearing a pensive but suspicious look. The lieutenant was right in front of him, holding something in his hand. Pruett's shotgun. "How did you know?" he was saying, his eyes unable to mask his own suspicion. His own fear. "How did you know it wasn't Pruett? How?"

Stiles's mouth moved but he didn't answer. He didn't even try. Instead he looked past Wilkerson's shoulder and past the men to a figure standing away from the others, back in the shadows behind a shell-pocked tree. "Tell them," Alex said. "When you get back, call home. Tell them where I am."

"Where are you?" he asked. The men exchanged puzzled glances and looked to see who he meant.

"The park," said his brother, his voice cracking. "Central Park. Tell them to come and find me. Don't leave me there."

There was a sudden flash of lightning in the storm beyond, and a stencil of it reached the floor of the rain forest. For a brief instant it chased away the cloak of shadows and gave Chris the first glimpse he'd had of his brother in years. Alex wasn't the same. Parts of him were missing. But it wasn't that, nor the gleam of his bare cheekbone or the jutting ribs or the blood that matted his hair and clothes that made Chris's guts twist the most. It was the cause of his condition. Something had been at his brother. The teeth marks were evident even from a distance.

"Tell them where I am, Hoss," he repeated as he started to fade.

"But where? Where in Central Park?"

For the first time some spark of emotion came from the phantom. A sob racked his mangled frame. "The whole park," he cried. "I'm all over it!" Then he faded, and the jungle was silent again.

Stiles didn't so much wake up, since he had not been sleeping, as suddenly come alert. His eyes were still glued to the roadway but they had failed to notice the subtle lightening of the eastern sky. As the realization sank in he rubbed his tired eyes and checked his watch: 5:30 A.M. *Christ, have I missed anything?*

He got out of the van, one hand hiding the Uzi beneath his overcoat, and ran through the trees to the culvert. The scene was undisturbed; the hand was still visible, still frozen in place. Disgusted, he bent the rigored limb back out of sight, though not so far that he couldn't pull it forth again. He'd need his marker again tonight.

Five-thirty, he thought, stretching his cricked spine. That ought to give him enough time to shower and sleep and then think of what to tell Billie before his vigil started again. Grumbling, he greeted the sun as both friend and enemy and walked tiredly back to the van.

On the way back to town, he thought about stopping for cigarettes but he fought the urge until it faded.

Chapter Nine

"Billie?"

She snapped out of her daydream, stopped mopping the counter, and turned slowly to where Sharon Lou stood at the far end. Seated across from Sharon was Carol Gastineau, a sturdy woman in a snappy tweed business suit with a briefcase laid next to her coffee cup. "You've been off work for fifteen minutes now," Sharon reminded her. "Why don't you go on home?"

Billie smiled tiredly, took her apron off, and went around the counter, but only to take a seat on one of the empty stools. "The boys have been out since this morning, playing football I imagine. I'd just as soon hang around here than be in the house alone."

"Is that old house bothering you, honey?" Carol said with a smile and a gleam in her eye and Billie knew she'd said the wrong thing. Carol was the local real estate agent, and land was her life. "You be sure to tell me," she went on, "because if it is, I just know we can come to some kind of arrangement." She drummed her fingers on the genuine imitation leather of her case as if it contained all of the treasures one could ever wish for. "I'll bet I can get you a good price for your old place, well, not *too* much, but a decent price just the same. Now," she snapped the clasps on the case and arched her eyebrows, "what kind of house do you have your heart set on?"

"Put your teeth back in your mouth, Giggy," Sharon said sharply, "she didn't say she was selling or buying."

Carol huffed and sipped her coffee. Giggy had been her nickname in high school, back when she was a cheerleader and one of the popular girls while Sharon Lou Moore was just a face in the crowd. But nowadays the only person to remember *was* Sharon, and she twisted it like a knife every chance she got.

"I was only trying to help," Carol muttered into her cup. "And you know, this coffee's cold. Lou honey, would you be an angel and warm this up?" It was more a command than a question, a reminder of who was being served there and who did the serving.

Sharon shrugged it off and, with a bigger smile, overran her cup. "Oh. Sorry about that. Giggy."

"I appreciate the thought, Carol," Billie said, signaling a truce. "But I'm not really interested in getting rid of my house right now."

"Then what's bothering you?"

"That new boy in town," Sharon said, then caught Billie's look. "Excuse me . . . new man. Billie's kinda taken up with him."

"You don't have to make it sound so back alley," Billie complained. "He's just a nice guy's all."

Sharon leaned across the counter as if it were a back fence. "You never did tell me about the other night when he went home with you 'uns."

Carol stopped brushing microscopic lint from her outfit and arched a thin brow. "What's that? With a stranger?"

"Nothing happened," Billie shrugged, "at least nothing to feed your libidos. We just talked is all."

"About what?"

"Well . . . things."

"Are you seeing him again?"

Billie just shook her head. "We were supposed to go out last night but he called and canceled at the last minute. I haven't seen him since."

"Deadbeat," Carol said, offended. "Isn't that just like a man, wheel into town and then back out, leaving a woman high and dry?"

"Whoa there," Sharon warned, "both of you. You act like it's been days instead of the roughly, what," she checked her watch, "eighteen hours since he called? Give him time, Bill. He's not on the clock, you know. He'll call." She leaned closer. "Or you could call him."

Carol huffed. "Well, I wouldn't. Men don't like pushy women, Billie, take my word on that. Why, when I was seeing my husband Jim Gastineau, God rest his soul, I gave him a long leash, if you know what I mean, and sooner or later he'd come sniffing around. . . ."

"Roll up your pantlegs," Sharon cautioned, "the shit's getting deep. Remember, dear Giggy, that I was around back then. That man couldn't take two steps that you didn't have a bulldog headlock on him. The way I heard it, the poor sap only married you so he could get a little rest." Carol inflated with indignation but Sharon held her at bay with a raised hand. "Billie, you do yourself a favor and go after him. There ain't many in this town or anywhere else worth a hill of beans, but that one's special. Take my word for it." Then Carol couldn't hold it in any longer and a storm rolled across the counter that probably showed up on the weather radar in Indianapolis.

"How dare you, Sharon Lou Moore, how can you set there and insinuate that I would *blah blah blah . . .*"

Billie tuned out the festivities. She'd heard it all before; Carol was a regular customer, coming in like clockwork every day to "wait for a potential buyer" who invariably never showed. Billie knew she was trying to rub her job in her old rival's face, but Sharon seemed quite content with her own store and her job and took none of the other's guff. So the friendly feud went on, week to week, and sometimes customers showed up for ringside stools just to listen to the meowing and hissing.

Billie's eyes strayed to the door, though the bell hadn't rung to attract her. Nonetheless, she found Chris Stiles standing in the doorway, watching her for a reaction before daring a smile of his own.

Carol Gastineau saw him as well. "I wonder if he'll be staying on," she pondered aloud and reached for her briefcase but Sharon smacked her hand.

"I didn't know if you'd be talking to me," he said as he came across the store.

"Why not?" Billie shrugged. "Things come up, I know. It happens." She became aware of the stares burning into her back "C'mon, let's sit down," she motioned to a table nearby, but not before glaring back at the counter. Sharon was suddenly busy wiping glasses, but Carol still gawked openly and with a smirking grin. Sharon had to snap her with the dishtowel to get her to turn around.

"So," Billie began, "how did it go last night?"

He stiffened. "How did what go?"

"You said you had something to do."

"Oh that. Yes, that's what I came over about."

Uh oh, she thought. *Here it comes. I'm sorry, Billie, but I'm going to be busy again tonight . . .*

"I'm sorry, Billie, but I'm afraid I'll be tied up again tonight. Can I get another rain check?"

She shrugged. "Sure, no problem. We don't even have to go out if you don't want, really, I—"

"Billie," he said in a firm tone that brought her eyes up to meet his own. "I want to. Really. This is just very important stuff, and it can't wait, that's all."

"What is it?"

He grinned and hoped she didn't realize he was scrambling for an answer. "Research. The book, remember?"

Her eyes lit up. "Really? You mean the scary stuff? Great. I'll come along."

"No, I don't think so."

"Oh, come on. I ain't 'fraid of no ghosts."

Stiles was adamant. "I said no. It could be dangerous. I won't take that chance. Not with you."

There was a protective tone in his voice that she liked, but she began to bait him anyway. "Oh, yeah? Well, how do I know this isn't some kind of stall. I mean, there are other women in this town, maybe you're seeing one of them. . . ."

He reached across the table and cupped her chin and pulled her toward him. She gave no resistance. His kiss was insistent yet tender and convinced her that yesterday morning had not been a dream after all.

Giggy yelped from being snapped with the towel again and turned back to the counter reluctantly.

Stiles stood to leave. "Do you think you'll get it done tonight," she asked, "whatever it is?"

"Possibly. Or it could take another night, or two. There's no way to tell."

She took his hand. "Well, whenever you're done," she lowered her voice to a whisper, "stop by. Okay?"

"No matter how late?"

Her smile widened. "If I'm in bed, get me up."

He turned and waved to the ladies at the counter before he left. This time the bell sounded.

Charlie Bean eased the squad car down the main drive of the Nevermore, then slowed near the rear of the park. A police cruiser just like his own was once again parked outside the beat-up Windsor trailer—Rusty Sanders was not known for his subtlety. Bean wondered how the other residents, mostly conservative, God-fearing folk, perceived Sanders's blatant immorality, but there had been no complaints to his knowledge. Surely their disapproval had been tempered by the security a police car conveyed.

A mischievous thought flickered through Bean's mind. He wondered how Rusty would like it if his distributor cap disappeared or someone stuck a banana up his tail pipe.

Or up his ass, he thought, a bit more irritated after he remembered running into Georgetta Stovall last night. When he stopped by the A & W for a few burgers and a root beer he saw her there, eating with some youngster he didn't recognize—probably from out of town, and barely eighteen if that old. Her condition had immediately caught Bean's eye. Georgie was always a bit too made-up for his taste but last night her rouge was deep enough to plant corn in and the glistening lip gloss did nothing to hide the gash in her lower lip. In fact, the makeup did more to enhance her contusions than hide them. Somebody'd bounced her around pretty good, and he doubted it was her adolescent suitor. Georgie was a big, buxom woman and could have spit in the boy's ass if she'd wanted (or if he'd ask). He could think of only one person who patronized her little Windsor on a regular basis and seemed capable of such treatment. And Rusty's name seemed all the more logical when she reached for a cigarette and he saw the handcuff bruises on her wrists. He questioned her about it, hoping she might swear out a complaint or give him any reason at all to hang the little bastard's butt on a nail. But she just smiled sweetly if a bit vacantly and said nothing.

I swear, Charlie thought, *if he's using that badge for coercion I'll pin it to his spleen. Personally.*

He thought about the banana again and his second use for it and the idea began to appeal to him. He couldn't stomach a woman-beater. Hell, he'd been married once and had three different relationships since, and not once had he raised a hand against any of them, not once. Not that he didn't want to on occasion. Take last night for instance. Especially last night, he thought. It was probably the worst row he and Susie had to date. But he didn't lose his temper.

No, he told himself cynically, *all you lost was Susie.*

Scowling, he put the car in gear, left the trailer park, and headed back across town. His watch beeped but he couldn't remember why he'd set it for seven o'clock. It was almost dusk.

He found Isherwood just as he'd left it earlier. Restive. Sleepy. Catatonic. The main street saw few cars and the shops even fewer customers—what shops were open. Many hadn't even bothered. The apparent emptiness of the town didn't cause any great concern in Charlie Bean. Isherwood was never a lively place except for special occasions like Christmas or the Fourth of July or when the Hoosiers won the NCAA title. But the shops were normally open, all of them, rain or shine, waiting for that one tourist who might wander through and leave a buck or two behind. He slowed the car and peered into the darkened windows that lined the block. The lights of the barbershop and the Woolworth's were usually out by seven on a Sunday, but the knowledge that they and others had not been on at all today bothered him. Across the street Moore's was still open—a Sherman tank couldn't keep Sharon Lou from her business—but only for the moment. The lights in the rear were winking out in succession, and he realized how much slack the drugstore had been taking up. With its closing, the street was plunged into a gloom that only deepened with the flight of the sun.

He shivered. Must be something going around, he thought. Another Asian influenza, maybe an epidemic. Hell, the marshall hadn't even made it in today. Bean coughed by association and felt his forehead and made a mental note. Nyquil and vitamin C and a lot of zinc. Stop by the IGA before it closes.

He couldn't get his mind off Susie. *Why don't you call her*? a voice kept nagging, though another retorted that she wouldn't talk now any more than the five times earlier. She had ran off to Bedford last night after he'd gone to bed, and her parents' home was as much a recognized sanctuary as the church. Norman and Bernice were always cloyingly protective—her mother had already rebuffed each of his calls, answering in a burst of short, staccato yesses and nos. Another call would not change anything. Why waste the time?

Yeah. Why?

He steered into the Sunoco station just as it was shutting down for the night. The sign was still lit and the doors open, but Kenny Houter was already out front in his stained coveralls, pulling the heavy tire displays toward the bays and struggling to make headway as the wiggling casters kept catching in the rutted asphalt drive. The young man grinned when he saw the deputy get out to help him. "I 'preciate the hand, Charlie," he sighed. "These babies can be a bitch by yourself."

They tugged the obstinate display free. "Where's Myers?" Bean asked once they were inside the empty work bay. "I thought he usually works on Sunday."

"So did I," answered Houter, disgusted. "Probably sleeping off a drunk someplace. I hope the boss fires his ass." He looked at the squad car outside. "Anything I can get you 'fore I close up?"

"No thanks. I just wanted to use your phone."

"Help yourself." He headed back toward the drive. "I've gotta get busy or my supper's gonna be cold by the time I get home."

Bean used the phone in the back room of the station and dialed the Swango's number from recent memory, no longer needing the dog-eared paper from his wallet. But there was no answer at the other end, just a busy signal. Probably off the hook. Damn. This thing was dragging out too damn long, and he didn't like it. The apartment seemed too quiet already and he wasn't even there yet. For a change he really dreaded going home.

"'Scuse me, Charlie," Houter said from out in the middle of the bay, where he was setting water cans and an unplugged air hose atop the dormant lift. "I wonder if you could do me a favor?"

Bean looked at the phone in his hand, considered calling again, but hung up instead. "Sure, Kenny. Shoot."

"Well," the attendant hemmed and hawed, "it's not really for me. It's for Poop-deck Pappy out there." He nodded out toward the pumps to where a familiar scarecrow loitered. George Bailey stood in the middle of the island clutching an Isherwood Hardware bag in one hand and a small gas can with the other, barely keeping erect against the stout breeze. He was staring away at the horizon, his pinched and scowling expression matching the disarray of his silvery hair. He looked like a refugee from a Frankenstein movie or, better yet, from an old issue of *Creepy* magazine.

"Oh, that weird duck," Charlie said. "He's ornery as hell. What's he want?"

"Well, he was wanting me to call him a cab, but Lorene at the switchboard told me two of their drivers didn't show up and the other's on a call all the way to Bedford. Mr. Bailey could be waiting out there for a good while and I'm almost ready to close, so I was in hopes you'd give him a lift. It's not too far, just up to the old folks' home."

Bean thought about it. "I don't know. Why are you so worried about this crotchety old bird?"

Kenny threw up his arms. "I figure I'm gonna be old some day, you know, an' I'll probably be pretty pissed about it myself. C'mon, Charlie."

"Might as well," Bean sighed. No one to hurry home to anyway. He slapped Kenny on the shoulder as he passed. "Give the little lady a flourish for me too, you hear?"

"That depends on what's on TV tonight," Houter laughed. "See ya, Charlie."

George Bailey was still staring at the dwindling light at the horizon and didn't realize the deputy was next to him until he spoke. "I've seen prettier sunsets. How about you?"

The old man staggered sideways and crashed into the "Unleaded" pump and would have fallen had Bean not caught him by the arm. "You sneakin' som'bitch," Bailey croaked, once he'd cleared the heart from his throat. "What do you want me to do, have a heart attack?"

"I'm sorry. I thought you saw me."

"Well, I didn't." He straightened himself on his cane and sloshed the gas can to make sure the cap was on tight. "Well? What do you want? I'm not under arrest, am I?"

Bean forced a laugh. "No, nothing like that. Kenny tells me there won't be any cabs available for a while so I thought I'd give you a lift back home."

Bailey turned his hawkish stare on the patrol car a few feet away, then glanced back at the horizon. The sun had abruptly sank out of sight behind the trees. Without a word he crossed to the car and climbed into the front seat, his sack on his lap and the can between his bony knees. "Well?" he called back. "What are you waiting on, the first snow? I don't have all night, you know."

Bean scratched his head and shot a perturbed glance back at Kenny Houter but the attendant wasn't in view.

"So," he said as they pulled out of the station and started through town, "did your car run out of gas or what?"

Bailey looked out the window. "Don't own a car." He kicked the can with a knee. "Lawn mower. Figure we might have to cut again 'fore it gets really cold. It ain't me that's gonna do it, by God. I'm just a gopher. I was going into town anyway, to pick up a few things. But goddammit, nothing's open. 'Cept the hardware store, thank goodness." He crunched the sack against him and said, more to himself, "I need these things."

"What's in there?"

"Just things."

"Oh."

They drove in silence for about a block before Bean started fishing for a conversation again. It was too quiet otherwise, and he was afraid that the old man might slip away when he wasn't looking and slump dead as a carp against the passenger door. He didn't need the aggravation. "You've been around here a long time, haven't you?"

"Long enough."

"Born here?"

"No."

"No? I was, on the other side of town. You have any relatives around here, Mr. Bailey? Any brothers or sisters, any children or grandkids?"

"No."

"Not around here, or—"

"Nowhere. I don't have any family."

Bean nodded solemnly. "Yeah. Me neither." He changed the subject. "So, what made you come to Isherwood then? When was that, back in—"

"I came here in 1950, for a friend's funeral. This looked as good as any other town so I stayed. My height is five-nine, my weight is one hundred and twenty-five pounds, and my hat size is seven and three-quarters. Now, is there anything else you'd like to know, Deputy, or should we just check my prints and have it over with?"

Bean laughed. "Just making conversation, Pops. You're a crotchety old fart, you know that?"

"That's what they tell me."

They passed the edge of town, turned onto Moffit Trail, and began the winding drive to the top. The boardinghouse was already in view, standing out against the reddened sky of dusk. It was still light enough to make out the big old structure with its vigilant elm tree out front, its ornate eaves and ivy-encrusted trellises and a honeycomb of shuttered eyes, some dark, others already glowing with lamp light. It was a homey-looking old fortress, had stood for nearly a century, and had functioned as a boardinghouse for about half that time. It had never had a formal business name, nothing you could look up in the Yellow Pages under "Room and Board." But the people of Isherwood had rectified that years back when they bestowed a moniker from TV. The name still stuck today—as long as *Petticoat Junction* lived in syndication, the big house on the hill would always be known as the Shady Rest.

Bean wondered what it would be like to live in such an airy old palace instead of a cramped apartment or mobile home as he had most of his life. "It must be great to have such a big old home like that," he said, mostly just thinking out loud. Bailey turned in his seat and looked at him as if he were stupid.

"Oh, it's wonderful. If you like to hear the pop of old, brittle bones and the creak of muscles as stretchy as sandpaper, the panting of people who've lost their breath and ain't likely to find it again. This ain't no home, friend. Ain't nothin' but a depot for the dying." Then, under his breath, "Well, not me. Not yet anyway." He kept muttering that until they pulled to a stop in front of the house.

There were people out front. Hubert Ranall was just finishing mowing the lawn. A woman not much older than he, Jessie Shively, rose from her flower bed and peeled off her rubber gloves, brushing soil from her knees. A handsome woman with gray hair and still very vital, she had just transferred several late bloomers from bed to pot and would take them inside to protect them as long as any mother could. On the porch was the only person Bean actually recognized by name, Avina Atchison, the house's owner, rocking with a sweater around her shoulders and some needlepoint on her lap. She was long-faced and dour, not quite as old as her boarders, but looked it. She kept her eyeglasses on a chain around her neck and owned almost as many wigs as Dolly Parton. Today her hair had a reddish hue. It almost looked real. She waved when the squad car pulled up. But none of them spoke when George Bailey climbed out and, without even a thank you or a nod, started up the walk. Bean grimaced. What a charming guy.

The frail old man stopped as he reached the porch and turned to the woman. "Viney," he said, looking at the darkening sky as if fearing rain. "Come in the house."

She looked up questioningly. "Did you say something, George?"

"I said you should come in now. And you too, Jessie. And Hubert. It's getting dark."

The woman looked from him to the black man and back again. "Since when were you so concerned with us?"

"Yeah, George," Jessie Shively said, coming onto the porch. "Besides, you don't have to worry. We're all grown up now. We aren't afraid of the dark anymore." She and the landlady broke up laughing. Bailey stiffened and hobbled on into the house.

Charlie Bean eased the car along the road until he was just across the little plank fence from Hubert. The big man smiled broadly and tipped an imaginary hat but did not take his attention away from his struggle with the bogged down push-mower. "Looks like hard work," Bean called.

"Ain't easy," Ranall laughed back. "But a little hard work never hurt nobody, right?"

The deputy nodded. "Wouldn't the power mower be a lot easier?"

The big man looked at him quizzically. "It certainly would," he said, "if we had one." Shaking his head, he untangled the blades of the ancient mower and continued his work, hurrying to beat the nighttime.

"What about the gas can . . ." Charlie started, but then he just shrugged it off, chalking it up to Old Man Bailey's senility. He drove back down the hill toward town as the sky darkened further, and didn't notice the figure standing in an upper floor window behind him.

Not that George Bailey was spying on the deputy; he was far too busy using his new tools from the hardware store. A few more whacks of the hammer and the window was nailed completely shut.

Stiles snapped alert. It was even darker out now, fully night. He checked his watch—8:30 P.M.—as he reached for the scope and leaned it across the steering wheel.

No change at the culvert. Larry Hovi still waved from his hiding place. Then what had alerted him?

His eyes were drawn to the right, along the edge of the road. A shadow splashed across the shoulder and then it was gone. But a branch still swayed there.

The adrenaline began to pump, as suddenly as if he'd flipped a switch. He worked by rote: securing his combat vest, flipping the Uzi's safety, making sure the Dome-Lite button was still taped down as he opened the door. He slid quietly into the night and glided through the trees toward the road.

Another veil of clouds was pulled across the moon. The countryside went almost pitch black.

Stiles crouched beside a tree and pressed his back to it and gave his eyes time to adjust. He was only a few feet from Sykes Road—the culvert was to his left, fifteen to twenty feet at the most. Hovi's hand was beyond his view. He watched instead the other shoulder where the bushes had moved. It was still now.

Easy. Danner could be anywhere. Take it slow. Remember, he's blind. You have the advantage..

He checked the clouds again to make sure they would cover him, then scrambled, low and spiderlike, across the road and into the underbrush on the far side.

He rolled to his feet, his ears perked like parabolic mikes, sweeping the darkness around him. There had been a footstep nearby but now there was no sound at all.

Listen.

There was something . . . breathing. Quick and raspy, either nervous or emphysemic or rattling through a shot-up windpipe. Did vampires actually breath? He'd never thought about it. Alex was dead and he didn't, but then again, since when did ghosts and vampires have to play by the same rules?

The breather took a step.

The bushes directly ahead parted. A hunched figure stepped past just as the clouds broke up and let the moon's stunted glow spill through.

The soldier's two quick steps crunched in the crepe-paper leaves as loud as gunshots. The stalker whirled about just as Stiles left the ground and the edge of his foot pistoned into its unprotected cheekbone with merciless force. The figure sprawled backward with a groan and the soldier was right on top of it, sweeping the Uzi across the prostrate form with a controlled, almost surgical burst.

But at the last instant, he turned his hand. The spitting machine pistol ripped up the soil instead, but it was close enough for Charlie Bean to throw down his revolver, cover his head, and yell, "I give up! Jesus, don't shoot!"

Stiles stood over him, glaring. "Goddamn you," he fumed, visibly shaken himself. He'd barely averted the fire in time. "What the hell are you doing out here? I could've blown your fucking head off!"

The deputy sat up and cradled his aching face in his hands. "Mr. Binford . . . lives out yonder . . . stopped me in town, said he saw somebody parked back in the trees out here. I came out to . . . hey, you sonuvabitch! I should be asking the questions here!" He crawled toward the gun he'd dropped but Stiles was already past him and picked it up instead.

Bean watched him hesitantly. "What're you gonna do?"

"I don't know. Yet."

He motioned to the Uzi. "Full auto, huh? That's illegal. I hope you know that."

"I do."

Bean fidgeted. What did he have on his hands here, some kind of psycho? A terrorist even? "Wha . . ." He cleared his throat. "What do you need something like that for?"

"It's just a tool," Stiles said evasively, but the more he stood there facing the law, the more he realized he would have to tell the deputy something, anything, any kind of explanation. It was either that or get sent up for illegal weaponry and assault on a police officer.

Or he could kill him.

He weighed all his options.

"I'm going to confide in you, Charlie," he said simply. "I'm a hunter."

"With that kind of armament?" Bean laughed, but then it dawned on him. "Oh. You mean a bounty hunter?"

"Of sorts. I'm after somebody right now, and I'm waiting for him to return to the scene of the crime."

Bean looked around him. "Crime? What crime?"

Stiles was blunt. "Murder. There are three bodies stuffed into that culvert over there. And I have a feeling their killer will be back."

The deputy stared at him blankly before inching his way toward the culvert, though never taking his eyes off Stiles or turning his back. He took the police light from his belt and stooped to look into the concrete tube. Stiles prepared for the retching sounds to come. Even a seasoned officer like Bean would never have seen anything like that.

"Mr. Stiles?"

"What?"

"There are no bodies here."

Stiles scrambled across the road and dropped into the culvert beside Bean. The tube was indeed empty save for the trickling of backed-up water. There were no twisted limbs, no grinning throats, no gaping, pained faces. No blood to stain the water or the concrete walls.

Nothing.

"I repeat," Bean said from right beside him, wondering whether he should try jumping the guy and wrestling for his gun, "where are the bodies?"

Stiles stood up and laid the Uzi muzzle against Bean's lapel. It was not a threatening gesture, though it did make the deputy swallow very hard. Stiles was just motioning to him, for his mind was on other matters. "Quick," he said, "where's your car?"

"Just down the road," Bean stammered, pushing the barrel gently away.

"Well c'mon then," Stiles nudged him in that direction, "we've got to get back to town."

"Now hold on just a damn minute here. I'm not going anywhere until I get some answers—"

"Look!" Stiles barked, and his intensity backed the burly officer up a step or two. "They're probably heading back toward town now, cross-country. That means they'll beat us there, and they'll probably . . . oh, God, Del and Bart! They could be after the boys!" He hurried down the road, all but dragging the deputy behind him.

The squad car squealed into reverse and did a one-eighty in the middle of the road and raced back toward Isherwood. It was 8:50 P.M. The night had just begun.

Chapter Ten

Del was still in front of the television, as he had been for several hours, quiet, watching but not seeing. Once every fifteen or twenty minutes, when his mother wasn't looking, he would run to the window and peer outside, looking first to the driveway for a white van and then into the darkness for something else, something altogether different. He came back, scooted over near the couch where his brother lay with an *X-Men* comic book draped over his face, half-snoring. Del didn't say anything, just sat there, but his presence was enough to rouse Bart. "Cap," he sighed through the comic book, "would you settle down? There's nothing to worry about."

"Nothing to worry about?" the boy snapped, lowering his voice so it wouldn't carry into the kitchen to their mother. "This is two nights in a row. There's trouble, admit it."

"You're your own worst enemy, Delbert. If there was anything wrong, Chris would've told us. So just settle down. He probably had something to do or someone to see. Maybe he hooked up with another woman—I wouldn't put it past him."

"Nope," Del was adamant. "He was going to look for Danner, he promised me, and now there's something wrong. I know it."

"Stop borrowing trouble. Everything's gonna be fine. You just need to think about something else for a while, get your mind off it. Isn't there anything on television you could watch?" The younger boy shrugged. "Well, how about a game or something? Anything to shut you up."

Del brightened. "How about Dungeons and Dragons?"

The older boy frowned. "Hasn't your imagination been satisfied for the next couple of centuries? Pick something a little tamer."

The boy thought. "Stratego? Trouble? Life, chess, backgammon, crazy eights, euchre, Battleship, Monopoly . . ."

"Hey, Monopoly. I haven't played that in a coon's age." He yelled, still without moving the comic book, "Hey, Mom. You want in on some Monopoly?"

Billie's voice called back, "No thanks. Somebody's gotta do dishes around here. Besides, you can only play a short game. Tomorrow's school, remember?"

"Aw, Mom," they groaned in unison. As children, they were obligated to do so.

"You heard me." Her tone was no-nonsense.

"I think it's in my closet." Del said as he went out of the living room and down the hall, almost to the back door before turning into the last bedroom.

The boy's room was just that; a boy's room. The mere identification encompassed not only its condition but its contents. Dirty clothes were puddled everywhere except in the hamper they'd been thrown at. Magazines and comic books were spread liberally about—*Popular Science* and *National Geographic* (gift subscriptions from Grandma and Grandpa), *National Lampoon*, a *Mad* magazine or two, an amalgam of superheroes, from the *Teen Titans* to the *Thundercats* to *The Savage Sword of Conan*. Absent were *Fangoria* and *Famous Monsters* and his other horror books. Those were stashed by the closet door with a blanket thrown over them.

He crossed the mine field he called a floor and dug into the closet, stepping around the covered stack as if it were a basket of snakes. The Monopoly game was buried at the very bottom of his game stack. With patient prying he got it loose without tipping the rest of them, then went back into the hall.

What was that? He heard something and turned automatically toward the back door. It was coming from the backyard. He listened for a second . . . A dog barking. Bruiser, the pit bull next door. But what's he carrying on about? Then a knock came to the back door, not six feet away. Delbert jumped, and the scarred old game box came open and sent deeds and tokens and a rainbow of money scattering across the rug. He ignored it all and took a step toward the door. Through the small porthole window he could see that the screen-door was open and someone was standing out there, just out of view.

The knock came again, insistently.

"Wh . . ." He swallowed. "Who is it?"

"C'mon, honey," Billie's voice called. "Open the door, will ya?"

The boy's sigh of relief was so pronounced he almost wet his pants. "Jeez-o'-Pete," he laughed, "you scared me half to death. I didn't know who it might be." He went over to the door and reached for the knob but realized at a glance that the button on the handle was not depressed. "Hey, it's not locked, lazy. Open it yourself. I gotta pick up this game you made me drop." He went to his hands and knees and scooped money into a pile.

Billie became terse. "I can't open it, Del. My hands are full. C'mon, let me in."

"Full of what?"

"Clothes. From the clothesline, all right? Now let me in."

"Clothesline?" he said, rising slowly. "What's wrong with the dryer?"

"Delbert," her voice was sharp and angry. "You open this door for me right now or you will regret it, young man. I'm going to count to three. . . ."

"Why can't you let yourself in?" he wanted to know. Panic was rising in him.

"One."

It's just your mother, stupid. You don't want her standing out there in the night, not when something might be out there too, ready to grab her . . .

He took a step toward it.

"Two."

No, don't open it, because Mom hasn't used the clothesline, not since we got the dryer and sure as hell not when it's getting cold outside and she's scared of Bruiser getting loose, but there's no fear in this voice none at all and none of this is making any sense . . .

He stepped backward, away from the door.

"Three!"

Someone grabbed him from behind. Delbert yelled and swung his fist so hard that Bart felt the wind as it missed his jaw. He shoved the boy into the wall and doubled his own fist but the frantic look in his brother's eyes brought him up cold. "What the hell is it?'' he said, his sudden anger giving way to an icy dread. ''What is it?''

Del stammered and pointed. ''Someone's at the door. It sounds like Mom, but . . .'' He shook his head.

The older boy stared at the door and crept over to it and started to raise up to look through the small window but stopped himself. *What if it isn't Mom? What if you don't like what you see?*

He turned, went back down the hall. ''Mom?'' he yelled through the living room to the kitchen beyond. ''You sure you don't want to play?''

There was no answer.

He looked at Del, then stepped closer to the corner and the foot of the staircase to get a view of the kitchen door. ''Mom? I said do you want to—''

''I heard you, Bart,'' Billie said from so close that the teenager all but jumped out of his skin. She was coming down the stairs and almost beside him now. ''Sorry about that, sport,'' she grinned. ''I didn't mean to scare you.''

Bart was relieved and worried at the same time. He looked from her to the back door. ''How did you get up the stairs without me knowing it?''

''You were half-asleep under a comic book, remember?'' she laughed and swatted his nose. ''I walked right past you, honey.'' She turned to Del, expecting him to start needling his brother as he did incessantly, but the boy was not laughing or barely paying attention. He was standing amid the guts of the Monopoly game and staring at the back door. ''Del, is that where you found that game? Now, start picking that up, young man, before I . . . Del? Are you listening to me?''

He looked at her, wide-eyed, his face drained of color.

She knelt beside him to feel his forehead, but then she heard Bruiser barking and her eyes strayed to where his had been and she saw through the little window that the screen door was standing open. ''Is somebody out there? Who is that?'' She started for the door.

''No!'' the boys shrieked in unison. ''Don't open it!''

She looked at them suspiciously. ''And why not?''

Del stammered. ''Well . . . because. Just because.''

There was a knock.

Del and Bart exchanged glances full of dread. Billie took

another step toward the door but the boys' hesitancy had infected her and she stopped her hand just short of the knob. She rose onto her toes and peered through the porthole. "Can't see . . . Who is that out there?" She called out louder. "Who is it?"

There was a pause, then, "It's me, Billie." The tone was familiar. "Mrs. Schloesser, from down the street? Our phone's out. Could I use yours?"

The boys whispered to her urgently. "Say no, Mom. Say no." This was ridiculous she thought, it was just that kind lady from a few doors down who was always bringing cookies over for the boys and who canned her own preserves and brought some for her neighbors every Sunday when she sat in the front row at services and sang hymns the loudest and the most off-key. So why couldn't she invite her in?

She reached for the knob but stopped. *Why can't I invite her in?*

The knock came again, insistently. "Billie? Can I come in?"

Billie reached again for the knob. And pushed the button in to lock it. "I'm sorry. Our phone's out too."

The knock came even harder. "Let me in," the voice said, only now Mrs. Schloesser's voice was much deeper, angrier. Billie stepped back with the boys. The knob was turning, back and forth, jiggling.

"Who are you!" Billie yelled.

Then the whoop of a siren erupted out front like a sudden storm. It drowned out the creak of hinges as the screen door swung shut. Flashing lights stabbed through the living room drapes and painted the walls red. The boys took their mother by the arms and pulled her along with them, away from the back door.

Del ran to the window. "It's Charlie and . . . Chris!" He ran to the door and out onto the porch just as the two men were climbing from the patrol car parked half on the curb and half off. "Chris! There's something in the backyard!"

Stiles flew up the walk with long strides, his face set, the Uzi held close to his side. He was past Delbert in an instant and through the house, jerking open the back door without hesitation. The others hurried to catch up.

They found him standing in the backyard, shining his small flashlight into the shadows where the porch light didn't reach.

There was no one else in sight. Even the neighbors' unseen pit bull had settled down behind the tall shrubs and was just growling deep in his throat. Stiles walked to the big shade tree near the back of the lot where the tire-swing still turned in slow, dizzy spirals. He reached out and stopped it. "There's no one here now." He motioned them all back inside.

Billie was exasperated. "Would someone tell me what the hell is going on here?"

"I don't know," Charlie Bean told her, "but we're damn sure gonna find out." He pointed at Stiles, forgetting momentarily that the latter still carried the only guns between them. "You stay right here, mister. You've got some talking to do." Then the deputy went back out to his car to shut off the lights and assure the gathering crowd of neighbors that it was all just a false alarm.

Stiles sighed and hung his head, letting the tension ease from his shoulders and neck. He'd been so afraid . . . He smiled to reassure Billie, reached out for her. "I'm glad you're okay—" he started, but the words stuck in his throat. Billie was backing away from him. Her eyes were on the Uzi. "Chris?" she stammered as if unsure if he were really there in front of her. "Chris, what's going on? Why are you carrying a machine gun?"

Bart stood nearby, dancing anxiously as if he had to pee. "Was it him, Mr. Stiles? Was it Danner, do you think?

Del hugged Stiles's leg and started to cry. "It talked to me, it tried to get me to let it in. But you said it was over. You said it was over!"

Billie came over and drew Delbert away from him. "What's he talking about, Chris?" Her tone was losing its surprise and gaining in anger, growing maternal and protective. "Just what is this all about?"

"Yes, Mr. Stiles," Deputy Bean said from the doorway. He shut the door and locked it. "Tell us what's going on here, and don't leave out anything. Understand?"

"Is that a threat, Deputy?"

Bean didn't flinch. "If that's what it takes."

Stiles regarded him coldly, like a shark, and in that moment Bean would not have been surprised to see the man raise his weapon and fire. Instead he looked from the officer to the woman in front of him and then to the boys, one in his mother's arms and the other standing at his side. Finally he said to Bart, softly, "Tell them."

"Everything? You sure?"

He sat down on the couch and laid the Uzi on his lap. "Everything."

Bart started slowly. "Well, first off, we didn't get beat up by out-of-town guys the other night, and we didn't go over to Jay's either. We had a bet with some guys from Seymour that Del and me could stay all night Friday in the old Danner place."

"The what?" Billie gaped. "Young man, you should know better than that. That place is falling apart. You could have been hurt, both of you—"

"Would you just let me finish?" he snapped. He glanced back at Stiles, rolled his eyes, and sighed, "Adults!" as if the man wasn't included in that group. Then he continued with his story. "So we jumped the gate and got to the house and everything's cool. We put down our bags and ate some sandwiches and then we go poking around the house. That's when the shit hit the fan."

Bean listened intently. "What did you find?"

"Well, down in the basement there's this . . . this thing, fighting to get out from behind one of the walls. It grabbed me here," he pointed to his still-swollen wrist, "and I thought, Jeez, I'm never getting away from this joker, he's so strong. You ain't never felt anything like this, it's superhuman."

"PCP," Bean said matter-of-factly.

"This ain't *T.J. Hooker*, Charlie," Bart sounded annoyed. "You want to hear this story or not? Anyway, Del helped me get away from him—it—whatever—but here it comes after us, tearing apart the wall to do it. We tried to get away and get outta there but it cornered us outside and forced us back into the house. That's when we got a really good look at it. At him. It was Sebastian Danner."

The woman and deputy looked at one another. "A ghost?"

"A vampire."

Billie just stared at them but Bean couldn't hide his exasperation. He rubbed a hand through his hair and gave the boys his best "you've-been-speeding" glare. "Cut the crap, you guys. What really happened?"

Bart was indignant. "This is the God's honest truth! Why

would I make up something so stupid and unbelievable? Cut me some slack, Charlie! That . . . that thing, Danner, he nearly killed me and Del. Hell, look at me. My jaw, my wrist . . . I'm a mess. Where do you think I got these gashes in my neck?"

"You said you got poked with a stick fighting those—"

"I lied, okay? That damned thing bit me. If it wasn't for Chris, we'd be dead, period."

Bean looked to Stiles. "So this is where you come in?"

Del leaped to his defense. "You bet. Danner knocked Bart out and had me by the throat when Chris came in and blasted him. Ba-ba-ba-ba-bam! Danner's face just blew up, I swear." Some of the horror came back to him then, and the excitement drained from his voice. He edged away from his mother and closer to Stiles's seat and kept looking to the hallway that led to the back door. "Danner kinda stumbled away and we lost him in the woods. I wanted to go back and kill him for sure but Chris said that he was the expert and knew how to handle it."

Bean's eyebrows arched. "Expert?"

"Sure," the boy nodded. "He's fought all kinds of monsters, vampires too, I don't know how many times. Right, Chris?

The deputy smirked. "Is that right, Chris? And how many of the big bad vampires have you fought?"

The stranger's eyes furrowed as he stood, and Bean stepped back, thinking he'd just screwed up and pushed the psycho a bit too far. But Stiles pointed only a finger at him. "You stick your sarcasm up your ass, buddy. I'm trying to help *you* here, not the other way around. This town and you people are in danger. The boys who were with Del and Bart the other night? They came back later, after we were gone. They tried to get to the house but, once they were in the woods, they came across Danner first." He looked at the boys sympathetically. "I found their bodies yesterday afternoon."

"Sweet Jesus," Bart whispered. Del started to cry again, and Billie held out her arms to both of them.

"Charlie?" she asked. "Is it true?"

"He didn't see the bodies," Stiles admitted before the deputy could answer. "I'd been staking them out since last night but because of Charlie's interference, they got away."

Del shivered. "Got away? They're vampires too?"

Chris nodded. "That was probably them in the backyard. One

was on the porch, another just to the side. I found the prints. The third was playing on that tire swing by the fence.''

''Why didn't they just break in?'' Bart started, then answered himself by remembering, ''They have to be invited in, don't they?''

Stiles nodded.

Billie kept her eyes on Bean. ''Is it true?'' she repeated.

''I never saw any bodies.''

She met Stiles's gaze. Even in the brief instant of contact he found in her eyes not what he wanted—belief, faith, a modicum of trust. Instead he found only what he'd come to expect over the years. Skepticism. Anger. Mostly fear.

''At least believe your children,'' he begged her. ''For their sake.''

''Chris . . . Mr. Stiles . . . I think you'd better go.''

''Billie, I . . .''

She hugged her boys close, despite their protests. ''I don't know what games you're playing and I don't know what influence you've got over my children. I'm not sure I want to know. But I do think you should leave.'' She wiped her eyes. ''Now, please.'' She saw the pain in his gaze and turned away. ''Charlie? Get him away from us.''

''Mom, listen to him!'' Del cried, but Billie wasn't listening.

The deputy took a hesitant step toward the soldier. ''Mr. Stiles? If you're about ready—''

''Just a minute.'' He went over to Billie and the boys and kneeled down in front of them. ''Listen to me, just for a second.'' He pulled her chin around to face him. ''So I'm a nut, or a serial killer, or whatever you want. Hell, I don't care. Just do me one favor. Leave town. Just pack up a few things and get out, all of you. Take Charlie if he'll go. Just stay away from Isherwood. Please.'' He reached for her hand.

She pulled away.

''This is my home,'' she told him. ''Our home, our neighbors, our friends. And I'll not pack up and leave it just because some . . . some stranger tells me the sky is falling . . . or that there are monsters around.'' She looked away, and her voice softened. ''Just . . . just leave, Chris. Please.''

He stood soberly, resignation masking whatever emotions he felt. ''Suit yourself.'' He turned and walked toward the door with the deputy in tow but paused just before leaving. "Boys," he said to Del and Bart. "Try to change her mind. And soon. By the end of the week, Isherwood will be a ghost town." Then he was gone.

The two men got into Bean's car and sat for a few minutes, silent, each wondering what the next move should be. "Are you gonna give us any trouble, Mr. Stiles?" Bean finally asked. "'Cause I've got a feeling you could do a heap of it if you set your mind to it."

Stiles shook his head. "Nope. I tried to help but fuck it. I'm out of here tonight." He reached over and started the motor for him. "Take me back to my van," he said.

They rode the distance to Sykes Road in silence. Neither spoke until the squad car was parked once again on the shoulder near the culvert.

"There's blood back there in the woods," Stiles said, his tone dull, resigned. "And there's always Danner's basement wall. But I don't suppose you'd want to go look." He saw Bean's pained expression, saw him rub his eyes and check his watch. He nodded. "I didn't think so. Tell me, Charlie. Just what am I? A crazed vet still fighting the war? A tormented soul begging for attention? A psychopath fighting his own demons? Come on, I want to know."

"I'll tell you just what you are," Bean said flatly. "You're a problem I can do without. S'funny, I've always dreamed of a little action in this neck of the woods, a little oomph, you know? Guess there's a little Barney Fife in me after all. But you . . . I hate to say it, Mr. Stiles, but you scare the holy hell out of me. And I don't like that." He leaned over the soldier, slowly so as not to look like he was going for his gun, and pushed open the passenger door. "Go on, get out. And don't make me regret this. I don't want to pick up the Bedford paper and find out you've shot up a grocery store or something." He held out his hand. "Can I have my gun back?"

Stiles took the Ruger out of his belt. "Promise me time, Charlie. To go back to town and get my stuff. Then I'm gone and you'll never hear from me again."

Bean nodded. "Sounds fine to me."

He put the revolver in the deputy's hand and walked back through the trees to the van. A cursory search told him it was secure. Bean was still waiting when he pulled out onto the road. The squad car followed him all the way back to town and even into the all-but-empty motel parking lot, staying right on his tail the whole time. Stiles got out, fuming, walked over and leaned in the cruiser's window. "I thought we had a deal," he said, irritated. "I trust you, you trust me. Remember?"

"I'm not giving you no trouble," Bean said. "Yet. I just want to make sure you get out of town."

Stiles's tone was clipped and full of warning. "Get off my ass, Charlie. I said I was going." He leaned in closer, enough that the deputy could feel his breath, and he grinned. "You don't want to get the psycho mad, do you?"

Bean glared back, but his confidence was shot and he quickly looked away. It wasn't that he was weak or afraid; in fact, he was short on neither strength nor courage. But he was fiercely practical, and the idea of starting a battle with this man served no logical purpose, except, perhaps, for a death wish. His face still smarted from that kick earlier, the one he never even saw coming, the one that hit him harder than he could remember ever being hit; with or without a weapon. Because that's what Stiles was, basically. A weapon. Bean hadn't seen it in town when they'd first met—Stiles had been hiding it then—but now he could tell, just by the way the man walked and moved and breathed. He was like those lions that Jim and Marlin chased across the veldt for *Wild Kingdom* every Saturday in syndication. Superior and strong. A born hunter. A killer.

Bean was a practical man. And he knew when to back away. "Till morning," he said, retaining his composure and hoping it sounded like a threat. He put the car in reverse and started to pull out when Stiles reached in and caught his arm.

"A little advice," the soldier offered, "on the house. In the middle of the night, if someone comes to your door or taps at the window, whatever you do, don't invite them in."

Bean glared. "Vampires again?"

"No matter who it is," he continued. "They can't enter unless you let them in. Remember that." He patted the deputy's shoulder and smiled. "Goodbye, Charlie. Good luck. You'll need it."

Charlie Bean left the motel and headed back to the ofice, where he would go off duty and take the near-full bottle of Jack

Daniel's from his desk drawer and get as shit-faced drunk as he could. Because tomorrow he would have to come back here to make sure this nut was gone. And there was always the chance that he wouldn't be.

Stiles stood alone in the parking lot and closed his eyes and wished that he'd been dreaming all of this, that when he opened them again he would be back at the culvert and Larry Hovi would still be rigid and ever waving and he would still have a semblance of control over the situation. But as it stood there was now a virulent affliction afoot with not one but four vectors running rampant. He wanted to run door to door and yell at them—Hey, you fools, wake up! You're in danger!—but he knew the reaction he would receive. Charlie and Billie had been effective examples of that already.

Billie, he thought with dismay. She'd been so quick to condemn, even with her children defending his veracity. It was over once that label had clicked into place. Vietnam vet. In fact he'd been amazed at her acceptance of it the day before. But let the least idiosyncracy show itself, the smallest glitch in his character or behavior and suddenly he wasn't a man anymore. He was TV's villain of the week, the poor, disturbed crazy-as-a-loon veteran, a shell-shocked loser who's hash-hazed mind couldn't distinguish between present day and 1968. He could even evoke sympathy if he weren't so busy looking for someplace to explode.

He was disappointed. He'd expected more from her.

Maybe your expectations were just too high, his conscience reckoned. *You've got a lot of room to talk. Look at yourself. The Uzi, the pistols in your shoulder holsters, the bali-song in its belt sheath. Don't sound so self-righteous. If anything, you propogate that myth as much as Rambo ever did, if not more. Just how did you expect her to react?*

He couldn't deny it. He considered going back to explain, but just as quickly he laughed at the idea. *She'd have you locked up, idiot. You heard her earlier, saw the accusation in her eyes. She came that close to saying you beat up, even molested her sons. It was just a germ of suspicion but the only rational excuse to explain her boys' condition and behavior. If she sees you again, that germ could fester into a full fledged warrant for your arrest.*

Get out of town. It's your only option.

But he knew that wasn't an option at all. He would have to play his leaving-town-in-the-morning act carefully; Charlie Bean was not stupid. But he would stay within reach, along the fringes of Isherwood, and he would get word to Del and Bart not to worry, that they had a guardian angel watching over them and their mom. And then he would wait for the dying to begin. It was inevitable; sooner or later others would fall victim. Isherwood would finally acknowledge its plight and welcome his aid openly.

He hoped that was soon. Before the infected cadavers began spreading their thirst beyond the city limits.

The thought gave him a chill—Indiana crawling with the undead—and he expected to have a full-blown nightmare on the subject later, but by the time he got the key into the lock and shambled into the dark motel room, he knew he was too tired to dream of anything. The room helped too. The heater had kicked off or failed to come on at all and the chill of the air made him long for the warmth of bed. Billie fluttered through his mind in association but even that failed to fully arouse him. Only the total limbo of slumber could soothe him now.

He flicked the wall switch and the two lamps on either side of the wall mirror popped to life, though he almost had to light a match to see if they were lit. The bulbs were cheap and barely illuminated the room's sparse furnishings. He punched the TV with his elbow. There was a war movie on somewhere behind the curtain of snow but he was unable to find it and cared to even less. He threw his Uzi and holsters on one of the single beds and draped his shirt over the back of a recliner and leaned across the chair to flick on the hanging lamp over the table. Just then the heater decided to come to life and blow a puff of warm air against the side of his face and neck.

He caught the smell of that warm gust and found it nauseatingly foul, like a roomful of bad eggs, and wondered in that same split second how anyone's breath could possibly be so bad.

Breath. Not the heater. His fatigued senses finally registered the presence in the chair.

Stiles grabbed for the only weapon within reach, the bali-song on his belt, and a flick of the wrist had the knife out of its case and snapped open. But powerful hands caught him and physically flung him the length of the room. He sailed over the beds and hit the wall with an audible crunch. His head left a melon-sized crater in the woodgrain paneling.

Fireflies danced before his eyes in sync with the sound of big guns on the television. He floundered on the carpeting, disoriented but desperate to regain his footing before the attack continued. But it did not. There was only John Wayne on TV, leading his men onto the beach.

He lunged for the lamp on the bedstand and slammed into it, knocking the vibrate-a-bed machine and his alarm clock onto the floor and spilling the lamp onto the bed. It flashed to life and floodlit the other side of the room.

The intruder was still sitting in the chair, one leg crossed casually over the other. It was just a kid, Stiles thought at first glance. Early twenties, with short blonde hair and a stern, midwestern face and eyes shadowed beneath a heavy brow. But then he noticed the clothes. They were the same tattered coat and torn trousers, the same dried and cracking boots. *No, it can't be*. The soldier studied the face again. This time he saw the cross-shaped scar on the cheek. This time he saw the eyes. The cold, the black-within-black emptiness. His jaw went slack. It was Danner's face, the one from the ancient newspaper photo, youthful and vigorous and full of life if not for the stricken pallor. Only the cheeks held color. He had fed recently.

"How . . ." Stiles stammered, unable to believe his eyes. How could he change, how could he regenerate an entire face? But how he'd done it was now academic. He quickly changed his tact. "Get out!" he ordered, his eyes already searching for the knife he'd dropped or the Uzi and pistols that had fallen from the bed. Anything he could use to fight.

Danner smiled. His movements were still jerky, but he managed to spin a keyring around one long-nailed finger. "The owner was most helpful," he said, and his voice raised the hackles on Stiles's neck. "It's his invitation that counts, you know?" The smile turned to a thin grimace. "You will regret what you did to me, Mr. Stiles. You will curse the day you were even born." He stood with stuttering movements, insectlike, and stalked forward. His foot brushed the Uzi on the floor and knocked it spinning under the bed.

"Then come on, big mouth." Stiles dropped into a ready stance, muscles bunched like coiled springs. "C'mon, you fucking pussy. Let's see what you've got."

Danner snarled, his reformed mouth flexing into a startling display of overlarge incisors. He reached for Stiles blithely, unconcerned by what this unarmed man could do, intent only on reaching that muscular throat . . .

Stiles stepped into the attack and drove a punishing front kick past those groping limbs, growling with satisfaction at the sound of breaking ribs. The vampire staggered back a step or two, but the soldier wasted no time. He spun to the right, his leg arcing around to dig a heel into the creature's jaw, then reversed himself and landed a similar kick to the other side of its face. He pressed his attack like a berserker, bellowing in rage as he pummeled the foe again and again with a barrage of reverse punches and ridge hand blows and two successive backfists that spun the vampire like a top. Danner tried to grab him, but his hands found only empty air as Stiles ducked beneath them and broke one of his elbows, then came up from his crouch and drove both palms into the vampire's chin. Vertebrae crackled as Danner's head pitched backward, stemless, then lolled forward onto his chest at an impossible angle. But he still didn't fall.

Stiles's peripheral vision told him that he'd fought within reach of the Heckler & Koch on the desktop. He ended his flurry with a battering side kick that exploded into the fiend's chest, collapsing it like a dented car fender and throwing him all the way to the front of the room. Stiles instantly dove for the rifle and snapped off the safety even as he whirled.

His wrist froze in midair, caught in an icy vise of a grip that grated the bones together and shook the gun from his numbed grasp. Danner was somehow standing right in front of him, a hairsbreadth away, and Stiles would certainly have felt that rancid breath in his face had the vampire's head not been jackknifed onto his chest like a hanging bag. But Danner was watching him. He was looking up from the corners of his eyes, totally coherent.

And he was grinning.

Danner's other arm, shattered at the elbow and hanging limp, proved still operable after all. It suddenly seized Stiles by the crotch in a merciless grip.

The pain rolled up through Stiles in a wave, engulfing everything in its path, cutting off his breath, blacking his vision. His arms and legs went numb. A scream tried to reach his lips but was drowned by the rising bile in his throat. For the few seconds that he was still conscious, it felt like his pubic bone would go through the roof of his mouth. Then the wave engulfed him totally, and there was only the merciful darkness.

Chapter Eleven

Isherwood did not sleep well. The nightmares began just before midnight.

On Cayuga Avenue there was an anxious tapping on a windowpane. Ten-year-old Nate Haskell awoke and reached for his glasses on the nightstand, only to find familiar faces pressed against the window. He could hardly believe it; there was Joey Lipp and Freddy Felder and the Yeager twins, and Andrea Hart was with them, too. Andrea Hart, who was about as hot as a ten-year-old could get, bar none. She even had tits, or at least the starter kit. To Nate she was a goddess. Hell, they were all special—each one a member of the fifth-grade elite, and not one of them had ever deigned to give him the time of day.

No, that wasn't true. Andrea had said thank you once when he gave her butts in the lunch line, and Freddy had called him a fat-nerd-four-eyes-dipshit once last year on the playground. But nothing since.

So what were they doing here?

"C'mon, Nate," Joey whispered urgently, looking back to make sure the lights didn't come on in the other window further along. "Let us in. We gotta . . . talk to ya 'bout something."

"Yeah, talk," the Yeagers, boy and girl, both giggled.

"About what?" he asked. "Can't this wait till school tomorrow?"

"No, it can't wait," Freddy sneered, showing a momentary flash of anger and teeth. Andrea swatted him and his smiling, friendly face returned.

Turn it off, Freddy, Nate wanted to say. *I've never liked you anyway.*

"Nathan," Andrea said lyrically, brushing up against the window so that the budding breasts beneath her sweater flattened out and looked larger. It was a cloying caricature of adulthood. "We just want you to be in our club, that's all."

"Right," Joey said over her shoulder. "A club. You can be one of us."

Nate brightened behind his too-thick glasses and looked at Joey with amazement, but not for too long. His eyes couldn't stray far from Andrea. "You want me to be . . . one of you? C'mon, you guys, what's the catch? You want me to do your homework or what?"

"No catch," Andrea cooed. "We just want to be . . . friends. We can make you just like us."

"Just like us," said the Yeagers, in perfect unison.

Joey pressed his face to the glass. "What do they call you at school, Nate?"

The chubby boy hung his head and said nothing.

"Do they call you fatso?"

"Do they call you four-eyes?"

Freddy laughed. "Nerd? Pigshit? Brainiac? Lard-ass?"

"Yes!" Nate hissed. His eyes were watery, and a few tears had begun a slow slide down his pudgy cheeks.

"Nate," Andrea whispered, "you don't have to take it. Never again."

"I don't?"

Joey looked feral in his glee. "None of it. No one'll ever call you that again. You'll be one of us. You'll be a big shot."

"Open up, Nathan," Andrea smiled. "Let us in. Don't you like us?"

"I like you, Andrea . . ."

"You know," she said, pouting adolescent lips, "I never did thank you for letting me in line that one time. Remember? I mean really thank you. Let me in, Natey. I'll give you a little kiss."

"Let us in," Joey urged impatiently. "We're buddies, aren't we?"

Nathan Haskell felt a tingling at the back of his neck, the warning that they were out too late, that their skins were too white, that they somehow clung to his second-floor window with no ledge to support them. It was a trick, he thought, all a trick. They were trying to make him out to be a fool, making fun of him. But their offer . . .

Andrea wouldn't lie to me. The others might, but not Andrea.

He went to the window. "You can come in, Andrea," he said as he slid up the sash and loosened the screen. "But only Andrea. I'm not sure I can trust you guys."

The rest of the children hissed angrily and dropped away from the window. Andrea Hart smiled and took Nate's hand and climbed into his room.

"You wouldn't lie to me, would you, Andrea?"

"Never," she cooed, and came toward him. Nate welcomed her with open arms.

His parents didn't have the same choice.

She was in the house for almost two hours, and when she finally left she used the front door. The other children were waiting on the porch, brooding and hungry. Andrea calmed them with a smile and let a few of them lick her fingertips and chin. Then she took the rolled-up elementary-school yearbook from her jacket pocket and used a Magic Marker to cross out another face in it, this one pudgy and wearing thick glasses. There were more faces to go. Three whole pages of them.

The others nodded and licked their lips anxiously.

A few streets over, on Ritter, Frank Sipes was just getting home. He was on foot, which was not so unusual. He often left his car at the tavern. He sauntered up the steps, surprisingly staggerless, and rang the doorbell.

A pinched face peered through the glass, then the door opened a crack, the farthest the chain would allow. "Decided to come home early for a change," Irene Sipes observed, hiding her surprise at his appearance. She was a frail but threatening woman on first glance, with a wide forehead and eyebrows that grew together in the middle. Frank's drinking became surprisingly understandable in her presence.

"In the mood for pitching a little woo?" Frank asked slyly and held out a handful of flowers he'd picked.

Irene yawned. "Whose trash did you get those out of?"

"What a darling sense of humor," he chuckled, pushing at the door. The chain popped and hung loose. The door swung open. But Frank stayed outside. "May I come in?"

She looked from the busted lock to Frank and back again. "Have you been drinking?"

"Nope," he said, holding out a hand. It did not tremble. "See? Not a drop." He held out the flowers again. "For you, my love."

Irene looked into the deep redness of the roses and then into her husband's eyes and in the latter she thought she saw the spark that inebriation had extinguished long ago. The hunger. She blushed. "Come on then," she said, taking the flowers in her arms and pushing at her hair as if it could be kneaded into a more becoming style. She loosened the belt on her flannel robe as she mounted the stairs. "Give me a minute to freshen up, then . . ." She giggled and rushed up the steps. At the top she called back, "Frankie, are you sure you haven't been drinking?"

"Not yet," he grinned, starting up the stairs after her.

There were several cars parked at the Tunnel, despite the chill in the air. A new kind of game was being played. Every few minutes or so the passenger doors would swing open in unison and teenage boys and girls, giggling mischievously, would run past each other and switch cars. The doors would slam and there would be quiet for a while, then the change would take place again.

It wasn't that the morals of the young in Isherwood had deteriorated to partner swapping.

It was more like a buffet.

Bean had to concentrate before he could realize that the ringing wasn't inside his head. It was the phone hidden amid the pile of dirty clothes that Susie hadn't been around to pick up.

He stood and stretched tiredly and didn't realize the countless shots of Mr. Jack's Old No. 7 had had any effect until he took a step and found his legs now jointless and made of rubber. He crumpled to the carpet and floundered there, having to crawl hand over hand to reach the phone. He finally managed to pluck the handset from its cradle on his third try. "Su . . . Susie?" he slurred hopefully.

The voice at the other end was a deep baritone. "No, it's me, Charlie. Ron, over at county. You okay?"

Bean sat up and wiped at his face as if to uncover a patch of sobriety that lay hidden beneath his slack expression. "No, I'm fine. Just caught me nappin's all."

"Ooh, sorry about that."

"'S okay. What can I do ya for?"

The voice sighed. "We've been getting a few calls tonight from over your way."

Bean thought for a moment, trying to remember why that should sound so familiar. "Wait a minute . . . let me guess. This time of year—"

"Yep. Mrs. Conder. The kids are bothering her again, probably soaping her windows or corning. Happens every year this time. We send a car and they're long gone before we get halfway there."

"She's an old woman," Bean offered as an excuse. "She scares easy."

"I can understand that," Ron said, "it being this close to Halloween and all. My mom's the same way. Trouble is, we've had some flu going around and I really can't spare the manpower tonight. So I was wondering if maybe you'd check this one out. I hate to bother you after hours, but I thought you'd be up watching TV or something."

Normally Bean would've let him simmer a while before agreeing, and not without a good speech about dereliction of duty and plumb laziness. But tonight his brain cells were too steeped to answer anything but yes or no. He said yes, not realizing he had saved a county officer's life.

"I appreciate it, Charlie. And I owe you one."

Bean hung up and staggered across the room to where he'd shed his pants and holster and began to redress himself. He was feeling a little better; maybe he could make it out there to the trailer court, just to check things out.

He inhaled deeply to get his pants snapped and that's when the room started to spin. He stumbled back and fell across the hassock and felt his stomach begin to roll. *You're gonna puke,* he assured himself, *unless you pass out first. Which is it gonna be?*

Bean hated to puke. So he relaxed and let himself black out and never realized that, by doing so, he'd saved a second life tonight. His own.

At least for a little while.

Rusty Sanders turned up Hank Williams, Jr. on the squad car's radio as he veered onto the Nevermore's main drive. As he did so, he caught a glimpse of himself in the rearview and had to laugh at the stupid grin of expectation he found. "Tonight's the night, bucko," he said, slicking his hair with a little spit on the palm. He was off duty tonight and dressed to the teeth, with his snakeskin cowboy boots and his tightest jeans and the thick trucker's wallet in his back pocket, its chain dangling from his belt. His Aqua Velva was strong and his breath sang of Lavoris. What a killer, he thought. Was she lucky or what?

He drove all the way to the back as usual, past the rest of the darkened trailers, past Mrs. Conder's Hollypark where the front door stood wide open to a dread and lifeless silence. He didn't notice the shadowy figures in the glow of the dim security lights, scurrying from yard to yard. He was too preoccupied. He pulled the cruiser into the ruts worn alongside Georgetta's mobile home. "Here we are," he sighed, unable to keep the giggle from his voice.

He reached for his gear bag which lay open on the passenger seat, picked up the paddle from amid his paraphernalia, and swatted his palm with gusto. "You've been a bad little girl," he rehearsed with expectant glee, his mind filled with visions of frilly cotton and lace and patent leather shoes and sheer undies. "Daddy doesn't like to spank you, but it's for your own good." He giggled again. "This is gonna be great."

He got out and went to the dilapidated old trailer. The key was just where it always was, beneath a well-traveled mat, and he let himself in.

The sound of the television greeted him, and the interior was awash with its solitary light. He had to shield his eyes against it to find Georgetta sitting with her back to him. Her attention was fixed on the channel four late movie.

"Whaddayasay, honey bunch," Rusty purred, taking off his jacket and unbuttoning his shirt. "Did you miss me?"

She looked back over her shoulder and smiled. "Of course I missed you, Russy honey."

"How's the eye?"

She reached up and touched her face. "It's fine."

"Georgetta, I'm sorry about that," he shrugged. "It just happens sometimes. I guess I get a little carried away. But I only do it because I love you, honey." He gave a sly little chuckle. "Besides, you know you like it."

"I do?"

"You know you do." He wetted his lips. "Well? Did you get the outfit?"

She nodded. "Yes, Russy."

His grin widened. He picked up the paddle and flipped it from hand to hand. "Are you . . . wearing it?"

"Of course."

He was getting hard already. "Show me."

Georgetta stood and stretched, catlike, then flicked off the television. The room went black, leaving only the angled glare of the security light outside to see by. She came slinking through the dark until she was framed in the window's luminescence.

Rusty's jaw went slack, and so did his crotch.

There was no frilly skirt, no bows or ankle socks or buckle-over shoes. There was only leather, jet black and gleaming in the light. The spike heeled boots reached past her knees and the gloves past her elbows, and the tight corset wrapped around her middle like a second skin, thinning her waist and showcasing the pale breasts that bulged out and over it like twin moons. The black hair that cascaded over her bare shoulders gleamed like wire in the light, and likewise the curls at her naked crotch.

"Wha . . . what the hell's this?" Rusty said, annoyed and quickly building to completely pissed off. "This ain't what I wanted."

"No?" she pouted, rubbing her pale breasts, playing with the nipples, urging them erect. "But Russy . . . I want to play this game." She stepped closer to him, purring out loud like a cat. "You really don't like it?"

"Take it off," he said angrily. "You know what I wanted."

She laughed. "The little girl thing? But Russy honey, that's so . . ." she stepped even closer, "sick."

The deputy began to snort through his nostrils like a miniature dragon. "I said take that shit off. Now."

She tilted her head to kiss him and whispered, "No."

Rusty hit her, not an open-handed slap, but with a clenched fist and very hard. The blow snapped Georgetta's head around just like the night before, just like all the nights in the past. But, surprisingly, it did not back her up a step. She turned back to him slowly, and he was shocked to see her grinning. Then her own fist came up, straight from her side, and the back of it caught Rusty flush in the mouth. He staggered backward, shocked, blood seeping from his split lip. Georgetta's eyes flashed and she was on him all at once, grabbing him by the hair and pulling him into her kiss.

Rusty squirmed to get away as she sucked at his lips and licked at them and pried them apart with her own. Her mouth was cold, like ice, and the taste of her was bitter. He clenched his teeth but she worked them apart and her tongue invaded him, pushing and prodding, raspy and dry, and not like a tongue at all, but a snake or some giant millipede that had crawled into her mouth and taken up residence. His stomach turned and he tried to shove her away, but she clung to him frantically. He drove a fist into her gut once, twice, but it just seemed to spur her on. When she did let go it was only to cuff him about the ears with an open hand, and the blows were hard enough to jangle his senses. "C'mon, Russy," she taunted him, "you like it rough, don't you? You know you do." He tried to stagger toward the trailer door but she caught him with a full-fisted blow to the side of his face, and the supple leather over her knuckles opened a gash above his cheekbone. She was back on him in an instant, her tongue running across his face and cheek and finding its way back to his mouth and forcing its way in.

He whined and tried to push her back, and his hands landed on her breasts. They were stiff and slick, almost waxen, and frozen to the touch. Georgetta stepped back, her wide expression visible in the light from the window. There was passion in her eyes, wild and unyielding. At least that was what it looked like.

"You want these, honey?" she said, kneading her tremendous

breasts with first her own hands and then forcing his to do it. "Oh, baby," she moaned in a pathetically emotionless voice, "I want you. Sooo bad."

"Georgie, please . . ."

She shoved him back into a chair, and her hand slid down his chest and stomach to tear the snaps off the front of his pants. "Oooh," she sighed, mocking disappointment as she took him in hand. "What's wrong? Don't you love baby no more?" She stroked him roughly, almost angrily, and he flinched with each jerk of her gloved hand. He tried to fight her but she caught his wrists and pinned them to the arms of the chair. Then she knelt in front of him, locking his legs down with her hips, and her expression was a feral smile as her face lowered toward his lap. "Show me you love me, Russy," she said softly.

He closed his eyes and whimpered. Her mouth was on him, that obscene worm of a tongue wrestling with him, entwining and tugging, fouling him but bringing him up. He fought it, tried to conjure images in his mind, things that would stem his arousal. Yet, despite his revulsion, somewhere deep inside on a purely mechanical level, he felt the physical sensations and reacted to them.

Georgetta sighed mock-happily. "Oh, Russy. You do love me."

"Please, Georgie," he stammered, "please, don't do this. In God's name . . ."

Putting a hand on each cheek of his buttocks, the big woman picked him up from the chair and carried him to the bed. Her mouth found his again for a long, probing, soulful kiss, but there was no soul to it. It was a cold, violent act, offensive in the extreme, not like love or passion or kissing a woman at all.

It was like kissing a man, Rusty thought.

A dead man.

Rusty Sanders knew then, and he began to cry.

She laid him back on the bed and straddled him. "I want you in me," she licked her lips. "All of you."

"Please . . ." he sobbed. "Please . . ."

"But, Russy," she purred playfully. "I only do it because I love you." Then she laughed and eased herself down.

He was deep inside her when she started to feed.

* * *

Across town, at the Tri-Lakes Inn, in the Walnut Suite two doors down from the clattering ice machine, Chris Stiles began to stir.

Chapter Twelve

➢

He awoke slowly, in stages: his numbed senses were cognizant of little more than a dull buzzing in his ears. But it became steadily louder and more distinct. Marching music . . . laughter . . . The television set.

Gomer Pyle came to Stiles's ears, and at the same moment: Pain.

It was a dark and angry being, this pain, and it waited for him to surface with unerring patience so it could caress him again and flay his senses raw. It centered mostly in his crotch and throbbed in rhythm with his heartbeat, but just out of sync with the diesel rigs that roared between his ears. The nausea was thick as well, clogging his nose and throat, making it hard to breathe. But he fought it. He fought hard and he pushed it back into a corner and held it there. Only then could he feel his way outward and take stock of himself and his situation.

Without opening his eyes, he knew there was blood on his face. Spots were still warm and sticky, especially around the gash in his brow, but the rest was drying and cracked with the slightest twitch of a facial muscle. There were bruises too, all over him—he didn't have to move to know they were there. But at least nothing felt broken. His left eye was nearly swollen shut and his jaw felt rubbery, though he couldn't remember being struck in either place. He couldn't remember much of anything, in fact. Not yet, anyway.

He knew he was on the bed—the detergent scent of the sheet and pillows was a sharp contrast to the gastric odor still lingering in his nostrils. He was flat on his back, spread-eagle, and could not change his position. Taut nylon (*your own rope, goddammit!*) cut into his wrists and ankles with the slightest movement.

The room was silent except for the TV. He opened one eye just enough to look around.

He couldn't make out much at first; the only light was that of the television, and its snowy picture rearranged the shadows with each flicker and roll, making the room seem alive with phantoms. What he could see was a shambles. The bureau was tipped against the wall, its drawers askew and spilling clothes onto the floor. One of the Walnut Suite's two lounge chairs seeped fiber entrails from a mortal wound in its upholstery. Even the bed he was on had suffered a broken leg, so it lurched to the left like a sinking raft. The walls were a mess; at least the extensive cracks and dents and streaks of blood explained his further injuries. He'd been bounced off those walls more than once.

The memory of it was suddenly upon him then—the pain swelled in response, and so did his panic. His eye scanned the room frantically, searching, for not only was his raft sinking but there was a shark still out there in the darkness, waiting . . . *Easy. Slow and methodical or you'll give yourself away. Now think, dammit. There has to be a way out of this.*

"Sur-prise, sur-prise, sur-prise!" Gomer exclaimed, and the canned laughter rose appreciatively. It and one other. The accompanying chuckle was deep and distinct and only a few feet away.

A sudden chill raced along Stiles's spine.

The second lounge chair was turned away from him toward the television, so he hadn't noticed the dark figure still sitting there. The vampire was not looking at Stiles; his eyes were on the television, glued there with a sort of bemused awe. And as he watched, he rolled his head from side to side, turning it slowly, aligning the reformed vertebrae and audibly grinding the cartilage until the fit was secure. His movements were still jerky, made worse by the damage Stiles had inflicted, so it appeared all the more unnatural when that once-broken neck craned around to glare at him. The face was shadowed, backlit by the television, but Stiles could feel those empty black eyes on him, never blinking, boring into him. It was all he could do to fight back a shiver and continue to feign unconsciousness. Danner watched a little longer, then cocked a thumb at the TV. "This is really something," he said in a distinctly Hoosier drawl, though there was nothing at all folksy in his tone. "How does it work?"

Stiles stayed silent.

With a sigh of exasperation the vampire stood and stretched his young, lanky frame. Then he stepped over to the bed and jabbed a vicious finger into Stiles's crotch. The prostrate man clenched his teeth to conceal a whimper and tried curling into a ball, but the ropes refused him. Danner just laughed. "I thought that would get your attention. Now, how does the TV box work?"

The soldier strained against his bonds. "Go fuck yourself," he hissed.

"Still defiant," observed the younger-looking man with a mechanical nod. "Good for you." He turned back to the television now that Gomer and his sergeant had segued into an armed forces recruitment ad. The Blue Angels arched across the sky in formation, leaving puffy jet trails in their wake and Danner mesmerized by their mere existence. "Amazing. So many things have changed." He patted the top of the TV. "This could get to be a habit. I hope it doesn't interfere with my hunting time." He leaned closer. "Or I could just 'order out', eh?" He sang the "Domino's Pizza Delivers" jingle and chuckled to himself. Stiles was silent—hearing the song in that dead man's voice made his skin crawl. "Come now. Where's your sense of humor? Oh," he snapped his fingers, "that reminds me. I've been saving something just for you." He shed the ragged remnants of his coat and vest and pulled off his shirt to bare the pale flesh of his chest. There, just to the right of his sternum, was a dent the shape of Stiles's foot, nearly a quarter-inch deep. "You kick like a mule, friend," Danner said, "but it doesn't mean much." He closed his eyes and pursed his lips, concentrated, and the dimpled flesh suddenly popped back into place like a child's plastic ball. The vampire grinned boastfully as he stole a sweatshirt from among Stiles's things. But then he saw the soldier shrug with indifference. "Oh? You've seen such a thing before?"

Stiles continued to hide his shock. He just shrugged again.

The vampire gritted his pointed teeth. "I'm afraid the years have thinned my patience," he said as he rose from the chair.

He reached out and weaved the ring finger of Stiles's right hand between his own and, with no more warning, snapped it like a pencil. Stiles went rigid but would not allow himself to cry out. The tears rolled down his bloodstained cheeks. "Oh, go ahead," the creature urged him. "Cry out. Yell your hardest. No one will hear you."

Stiles gasped for breath, fought to focus his senses again and will the pain away with the rest. "Ass . . . hole. The deputy'll be back . . . to check. Probably bring the marshall."

Danner smiled as he perched himself on the edge of the bed. "I'm inclined to doubt that," he said, reaching into his pocket. He took out a small metal oval that gleamed in the flickering TV light. "You see, I met your Mr. Larson last night." He leaned over and pinned the town marshall's badge on the pillow next to Stiles's head. "And I wouldn't count on the deputy either. The marshall should be stopping by there any time now. For a midnight snack?" Smirking, he went to the Walnut Suite's big picture window and pulled open the drapes. Against the TV's glow, the window was a canvas of flat black, and the vampire drank it in like the most glorious sunrise. "I met many people last night," he told the soldier. "Yes, indeed. And you—you amused me. Sitting there in that great box of an automobile, watching those turds I stuffed under the road. I could've taken you then, my friend. I could've had you any time."

Chris smiled through his pain. "You should've tried."

"Why?" He motioned out the window. "I had other business out there. With them. An entire town to slake my thirst and, by damn, I was thirsty. Seventy-five odd years will do that to you. So I drank, my friend, long and deep and I haven't stopped yet. There is so much more prey these days; everywhere you turn. Men, women . . . children." He chuckled low in his throat. "I so enjoy the young ones. They're so . . . so soft, so . . ."

"You sick motherfucker."

The vampire looked back at him and this time his young, stark features were drawn tight. He came back to the bed in two long strides and glared down at his prisoner. "You'd judge me?" He grasped the pinkie finger of the man's already injured hand and started to bend it backwards, as slow as he could. Unrelenting. Stiles struggled and bucked and buried his face in his shoulder to muffle the cries he couldn't hold back. But it was still several seconds before the bone finally gave. He collapsed and sank back into the mattress, gagging on his bile, spitting blood from where he'd bitten through his bottom lip. Danner's palid face was hovering just above him; its breath was fetid. "You have a big mouth, friend. I suggest you shut it while you still have some . . . fingers left. . . ."

Danner's expression changed in midsentence. His eyes widened, and the pupils, like dark empty holes, suddenly flashed with rims of silver. His breathing increased, panting, and his lips quivered with expectation. His nostrils flared at the scent of . . . *oh, Christ*. Stiles suddenly realized. Blood. The vampire leaned closer and muttered something soft and excited under his breath, and a pale, raspy tongue licked out at the cut in the prisoner's lip. Stiles spat at him in disgust and pushed himself deeper into the mattress but the thing followed, tracing a path along his cheek to the gash above his eye. Danner started to purr in his throat as he sucked at the wound, and his breathing grew faster and the purr became a growl and he grabbed the soldier's hair and wrenched his head to one side. "NO!" Stiles yelled in disbelief, his tone becoming frantic when he felt the clammy lips fasten to his throat.

But suddenly Danner threw himself back from the bed. He stood there, tensed and glaring, struggling for control, and in that instant, in the flickering cast of the TV, he looked starkly different. He was no longer the fresh-faced young man from the picture in the newspaper; it was as if that image had become transparent, and Stiles could stare through it to the creature beneath. It was the same creature he'd faced two nights earlier. Its frame was rigid, its shoulders hunched, and the head jutted forward at an unnatural angle. Its eyes were wide and livid, and the long teeth bared in a feral smile. "No," the creature hissed, more to itself than Stiles. It stalked toward the window and looked away, and slowly its composure returned. When Danner looked back, his youthful facade was reinstated. "No," he sighed, calmer now. "Not yet. There's time enough for that." He stepped closer to the bed, paused to lick a smear of blood from his fingertip. "It won't be that easy, Stiles. Not by a mile." He went back to his chair and settled himself. *Gomer Pyle* had been replaced by *Hogan's Heroes*, but it didn't seem to bother him.

Stiles lay shivering and finally managed to swallow the knot in his throat so he could breath again. That image, that devil's face still lingered before his mind's eye, the feel of that mouth on him . . . *Dammit, man. Think! There has to be a way out of this!* He surged against his bonds again, hoping in desperation that this time, somehow, they would give. But a new, stinging pain brought him up short. He found his wrists torn and bleeding; during the struggle the ropes had slipped halfway over his hands, taking a layer of skin with them. Despite further burns and the pain to his broken fingers, he was sure he could pull free. But what then, he wondered. His legs were still held fast. What would he do?

He searched the room for weapons, for a gun or a knife. But his spirits sagged just as quickly. The Heckler & Koch was on the desk across the way, beside his holsters and the open butterfly knife. Even if he freed his arms, and his legs too for that matter, he'd never make it across the room. But wait a minute . . . where was the Uzi? It wasn't on the desk. He could remember carrying it into the room, dropping it on the bed, seeing it on the floor during the fight.

Danner's foot kicking it as he passed . . .

Stiles shifted as far as he could, careful not to attract Danner's attention, and craned his neck to see over the right side of the bed. Nothing. He stretched back to the left, where the bed sagged from its broken leg, and he peeked over the edge. It was dark along the floor, but . . . was there something down there? He waited for the TV picture to brighten again. When it did, just enough light slipped beneath the bed for him to recognize the corner of the Uzi's extended magazine. It was within reach. If he could just get his hands free . . .

"And now for a few words of inspiration," said the television announcer as programming finally ended for the day. A small, balding man from an Indianapolis church stood before a stained-glass backdrop and smiled wanly. But before he could open his mouth, the vampire's fist lashed out and shattered the picture tube in a spray of glass and sparks. Stiles was startled; he ceased his struggles just as Danner turned to look at him.

"You know," said the creature, "you never answered my question. Have you come across anyone like me before?"

"Oh, I've met lots of assholes over the years. . . ." Danner started to get out of his chair. "All right, all right. I haven't. Satisfied?"

The vampire smiled. "I knew it the moment you saw this face, the look in your eyes . . . It was almost worth the trouble. Almost." He turned his chair toward the bed and perched on the edge. "There aren't many like me, friend. Because I'm the real thing. A vampire. Those things you're familiar with, the ones running the streets right now, they're simply cadavers. The by-product of my existence; my bite passes along the thirst just as a dog may pass on rabies. It alone drives them; it is all they think about, all they dream of. Personally, I don't condone their existence. In all honesty, they deplete the food supply from time to time and I have to destroy a few. But on average they do as they're told, and they come in handy now and again."

"And what makes you different?"

The vampire beamed. "I'll tell you the secret." He leaned closer. "It's in the blood. There's a ritual, a bonding and pledging and damning of oneself, all in one exquisite act. The Master partakes of the initiate's blood, and the same in return. That is where the power comes from. The strength, the abilities. The magic."

"A pact with the devil, then."

Danner scoffed. "Some things are worth the price. I, for one, was never satisfied before. I needed more, always more—knowledge, excitement. More . . . life?" He smirked. "I left this backwater state as soon as I could, to travel and explore, to dabble in matters both dark and fascinating. I saw things in those days that would curl your toes, Mr. Stiles. Some were perverse even to me, like that damn voodoo nigger magic. And none of it appeased me. So I took my curiosity abroad."

He leaned back in the chair, all but lost in recollections that stretched back three-quarters of a century. "I came upon him in Paris. He had been stalking men for centuries even then. He told me he was from Britain, just after the Roman invasion. He was tall and thin and not particularly attractive, but his presence . . . it was magnetic. I was easily obsessed with him, even before I knew who, or what, he was. I began to follow him, to his resting houses, his hunts. His kills. But I wasn't shocked by it all. I was excited. One night he found me watching, yet he didn't raise a hand against me. He said he saw something kindred in me, what was it . . . ah. A questing soul. So he let me stay with him. I became his familiar, then his companion. Ultimately, his lover. I entered into the rite of blood quite willingly, and I reveled in it. That night, I became more than human."

"You became very dead," Stiles said disdainfully.

Danner frowned. "Semantics, my friend. How should we judge life? By the warmth of the skin, by the mechanical lumbering of a fragile heart? I am superior now. I have six times your strength. I can hear better, see farther. I can remember any passage from any book and I will be around long enough to read them all. I can experience undreamed-of changes, discover new times and new worlds where there are television boxes and movies with sound and great iron vehicles that rend the skies above. I can even fly one, and shall, in time. And," he leered, "no matter what the year, whether this century or ten centuries from now, I can hold the lives of men right in the palm of my hand. You are a hunter, Mr. Stiles. You know what it is like. That tinge of excitement, that heady thrill that the kill brings."

"No," Stiles said flatly, hiding his own self-doubts. "I don't like killing."

"Really? Come now, my friend. We are too much alike."

"Not hardly."

Danner wore a viper's smile. "We shall see. For that's the purpose of my little confession." His expression became malevolent as he came to the bed and sat down on its edge. "You. Hurt. Me. Mister. Stiles," he hissed, punctuating each word with a finger jabbed into the soldier's ribs. One of them gave an audible crack, and the soldier winced. Danner continued talking. "I thought imprisonment was the most grievous wrong done me but you went one better. It took all I had to recover from your attack, to regain my strength, to heal myself. You will suffer for that. You will rue the day you raised your hand against me."

He reached over and smeared his finger with blood from Stiles's lip and licked it off with rapturous delight. "I could take you now. I could bleed you dry and leave you a mindless husk like those out there. But that seems so . . . simple. You wouldn't be able to comprehend your plight, would you? No, I want you as I am: fully conscious and able, with all of your faculties and wits intact. You will need them." He leaned over him. "For this fate can be many things—blessing to some, curse to others. Imagine an unquenchable thirst, and the vile acts you must commit to appease it. Could you bear the shame, the guilt? A moral man, a righteous man, would be tormented throughout eternity." Then he smiled. "Or at least until he learned to enjoy it. And you will, Mr. Stiles. We are that much alike."

Stiles strained at his ropes openly. *If only I can get to the Uzi* . . . "You're screwing up, Danner," he stalled. "Making me like you would be your biggest mistake. Then I'd have your powers, and I'd use them against you. I'd can your ass, so help me God."

Danner laughed. "No vampire can use his powers against his master. Never."

Stiles managed a disturbing grin. "Just wait and see."

The vampire's smirk vanished. "Enough talk," he snapped. "It's time." He stood and stretched like a cat before its meal. "You know, traditionally, the apostle would drink from a wound in the Master's neck or breast. But for you . . . I've another vessel in mind." He unbuttoned his pants and reached inside. The thing he took in hand was pale and bulbous, like a slug born to darkness. When he ran a fingernail across his penis's sallow head, it left a ragged scar as if in wax, and, slowly, stolen blood began to seep through the laceration. Stiles squirmed frantically, jerking and tugging at his bonds, but they wouldn't come loose, not fast enough. Danner seized him by the face and pressed at the jaw hinge, squeezed hard until the soldier had to unclench his teeth and open wide or hear yet another bone crack. "Drink, Mr. Stiles. Drink deep."

A voice sounded from over near the door. "Put your dick away," it said. "Nobody wants to look at it."

Danner wheeled with a snarl. But there was no one there.

"Alex?" Stiles muttered.

"Who is it!" barked the vampire. "Show yourself!"

"Back here, Smiley." The voice came from the bathroom. "Catch me if you can."

Danner buttoned his pants and stormed across the room with a low growl, battering in the lavatory door, knocking it off its hinges. But there was no one there. The voice had already moved on.

"Over here, Smiley.

"No, over here now.

"C'mon, Smiley. You're getting cold."

"ENOUGH!" Danner went back to the bed and caught Stiles's windpipe in a vise-like grip. "Show yourself," he ordered, "or he dies now!"

There was movement near the front door; an indistinct figure was suddenly standing there, hiding in the gloom, a shadow among shadows. "Whoever you are," the vampire hissed, "you're a dead man."

"Lucky guess, fucknuts," Alex replied. "Now, move away from the bed."

"Or what?" Danner picked the lifeless television from its stand as if it weighed nothing and flung it at the intruder, smashing it into the corner and destroying both wallboard and appliance alike. But the shadow man standing there was untouched. "But . . ." the vampire stammered, "how could . . ."

"You're a little slow on the uptake, son. I'm a ghost, get it? A spirit, a specter, a haunt?"

"That's impossible."

"You should talk. Now, I suggest you leave while you can."

Danner managed to control his shock. He even laughed. "Is that a threat?"

"Gosh, it sounded like one to me."

The vampire shoved the lounge chair across the room, where, like the TV, it passed through its target and rebounded off the wall. Then he laughed. "You have no substance, spook. How do you plan to hurt me?"

"I can't," the shadow man replied. "But he can." He pointed behind the fiend. Toward the bed.

Danner's eyes widened. He suddenly knew that the phantom was no threat—only a diversion.

He turned just as the prisoner sat upright on the bed, pulled the Uzi into view and opened fire. The short, static burst started low and swept upward, opening the vampire from crotch to collarbone. But Danner stayed on his feet. He looked down at the widening fissure in his chest and stomach, saw his captured blood spilling onto the motel-room floor, and he shook with sudden rage. His mouth opened wide and kept going, seeming to fill with more and more jagged teeth, until he gave a guttural cry and lunged toward the bed.

Stiles ignored the pain of the Uzi's recoil in his hands and fingers and fired again, this time sweeping from side to side. The first pass cut a dotted line along the creature's throat but didn't slow him; the second enlarged the perforation and made Stiles's intentions obvious. Decapitation. "NO!" Danner croaked, mostly through the rent in his throat, as he turned and threw himself through the picture window in a rain of glass.

The Uzi had hit empty but Stiles kept it ready nonetheless, at least until the footsteps outside staggered away and faded from his ears. The vampire was gone again, but for how long? He was getting stronger, Stiles could feel it. It was just a matter of time.

He struggled with the ropes at his ankles, cursing them and his aching hands, and finally freed himself completely. But he collapsed like a stringless puppet as soon as he left the bed. He looked to the specter still lingering in the shadows. Even Alex looked haggard and spent—what Chris could see of him—and he was already fading. But he managed to smile anyway. "How're you doing, Hoss?"

Stiles nodded. "Pretty shitty, but I'll manage. How about you?"

Alex faded a little more. "I guess my Casper act . . . took a little more out of me than I expected."

"But why? Why'd you come back to help? You never did that before."

The specter tried to shrug. "I guess you never really needed me until now." He was little more than an afterimage now. "I'm used up, Hoss. I won't be back for a while. So it looks like you're on you own."

"I'm used to it," Chris replied. "And Alex . . . thanks. You know?" But by that time the shadow man was gone. Chris couldn't tell if his brother had heard him or not.

Chapter Thirteen

Billie lay wide awake in the cocoon of her comforter and stared a hole in her bedroom ceiling, waiting for sleep that was already three hours late. She wasn't asking for much, just a brief respite, a chance to elude the worries that, since earlier in the evening, had begun to gather like bloated specters at the edge of her imagination. She was exhausted, and desperately needed the rest. But the arms of slumber would not comfort her. Chris Stiles just wouldn't allow it.

He had taken up residence in her mind and she could not force him out, no matter what his incarnation. First the rugged stranger with the easy manner and the quick smile, then the quiet loner on her porch swing, fumbling with his solitude and wanting, needing to reach out to someone. To her. That was the man she was quickly learning to care for, learning to . . .

To like a lot, she was quick to finish. *I just liked him a lot. Past tense*.

For that man's face was blurring now, and another was taking its place. This one was a parody of the former, an identical twin whose features shifted schizophrenically with wide eyes that saw, what, jungle enemies from a war long over? Or something more seriously unbalanced, like demons or ghosts, or vampires?

Maybe a cup of hot chocolate would help her sleep. She slipped into her housecoat and scuffs and shuffled down the chilled hallway, careful to avoid those worn spots in the floor lest she wake the boys.

She was two steps down the staircase before she heard sounds from the darkness below.

It was soft and continuous, like the low drone of an insect. Her throat constricted. Voices. Muttering just softly enough for her not to identify them or make out what they were saying. She backed up a step, hoping she could make it to her room and the telephone without setting off one of those land-mine floorboards and giving herself away. But then the voices downstairs turned to clapping and her alarms deactivated with a sigh. Unless the intruders had brought a studio audience, she realized, it must be the television set. And where there was a TV on . . .

She crept the rest of the way down and peeked past the wall into the living room.

A late night episode of *Happy Days* was about midway through, and the studio was still alive with whistles and applause at Fonzie's entrance. The home audience, however, was not so enthused. Del was sprawled on the couch in his pajamas, cradling something (probably He-Man or Skeletor) in his arms like a football player protecting the ball. Bart sat in the recliner before the television and nodded his head erratically, swaying and dipping, the same way his dad used to do when he just couldn't stay up for those late-night westerns.

Billie felt a flash of motherly anger at being disobeyed—they were sent to bed hours ago—but her temper was quickly squelched by even stronger maternal concern. *What's wrong with you*, she snapped at herself. *Have you been that wrapped up in your own worries and disappointments? What did you expect, two scared boys to sleep in their own rooms, alone, in the dark? They're your children, dammit. Act like it.*

Bart's chin finally tipped forward onto his chest and stayed there, snoozing fitfully. She came up behind his lounge chair and tilted it slowly back. The boy conceded to the change in body position without opening an eye or breaking rhythm in his snoring. Only then did Billie notice what he'd been doing: a grocery sack full of wood shavings sat between his legs, as did the broken head from her best broom. The shaft of it lay across his lap, one end whittled to a threatening point. She took his pocketknife away and laid it on the coffee table, then eased the makeshift stake from his grasp and looked it over. A glance toward the couch told her Del had a weapon too, of sorts. The "toy" he'd been cuddling was the remainder of the garlic bread from supper a few nights back. Vampires, she sighed wearily. They just wouldn't give it up. They were so adamant about it earlier, almost frantic, insisting that she believe them. Was it so much to ask, she wondered now. *They are your children—don't you owe them that much?*

No, she reminded herself emphatically. Humoring them wouldn't do any good, not for them, not for anyone. Not even for Chris. Because that was who this all boiled down to, wasn't it, whether she wanted to admit it or not. The stranger had some kind of hold on the boys; just what it was she couldn't say and was afraid to even guess. But they would never uncover it if they hid their heads in the sand and blamed it all on imaginary monsters. Maybe they should get out of town after all, she considered, just for a little while. But not because of Stiles's warnings. They would go because the boys needed help, either medical or psychological or maybe both, and they wouldn't get it in Isherwood. Maybe they'd go to Mom and Dad's in Ellettsville, and stay there for a few days. There were plenty of doctors in nearby Bloomington, and Indiana University had a whole department of psychology if they needed it.

Billie kneeled down beside Delbert and brushed the hair from his brow, finding his skin cold to the touch. No sense getting him up, she thought, so she went out into the hall to get a blanket from his room. She picked her way through the mess of adolescence like an experienced adventurer, stripped the top blanket from the bed, bundled it under her arm, and went looking for one for Bart. There was bound to be another around there somewhere.

She saw a cover in the closet doorway, picked it up, and spied the carefully hidden stack of horror comics beneath. "What the hell?" She kneeled down beside the magazines and books and felt her face flush with anger as she sifted through the *Fangoria*s and *GoreZone*s and *Famous Monsters of Filmland*s. Many of them were emblazoned with dripping monsters and hideous mutants and imaginatively dismembered victims.

"Dammit, Delbert," she muttered as she leafed through one of the magazines, "how many times have I told you not to buy this junk?" She dropped the book as if it might bite her fingers and just sat, fuming. No wonder the boys were so rattled. How could any normal child read such trash and not be affected? A horrible thought struck her—what if she'd been placing the blame on Chris unfairly? What if she'd had it backward all the time, that Del and Bart had convinced themselves that it was a vampire who beat them up, and when poor troubled Chris came along he was unwittingly drawn into their fantasy world?

They all have to go, she fumed. *I won't have this trash in my house*. She scooped up the whole stack, wrapped it in the blanket, and went out into the hall. The trash cans were out back, along the side of the garage. But when she got to the back door, she hesitated. She felt a twinge of fear, though not because of the vandals who'd been out there earlier. They were long gone by now, she reasoned. Seeing a nut with a machine gun would have put the fear of God in them readily enough. No, this was a more familiar fear, one she knew most every day. Namely, fifty-five pounds of canine muscle named Bruiser. The Citozzi's pit bull next door always made her nervous, even out of sight behind a boundary hedge and a tall chain-link fence. Del had assured her that the dog was docile, but she had seen too many news reports on TV . . . She turned and crept back into the living room just long enough to retrieve Bart's customized broomstick. Then she unlocked the back door and stepped outside.

It wasn't as dark as she'd expected; the security lamp on the corner of the garage to her right did a good job of keeping the night at bay and spilled a cone of liquid light across the backyard. It illuminated the tire swing on the lowest branch of the big oak and the grill that hadn't seen charcoal since two summers ago and the lawn-darts set that the boys seemed incapable of putting away. The mower was in the middle of the yard, its last meal digested and waiting to hibernate in the back of the garage until spring.

She listened to the night around her and heard nothing beyond the rustling of branches overhead, the whistle of the chilled breeze through the hedge. No dog so far. She started down the stone walkway slowly, scuffing her feet louder than necessary just to have a little audible accompaniment. But still no growls. Not even a whimper. *So what were you so afraid of*? she chastised herself. *A brass band couldn't rouse that mutt*. She looked at the stake in her hand and felt stupid. So when she got to the plastic garbage cans along the garage, it was the first thing to go in.

She unwrapped the blanket and found herself staring at one particular cover in glorious color. The title identified the movie as *Fright Night*. The woman pictured was blond and clad in a wispy white gown, but that was all so much detail. It was her feral face that dominated the picture, especially her mouth. The lips were peeled all the way back to the nose, baring an unprecedented jawful of teeth. Including the requisite canines.

A chill edged along her spine.

Staring into that face out there in the dark, she realized that what seemed ridiculous in the confines of her home a few minutes ago was a wholly different situation out here. In the silence. In the dark. She still didn't believe in vampires, at least not in the classical sense. But there were human monsters, weren't there, not just criminals but blithering psychopaths who strained the boundary between man and beast. Hadn't she seen tribesmen somewhere, in the *National Geographic* maybe, who filed their teeth to vampiric points? And weren't there documented cases of madmen who killed for blood, like that guy she'd seen in a *TV Guide* book ad once. What was his name . . . the Vampire of Düsseldorf?

She stared at the picture and wondered if someone like that had come upon her boys at the Danner House. And if that someone might still be walking around loose.

A low growl sounded from beyond the hedge at the side of the yard, not ten feet away. It took Billie by surprise, jolted her. The menace it conveyed raised the fine hairs on her neck. "Ssh, Bruiser," she whispered, trying to stay calm. "Easy, boy. It's just me." But the growling continued, deepening until there was no sound at all, just an angry rasping of breath. Billie backed up a step. *What is it?* Her mind raced. *Is it me, or is there something else?*

The first yelp was so unexpected that it struck Billie like a physical blow. Another followed soon after, but this one did not end. It was a shrill ululating cry of pain, and it froze Billie in her place. All she could muster was a whispered, "Dear God . . ."

The whimpering ended swiftly, in midcry, and then the quiet of the night returned as if never disrupted. Billie stood gaping at the blank wall of the hedge, disbelieving all she had heard. Where was the sound of doors and windows being thrown wide in alarm? Surely everyone had heard that noise . . . hadn't they? Hadn't she? She took a numbed step toward the hedge.

"Bruiser?" she half-whispered even before she realized what she was doing. Her voice seemed impossibly loud. But then, so did the furtive whispers and snickering that answered.

Her breath caught. In her mind's eye, she could almost see through the hedge to the mob of elfin figures crouched in the yard beyond, as they looked up as one from the dog's body and craned toward her, and their eyes . . .

She turned and ran for the porch and felt as if she were wading in molasses, moving impossibly slow and fighting for her balance and losing a slipper but not worrying to recover it. *You'll make it*, she panted, *you're only a few feet away and the door is still unlocked and besides, they've got to go around the fence . . .*

Chain links popped. One after another, quickly, like ripping metal fabric.

She reached for the doorknob even as she chanced a backward glance. The hedge was moving.

She turned the knob, or tried to. It didn't budge. With both hands she frantically grabbed at the knob and twisted and threw her weight against the wood and this time it gave. The force sent Bart crashing back down the hallway and Del screamed as she plunged inside.

"Are you nuts?" Bart was incredulous. "You went outside?"

"Close the door!" Billie cried even as she launched herself at it and slammed it shut and pushed in the unbelievably feeble lock button. "Get a chair from the kitchen," she said frantically. "We've got to block the door. Who knows how many there are—"

"How many what?" Bart tried to get past her to see out the door window. "Did you see them? We tried to tell you!"

"I didn't see anyone!" she snapped. "I just heard someone —I think they killed Bruiser and they were coming this way." Her eyes widened. "The windows! Are they all locked?!"

Del, still clutching his garlic bread, put a hand on her shoulder. "Don't worry, Mom. They can't get in. They've got to be invited."

"Wha—dammit, Del, would you two stop with the monsters? This is serious! Get to the phone and call Charlie at home. He's closer than the county sheriff. . . ."

Bart nodded. "I'll call Chris."

"You'll do no such thing—"

"Both of you, shut up!" Del held a shaking finger to his lips. "Listen!"

The three of them sat there crouched on the floor in silence, waiting. Billie expected to hear the scuff of feet on the porch just outside, the jiggle of the knob right before her face. Instead they heard a distant knock. It was on the front door at the other end of the hall.

"Don't answer it!" Bart hissed, moving halfway down the hall to switch off the lights. "They've got to be invited in! They can't come in unless we ask 'em!"

The knock came again, this time insistent. Powerful. It shook the heavy door on its hinges. Del started to cry; Billie pulled him close, wanting to join him but staying strong for their sakes. She motioned to Bart and mouthed, "Get to the phone," but the teenager's attention was fixed with morbid fascination on the front door as he awaited the next knock.

It did not come. Not for several minutes, or at least it seemed that long.

There was a muffled report, like a string of firecrackers, and part of the door splintered inward with explosive force. The knob and dead bolt fell to the ground, still connected to a single chunk of wood. The door swung open, and the Millers stared at the shadowy figure in the entrance, framed by the sterile moonlight beyond. No one moved. Not until Stiles's low, but harsh voice echoed through the house. "Everybody out!"

Billie stood hesitantly. "Chris?"

"I said move!" he growled, limping down the hallway and shifting the H & K to one hand so he could grab Bart by the collar and shove him toward the door. Del ran to the man and hugged his waist but Stiles caught his arm and guided him along after his brother. Then his powerful hand caught Billie's and she had to move quickly to keep from being dragged through the house.

"Hold on just a minute," she said defiantly, though not fighting him. "Just where do you think you're taking us?"

As they came through the front door he turned and looked her in the eyes and she saw his face in the moonlight. It brought a gasp in reaction; she reached out to touch the swollen eye and bruised flesh but he caught her wrist. "Boys," he called to them, "put your mom in the van."

She noticed that his eyes were no longer focused on her. He was looking away toward the side of the house. Del and Bart grabbed her arms before she could turn and they hustled her across the yard, moving so fast she couldn't even spare a look back. Not until she reached the van. Only then did she get a good look at the figures standing at the edge of the house.

There were not six or seven as she'd expected from the dog's cries and the destruction of the fence. There were two. They were little more than slight shadows standing just beyond the bushes there, watching. Stiles stood in the middle of the lawn facing them, and his whispered taunts were so angry they reached even her ears. "C'mon, fuckers. Let's see how bad you are." He even lowered the carbine as invitation but still the figures would not move.

Billie looked around the rest of the neighborhood. Stiles's curses, like the dog's yelps, should have awakened everyone in the immediate vicinity. But there were no lights on in the Citozzi's house, or the Schloesser's or the Ingrams or the Chastains or any of them. "Somebody, help!" she yelled. "Call the police!"

"Shut up!" Stiles barked at her, turning. "Do you want to get someone else killed?"

With his back turned, the dark ones in the bushes came rushing on.

She tried to shout a warning. But the sight of those dark figures scurrying like human spiders across the lawn stole her voice. But Stiles was already turning, expectant. The sighting beam swept across the figures at waist level and the H & K played another riff. One figure reacted like a movie stuntman and pitched backward as the rounds slapped into its gut. Just as quickly it was back on its feet and running, this time in the opposite direction. The other figure was caught at waist level and the shock of impact made its feet dig in and skid to a stop. The rest of it, however, kept on going and the cleanly separated torso spilled onto the lawn like a crab thrown from its perch. It flailed about before finally righting itself and scrambling back into the darkness of the hedge, an obscene insect leaving its lower limbs to writhe alone on the moonlit grass.

Stiles hobbled to the van while he changed magazines and forced the stunned Billie inside with the kids. He climbed into the pilot's chair with obvious discomfort and gunned the engine. "Charlie's in trouble," he told them. "Hold on and we still might make it." He stomped on the gas. The van jolted away from the curb and careened down the sleepy neighborhood street, then squealed around the corner and headed toward the middle of town.

Billie leaned her head against the window and kept telling herself that it was all a dream, that it wasn't real, that Rod Serling would step out in a minute to explain the plot before station identification. Even the town was different; she watched it whirl by and somehow knew this was not her home. It looked like it, right down to the smallest detail, but it didn't feel like it. That's what gave it away. It had no life. It was a facsimile, a facade from a Hollywood back lot that looked completely real from the front but concealed two-by-four bracing and rigging lines and technicians doing sound checks.

There were people up ahead, milling about on the sidewalk, both children and adults. The headlights flashed across them and for an instant each had cats' eyes, reflecting red and silver, and then they were all running like Halloween pranksters and the van was suddenly past them and turning onto the main street.

She closed her eyes so tight that dark purple spots danced before them. *Just a dream. Just a dream.*

"There's Charlie's place, Mr. Stiles," Bart pointed as they wheeled around the corner. "The apartment above where the pizza shop used to be. See his squad car?" Stiles's reply was to steer the van right for it, barely wasting time to brake. The tires screeched and the rear end swung around in the middle of the street, and Stiles was out almost before it had come to a full stop. "Which way in?" he called back, cocking the Uzi pistol he now carried.

Bart pointed to the doorway between the two shops, but his shouted directions were drowned out by a sudden explosion of glass.

A uniformed body hurtled backward through the upstairs window and arched toward the ground as if in slow motion, twisting and turning amid a rain of sparkling shards. The flight ended abruptly as he landed head first atop the police car parked below. The impact crumpled the roof like a tin can and popped the windshield out of its frame and shattered the red flashers. It even coaxed a dying mewl from the loudspeaker. And intermingled with that cacophony was the unmistakable sound of breaking bone. The body flopped limply to the side, end over end like a rag doll, and came to rest across the engine hood.

Stiles went slowly forward, wincing from the pain of each step. "Charlie?" he whispered, reaching out to the motionless form.

Dutch Larson sat up and smiled toothily. "Fix that desk yet?" the vampire said before it launched itself at the startled soldier.

Stiles tried to bring the gun up but Larson knocked it spinning away and went for the throat, clawing and catching Stiles's shirt and pulling him into a bear hug. Stiles went with the momentum instead of fighting it and drove his head straight into the vampire's mouth. It bought him a second or two of surprise, just enough time to slip Larson's grip and to lock one of those meaty arms behind him. Then, with a bit of leverage and a handful of hair, he spun the marshall completely around and drove his face into the fender of the patrol car, again and again.

Larson shoved him away and shook his head to clear it, then laughed. "That the best you can do, boy?" he taunted, despite his own physical condition. Stiles's defense had pulped a cheekbone and spread out his nose like a pad of butter, but those were the least of his injuries. A point-blank shotgun blast had left a cavity in his chest big enough to stick a cat through, and the fall had rendered his balding head even balder, this time clear to the bone. Hitting the light bar atop the cruiser had sheared off most of his scalp; it now hung in his face like a displaced toupee, connected only by a few strands of flesh. His shirt was tented by jutting rib bones and soaked with blood from some previous victim.

Charlie? Stiles glanced at the window upstairs with dread.

"What's wrong, boy?" Larson said, stalking him. "You don't look like you feel too good. C'mon." He yawned like a bear trap and oily spittle ran down his chin. "I'll make it quick, I swear. C'mere."

Stiles made a lunge for the van but Larson anticipated it and scrambled into his path, arms outstretched. In reflex the soldier jumped into the air, spun and buried a heel in the marshall's mouth. But the move sent a flash of pain through his own body, straight from groin to brain, and it stole his balance. He came down on his pivot leg that now wobbled like rubber, and he collapsed, his vision blurred, his mind swimming. All he could see was Larson's leering face coming at him again, spitting teeth along the way but retaining the two important ones. "Good try, boy," he smirked, "but no ci-gar."

Then Dutch flinched. He backed up a step, looking about perplexed, and then he flinched again as if stung by a wasp and he rubbed at his eye. The red dot that appeared on the back of his hand was comparatively weak as lasers go but still strong enough to burn the optic nerve. Larson turned his half-blind eye on Billie, standing a few feet away with Stiles's carbine at her shoulder. "Stay back, Dutch," she warned, "or so help me God, I'll kill you."

"Kill me?" he said, and for a moment his face slackened. Like a cloud passing before the moon, he lost that feral glint. "Kill me, Billie?" he whispered. "Why, I almost wish you could." Then his eyes narrowed and the grin returned, fracturing his face from one ear to the other.

"Shoot him, Mom!"

"DO IT!" Stiles yelled.

Billie's finger tensed on the trigger. But there it froze—she couldn't pull it through. And by then, Larson was already on her. He charged and brushed the gun aside, caught her by the shoulders. Stiles was already on his feet and struggling toward them, but he was just too far away.

Dutch pulled her head to one side and she could do nothing to stop him; she was rigid with terror. She could only whimper as he licked her neck, a big sloppy dog kiss, oily and tainted, and then he laughed and bared his teeth—and gasped.

He drew back and grabbed his mouth, which was smoking inexplicably, then flung the woman aside and began to run. Stiles reached Billie a half-second later, jerked the rifle from her numb hands and ripped open the fleeing figure's back with an erratic burst. But it only knocked the vampire on his face; a moment later he was up and running again, around the corner and out of sight.

"I . . . I couldn't move," Billie mumbled as she leaned against Stiles for support, too shocked to even cry or be afraid. "I looked at him and I just looked and looked and I couldn't move, not even when he . . ." She grimaced with disgust and wiped at the wetness on her throat. Even the little golden crucifix on her necklace was slimy with his spit. Her eyes widened; she pulled the trinket from her neck and gaped at it. "This? He touched this? Then that means . . . he really is a . . ."

Bart sighed to his brother. "It's about time."

"I don't get it," Del said, staring at her crucifix. "It didn't work for me."

Before Bart could say a word Stiles had shoved the carbine into his arms and, recovering his own Uzi, they went through the doorway between the shops. The door at the top of the staircase was standing wide open, beckoning, inviting them in. To see what, Billie wondered, fighting back her chill. Stiles went up the steps without a sound and slipped inside. He returned in a minute and motioned for them to come up.

Charlie Bean sat on the couch in the middle of what was once his living room, amid overturned furniture and broken glass. He held a pump shotgun across his lap and stared vacantly into space.

"Charlie?"

Bean turned his head toward the doorway slowly, his expression blank, and he turned the barrel of the Mossberg as well. "It's okay, Charlie," Chris said. He gave the Uzi to Del and then held up his empty hands. "See? Now I'm going to come over there, okay? Just lower the gun." He started across the room but the shotgun did not lower. If anything it actually raised, so that halfway to the couch Stiles realized that it was trained on his face. "Put the gun down, Charlie."

"Open your mouth," the deputy ordered.

Billie called to him, "Charlie, please . . ."

He racked the pump on his gun. "Open your fuckin' mouth!"

Stiles yawned for him. "See? No fangs." He nodded to the others and they did likewise. "Now, satisfied?"

For the first time since they'd arrived, Bean blinked. The hands holding the shotgun began to shake, violently, and he stared at them as if they belonged to someone else. Stiles took the weapon from him. "Oh, Jesus," he muttered, cradling his head in his hands, "Oh, Jesus, what if Susie'd been home . . . what if she'd been home . . ."

Billie dug a blanket from the closet and put it around his shoulders, while Bart and Del made a fresh pot of coffee. She found a bottle of tranquilizers in the bathroom medicine cabinet. It took three of them before Charlie would finally calm down.

Stiles was standing at the shattered window, looking out into the night, when Billie came up behind him, put her arms around him, and hugged herself to his back. But he barely acknowledged her presence. His attention was focused on the dark, deserted street below. "How many do you think are out there?" she asked.

"You don't want to know," he said somberly. He motioned to the street. "Look at it. This place is already gone, or most of it at least. It isn't even a town anymore. It's a battlefield." He was looking away from her when he said that, so she did not see the flicker of a grin drift across his bruised and bloody features. "A battlefield," he repeated to himself in a bare whisper, and the grin became an unsettling smile. "I've come home."

Chapter Fourteen

Billie awoke with a jolt. The nightmare had been so vivid that she was still wiping at her neck where Larson's tongue had fouled her. But the sight of sunlight spilling through the window across the room was a relief. It eased the tension from her shoulders. *Just an awful dream after all*, she thought, lying back and closing her eyes. *Just an ugly dream*.

"Mom? Are you okay?"

Bart was standing at the foot of the couch, looking down at her in concern. "You yelled just now," he said. "Are you all right?"

"Yes, I'm . . . uh . . ." Details finally started to seep through the fuzziness surrounding her mind. Like the fact that her oldest son was cradling a machine gun in his arms. She looked around the room again, this time realizing that it wasn't her bedroom after all but Charlie Bean's apartment, that she was lying on the couch and that one of the windows, the one Dutch had been blasted through, was now patched with plywood slats and plastic sheeting. Then it wasn't a dream. She suddenly felt very cold inside.

"Mom?"

She forced a smile. "I'm okay, hon. Just a nightmare." Another glance around. "Where is everyone?"

"I guess Charlie's still in bed," the redhead replied, "I haven't seen hide 'ner hair of him all morning. Chris left as soon as it got light out, and Del's in here with me." He turned and walked back into the dining room.

Billie caught up to him just as he laid aside the H & K and sat down next to Del before a tall piece of equipment that had been bolted to the dining table with C-clamps. The reloading machine looked in passing like a drill press from Sears, but a second glance noticed the powder measure and the 9mm dies and a cylinder in the center where empty brass stood. Billie's two boys were hard at work like a miniature assembly line: Del would prime each casing with a handtool, then pass them along to Bart where they were inserted in the press and the powder charge added automatically. Then, with a pull of the lever arm, the bullet was seated and the casing crimped to hold it. This was all done in a quick, practiced succession, and the plastic bin that caught the finished rounds was filling steadily.

"Hi, Mom," Delbert said, barely taking his eyes off the work before him. "We're up to sixty rounds an hour, but Chris says we can hit a hundred easy." He scooped up the pile of finished rounds and transferred them to the open ammo can on the floor between his feet. It was almost half-full.

"You say Chris left?" she asked. "Where?"

Both boys shrugged in unison. "I guess to look around. He took the rest of his guns with him, though he left the rifle for me." Bart pointed to the H & K. "Just in case."

Concern welled up within her, though she hid it from the boys. Chris knows what he's doing, she assured herself. He can handle it. Nothing will happen to him. But then she thought of that rugged, handsome face, now beaten and cut, swollen to an angry hue. *Please don't let anything happen to him.*

She shrugged off the thought and continued to watch the boys. She was proud of them. They'd grown up quicker than she'd ever realized, and most, she suspected, in the last few nights. Still, somewhere inside her, she almost wished they would act their ages and behave like the little boys they were; frightened, wanting, no, demanding that they all run away and get as far from this place as possible. It was less a maternal need for dependency than a desire to allay her own guilt for having those same feelings. But they didn't complain. They knew. Without Chris having to explain it as he had to her, they knew that they had to stay, every one of them, and they accepted it. They understood the horrors around them so much more clearly than anyone else. Such was the grace of childhood, she thought. The innocence to believe in the unbelievable without qualification or argument and to go on from there while she and Charlie struggled with their rationalizations and logic. Maybe they could learn a few things from the boys.

The monster magazines crossed her mind. It worked for them, she thought, and she was sorely tempted to go back to the house and dig them from the trash can and get to know her enemy better. She could just see herself, a student pouring over her *Fangoria* Cliffs Notes, sharpening a stake for her homework . . .

Don't laugh. It's not that implausible. Nothing is anymore.

The bed creaked in the room down the hall, and she heard the ratchety sound of a rotary phone dial turning. Then a receiver slammed down angrily, enough to sound the phone's bell, and Bean came stalking into the living room, wearing only his jeans and his gunbelt, carrying the ever-present Mossberg. He went straight for the phone but Bart saved him the trouble. "They're all dead, Charlie, all over town. Chris said he was going to cut the lines."

He gaped at them. "What! What the hell'd he do that for? Where is he, I want to talk to him."

"He's gone," Billie said. "But he'll be back in a little while."

Bean's anger couldn't mask the concern beneath. "But how am I gonna call Susie?" He snapped his fingers. "My car radio . . ."

"He took that too. Just settle down, Charlie. He knows what he's doing."

"But what about Susie, goddammit! I've got to tell hér not to come back here."

Billie sat the big man down on the couch. "What do you tell her, Charlie? That there are vampires here?"

"Are you kidding? I'll have to make up something better than that."

"But what can you say that won't scare her or make her suspicious? And what's the first thing she'll try to do if she thinks you might be in danger? That lady loves you, my friend, and come hell or high water she'll try to get to you. Is that what you want?"

He brooded a moment, but finally dropped his head into his hands. "Of course not."

"Don't just think of Susie here. Think of the entire town. Think like Chris does. We've got to be cut off, Charlie—phone, road, everything. We've got to contain this disease. You let one word slip out that something's going on here and we'll have every cop and reporter in Indiana flocking to us. And come nightfall, you might as well slap 'em on a plate and stick an apple in their mouths. They'll never know what hit 'em."

He looked up and gave her a frustrated smile. "You've got this all figured out, haven't you? When did you get so level-headed?"

She leaned close so the boys couldn't hear. "Are you kidding? I'm a mess. But Chris knows what he's doing. This time I think we should trust him."

"Chris knows, eh? Well, I'm glad of that, 'cause I don't have a blessed clue as to what's going on around here. All I know is I sat right here and shot a man with this shotgun, point-blank, and blew him through a second-floor window, only to have him run off down the street. Now, dammit, that ain't supposed to happen! Somebody's changed the rules to this game and forgot to tell me."

"You want to know the rules, Charlie?" Bart said, flicking yet another shell into the ammo can. "I'll tell you what I know. Those things out there, Larson and the rest, are vampires. And don't make that face to me, 'cause you saw Dutch last night. You know it's true. And once you accept that, you can fight them." He pointed to the deputy's shotgun. "If you're gonna use that, you'd better learn how. Because what stops a normal man just won't work here. You've got to cripple them, or they keep right on coming. Blind them or blow off a leg or both arms. Take their head clean off.'' Billie's expression soured; she was suddenly nauseated. ''Sorry, Mom, but it's the truth. Chris said that guns are only effective if used that way. Except against Danner, that is. He's some kind of special vampire, like Dracula or something. He doesn't stay crippled, he . . . rejuvenates. He grew back his face in just two nights, and Chris says he's even stronger than that now.''

''Aw, what a load of horseshit,'' Bean muttered, but the others could tell from his expression that it was his last stab at rationality, and even that was half-hearted. Begrudgingly, he believed. After last night, he couldn't afford not to. He finally threw up his hands. ''Okay, okay. So how do you kill them stone-dead? Or can you?''

''There are ways,'' the older boy told him. ''You've seen them on the late show—wooden stake, sunlight, fire, decapitation, a silver bullet—''

''No,'' Delbert corrected. ''Not silver. That's werewolves.''

''Vampires too, you little goof. I saw it in a movie a while back—I think it was *House of Dark Shadows*—where the police were given silver bullets to hunt down Barnabas Collins—''

''Nuh uh, they got it wrong then—''

''How would you like a good rap in the mouth—''

''Boys,'' Billie said in a stern tone. ''Settle down.'' The two frowned at each other but nodded and went back to bullet-making.

Bean leaned forward and rested his chin on his hands, thinking. ''Silver, huh?'' was all he said.

Billie wandered to the one unbroken window in the living room and looked out over the lifeless street. She thought the morning light would have made it less foreboding, but instead it seemed even more so: the total lack of movement out there was unnerving, like being the last people on earth. She hugged herself, thinking aloud, ''I wish Chris would get back.''

''I don't want to rain on your parade, Billie,'' Bean said from behind her, ''but what if he doesn't come back?'' She turned with a knitted brow and glared at him. ''Hey,'' he said, ''it's not his town. If I were him, all busted up and such, I'd hit the highway and keep going.''

''No, you wouldn't,'' she said, ''and neither will Chris.'' Her tone was adamant, but the seed of doubt had been planted. She realized that the boys were both looking at her and even Del had an expression of uncertainty. But not Bart. He winked at her and reached down to pat the Heckler & Koch. "That's right," she said, relieved, and rushed to pick up the rifle and hug it to her. "He wouldn't leave this behind, would he? Or his bullet machine? Or his pack?" She went across the room and tried to pick up the frayed old Alice pack but found it too heavy. "He wouldn't leave us behind, Charlie. He's coming back. Don't you worry."

"Maybe you're right," the deputy said, though still a bit skeptically. He went over and unzipped the pack and started sifting through the contents. "Look at this," he said in amazement. "Saltpeter and sulfur and carbon . . . that's black powder. And he's got cannon fuses and solenoids and electronic triggers and detonation cord . . ." He held up what looked like a large block of clay. "Jesus, do you know what this is? It's C-4. Plastic explosives. This shit is Army issue—not even blasting companies can get this. Just who is this guy?"

There came a rumbling in reply, the sound of an engine out front. Not an unusual phenomenon in itself, since the apartment overlooked Isherwood's only thoroughfare, but it was the first new sound they'd heard all morning. Del jumped from his stool and raced to the window. "A-ha," he called back to Bean, "now who's butt's the blackest? Chris is back." He looked again. "And he's got somebody with him."

They all went to the door of the apartment and waited.

Stiles came up the staircase, a Moore's Drugs sack clutched in one arm and the Uzi in the other. He looked worse than the night before; aside from the same blood-stained clothes, he had shaved his beard off earlier and the bruises beneath were now even more jarringly visible. He climbed the stairs with quick, easy steps but the thin line of his mouth and his knitted brow bespoke his discomfort. Billie stepped out to help him inside but he just brushed past her. Following close behind him was a worried-looking Ted Cooper, carrying his favorite Louisville Slugger cocked hobo-like over one shoulder. When the boy looked up and his eyes met Bean's, his face flushed and he almost started to cry. "I can't find Doreen," he said plaintively.

They held out their arms to him and ushered the teen inside.

"I went over to her parents' house this morning," he explained, "but no one was there, nobody, and I didn't know who to call 'cause Mom and Dad are outta town and the phones're dead anyway. C'mon, Charlie, we gotta find her."

Bean looked to Stiles for help.

"Sit down, son," the soldier ordered.

"But we're wasting time—"

"I said sit down. Charlie has something to tell you." Stiles turned to the deputy and whispered, "Tell him. It'll be good practice."

"What's that supposed to mean?"

"I put up signs on every road, in and out. As of now we're supposedly quarantined. That should buy us some time—at least one night. As for those I came across, they'll be waiting for you at the church around nine." He checked his watch. "You've got an hour to rehearse."

"But what do I tell them, the truth? They'd never believe it."

"I don't give a shit what you tell them. I just don't want a panic, and I don't want anyone trying to get out of town. Think you can handle that?"

"No."

"Well, life's hard," he shrugged. "I'll be indisposed for a while. Don't bother me until about eleven." He took his sack and started down the hallway.

"Just a minute." Bean caught his arm. "I've been talking to Bart, and he's given me an idea. Have you ever used silver against these . . . against vampires?"

"Silver's for werewolves,. Charlie."

"I know, I've heard. But the kid sounds convinced, and if it's true, this could be a real edge for us. Now I'm not talking silver bullets—I don't think it would hold a proper rifling well enough—but what about shotgun shells?" He lifted the Mossberg. "Pellets don't need any rifling. Shape doesn't even matter—it's like the grapeshot they used to use in cannons. Anything that'll fit in a shotshell will fire. Besides that, shotguns have a big dispersal pattern. All you'd have to do is aim at the chest, and at least one pellet's bound to hit the heart. What do you think?"

Stiles leaned back against the wall wearily. "The theory's

viable, Charlie, but only if the silver works, and, unfortunately, there's just not enough time to test it. I've got to get a little rest before I start preparing for tonight—"

"Hell, I'll test it then. I'll just find one of them and—"

"No, you won't." The soldier was firm. "We need every hand we can get. There's a lot to be done before dark, and you can start off by taking care of the Cooper kid."

"But what about—"

"No buts, Charlie. Please. Help the kid, okay?" The deputy frowned but nodded. Stiles patted his shoulder and limped past him down the hall, and almost made it to the bathroom this time before being stopped again.

"Chris," Billie said, touching his shoulder. "Can we talk?"

He turned and looked into her eyes, coldly, hiding his emotions. Finally he gestured for her to follow him in.

"I hope you don't offend easily," he said, dropping his pants, "but right now I'm in no mood for niceties." He leaned over and scooped a wad of hair from the tub with a grimace, then turned on the spigots. "What did you want?" he said, perched for now on the edge of the tub.

"I . . . uh . . . just wanted to know how it is out there."

"In a word, rotten." He managed to get his shirt unbuttoned but needed her help to get it off. She gasped at the map of scars, both old and new, across his body. His chest was as black and blue as his legs and face. A thick bandage was wound tight about his injured ribs. She helped him off with that as well. "There are more of them out there than I expected. It's spread too fast. Shoots the hell out of that old legend about it taking three days for one to rise from the grave. Hell, we're talking next night here, maybe even same night. In one weekend we've lost most of a town."

"What about the rest? Are there any others like us?"

He took a carton of Epsom salts from the sack and began pouring it into the tub water. "They're out there. Confused. Scared. At least the sane ones. Believe it or not, some are just business as usual, disgusted because they can't get to work or use the phones, unwilling to open their eyes and look around them because it might disrupt their complacency. Kinda the way you were last night when you threw me out." She turned her face away. "Sorry about that. Cheap shot. But there are a lot of them out there deluding themselves. Your preacher, Knutson, he's one of them. Gone completely bugshit. Slammed the door in my face this morning. Most of them just want to leave, whether they know what's going on or not. But we can't let them. It may sound mercenary, but we need them here. As bait. Because once this town is empty there won't be any supper on the table and those bastards'll start looking elsewhere. Bedford. Seymour. The whole fucking state."

Billie's face darkened at the pessimism of his forecast. "But how can we stop them?"

"All in one night," he told her point-blank. "Danner first. Without him they have no collective consciousness. They'll just scatter like roaches. Hunting them then will be a cinch. The hard part's finding Danner." He leaned back, hissing painfully, to check the water with his hand. "I couldn't find him this morning, not even a clue. He knows I'm looking, so he won't make it easy. But I'll find him, even if it means face to face after dark. And when I do . . ." He stood to skin out of his shorts and groaned again, once too often. He retrieved his drugstore sack and poured several pill bottles onto the counter by the sink. Billie picked one up. There was no actual label; he had just written *Demerol* on a scrap of paper and taped it to the outside. He took it from her and uncapped it while she inspected the others: Percodan, Methadone, Dilaudid. "These are all pretty strong."

"So is the pain. I've got to get some rest now, Billie, so if you don't mind . . ."

"What I really came to say," she finally managed, sitting down on the closed toilet and wiping her eyes, "is that I'm really sorry. I should've trusted you, and I'm just . . . well, I'm confused and . . ."

"It's okay," he reached out and touched her cheek. "Really. You were scared. I understand."

"I'm still scared."

"So am I."

She perked up. "You are?"

"Sure." He slipped into the soothing womb of the tub. "Is that so surprising?"

"So how do you cope with it?" she asked.

"Experience, my dear. I'm used to it by now."

She leaned closer. "I've been meaning to ask you about that. Just how did you get into this . . . business?"

"I guess you could call it family connections. My brother Alex got me involved. You remember I told you he was murdered while I was in 'Nam? Well, he still comes back from time to time."

"Comes back?"

Stiles nodded. "That's right. He's a ghost."

"Oh."

"The thing that killed Alex wasn't exactly human, and his spirit can't rest until I find it and destroy it. That's what brought me here—looking for the Enemy."

"So the thing that killed your brother was a vampire?"

He shrugged. "We don't know what it is. Its attack was so sudden and vicious that Alex never even saw what hit him. All he can remember is a choking sense of evil. So that's what attracts him now. Evil. He seeks it out, and I take it from there."

"Sounds a little one-sided to me."

"Tell me about it." He shifted his position in the tub, grimaced at the discomfort it brought. Billie looked concerned.

"I'll let you rest," she said, moving to the door.

"Billie," he called as she slipped from the room, "don't worry. It's going to be all right."

Bean was waiting for her in the hallway. He had put on not only his shirt but his jacket and cap as well. He still carried the shotgun. "What's wrong?" she asked.

"Teddy didn't take the news too good," the deputy told her. "He bolted as soon as I told him. Thinks I'm full of shit, more'n likely."

"So you're going after him?"

"Nope. Ted's a big kid now, he'll have to fend for himself. There are other things to be done." He lowered his voice so it wouldn't carry through the bathroom door. "You have a silver service, don't you?"

"Yes, but . . . Wait a minute. Didn't I overhear Chris telling you to leave that silver business alone? I think we'd better listen to him, Charlie—"

"Screw him," the deputy huffed. "He's just a man, Billie,

one lone man, and he's in a lot of pain. We can't all depend on him. We've got to stand up for ourselves, in case something happens to him, and now's as good a time as ever. Now, where's your silver?"

She thought it over. "I'll have to show you."

"Oh, no," Bean told her, but he could tell she'd already made up her mind. "Oh, all right then, but just as far as your house. The rest of the time you stay in the car."

Bart looked up from the reloader to see his mom slipping on her coat. "Where are you two going?"

"To check on a few things," Bean said casually. "Stay here with your brother, keep an eye on things."

Bart's expression was knowing. "Then you'd better take this," he said, chambering a round into the assault rifle like a seasoned fighter. "You might need it."

She pushed it back into his arms and hugged him and Del too. "Chris left that for you. Keep it. We'll be all right." She joined Bean at the door. "We'll be back before nine," she told them, smiling for Del's sake and for her own. She wanted to warn them, the same way she did every time she drove out of town or took a plane ("This is where the insurance policy is and this is who you can call"), but she didn't want to make Del worry. In the end she didn't have to. Bart read her intention just the same. He nodded. He would bring Chris if there was no word.

Outside the apartment Billie stifled a sob. Bean told her once again that she didn't have to go. But she climbed into the windshieldless squad car just the same, and they drove to her house in relative silence.

Billie's misgivings had free rein even before they turned onto Greenbriar Avenue. She averted her eyes as they pulled up out front. "Is there anything on the lawn?"

He looked around. "Such as?"

"Oh, I don't know. Maybe a pair of legs, a spare torso, something like that. Anything?" Bean just shook his head, forcing her to look for herself. The lawn was empty save for the plastic ducks near the mailbox. The legs were gone. That . . . thing must have come back after them, she thought as a chill raced up her spine. She didn't want to leave the car.

"I can get it if you'll tell me where it's at."

Her brow furrowed. "Don't fight my battles, Charlie. Please." She took a deep breath, flung the car door wide, and was halfway up the walk before he could even get his open.

"Hey, Rambo! At least wait up!" He grabbed the shotgun and hustled to catch her. She waited for him only after reaching the door, and she kept her darting eyes on the surrounding bushes. Her hand was on the knob and starting to open it when Bean motioned to her. "Let me go first," he said, racking the pump on the Mossberg. "To check the place out."

"There's nothing in here," she assured him. "Chris says they've got to be invited first." She pushed open the unlocked door. The drapes were still drawn throughout the house; a remnant of twilight still lingered within. Billie gulped audibly. Before entering she drew the Magnum revolver from Bean's holster.

It took her a few minutes to remember where she'd stored the silver, on the top shelf of the cabinet over the fridge. Bean pulled down the laquered chest, laid it on the countertop, opened it, and lifted a long, tapered cake knife from its satin recess. It felt good in his hand. It wasn't a Buck or a Gerber, but it would suffice. "This ought to do the trick," he said. They packed up the rest and headed for the car.

Billie sank into the passenger seat and sighed, "So far, so good. Now comes the hard part. Finding a guinea pig." She glanced at the neighborhood around her, at her friends' houses, the Citozzis next door and the Ingrams and the Foxes across the street and the Schloessers down the block, all with drapes tightly drawn against the morning sun. And she remembered how no one had heard the commotion last night and how no one answered her cries for help. "On second thought," she decided with a shiver, "the hard part won't be finding one. Just deciding where to start."

"I've already got one in mind," he told her, steering the squad car away from the curb.

Dutch Larson's house was only a few streets away.

It was a tri-level ranch half-again the size of Billie's house and situated to the rear of almost an acre of well-tended lawn. It was not an elaborate house, nothing that said "money" on the mailbox or merited a nod from *Better Homes and Gardens*. But in a small town like Isherwood it was the exception to small, cozy homes and its amenities were much envied. Bean sneered.

So this was what made Dutch more qualified to be town marshall. Money. Land. Community standing. No matter that he was sixty pounds too heavy and couldn't qualify with a handgun if he was two feet from the target.

Bean tried to stop himself, tried to swallow those pretty jealousies and put them in the past. But they kept coming, and finally he just gave up. His subconscious was regurgitating those feelings for a reason; he was about to go in there and stick a cake cutter into a man's chest. If he didn't go in hating him, he'd be scared to death.

Like last night.

"I'll be back in a minute," he said, stepping from the car with a shotgun and ceremonial weapon in hand. "If you hear any gunshots, get back to Stiles, okay?"

"Bullshit," Billie answered, getting out herself. "I'm going in there too."

"Oh, no, you're not."

"Try me. C'mon, Charlie. You think you're the only one here with something to prove? I know we're testing a theory—at least that's the idea—but that's not the only reason we came. It's to face him. You cracked up last night, Charlie, I saw it. You were lucky he didn't come back upstairs. And me—I couldn't even pull the trigger. I stood there with a gun on that bastard and my eyes kept telling me he's a monster, goddamn it, shoot him! But my mind said nope, that's just Dutch, and you can't shoot Dutch. I almost got us killed. Right now we're both liabilities, Charlie. And we might freeze again. Unless we prove otherwise." She laid the Magnum on the roof of the car, then reached inside the collar of her jacket and pulled out her crucifix. It dangled there in the open and reflected the precious sunlight. She took several breaths, then retrieved her gun. "Coming?"

There was nothing else to say to her except, "Yes, ma'am."

They started up the winding walk to the front porch, exchanging ideas on how best to enter. Bean favored the direct approach. He went up to the massive oak door and tried the knob. Unlocked. The portal swung open freely. It was still dark within. Billie reached inside and flicked the wall switch. The entry hall to the living room lit up, showing a carved wooden mirror frame, conspicuously mirrorless, and an ornate mahogany coat tree. The latter's burden was light; only two coats hung there. Bean reached in with his shotgun barrel and plucked what little remained of the dark brown uniform jacket from its peg. His hastily aimed blast had hit dead center and shredded the chest area, while the back was perforated up the middle with a dotted line of bullet holes. The material was greasy with blood, yet it had been taken off and hung up, nonplussed. The parody of normalcy chilled them. "At least we know he's here," Charlie whispered, his throat suddenly lined with sandpaper. He dropped the jacket quickly. "We'll go from room to room and open the curtains as we go. Okay?" He took a moment to psych himself and focus that hate. It wasn't working anymore. He was just scared. "Let's get this over with."

They crept around the corner and into the living room, Billie in the front with her revolver, Bean right behind with the shotgun covering either side of her. The room was cloaked in shadow, the furniture merely clumps of black against a field of twilight. It was impossible to tell if anyone was there. Bean wished he'd brought the Mag-Lite from the car. He felt along the wall for a switch but couldn't find it and, feeling vulnerable there against the light of the entry hall, began nudging Billie across the room in the direction of the bay window. The distance seemed to grow and every table and hassock and chair they maneuvered around threatened to loom up over them at any minute. Billie reached out, found the curtain fabric against her palms and jerked them open. Sunlight invaded the realm without fanfare, without a sound. But they were still taken aback by its entrance, its intensity. They looked around them. Dust motes swam in the light. Nothing else. The room was empty.

Bean shimmied out of his jacket and wiped the sheen of sweat from his face. "One room down, only seven or eight more to go."

"Wait a minute," Billie whispered. "Do you hear that?" Bean listened and this time he heard it too. An incessant murmur, far off. "A television?" she wondered. "It's coming from . . ." She turned to the stairway at the other end of the living room, well within the arc of sunlight they had invited. One arm of steps reached upward to the bedroom level above. The other led below, to the den or basement or whatever lay beyond the murkiness down there that lapped against the third step.

"Downstairs," Bean nodded, heading for the staircase. Billie caught his arm.

"Wait a minute. Shouldn't we check up here first? He could come down behind us."

Charlie pointed at the window. "The sunlight cuts this room in half. Nothing can come up, and nothing can follow us down." He looked into the murk awaiting them and swallowed hard. "Ready?"

They slipped down the staircase without a sound, immersing themselves in the inky dark. But once they reached the foot of the stairs, away from the bright sanctuary above, the cloaking gloom eased. They were in a shallow hallway, lined with several doors. The door at the very end was ajar, and bars of lamplight framed its edges. The television sounds came from there.

The adrenaline was pumping hard now. It blinded them to the empty doorways they passed, deafened them to all but the sound of their own breathing. They glided to the door like well-armed wraiths and peered through the crack.

They could see bookshelves and wood paneling, the corner of a pool table to one side, and a console television to the other. A coffee table sat in front of the couch, sporting magazines and a reproduction of a Remington bronc-buster. Willard Scott was saluting the elderly on the *Today Show*. But there was no one else in sight.

Bean edged the door open with the shotgun . . . a little further . . . a little more . . .

A limp figure was sprawled on the carpet in front of the couch, a female, lying facedown. She was naked except for her panties and her arms were bound behind her back, though the handcuffs were hardly necessary. The pale cast of her skin told them she was beyond struggling. Bean slipped into the room and scanned it once more before moving to the girl, and Billie stayed right behind him. "I don't want to do this," he whispered, but he reached out and touched the girl nonetheless. Her skin was stiff and turning cold. He pulled her onto her back, where they could see the young face with its glassy eyes open and its mouth frozen in a grimace, and they found the features only too familiar. Billie started to gag and all Bean could mutter was a low "No . . . oh, God, no . . ." as he felt for a pulse in Doreen Moody's puckered, much-bitten throat. But there was none. He sighed with frustration and sat back on his butt. And then he realized his fingertips were still wet from touching her, almost oily. Not blood. Saliva. The bites were fresh.

"Ah, company," came from behind them. Both flinched and whirled about to find Dutch Larson standing in the rumpus room doorway, blocking their retreat. He wore only his jockeys and a clean T-shirt, or at least it had been clean when he put it on. Since then his ventilated chest had leaked a steady dribble of Doreen Moody's blood across his bloated stomach. He had washed his face since they'd last met and combed the hair on his loose scalp, and he'd even pushed his jagged ribs back into place. But he looked no less nightmarish.

Bean tried to rise and bring up his shotgun but there wasn't time: Larson charged across the room hissing and bowled him over, knocking the Mossberg in one direction and the cake cutter in another. The creature's momentum carried them onto the couch and over it and onto the floor, and Dutch came out on top. He hammered at Bean and clawed at him, knocked his hands aside so he could get at that thick, luscious, bull-like neck. Bean tried frantically to throw his attacker but he was pinned by Larson's weight and couldn't gain any leverage. He swung again at Larson's leering, flat-nosed face, but the marshall caught his wrist, forced it to the ground, and held it there, and all the while squealing in anticipation and raining oily spittle onto the deputy's face.

"Dutch!"

Larson looked up at Billie's command, just as she fired the Magnum from a few feet away. Thunder shook the room as the hollow point round tore its way through the left side of the marshall's forehead and out the back, spraying the far wall with flecks of blood and hair and dead gray matter. The impact almost knocked him off of Charlie. But he just shook his leaking head, looked up at Billie, and growled, "Wait your turn, bitch," before attacking Bean again.

"The knife!" Bean screamed. "GET THE KNIFE!"

Larson laughed at that, and it grew into a mad cackle that made the deputy's flesh crawl. "Sorry, Charlie," he said, a rivulet of viscous fluid and brain cells running down his face. "Knife won't do you no good. What's a knife gonna d—" He stiffened as the tapered blade of the cake knife pierced his already shot-up back, and groaned even louder when Billie put her weight behind it and drove the point as deep as she could. Dutch fell away from Bean and writhed across the carpet, his limbs rigid and jerking. And then, just as suddenly, the spasms ceased. There was one last exhalation, and the corpse was still.

Bean climbed to his feet unsteadily and found Billie standing over the body, her look a mixture of vengeful satisfaction and outright disgust. She was trembling. "Are you all right?" he asked.

"I . . . I think I'm gonna puke. Excuse me." She staggered into the corner and dropped to her hands and knees.

Charlie knelt next to the marshall's body. Dutch's features were already softening, losing their savage mien. It worked, the deputy thought as he inspected the killing wound with clinical thoroughness, cautious not to remove the knife, no matter what. *Now we can fight these fuckers. Eat your heart out, Stiles.*

When Billie recovered, she found Bean picking Doreen's body off the floor. He laid her gently on the couch. "Why don't you go out in the hall," he said, throwing Billie his shotgun. "I'll be through in a minute."

"I'm staying," she said.

He pulled the slipcover loose from the couch and draped it over the girl to form a flowered shroud. He made sure her face was covered; he didn't want to see it again. Then he went to the pool table and picked a cue from the wall rack, laid it against the table, and stepped on it. The stick shattered. He took the sharper end back to the couch and plunged it into Doreen's body. The first try glanced off the ribs and missed; pulling it out was the worst part, and that was when he started to cry. But his subsequent aim was better.

Before leaving, Bean busted the glass on Dutch's gun cabinet and they cleaned out his shotgun collection. Then they beat a hasty retreat upstairs to the purifying light of day. But even there it did not feel safe. Not until they were out of the house entirely.

They sat in the car in silence, feeling the fear that only now was catching up to them. Bean wiped the blood from his watch face. Ten to nine. He started the engine. "I'll take you back to the boys," he told her, "before I go to the church. There's bound to be some people waiting."

"What are you going to tell them?"

"The truth," he said flatly. "They have a right to know. Besides, we need more people on our side, to round up the silver, to melt it down and load the shells. There's a lot to do before dark."

"They'll never believe you."

He looked back at the house as they pulled away and nodded. "I think they will."

Billie fidgeted in her chair, checking her watch every few minutes or so. Almost ten. Charlie had been gone over an hour already. Maybe she should go past the church to check on him . . .

She was immediately disappointed in herself. *Any excuse, right Billie? Any reason to get out of this apartment, to get out of the same room with Ted Cooper.* But she couldn't help it. His presence made her antsy, almost sick to her stomach. According to Bart, Ted had come back shortly after she and Charlie had left, carrying not his baseball bat this time but a stout ax. He held it even now as he sat in the corner of Charlie's living room, not saying a word. He didn't have to. Anyone who looked at the burly young man could see that he had changed. The concern for his girl had turned into grim resignation and, since then, something darker. He sat hunched forward, ax across his lap, his muscles taut, like an animal on the prowl. The thoughts behind those hard, staring eyes were bitter and angry and anxious for release.

She didn't like keeping Doreen a secret; it was eating away at her insides. But she knew better than to tell him.

"Are you gonna tell Chris?"

She turned. Del was standing beside her. "Tell him what, honey?"

"About the silver?"

She breathed a sigh. "When he gets up," she said, kissing his cheek. "He's pretty tired. Let's leave him alone for now. We'll wait for Charlie to get back, okay?"

"It's all right," Stiles said from the hallway. He was coming out of the bathroom in just his jeans, toweling the water from his chest. "I'm up now. What about the silver?"

She related the story to him for the first time and to the boys for a second, leaving out the graphic details for their benefit and Doreen's death for Ted's. The soldier listened intently, angry at first at Charlie's hardheadedness but taking in her every word, even inspecting the rest of the silver service she had brought back. When she was finished he said, "Well, I'll be damned." He looked at her and smiled, and pulled her into his arms. "You know, I ought to kick your ass for not checking with me first."

She nuzzled against him. "Would you have been worried?"

"Who me? Are you kidding?" He kissed her, unconscious of the stares and smirks around them.

"OKAY IN THERE. CUT OUT THE HAPPY HORSE-SHIT."

They all jumped. Bean was standing in the doorway with a speakerphone in one hand. "Nice to see you up, Mr. Stiles," he grinned.

"How did the meeting go?" Billie asked.

"See for yourself." He motioned toward the window.

A small crowd of fifteen to twenty people, men, women and children, were milling in the street below. Many carried shotguns and axes and shovels and any other weapon they could get their hands on. Others carried boxes and sacks of supplies. Like silver.

"They actually believed you?" Billie was astonished.

"It wasn't easy. A few still wanted to run, so we had to lock them up down at the jail. We're going from street to street now. If anyone comes out they can join us. We're also rounding up silver and taking it over to Pete's Radiator Shop. He's got some acetylene tanks we can use to melt this stuff down and flux out the alloys to get it as pure as possible." He tapped Stiles on the shoulder and said softly, "You and me and Billie, outside. Okay?"

They went out onto the stairway and closed the door. "Did Billie tell you what happened?"

"Not about Doreen," she was quick to say. Then to Stiles, "We found Ted's girlfriend there. Larson had been feeding on her."

"Christ."

"She was dead. Charlie made sure she stays that way."

"Temporarily," the deputy interjected. "That's what I wanted to tell you. Some of the others wouldn't believe me at first. So, I took them over to Dutch's house to prove it." His face was pale with the memory. "He wasn't there, Billie. Him or Doreen. I found the broken pool stick on the floor. And this." He drew a bundle from inside his coat and unwrapped the cake knife. "Look at the handle."

Stiles held it up with two fingers to avoid the gore-stained point and inspected the hilt. It was coated with a blackened, gauze-like substance. "Skin?"

Charlie nodded. "Whoever grabbed this burned the flesh right off their palm. That means someone else was in the house all the time. Like his wife. Well, I didn't have to think about it twice—we got the hell out of there. Fighting one's a God's plenty. Two, maybe three—forget it."

"Just stay out of houses from here on," Stiles warned. "We've got enough to keep us busy until nightfall." He looked at the sun. "Probably another eight, maybe nine hours. It's not much." He turned to Billie. "I've got a job for you. Take the boys and Cooper, maybe some of Charlie's people, out front. Find some lumber—slats, tomato stakes, whatever—and make crosses out of them. Big ones, waist-high or so. We'll need a cordon to isolate the town after dark. Living people will honor a quarantine sign but dead ones won't. If we string them across the roads out of town and out into the surrounding fields, we might at least slow them down. But be very careful. The others can help you make the crosses, but you have to put them out yourself. You and you alone."

She was visibly confused. "Why just me?"

He lifted the crucifix around her neck. "This is why. Faith. You've got it. You proved that last night when Larson ran off. Anybody can say they've got faith or play at it or even convince themselves of it, but you're the only one we're sure of. You put up a cross and they'll back away. We can't take the chance with anyone else. Can you handle it?"

She saluted. "Yes, sir. Crosses, coming up." She sneaked a quick kiss before disappearing back into the apartment. Stiles turned his attention to Bean.

"I like your approach to this. Do you have enough shotguns? How about reloading gear?"

"All taken care of," nodded the deputy. "We've got plenty of hunters around these parts and they know how to reload. We're leaning toward light loads, just enough to puncture the chest. Anyway, we've got three presses so far, and we've already got a mess of shotguns. I'm on my way to the office to get some more. I'll pick you up a couple.'' He started down the steps but turned with an errant thought. ''Pardon me for asking, but what are you gonna be doing while all of this is going on?''

''Planning a surprise party,'' was all Stiles would say. Bean caught an icy gleam in the soldier's eye and decided not to ask again.

It was nearly 10:30 A.M. The morning was almost gone. Nightfall was not far away.

Chapter Fifteen

The sun was losing its grip on the sky. With each glance Ted took, it dipped closer and closer to the tree-ragged horizon. It would be night soon. ''About an hour left,'' he said so everyone in the commandeered bakery truck would hear him. ''We should have time to kill a few more 'fore it gets too late.''

Billie was anxious enough with dusk so close and trying to keep her eyes on the road, but the teenager's words and manner unsettled her. ''Haven't you been listening, Cooper?'' she said, perturbed. ''Chris told us to stay out of the houses and that's what we're going to do. It's too dangerous.''

He waved her off. ''You ain't my mommy. If I want to do some hunting, I'll damn well do it.''

She was incredulous. He'd gotten so cocky. ''I'll tell you something, big man. If you want to get yourself killed, fine. Jim-dandy. But you'll not get someone else hurt in the process. You go hunting, you do it alone. Understand?''

He just shook his head, muttered something under his breath, and went back to staring out the window.

She glanced into the rearview mirror to check on Del and Bart. They were on the floor of the truck amid the trays of bakery goods that would never be delivered, Bart poking at a day-old Danish before tasting it, while Del sat propped against a row of bread shelves. Both were quiet and obviously exhausted, a feeling she heartily shared, but Del was more sullen than normal. He held the last of the tomato-stake crosses, turning it over and over in his hands, gazing at it as if it were some complex puzzle he couldn't quite fathom. Then he shook his head. "No way," he murmured. "No way these'll stop 'em. I mean, those things aren't stupid. They see that cordon, they'll just walk forty or fifty feet off the road until they find out it doesn't reach everywhere. Then they'll just go around it and what then?"

"There's no way we could've fenced in the entire town, Cap," Bart said through a mouthful of pastry. "That's not realistic. Hey, you ought to try one of these, they're not bad." The boy shook his head no.

"Bart's right, honey," Billie agreed. "Chris only wanted us to slow them down, that's all. And that's just what we've done."

His tone was skeptical. "You mean with these?" He threw down the cross contemptuously.

"You can't give up on faith, sweetheart," Billie assured him. "You've got to believe in it, if only to offset the evil. There is goodness out there. Why do you think they have to be invited into a house? Because there is an inherent good to every home —it's presupposed, taken for granted. Only when evil is invited in, accepted willingly, can that sanctity be violated. It's faith that wields the cross, too, not you or me. . . ." But the boy had already made up his mind and his attention was elsewhere. She frowned with worry and turned back to the road.

The Todd's Bakery truck rolled into the heart of town and found it not much different than before. There were no shoppers, no loitering old men. No cars running. For the latter she figured Chris was probably responsible. He told her earlier that any fool could drive a car. Even a dead one. And her fence of crosses wouldn't stand up to a vampire in a plummeting Honda Civic.

"Charlie's car's not there," Bart said, coming up from the back of the truck. "He must still be over at Pete's with the rest of 'em. Maybe we'd better head over there."

She pulled the truck into Bean's parking place just the same. "In a minute. You guys stay put. I want to see if Chris is back."

By the time she was out of the truck Bart had already slipped through the sliding door on the side and unshouldered the carbine.

"Hey, Mom?" Del leaned out the window and pointed across the street to the drugstore. "Can I go get some candy? The door's still open—Chris was there, remember?"

She looked at the empty store skeptically. "I don't think so."

"Aw, c'mon. There are windows everywhere. There ain't no way one of them can be in there. Please?"

"Oh, hell," Ted said, climbing out of the truck. "I'll take him. Shouldn't be five minutes." He shouldered his ax. "C'mon, little guy."

Billie finally relented. "All right, but just for a minute. And you leave money on the counter for anything you take." Then she sidled up next to Ted and breathed into his ear, "You let anything happen to him, kid, and I'll slit your bag and stick your leg through it." He answered her with a laugh as Del slithered out of the truck and walked alongside him across the vacant street. Billie watched after them anxiously, even after they were inside. Bart had to touch her shoulder to get her attention.

"They'll be okay, Mom. It's light in there." He started for the stairs and she finally followed after him.

The apartment was still unlocked, but no one was inside. Bart was the first to notice, vocally at least, that Stiles's things were gone. The reloader, the guns, the pack of explosives, and anything else that might even hint that he was ever there. Billie felt a sudden pang of distress at the discovery but said nothing. Bart was not nearly so controlled. "Looks like he packed up and left," he said, half-indifferent, half-frightened by the implication. "You think he'd really take it on the lamb like that?"

"No, I don't."

He shrugged. "Me neither. But I wouldn't blame him if he did."

She was adamant. "Believe me, he didn't, so let's drop it and go find your brother." She turned then and started for the door, inadvertantly knocking a photo from the end table with her elbow. She picked it up. The photo had been taken at Kings Island—the Eiffel Tower and person in the Scooby Doo suit in the background were the giveaways. In the foreground was Charlie, wearing a law enforcement cap and a T-shirt that read, CALL

911 TO MAKE A POLICEMAN COME. He held a woman in his arms, a clowning knight with his mousy damsel, and the two of them together were a study in contrasts. Where he was beefy and stout, she was petite. Where his manner, even frozen in the photo, was flamboyant and garrulous, hers was retiring and shy, eyes avoiding the camera. But she was looking at him, and Billie could read the emotion in that look. It choked her up. She kept connecting it to the Toyota wagon they'd found out on Croglin Way—Susie's wagon, off the road but with the nose pointed homeward, the doors open and the driver gone. Billie tried to think hopefully, to believe that Susie might have made it to safety. But she failed.

"You okay, Mom?" Bart asked, but then he saw what she was staring at. "Oh. Are you going to tell him?"

She sat the photo down gently, like a fragile, precious thing, then wiped her eyes. "No. Not till later." She held out a hand to her son. "Let's go find Del."

As they came down the stairs, they found Delbert and Ted sitting in the well of the truck's big side doors, the younger with a large sack perched on his lap. Del rifled through it and produced a handful of candy bars for their examination. "What do you want? We've got a Kit Kat, a Mounds, a Nestle's Crunch . . ."

Billie was indignant. "I thought I told you to leave money for anything you take."

Del grinned mischievously. "All of these were on sale. Hey, everybody check this out." He stuck his head down into the sack and when he looked up, his smile had changed. It was now huge, bulging his cheeks, and his incisors had grown long and tapered. The "Vampire Teeth" were obviously plastic, but that fact didn't spare his mother any discomfiture. Bart had to intervene to keep her from smacking them out of his mouth.

"Delbert, I don't want to see that stuff again, do you hear me?"

"But Mom—"

"It is not funny, young man. Now get in. We're going to find Charlie." She started around the front of the truck.

"Way to go, Cap," Bart said, giving him a noogie on the noggin.

"But she didn't even give me a chance to explain—"

At once all three boys suddenly became alert, ears primed,

like hunting dogs on the trail. It would've been almost comical had the sound that stirred them not been so distinct. A woman's gasp. "Mom!" Del cried, scrambling through the truck and picking up a claw hammer on the way while Bart went around the back and Ted around the front. They converged on the driver's side like the troops at Normandy.

Despite her exclamation of surprise, Billie already had the situation in hand: to be precise, she held a man at bay with a gun barrel halfway up his nose. A sane person in that position would have gasped and recoiled himself, but this man just smiled wanly. He was not old, but looked it at first glance. His face was haggard and his hair unkempt and his eyes were so red they looked ready to pop from the sockets. His dress shirt and tie and slacks were the same he'd worn at services the day before and were well wrinkled and dirty by now. In fact, his whole appearance was so disheveled that at first they barely recognized Reverend Knutson. The Bible in his hand was the only real clue. Even his pastor's smile was different. The warmth was misplaced, leaving it distant. Vacant. And he did not flinch at their abrupt defensive posturing. Instead he held that smile and reached out to touch Billie's shoulder. "Did I startle you?" he asked.

She lowered the weapon, embarrassed, and had to slap at Ted to get him to shoulder his menacing ax. "I'm so sorry, Kevin," she apologized. "I guess you did kind of sneak up on us. What are you doing out here?"

"His work," he said with a subdued exhaltation as he waved the book in front of them as proof. "At least I was trying. I thought I'd look in on some of the congregation, the ones who didn't make it to church yesterday and all. But I can't seem to find anyone home. It looks like we're the only ones who didn't go."

"Go where?"

"To Bedford. For the fireworks." They exchanged puzzled expressions, which seemed to weaken the man's own confidence. "It is tonight, isn't it?"

"It ain't even July," Del blurted before Billie's glare could cut him off. The minister heard him though and nodded and tried to smile. He just looked lost.

"Kevin," Billie said, stepping closer. "Are you okay?"

"Oh, I'm fine. Never better. The doctor told me just this morning that I'm in tip-top shape. He—"

"The doctor's office was open this morning?"

"Certainly. Dutch gave me a ride over first thing this morning. Then I went to the diner for breakfast and called on a few doors but . . ." He shrugged but still wore that same blank smile.

Billie looked at the diner across the street. It was still empty, still unopened for business, the door ajar only because Chris had jimmied it this morning. And Dutch . . .

"Sounds like somebody's slipped a cog," Ted whispered to Bart, but she heard it too.

"Listen to me, Kevin," she said, taking the man by the shoulders. "You've got to snap out of it. We need your help right now, so listen. None of that happened. You didn't see the doctor today. You didn't see Dutch."

"Billie, I just told you—"

"Dutch is dead, dammit. Maybe the doctor too. Most of the people aren't human anymore. They're vampires. Do you understand?"

"You too?" the ministered sighed. He pulled her into his arms and stroked her hair like a condescending parent. "Now, now," he soothed. "Nothing to be scared of."

She yanked out of his grasp. "Yes, there is something to be afraid of. They're here, now. I've seen them."

"NO!" His tone was suddenly violent, frenzied. Almost panicked. He raised the Bible as if to smite her with it. Bart stepped between them. "It's you who don't understand. I am strong. My faith is strong. Satan's touch cannot defile one of purity. He cannot!" His voice cracked. His confident tone rang hollow. "I am pure," he said emphatically, though they could not tell who he was trying to convince. "I am! And I will not let your own faithlessness draw down my flock." He turned, tucked the book under his arm, and started to leave. But Bart caught him by the shoulder before he could get too far and spun him around.

"Here," he said, forcing the last of the tomato-stake crosses into the minister's hands. "You might need it." Then he and his brother and Ted climbed back into the truck, leaving Billie and the irate reverend alone.

"Kevin," she pleaded, "come with us. We can use your faith. You can help us, and you'll be safe."

He looked around the town with the same dramatic flair he utilized at the pulpit every Sunday. "I don't see any evil, Billie," he said, but his eyes were still too glazed. It was no wonder he couldn't see. His insanity kept getting in the way.

"Please, Kevin. I'm begging you—"

"Send them to me, Billie," he said, striding off down the street. "Send your monsters, your vampires. Your boogeymen. Let them face me on hallowed ground." He laughed and headed in the direction of the church, to the sanctuary it offered him in more ways than one.

She was crying when she got into the truck. He had been a good leader, both spiritually and in the community, and despite his relative youth, it was still like watching a parent lose touch or drink himself stuporous. She climbed in the back with Del and let Ted take over the wheel. "It's okay, Mom." Del tried to be soothing. "He's just flipped out. There's nothing you could do."

"I say fuck him," Ted said, shifting into first and squealing off down the street. "Time's a wastin'. Look at the sun."

It touched the treetops and slid a bit past them. The light dimmed. Shadows festered and spread.

Pete's Radiator Shop was small and inconspicuous, just a block past the IGA store and the gas station on North Hickory. The little white building didn't even look like a garage; a painted plywood sign and arrow had to point out the two bay doors in the rear. Charlie Bean was standing outside with a cigarette and a Coke when they pulled up. "Nice truck," he said, half-facetiously. "So, how did it go?"

Ted looked to Billie, and she to Charlie. Then she managed a "Fine, I guess. Where's Chris?"

The big man shook his head. "Ain't seen him. I figured he was with you." Up close, he noticed Billie's reddened eyes. "You aren't telling me everything. What's up?"

She tried to smile reassuringly, but the picture from Kings Island wouldn't leave her mind. She just brushed past the deputy without a word and went inside. Bean looked to Bart, but the teen threw up his arms. "We ran into Reverend Knutson. The man belongs in a rubber rectory. I guess she's taking it pretty hard."

"I didn't know she was that fond of him," Bean said, "but

I know what you mean. He gave me some trouble at the church this morning. It wasn't easy convincing everyone else when he wouldn't even believe it.'' He flicked a butt across the gravel lot and leaned closer. ''You say you haven't seen Stiles?''

''Not a peep. We went back to your place and found all of his stuff gone.''

''Everything?''

''Every little thing.''

''Shit.'' He lit another cigarette and took a few anxious puffs. ''That's just great. What if that fucker's took off? What are we gonna do?'' Another puff, then he ground it under a heel. ''That's just fucking great.'' He stalked back through the garage door with the boys in tow.

They didn't recognize most of the people inside. That might have seemed strange for a town the size of Isherwood, but the days of knowing your neighbors had faded long go with the *Andy Griffith Show* and Saturday-night band concerts under the stars. They knew some of them by name, others by deed, and others by gossip, but they didn't really know them. And that felt strange. There they all were, some friends but mostly strangers, gathered around a pair of picnic tables and a trough of water as if it were the oracle at Delphi. A woman had donned Pete's welding mask and fired up the acetylene tanks to melt down the silverware. First it was fluxed to eliminate the other alloys inherent in the castings and to somewhat purify the silver content. Then the silver itself was melted, and the molten metal dripped into the trough at her feet. Each drop hissed in defiance as it struck the water and formed a perfect pearl of silver in the process. Then a man would scoop out the newly formed shot and lay it on one of the tables, where it became the focus of another reloading line. It was a slow process, limited by the speed of melting the shot, so another ad-hoc line had been set up on the other table. There metal snips were used to cut fork tines and silver wire and other pieces into smaller bits, irregular in shape. Like shrapnel. Then these too were loaded into shotgun casings. These loads weren't as pure as the melted shot, but it was better than nothing and too late in the day to argue. In all, a substantial number of shells had been finished, though not enough according to Bean. So there was factory ammo there as well, deer slugs and double-0 buck, just in case. The silver rounds were marked with stripes of luminous paint to distinguish between the two. If it glowed, it could kill; if not, just shoot for the eyes and pray.

Two men sat on stools nearby, sawing the butts and barrels off expensive hunting arms to make scatterguns out of them. Bean got one for Ted and Bart and one for Billie as well, then draped bandoliers of silver shells around their shoulders.

Billie was standing at Pete's work counter when she saw, among the tools and car parts and empty beer cans, some unusually altered shotgun shells. She picked one up. It had crepe streamers attached to the top and a cork with a nail through it glued to the bottom. The plastic casing had been scored and a length of tape wrapped around the middle. From the look of it, the tape had been impregnated with long silver clippings and slivers of wire. "What the hell is this?" she asked.

"A little home cooking," Bean said, taking it out of her hands and laying it back on the table. "They're fragmentation grenades. They land on the cork, and the nail detonates the shell. Since the casing has been scored, the charge blows outward rather than up, and that sprays the pieces of silver in every direction. Nasty little thing, isn't it? I thought Stiles could use them, but . . . doesn't look like that now, does it?

"What's that supposed to mean?"

"Bart told me about his stuff being gone. Looks to me like he's just took off."

Billie bristled at the notion. "You know what your problem is, Bean? You haven't got any faith. He said he'll be here. Okay?"

Bean had a cynical retort in mind but didn't get the chance to use it. He was interrupted by the sound of an engine outside. Del ran to the door, then came back with an I-told-you-so grin. "Wrong again, Chuck," the boy proclaimed.

Everyone stopped and turned their attention toward the doorway as a figure appeared there. Stiles was clad in black fatigues and knit cap and gloves. Even his face was smudged black, so that he looked like a shadow pulled loose from the ground. His mere presence had a distinct effect on the townspeople assembled there; a flash of relief, and of hope, swept through the room, but with it a tinge of fear. Bean could feel it. This dark angel might be their only salvation, but he also put them on edge.

The deputy felt empathy with them. Stiles made him nervous too.

Billie ran forward smiling. At least until she saw Stiles's face. No wonder the others were antsy at his appearance. She told herself it was the same face, the same bruised and swollen features. But there was something different now. The muscles were indeed more taut and the lips, despite the swelling, had become little more than a thin line. But it was the eyes that had changed the most. They burned with an open intensity, a thin, cold fury. He had psyched himself for the battle, she realized, and she didn't know whether to speak and risk breaking his concentration. So she stayed silent, and let the warrior stride quickly past her. He went straight to Bean and drew a piece of paper from his breast pocket. "It's time to move," he said, unfolding it to show a quickly scrawled map. "Do you know the two houses in the cul-de-sac at the end of Platter Drive?"

"Sure. That's in Pinecone Terrace, not far from here."

Stiles nodded. "The basements are well fortified. I've secured the upstairs doors, so the ones outside the basements will be the only entrance. Easier to defend." He turned to the rest of the people. "There's a school bus outside. I want all of you on it in the next five minutes. I've found a place for you to hide."

"Hide?" Ted said. "You mean all of us?"

"All of you."

Several of the men and even some of the women grabbed for their shotguns. "Not us," one of them said, and the others agreed. "We can help you out there."

Stiles seemed to ignore them. "I have traps set," he told them without looking. "You might blunder into them, trigger them prematurely. And I wouldn't like that." He looked to Bean. "Do you have my guns ready?" He noticed the streamered shells on the counter. "What the hell are those?"

Ted came up behind Stiles, still pushing it. "Stiles, you're not the only one here who can handle himself, so quit playing hero. We can do this." When the man didn't answer he cursed and called to the others, "You guys get the others into the bus and wait for me out there. If he doesn't want us, we'll just do this ourselves."

Stiles turned on Ted with an ominous glare and no one else moved. But after a long minute Stiles just stepped past him. Charlie handed him a chopped Remington semi-auto shotgun and a second one in a makeshift scabbard for his back. He nodded, grabbed a few bandoliers of silver shells from the table, and took Billie by the arm. "Come with me," he said softly as he drew her toward the door. They were almost outside before he said over his shoulder, "Charlie, get them to the shelters. I'll be there in a few minutes." Then he stopped and finally looked back at Cooper and the others. "If there's anyone not in a shelter when I get there, I'll kill them. At least that way you'll die quickly."

They went outside, past the soldier's stolen school bus, and climbed into the bakery truck. Stiles glanced at the setting sun. The rev of the pedal under his foot bespoke his urgency. Billie was watching him. "You were kidding back there, weren't you? I mean, you wouldn't kill any of them, would you?"

He said nothing. It was answer enough.

He steered the truck back to Elm and turned south, back across town. She intuitively knew where he was taking her. He crossed Main Street and turned at the next block, onto Walnut Street, and went one block more before parking in front of an older house with peeling paint and a hanging length of gutter along the front. The familiar Conestoga mailbox read MOORE across its wagon-cover. Stiles was already out of the truck and motioning for her to follow. He led her across the lawn.

Just off the porch and between the hedges there was a basement window well, reinforced with corrugated tin and just deep enough for the small pane to swing up. Barely enough room to show Sharon Lou's entire face on the other side. "Lou?" Billie exclaimed, kneeling down to the window. "Are you all right?"

Sharon's face disappeared abruptly and Billie suddenly found herself nose-to-nose with a double-barreled shotgun.

"I'm sorry, girl," the older woman said, "if it really is you. I just can't take no chances. Not after last night. Now back up there with your boyfriend."

She did as told. "I tried to get her out myself," Chris said.

"I knew she was a friend of yours, so I thought you might be able to convince her."

"Hell no, I ain't coming out," Sharon told them. "After what I saw last night . . . things I couldn't understand if I tried. I don't trust nobody. So I'll just stay put, thank you. I've got canned goods and blankets and a bathroom down here. And my gun. I can hold as long as I want. At least until the state police get here. Or the National Guard."

"But it's not safe enough," Billie said. "Come with us."

"It's getting dark," the older woman said, retracting her gun barrel. "I'm sorry, Billie. I've got to lock myself in."

"Wait." Stiles picked a handful of rounds from one of the bandoliers and dropped them into the well where she could reach them. "There aren't many. Use them only if you have to." He took Billie by the arm again and led her away.

"No!" she said, fighting him. "We can't just leave her there."

"Right now she's safer than we are. Look at the sun, Billie. There's no more time."

They hurried to the truck and he gunned the engine, and they covered the several blocks to the Platter Drive cul-de-sac in just a few minutes. The school bus was already parked outside. Stiles's van was where he'd left it in the driveway. Bean was standing outside the first house's basement, his trusty full-length Mossberg cradled in one arm. The extra belts of shotshells were in a pile at his feet. "They're all in," he said as the two approached, "and I mean all of them. You really put the fear o' God in 'em, bub." He pointed to the other basement, just across the side yard. "The others are secured already. Billie, you and the boys will be in here with some of the others." The heavy door was still open. She could see Del and Bart and Ted standing just inside.

She turned to the hard-featured man beside her and could not deny the obvious; in this present incarnation he frightened her. He was cold and stony-faced, an assassin every bit as familiar with death as his prey. But at least he was human. And somewhere deep inside him there was something more. Something she needed. "I don't really know what to say," she stammered, wanting his arms around her but not daring to ask. "Be careful." She started to go in, but not before throwing her arms around his neck and whispering in his ear. "I love you."

He put an arm around her middle but it was not holding her, not the way she wanted. But in pulling away, she saw it. Something in his eyes. A flicker perhaps, the slightest glimmer of what lurked behind that wall of armor. The man she knew. And he had heard her. It was gone just as abruptly, leaving only the look of the assassin in its place, but she had seen it. And she kept that thought with her as Charlie closed the door behind her and she threw the heavy bolt.

Outside, Stiles addressed the lone figure that now stood before him. "You too, Charlie," he said. "Get inside."

"Nope."

"You heard what I said earlier."

"Yep. And you scared me too. I don't doubt you'd do it, not for a minute. But just think about it for a minute. You're gonna need me. Look at yourself, man. You're a mess. You wince with each step, your ribs are busted, your face looks like hamburger, you're popping painkillers like M & M's. C'mon, I can help. Trust me."

Stiles just stared at him. Not angrily; no emotion showed on his masklike face. He just stared, and Bean thought he could almost hear the whir of mental gears computing the logic of his words. Then the decision was made. Bean could see it as the soldier bent down to pick up the remaining ammo belts. His eyes squinted for just a moment, and pain flickered through them. The point was conceded. He pulled a small tube of black face paint from his pocket. "Get that face covered," he said, "and help me get this stuff to the van."

They were loaded and ready to go when Bean first noticed the fog. It was starting in the low-lying areas, just down the street from them at the bottom of the hill, a pale and wispy grayness. "I don't like the looks of that," he groaned. "I guess it's too late to just torch the whole place and run like hell? Yeah, I know. It wouldn't get them all. Stupid idea."

"It wouldn't get Danner. That's the important thing."

Charlie shivered. The fog was spreading. "I still don't like the looks of this. Not one bit."

The sun lingered at the horizon, hanging on by force of will, just long enough for them to get into position. Then it was gone.

Part III

SHADOW WAR

Chapter Sixteen

The vampire had no problem getting Larson's patrol car into gear. Just push the stick to "D"—he'd learned that readily enough. But figuring just how much pressure to apply to the gas and brake pedals—that was a skill Danner had yet to acquire. He drove down the evening street in short, spastic little hops, squealing tires and screeching brakes, and it nearly brought a flush of angry redness to his pallid cheeks. The steering wheel sported finger grooves where it had not before, and the column groaned from the punishment he inflicted. But he refused to quit. He had to learn how to drive; it was the way of the world these days.

He gunned the engine and overshot the intersection at Sycamore and Cedar, and an overcompensating jerk of the wheel took him up over the sidewalk and across the corner lawn. But he managed to get the cruiser back onto the road, and the prowl continued.

He was hungry. Even after gorging himself the previous evening with such gluttonous abandon, the pangs were there, sharp and unrelenting. He had expended too much undoing the damage Stiles had inflicted. He was whole again, unmarked, but at what cost? He was drained. Once again he was a slave to the hunger instead of its master, as much now as when he climbed from his makeshift prison three nights past. He had to feed soon. He had to find prey.

But that was easier said than done. He'd been active for nearly half an hour already, and still no food was in sight.

The vampire fumed. Stiles was responsible. Who else could it be? He was hiding them, Danner was certain. Would he never learn? It was only a matter of time 'till he found them, all huddled together like a Thanksgiving feast. And Stiles would be there with them. After all, the man was no fool—ghost or no ghost, he wouldn't dare stay out past sundown again. Not after last night. Yes, he would be there, all right, cowering, hiding. Waiting to die.

Danner smiled at the notion. It gave him some solace, but not enough to overcome his needs.

He thought of blood, and he wished he'd made it home the night before. There he kept a reserve supply ready—he believed her name was Katrina, though it was of little import. But he just couldn't make it back there, not after Stiles had left him gaping like a sausage on the grill. So he had hid in a victim's basement and he had fed, and healed. And he had been confident that staying in town would guarantee easy prey the next eve. But now the notion seemed ludicrous. His eyes swept the empty street. Another half-hour, he thought. Then he would go to Katrina. At least she would get him by, tide him over till he could find Stiles and the others.

He tried the radio again—it was one of the few knobs on the massive console he could fathom—but little had changed from the last time. Sammy Hagar had been replaced by Bon Jovi; in short, he couldn't tell the difference. The music was strident and hard on the ears even with the volume low, and the lyrics were nonsensical to him. But he left it on just the same. Like the car itself, this music was a sign of the times. If he was to exist here, and thrive, he would have to acculturate himself. No matter how unpleasant that proved to be.

He listened a little longer, but the music did not improve. It reminded him that immortality did at times have its downside. And it reinforced his self-doubts.

He was apprehensive of this new world. The television box didn't only inspire him with wonder. It intimidated him. It overflowed with images that his turn-of-the-century mind fought to comprehend; not even the Master's gift had prepared him for it all. Perhaps, if he'd lived it, if he had experienced the changes as slowly, as deliberately as the rest of the world. But to be thrust into it like a naked foundling . . .

There was a voice in his head, and it whispered things that he did not want to hear. When he thought of moving on to the bigger city, away from this home that was never a home, this site of his misery and imprisonment, the voice said, *Are you sure*? And that kernel of doubt was enough to slow his advance. And when he thought of conquest and how the cities were like great gardens of fruit ever ripening on the vine, the voice said again, *Are you sure? Is it time yet? Will it ever be*? He'd struggled with the automobile as if it were some medieval dragon, while veritable children operated them with ease. This world was as alien to him as the moon—computers and calculators with their dancing blips of captured light and cameras that spewed color pictures and ovens that cooked in an eyeblink yet didn't brown the meat. Even the television box was still an enigma—he could turn it on and off, turn it up and change the picture, but its workings were as arcane as a brujo's spell. Yet such things were taken for granted in this world.

The voice was insistent and its questions were ones he could not answer. And when he ignored them completely, it changed its tact. *One more mistake. One more and you might finally meet the end you've eluded all these decades. Ignorance of the laws or customs or currency will attract attention, and in this day and age you can't afford that. Here, in a small town, one man has fought you to a standstill. What if there are more of him out there, not with crosses and stakes, but with guns like his that fire so fast they could chop you to pieces in seconds?*

Begrudgingly, he agreed with the voice. At least on that point. Stiles's impertinence had ingrained a certain wariness in him. He would be careful. He would approach everything slowly and deliberately, and he would plan before he struck. He already had a strategy of sorts in mind—he would stay in Isherwood as long as the food supply held, and he would use the time to learn. And only when he was ready would he venture to Indianapolis or maybe even Chicago. And there he would suckle on the teat of the city, thriving in its shadows. And his powers would grow, and the voice of doubt would finally fade. And then . . .

His body screamed with hunger, reminding him. One step at a time.

He drove on, searching.

There were crouched figures along the street ahead, and upon seeing the car they rushed it and tried to leap onto the hood. But then they saw the face behind the wheel and they scrambled away, letting the cruiser move past. Danner spared them little more than a contemptuous sneer. Half of him wished them away, the lumbering ill-witted shits. They were all so grotesquely stupid. They didn't even know when to wake, losing precious night hours. At times their wit and cunning could seem intact, but it was an act, and then only in relation to hunting their prey. Anything else, whether it be books or television or simply the weather, drew blank stares and mumbles. The dead were ever poor conversationalists, he had relearned of late. It was ironic; all of those years of solitude, hungering not just for sustenance but for company as well, for the spoken word of another, be he living or not. Anything but that perfect silence. But now he'd learned that words alone were not enough. He needed something . . .

He dismissed that notion out of hand. *I am a vampire. The vampire. I've survived for almost a century, and will do so for centuries more. I need nothing.*

Still, someone to speak to now and then . . .

He felt his rage at Stiles and sought to determine its core. Vengeance? Surely. Few men had ever hurt him so. But a tinge of disappointment as well? He had wrapped it in a film of retribution and used it to humiliate Stiles, but his offer of immortality had been more than that. Perhaps he should have killed the man when he had the chance, but he had felt something. It wasn't very strong—he did not care for this man, certainly not as he had for the Master. But there was something still . . . a recognition of likeness, perhaps. A kinship. Stiles would have made a good vampire, he'd seen that from the start. He would have accepted it, given time. And how he would've thrived.

But then the fanciful thoughts faded and he grumbled. Stiles was no longer an issue; kinship or not, he had stepped too far over the line. He had to die. And the vampire now derived a great deal of joy in planning just how.

The patrol car rounded the corner at Ritter Street and Danner immediately stomped the brake hard enough to nearly shove it through the floor. The wheels locked as he swerved to the side, barely missing the rusted white van that sat at the curb there.

Stiles's van?

He could scarcely control his anticipation—he ripped the driver's door off in his haste to get out and almost did the same to the other vehicle. The van, he found, was empty. But the color, the outer rust, the upholstery . . . it had to be. He crawled inside and sniffed the air, straining it through supernatural senses. It was Stiles all right. He could feel his presence around him, thick, almost palpable. It vividly brought back the scene of last night's confrontation. The scent of the soldier's fear.

The taste of his blood.

It was faint on the tongue at first, but the recollection grew until Danner could almost taste it anew. It made his senses swim, like a sip of rare wine, and it left him wanting more. Sadly, he could not use it to his advantage—he had not drank deeply enough to control Stiles or to bend him to his will (if that could truly be done), but . . .

Danner's eyes widened. He leapt from the van and stood there on the sidewalk, sifting the night air and finding himself still heady with the scent of the man's blood. So it wasn't the soldier's lingering scent that alerted him after all. It was the soldier himself! Danner closed his eyes; the taste of blood welled in his mouth and mind, and the perception of Stiles's presence grew sharper. The empathy was tentative; he could not pick up thoughts or mental images the way he could with others. But he could intuit the man's presence simply by detecting the flare of emotions. Excitement. A tinge of fear. And most of all, a cold rage.

He looked around. The feeling was close by—Stiles was near.

There were other cars lining the curb on either side of the street; their grouping in this otherwise deserted town was what had initially surprised him. The cars were closer to one house than any other. What did that mean? He started to smile, but remained wary. It just couldn't be that easy.

The windows of the Cape Cod–style house were still shaded, but Danner could see a sliver of light peeking between the heavy drapes. He started up the front walk and mounted the porch, astounded that this place was actually familiar to him yet not daring to suppose himself so lucky. Surely they weren't that stupid. He went to the front door and twisted the knob until the lock broke, only to find other locks and dead bolts in place. "Really," he smirked and gave the door a sound shove. There was a crack and it swung wide open, the bolts still intact but torn from the corresponding jamb. "Knock, knock," he grinned, "anyone home?" The entry hall, which led to what he knew to be the living room, was empty. "Ah. Then you won't mind if I come in."

He stepped across the threshold without invitation, for the one he'd received the previous night still held.

What were the odds, he gloated, that these simpletons would choose one of his houses—one already breached by invitation—in which to barricade themselves? And this was indeed their fortress, he no longer had any doubts. The pungent, stinging aroma of garlic had attacked his nostrils immediately upon entering. But instead of repelling him, it had an opposite effect. It only confirmed his suspicions, and it goaded him into searching further. He could feel Stiles. He could feel his own rage building.

And the hunger. Always the hunger.

The living room and kitchen were empty. But his discomfort grew as he neared the dining room. The garlic was stronger here—his eyes were streaming and his head pounded from the incendiary stench of the herb—but he would not back away. His anger, boiling now, was all that kept him there. It was also what blinded him to the perils of an obvious frontal assault, to the dangers that might lurk beyond the door if Stiles were there and if he were as well armed as before. The vampire was oblivious to all of it. All but the rage. It escaped his lips in a threatening growl as he catapulted blindly through the swinging tavern doors of the dining room.

The full strength of the wretched garlic hit his eyes like a wave of fire and he gasped and staggered off balance, colliding with a china cabinet and nearly toppling it. His fiery wrath was extinguished and he knew immediately that he was in trouble. He flailed about, trying to find the door and defend himself before a broomstick found his heart or Stiles opened fire. But there was no attack. After a few moments only his own grunts and stumblings could he heard, and he finally calmed himself. The return of rationality also helped him fight back against the effects of the garlic, enough that he could open his eyes and look around.

A string of garlic cloves lay on the dining table, peeled to release their aroma. He grabbed the table with one hand and overturned it, sending the hated herb into the far corner and letting him breath easier. But he still felt vulnerable. He scanned the room suspiciously and began to back toward the door. Something was wrong here.

Something brushed the back of his head. Danner leaped away and turned with a snarl while the other just swayed back and forth like a pendulum and gave off a soft shushing sound as his cotton garment scraped the wall. The man was wearing the same plumber's uniform that Danner had left him in the night before; the embroidered stitching said STEVE over the left breast, just above the heavy dowel that pinned him to the wall. The stake must have been driven solidly into one of the wall studs, for it alone held the body, a good six inches off the carpet, arms hanging limp, legs swaying.

Danner was livid. He held no special regard for the plumber—indeed, he would never have known his name had it not been emblazoned there on his chest. But to leave him hanging there as a warning . . . what gall! He grasped the stake and yanked it loose, tilting it so the body could slide off and crumple on the floor like a limp dishrag. A piece of paper that had been pinned to his chest fluttered to the carpet as well. Danner bent to pick it up.

It was a scrap of Garfield stationery, folded in the middle with a smiling happy face drawn on the outside. Inside, it carried a one-word message: *Boom*.

Steve the vampire-plumber was just struggling to his feet when Danner looked up at him anxiously. There were lumps under his coveralls, two just beneath the rib cage, two across the waist, two more in the side pockets on his thighs. And wire veins ran to each just beneath the cotton skin.

"Thank you, Master," Steve said, reaching out to fawn over him. Danner backed away, unable to identify the threat wired to his servant but recognizing it as danger and reacting by instinct. He was halfway across the dining room, almost to the windows, when his hypersensitive ears picked up the distant click of a toggle switch.

The room erupted like a toppled volcano, blasting out a cone of lateral fire. Steve, for all intent and purpose, disintegrated in the blink of an eye. The concussive force of the blast shot Danner through a window and didn't drop him for at least twelve feet. When he did come down, he sprawled end over end and rolled for another few yards, enough to snuff out the flames that danced along his back and shoulders.

The vampire lay there in the side yard of the house, his mind swimming, his face and neck peppered with slivers of glass. His back was blistered beneath the scorched sweatshirt but he couldn't heal it, not in his weakened condition. He could barely make it to his feet. Through the gaping hole behind him he could see the shambles of the dining room, its furniture destroyed along with its owner. But to his surprise, the damage was relatively minor. The house still stood, and no flames raged within; only the blackened walls were evidence of a fire at all. The charges had been directional—directed solely at him.

Stiles's handiwork was evident here, and so was his presence. The vampire could still feel him, close by. Was he still hiding . . . or could he be out there, stalking? "I'm still here, Mr. Stiles," Danner yelled, forcing a laugh. "Do you hear me? Still here! Why don't you come out and do the job right!"

He heard the scuff of footsteps on the street out front. The opening of doors. The drone of voices. The vampire gathered himself and walked around the house to where the crowds were gathering. His children, his offspring, had been awakened in number by the explosion and now milled about in front of the house, drawn by some remnant of human curiosity, or perhaps the primal expectation that where there's commotion, there might be a hot meal. There were between twelve and fifteen of them from the immediate neighborhood, some stalking through the ground fog in predatory poses, while others staggered about and wiped the sleep from their eyes. Most stood alone and eyed the competition warily, though some of the women and children did huddle together in unconscious recognition of their former family structures.

Of course, there was no sign of Stiles among them. The challenge had gone unacknowledged. Danner fumed. He would have to keep looking . . . and keep finding the bastard's traps. How many could there be?

How many could he survive?

The others had grown silent upon seeing Danner and now stood there stoically in the welling fog and the cold wash of moonlight, waiting before him like foot servants called to their master's side. It did not evade his notice. He grinned. Yes, that was it. His frustration began to ease. Perhaps they could be of use to him after all. He limped across the yard to the driveway pavement, in between a Datsun and a Chevy parked there, and approached them. Some backed away apprehensively, but not far. All listened. "There are people here," he said, his soft tone carrying up and down the street with remarkable clarity. "Food. They are here. But they are hiding." He leaned against the Datsun's hatchback for support. "You will find them for me."

Each licked his or her lips in unison with the others, like individual cells forming a larger, more malignant entity. They nodded their agreement.

"Then go. But mark me, no one is to feed." They looked at him blankly. "At least not until I do. I demand first blood. Bring them to me." His brow furrowed at any sign of discontent among them. His tone deepened. "Is that clear?"

All nodded. All but one. A young woman in ragged pink pajamas was standing near the front of the small mob, but she was barely listening to him. Instead she wore a puzzled expression and kept fingering a length of yellow cord that looped twice about her neck. It was apparent that she had not put it there. Others sported the thick strings as well; about their throats or waists, their thighs, even around their foreheads like rolled bandanas. The girl turned the cord over and revealed a thinner wire leading away from it down her back, where she couldn't see. But Danner could. A taped packet was pinned to the back of her pajama shirt, where a solenoid and miniature Radio Shack receiver were secreted.

He felt the same unease as before and started to back up, but the Datsun was in the way. Then he picked up the transmitter's trigger-click again and he thought he knew what to expect this time. But the result wasn't the same. There was no great explosion as before. This time it merely set off the whiplike cracks of detonation cord going off through the gathered crowd. He covered his face from the sharp flashes but not before seeing a dark object hurtle toward him. The pajama girl's head spun like a top as it sailed over his shoulder and smashed into the passenger window of the car. Other heads were rolling around at the base of the driveway like a child's marbles, and the bodies they left behind wilted and died. The three or four who remained were not so lucky. At least one staggered around in shocked silence, looking for his severed limbs, trying not to trip over the larger sections of cadavers on the pavement.

Another pop went off to Danner's right, near the Datsun's bumper. It didn't sound the same as the det cord, but its effects, at least to him, were much more pronounced. He felt the pain immediately; stinging, searing, right through his calf and thigh. He fell to one knee and ripped open a denim pantleg that was now marked by a rash of ragged pin holes. His fingers burrowed into the likewise punctured flesh like steel tweezers, reaming one of the miniscule wounds to get at the sliver of wire embedded there. Its silver content was not substantial, yet it was enough to cause him pain, even to burn his fingertips at the touch. Even as he extracted a single wire, a second jerry-rigged grenade came sailing overhead, and he caught the barest glimpse of it from the corner of his eye. The streamered shotshell arced out of the night and came down right behind him, hitting the Datsun's fender. The wire shrapnel sprayed in a circular pattern and caught him in the lower back this time, choking an angry curse from his lips. He pitched over onto his face and writhed there in the driveway, at least until more incoming streamers convinced him to move. He scrambled around the edge of the Datsun as the shells went off, peppering the fender wells this time instead of him. But he knew it was just a matter of time.

He looked to the patrol car. It was still in the road minus the driver's door. Larson's keyring still hung visibly from the steering column.

He gritted his teeth and pushed off from the compact car, threading his way through the other autos that clogged the driveway's mouth. His leg and back felt irrigated with liquid fire but he refused to stop, not even when more fragmentation shells rained down around him, not even when one exploded right in front of him. Needles of fire lanced his shins and knees but he waded through just the same. A few more steps and he all but fell into the driver's seat. He twisted the keys with a shaking hand and stomped the pedal as he shifted into reverse and coaxed screams and smoke from the back tires.

It was just as the vampire shifted back to drive that he finally caught sight of the note pinned to the crossbar of the steering wheel. His breath caught and refused to release. Another happy face. Only this one he didn't have to open. The C4 packed around the engine only minutes earlier went off before he got the chance.

The hood fluttered into the air like a windblown petal and the windshield shattered. The explosion triggered the gas tank in turn and with a sudden whoosh the car became a mobile bonfire. It careened down the block out of control, hit a truck and a mailbox before crossing the road to collide with a tree. There the flames consumed it. But not its driver. He lay senseless in the middle of the roadway fifty feet back, flanked by fiery streams of spilled gasoline. The blast had tossed him through the open driver's door, but this time he did not roll as he came down. He slid. A trail of skin marked the distance, and the left side of his face now shone clear to the bone. He sat up with some difficulty and tried to cradle his head in his hands but found only one arm willing. The other, from the bare socket down, still clutched the steering wheel of the inferno down the street.

Running footsteps came toward him. Faces hovered above, as pallid as his own, mimicking human concern as best they could. "Master?" these new arrivals said, "let us help you." Hands lifted him up from the pavement.

The stark report of gunshots, even after the many explosions Danner had heard that night, were startling just the same. The vampires on either side of him jerked backward as if pulled by unseen wires, and were dead when they hit the ground. The scatterguns' efficiency, and that of their silver pellets was spelled out in no uncertain terms on their ruined torsos.

He was there, Danner knew without turning. He felt him. He knew he would be there, right in front of him. All he had to do was . . .

Look up.

There was a demon in the road. It stood backlit by hellspawned flame, its wings folding and unfolding restlessly, its impossibly long arms drooped at its sides and reaching all the way to the ankles. But it was just an illusion of the fire. For in a few moments the vampire's eyes adjusted and he saw the truth. The wings were just the billowing tails of an overcoat. The arms, one of which raised to point at him, were not what they seemed; the middle section was in fact the man's forearm, while the lower extension proved not organic at all but cold steel with a 12-gauge bore. Still smoking.

One of the shotguns roared again. Danner staggered and fell, clutching his crotch or what was left of it. His cries were caused less by the blast than the silver it left behind. "How does it feel?" the avenging angel asked in a soft, vehement tone. Stiles's voice.

"HELP ME!" Danner cried out. There had to be more of his children in the area, there had to be! "Kill him! Tear him apart!!"

"Forget it, Sebastian," Stiles said as he strolled forward, both sawed-off shotguns pointed square at the prostrate figure's knees. "It's just you and me this time."

There was a bestial hiss from atop a car parked along the curb and the soldier turned just as the spidery figure there lunged. The shotgun blast caught the vampire squarely in the chest from point-blank range, but it could not halt the creature's momentum. The body slammed into him full-force and knocked him right off his feet. One of the shotguns slid away across the pavement. The soldier wrestled the cadaver aside and and killed it and went for Danner again, but by now there were others there to protect him, four of them at least, with more on the way. He caught the next one coming in with another chest shot, sidestepping the hurtling body this time. A female caught him from behind and immediately began frantically clawing for his throat. The shotgun flew backwards into her ribs with crushing force, over and over, and once the hold was loosened he turned and dealt with her permanently.

More of the creatures were starting to gather, almost ten now, including a pack of children who sealed Danner away from the action and seemed anxious to take Stiles in a solid wave. But handfuls of Charlie Bean's fragmentation shells came whistling into the street like New Year's favors and their swarming stings dispersed the monsters and sent them howling into the night.

While the deputy kept them from attacking en masse, it was

still Stiles who bore the brunt of the attack. And he bore it with an unsettling relish.

He was fighting even after the guns were empty, even as he reloaded, keeping two of them at bay with scything spin kicks until the shotgun could dispatch them completely. Danner watched him fight and could not believe that this was the same man he had tortured the night before. He did not move the same way, did not favor his crotch or the ribs and fingers that the vampire had taken perverse pleasure in breaking. He fought with a maniacal fervor that took even Danner aback. And worried him.

Stiles took out another adversary, this time only temporarily with a point-blank blast to the forehead, and then he looked back at Danner. In that one instant, as if rehearsed, the fireglow played on Stiles's face. They were the same bruised, puffy features, all right, perhaps even worse now. But their expression was different. His face was drawn and frozen in a mask of barely controlled rage, a face almost translucent, unable to hide the roiling emotion beyond. It was a madman's face.

And then it smiled.

"Your turn, Sebastian," he said almost casually, turning the shotgun one-handed in Danner's direction. The vampire froze —whether from pain already inflicted or not, he simply couldn't will his limbs to move. And in that split second, for the first time in decades, he was afraid. But then another of his creatures leaped onto Stiles from behind and drove him to the ground and the gunshot went wild. It struck Danner high on the left shoulder, just enough to rupture the deltoid and throw him into the fender of the car behind him. But the vampire did not cry out; instead he used the searing pain to fuel his movements. He scrambled away on his three limbs like a great wounded spider, across the yard's soft grass where Bean's antipersonnel devices couldn't reach him and then full out for cover. Despite the deputy's gunfire from somewhere in the darkness he made it to the corner of the house.

An anxious look back showed Stiles still down on the ground, wrestling and pummeling his assailant but not getting loose. Three more were moving in from behind him. Danner tried to be satisfied with that. "Make him suffer," he wished silently under his breath, but he did not wait to see further. He had learned better this night. He hobbled back along the side yard till he reached the chain-link fence that separated it from the neighbors to the rear and tore it aside with a groping hand. Another yard and another fence and a driveway later and he was crossing Cedar again and running along it to the next block, heading toward the main road. The gunfire was intermittent behind him and ceased altogether within the next five minutes but he would not slow. Instead he sent every vampire he came across back in that direction. "Two men," was all he would have to say before their hungry eyes would light up and their lips peel back from their canines in primal anticipation. They loped off into the night at the slightest mention, barely giving notice to Danner's condition or displaying any trepidations about what caused it.

They would find out, he thought. If Stiles were still alive, they would most certainly find out.

Danner stopped when he reached the small brick building of Isherwood High School and caught himself flattening against the wall for cover. The soldier couldn't possibly have kept up with him, he knew. Still . . . He closed his eyes and felt for him, reached out for his scent, his presence. But he couldn't find him. The vampire sagged against the brick in relief. It meant the man was dead, or at least out of range. Danner's confidence grew. It was only a matter of time, he reassured himself. Stiles and his cohort could only fight so long before running, and with all the vampires that Danner had set on their trail, they would not run for long. He regretted that he could not be the one to kill them. He would have relished it.

He almost slid to the ground and had to haul himself back to his feet. The pain was pervasive. For the first time he began to doubt his chances of getting home. But Katrina's face was suddenly there in his mind, that lovely form strapped to the table in the cellar, that soft young throat untouched save for that first nip he'd given upon finding her. What nectar. The image sent a ripple of anticipation through him. The thought of his lips on that neck, of her warmth flowing into him might have given him stirrings of excitement had there been anything left between his legs. At the very least it gave him purpose to leave that crutch of a wall and forget the pain, or at least ignore it.

The fountain beckoned.

His thirst was consuming, but it did not completely override his sense of self-preservation. He took the time to feel for Stiles once again before leaving cover. Still nothing. So he headed around the corner and along Main Street at a determined if haggard pace. But on foot and badly mutilated, it still took precious time to cover the roughly two blocks to the Tri-Lakes and then cross open fields to get to Sykes Road. He could have gone cross-country and saved himself some distance, but he could not afford the risk. The ground between the town and his own land was hilly and hard to travel, especially in his present condition. Besides, he'd had no time to reconnoiter that area—someone could have put up fences or other barriers over the years, or Stiles may have even booby-trapped such an obvious shortcut. So instead he stuck to the side of the road, in the shadow of the trees. It took him longer to reach the Tunnel and beyond, but at least it was a route free of obstruction, and he made it there unmolested.

He clambered over the wall of the estate at nearly the same place Tommy Whitten and his friends had gone over, but did so with considerably less aplomb. The pain was almost blinding now; the silver burned everywhere, in his legs, his crotch, his shoulder, and it grew worse with each step he took. But he kept on. His only thoughts were of that precious elixir awaiting him, crimson waves of it, washing over him, wearing down and vanquishing the wall of pain that was building around him, brick by brick. Blood would save him. Blood would conquer the pain, would bring back the power. It would make him invincible.

He quickened his limping pace, fell once, twice, scrambled like an animal on his hand and knees. *Not much further*, he assured himself as he tore through the underbrush. *Not much . . . further* . . .

The trees around him gave way to thicket and then ceased entirely, replaced by clear moonlight. The vampire broke into the open; the house lay just across the open field. The sight of it brought a mad cackle bubbling to the surface. He lunged into the thick grass and waded for home. Katrina was pounding in his temples already as he entered through the garden; he could all but feel her heartbeat as he mounted the porch and staggered through the doorway, swallowing in anticipation of each glorious pulse. He headed for the cellar door.

"Mrs. Daaaa-ner." The voice came from outside. It was almost as lifeless as one of his own followers. "Mrs. Daaaa-ner, can S'bastian come out and play?"

Danner froze. It couldn't be him. It wasn't possible. He concentrated again, rechecking what his pain-wracked senses already told him. There was nothing—no empathy, no contact. It couldn't be him. He hurried back to the doorway and peeked out into the night. A lone shadow stood in the overgrown garden, completely still. Only his coat moved with the breeze.

But it can't be him . . . I can't feel him!

As if in response, the man out there moved. He turned ever so slightly, just enough so that the moon could light his face. Then Stiles grinned. It was an entirely isolated expression; it didn't spread to the rest of a face turned stony and cruel. Like an assassin.

"No," the vampire muttered, backing away from the door. "It can't be . . . I can't feel you, I—"

Something sailed through the window of the dining room to his right—a white stick that hit the wall and rolled somewhere beneath the old dining table. Another stick flew into the hallway to his left, and he heard the clatter of a third as it cleared the balcony and landed in the bedroom upstairs, scaring a cloud of starlings into the night. But the last object came through the garden door right before him; it skittered across the floor and came to rest in a bar of moonlight. Almost a foot of PVC pipe, capped at both ends, one of them threaded by a short length of fuse. Burning.

"*Damn you to hell*!" was all Danner managed before the house went up.

Chapter Seventeen

Bean slammed on the brakes, skidding Stiles's van to a halt in the middle of Sykes Road. The soldier's sign was straight in front of him; a fluorescent arrow had been sprayed on the pavement, pointing to the right, straight at the wall of the Danner estate.

Don't go in there, Charlie boy, it's tainted land.

A chill ran up the deputy's spine as Papaw's words now rang true. But he couldn't let it deter him—there was no turning back now. Stiles might need him. He stomped on the gas and wrung black smoke from the wheels as he shot off down the roadway and around the next bend, until the front gate of the property came into view. He picked up speed coming down the straightaway, then turned in and rammed the gate full force. Metal crunched audibly and he was nearly jarred from the seat; the windshield shattered and part of it fell in his lap. But the vehicle's momentum won out. It tore both gates from their moorings and flung them aside, allowing access to the first vehicle in years. The van lurched to one side and almost hit a tree, then plunged into the darkness, torturing its suspension on the weed-choked drive. "Christ!" he muttered, fighting to control the van's wild bucking as he peered into the tree-lined blackness before him. "How the hell am I supposed to find him in here?"

There was a jarring clap of ground-level thunder in reply, and the flash of the explosion through the trees to guide him. "Holy shit!" he exclaimed, punching the gas pedal even harder. The van lurched forward, bashing a fender into the trunk of a spruce before turning the right way. The high beams found a thicket directly ahead; Charlie gunned it through to the open fields beyond. There, in the cold gleam of the moon, was Danner House. At least what was left of it. A few sections of wall and chimney were all that stood of the great structure now. It looked as if a great hand from on high had just mashed it flat. Small fires burned here and there, lighting the destruction further, but he could see no sign of Stiles. So he followed the remnants of the drive and skirted what was once the main entrance, circling around to the gardens and rubble-strewn courtyard. That is where the lone figure came into view. It whirled at his approach, leveling two sawed-off shotguns at the hip. They stayed there even after the van halted and Bean leaped out. "Whoa, simmer down there, bud," he said, not daring to take a step. "It's just me, okay? Look." He opened his mouth, pulled back his lips for a quick inspection. Stiles nodded and shouldered the weapons, and Bean breathed a sigh of relief.

"I was beginning to think you weren't coming," the soldier said.

"I almost didn't. Right after you went for Danner, the fuckers started pouring out of every nook and cranny. I've never seen anything like it. I even knew some of them." The recollection bothered him. He cleared his throat and stepped away, staring instead at the shattered remains of the house. "Was he in there?"

"Yes."

"Then we got the sonuvabitch!" Charlie said, his smile widening. "It's over, at least the first part. The rest of 'em won't be too hard to deal with, right? Right?" He noticed the other's cynical expression and it sobered him. His smile slid off his face. "Uh oh. What now?!"

Stiles was staring at the ruined building. It was hard to tell with his face so bruised and battered and smudged with paint, but his brow was knitted and his swollen jaw looked set in concentration. He looked as if he smelled—or sensed—something bad. "He isn't dead," he said. "Not yet. I can still feel him."

"Feel him? What's this shit?"

"You probably won't believe this, but we've got some kind of empathy going here, me and him—don't ask me how or why. But I can feel that bastard. That's how I tracked him as fast as I did."

"Empathy?" Bean repeated, considering the word. He finally shrugged. "Hell, why not? After vampires, things tend to go down pretty easy. Now, this empathy . . . does it mean he can feel you too?''

Stiles shrugged. ''I think so. When I let him. It's an old trick we learned in 'Nam. Some of the boys thought that Charlie—the Vietcong—could sense your fear, home in on it. It might sound stupid now, but it didn't out there in the bush. So we found a way to fix him. We called it shutting down. No extraneous thought, no emotion. Just put a lid on everything. I don't think Danner can see through it. At least he was surprised when I showed up.'' He took a few steps toward the rubble. ''I swear, Charlie, I can feel him. That bastard isn't dead yet.''

Bean looked at the man before him and saw a lull in his defenses, an instant when his facade slipped. He saw inside to the rage that drove him, and the pain as well, enough to force a man to his knees. And he could finally reconcile the image that tonight's battle had instilled in his mind: Stiles was no superman as he'd appeared earlier. He had simply kept his injuries bottled up all evening, by sheer force of will, and that in itself was somehow even more astounding. The pain was in there, roiling, waiting to take control again. But the merest flash of it and the defensive wall immediately went back up. Stiles blinked, and the blank look returned. He was shut down. He was safe again. He motioned to the deputy. ''C'mon. Let's take a look.''

They stepped cautiously onto the porch and began sifting through the splintered beams and bricks and roof shingles with the toes of their boots or their gun barrels. Stiles did not do so at random; he moved through the ruined house with a purpose. He stopped every few steps, stiffened, and swiveled his head like a hunting dog catching the scent. He picked at a pile of debris, first brushing aside the bricks and pulling at the fallen beams, then digging intensely, until Charlie joined in. They soon unearthed the fallen cellar door and, hidden beneath it, the partially caved-in staircase leading down into darkness. Stiles holstered one of the shotguns, drew a flashlight from his belt, and shined it down into the hole. From what they could see, the cellar was still intact.

''Is he down there?''

The soldier didn't answer. ''Stay close,'' was all he would say as he started down the fragile-looking steps.

"Now wait a minute," Bean complained, "I never said I was going down there. . . ." But Stiles was already disappearing into the darkness. The deputy looked around him and frowned. "You're an asshole, chum, I hope you know that." He racked the pump on the Mossberg, took out his own flashlight, and followed close behind.

His first impression was the chill. It was at least fifteen degrees colder down there, like a butcher's freezer. Bean's breath hung in front of his face like an arctic cloud, limiting what visibility he had. He was happy to reach the bottom and just be off the rickety stairs. He found Stiles already weaving a path through the decades of debris gathered there.

"Is he here?" Charlie whispered. "Do you feel him?"

"I don't know. It's faint, it's . . ." The soldier looked around, puzzled. "It's fading. But how? He couldn't have gotten out of here." He shined his light on the outside door to the cellar, found it still nailed shut and probably blocked by a ton of rubble as well. "He has to be here, Charlie," Stiles muttered in frustration. But then, suddenly, he tensed. He turned to the nearest wall and the crooked old bank of shelves that stood there, and without warning he raised his shotgun and fired. Compact thunder rolled through the cellar as the blast splintered two shelves and left a melon-sized hole in the thick back panel. It was certainly large enough to see through—not to a brick wall beyond, but to the blackness of a hidden passageway.

Bean helped him shoulder the creaking mass of wood aside and they shined their flashlights into the narrow opening. It revealed a cave-like chamber, dank and malodorous, the walls glistening with streams of seepage, and water standing in places on the floor. In its center was a table with thick ropes secured to the head and foot. "Oh, Lord," Stiles sighed as he inspected the ropes and saw how they had been snapped in haste. "He had someone down here. That's why he came back—for his reserve supply. Charlie, we can't let him feed!" He searched the chamber in earnest, found a crawlway opposite the entrance that was barely large enough for a grown man. But it didn't stop the soldier. He dropped to his hands and knees and scrambled into the darkness.

"Wait up, dammit!" Bean cursed, mostly for fear of losing his guide. He squeezed through as best he could, feeling particularly vulnerable in those tight quarters, but it was only a few feet before the crawlway opened into a much larger tunnel. He clambered to his feet to find Stiles standing nearby, looking about warily. It could have been a natural cavern—there were rock formations present, dribbling pale groundwater from the ceiling like mother's milk from limestone teats. But the cave roof was shored up in places, supported by big wooden beams that braced the ceiling and walls. "Well, this is something," the deputy said. "I never heard about any mine tunnels around here." He shined his light in either direction and saw that the passage split in two each way. "Well, at least you know how he got out ahead of the boys that night. Which way, Chris?"

"I don't know," Stiles sighed, and his shoulders sagged with the admission. "But he's definitely gone. I can't feel him anymore. And there's no telling where these tunnels end up. He could be anywhere. I fucked up, Charlie. He's already feeding again. Getting stronger. Damn!"

"Don't worry about it. We'll find him." Bean looked around. "Pretty old network, if you ask me. Could go anywhere. Too bad there's no one around these days who'd know just where."

Stiles glanced at him, and the deputy saw a gleam in his eyes. "Wait a minute," the soldier whispered, ushering Bean back through the crawlspace. He used both of their flashlights to illuminate the small chamber. The table and ropes had been moved there recently, but the rest of the debris present was older, much older, and gave the room a sense of identity. There was a smaller table, playroom size, with equally small chairs, all standing in a puddle of water and half-rotted. In the corner, a wooden box with an engraved lid was in much the same condition. There were rocking horses by the wall, two of them, each sitting crookedly on softening blades. Their wooden faces had grown whiskery with mildew. "Toys?" Stiles wondered aloud. "In a cave?"

Charlie accepted it all with a shrug. "Haven't you ever built a fort, Stiles? A clubhouse, someplace to hide out and play?" He looked around. "This would've made a really good one. If it didn't leak so much."

Stiles nodded. "Maybe it didn't, years back. This is connected to Danner's basement, remember?" He was standing by a rocky shelf in the wall, cluttered with odds and ends, the cast-offs of childhood. The shelf was dry and some of the things had escaped the ravages of mildew, like the wooden box perched there. Its exterior, like the horses, had grown green and fuzzy, but the interior still held little wooden cowboys and their horses, remarkably well preserved. The troop of cavalry soldiers, complete with bugler, were hand-carved and painted, and left with an endearing lack of detail. There were two of each soldier. He put them back and rummaged through the other things on the shelf, the two harmonicas, the slingshots, the toy six-shooters. Two of each. Two of everything. Even the books. Their time-worn covers were all curled and yellow, all but indistinguishable from one another. He could barely identify titles like *Treasure Island* and *The Adventures of Huckleberry Finn*, the usual adventures of youth, although most children don't enjoy first editions. Beneath them he found two copies of a school primer in somewhat better condition—at least it didn't crumble in his hands. He flipped open the parchment-like cover of one. In bold, young letters, the name *Sebastian Danner* was hand-printed. "We were right. This was Danner's playground."

He picked up the other, opened the cover. On the inside, in a slightly less legible scrawl, was *Nathan Danner*.

Bean caught the change in his expression. "What? What is it?"

Stiles grinned wryly, satisfied that the pieces were finally falling into place. The walled-up prison, partially disinterred. The old man Del saw in the woods. Two of every toy. "Maybe there is someone we can ask about the tunnels," he said, opening up the toy-soldier case. He held out two identical officers. "Don't you get it? Twins."

Chapter Eighteen

The residents of the Shady Rest boardinghouse gathered in the parlor at nearly one in the morning. All were dressed in their pajamas and robes, but none could sleep. Not with the peculiar happenings in the town below.

"It was strange enough with the phone dead all day," Jessie Shively said, sitting on the arm of Ida Fleming's chair and wringing her hands unconsciously. "But now, with someone lightin' off fireworks at this hour—"

"Fireworks, you say?" Jim Taggart grunted without knowing what the hell they were talking about.

"Wasn't fireworks, Jessie," Hubert said as he peered out the window. "Those were gunshots. And those explosions . . . well, who knows what that was all about."

George Bailey had a pretty good idea. But he sank into his chair and said nothing.

Why hadn't he done something before now? he wondered. He knew what was happening, what was going to happen. But he just cowered and hid his head, just as he'd always done. It was just a matter of time now, he thought. Till his nightmares came up the hill. He and the others had been lucky so far—he figured those things had been too busy preying on their own families and friends to think of the old house on the hill and its forgotten lodgers. But that would change. *Tomorrow we move*, he decided. *Tomorrow we get a car and we leave this place, this town, this entire state*. . . .

"Hey," Hubert said, leaning closer to the window. "I think I saw someone out there."

Bailey's eyes widened.

Jessie moved alongside the towering Mr. Ranall. "Where? I don't see anyone."

"Out there by the trees." He turned toward the door. "I'll just go see who it is."

"NO!" Bailey snapped, lumbering out of his chair. His stridency gave them pause. He went to the window and pulled down the shade. "Nobody goes outside."

"Why not, George?" Hubert wanted to know. "We can't just stay in here. I just want to find out what the hell's going on."

"Just wait till morning," the older man asked plaintively. "Please."

The doorbell rang.

Avina Atchison came down the hall from the kitchen and poked her hairnetted head through the parlor doors. "Who on earth could that be at this hour?" She headed for the door.

"Don't answer it!" Bailey wailed, racing to catch her.

He reached the hall just as the landlady was opening the door, nudging her aside even as he reached into his robe and drew forth his big rosewood cross. He thrust it through the open doorway at the figures there and commanded, "Get back! You are not invited, I do not invite you here! Get back!"

A hand reached out and plucked the crucifix from his grasp. "You won't need this, Mr. Bailey," Charlie Bean told him. "We just need to ask a few questions."

"Deputy!" Avina exclaimed, ushering him and his associate into the house. Then her eyes shifted to Stiles's black-and-blue face. "Good Lord, what's going on?" Hubert and Jessie came out into the hall just then. Ida stayed seated. Jim stayed asleep.

"What were all those gunshots, deputy?" Hubert asked before noticing that each man carried a shotgun. "What is this? Are we under seige?"

"You could say that," Charlie nodded. He looked at George. "We need to talk to you, Mr. Bailey. It's important."

The old man recognized the beaten-up Stiles from that night at the diner. He knew what this would be about. "Come to the dining room," he said softly. Then, to the rest of them, he warned, "Don't nobody open that door again, you hear me? Nobody!"

They followed him down the hall and into the dining room, where he turned to them with a look of resignation. "You know, don't you?"

Stiles nodded. "Who you are . . . but not which one."

Bailey sat down at the table wearily. "A long time ago," he told them, "my name was Sebastian Danner. I take it you've met my brother, Nathan."

"Oh, yeah," Bean said. "We thought he was you."

"A lot of people used to confuse us," he told them. His face was etched darkly with the remembrance, but the words flowed nonetheless. They had been held inside too long. "But we weren't nothing alike. Not inside, where it counts. There was always something wrong about Nate. Something bad. You know, the happiest day of my life was when he left here. He didn't tell anyone where he was going, not me, not our parents. He just left. And mind you, they didn't say so, but they breathed a great sigh of relief as well. It was like a weight had left our shoulders, freeing us. Well, our father got sick not long after that and died the next year and Mother the year after that. But Nathan didn't come back for either funeral. He may not have known about it, but I doubt it would've changed anything. He was just like that. I finally convinced myself to get on with my life, that Nate was dead. And in a way, I guess I was right.

"I was married not long after that." His eyes misted, and he turned away to hide it. "We'd made big plans. We were both of a mind for a large family. Lynn Anne was even carrying our first when I went away to Indianapolis on business. But while I was away, Nathan came home. She didn't realize it wasn't me, not until . . ." His voice cracked. The memories were vivid, even after so many years. "When I came back a couple of nights later, I found her waiting for me. In our bed! Lord God, laying her to rest was the hardest thing I have ever done. Ever completed, at least. Aw, but you were with me then, weren't you, Lord? It was with His hand on my shoulder that I hunted down Nate's other victims, his servants, and I killed them all, and then I found him too and he begged and pleaded for me not to destroy him then and there, and . . . And before God, I could not carry it through. We were . . . are twins. Despite it all, there has always been that bond between us, that damning tie. I mean, he was dark, evil. He had murdered my wife. But somehow, deep down, I still loved him. I imagine it's difficult to understand how two brothers can hate so well yet love so much."

Stiles said nothing. Bean continued the questioning. "So instead you walled him up in the basement."

Bailey nodded. "What else could I do? I couldn't just let him go, not after what he'd done to Lynn Anne. But I couldn't destroy him either. So I imprisoned him in the basement, and then I ran as far and as fast as I could. And I tried to forget. I went to Chicago, and then to the coast, and finally to Europe. I ran for forty years, afraid to come home, afraid to face myself, what I'd done. But always, down deep, I knew it was up to me. It was my responsibility. That was why I established a trust to take care of the house over all those years, and it's what made me come back in the long run. But I didn't want to be connected to that place or even that name. So I took George Bailey from a movie, and I moved back to town and I tried to work up the courage to finish the job, once and for all. But while I stammered and stalled, the years slipped by. I went out there maybe a hundred times, but I could never get past the basement door. I could feel him down there. Waiting.

"I stalled as long as I could. I kept secretly hoping I would die first and then the responsibility would be taken from my shoulders. But then the trust petered out and the land was condemned and they started talking about eminent domain and a housing addition—I knew I had to finish it once and for all, before any of that got started. Before they freed him. So I went back out there Friday night and I was determined this time and I . . . almost did it. I began to dismantle the wall and I was about halfway through when I heard him in there. He was scratching at the other side, digging, freeing himself. I froze. I peed in my pants, too. And I ran. Again."

Stiles had already figured as much out. "You came across the Miller boys in the woods, didn't you? It all fits. Well, let me fill you in, Mr. Danner. Your brother is out. He's taken about half of Isherwood already, and unless we stop him he'll take it all. Now, where do the tunnels under Danner House lead?"

Bailey's face slackened. "The tunnels? Lord, it's been seventy years, friend. I don't think I . . . Nope, I can't remember. I've slept since then, you know."

"Nathan hasn't."

That sobered the old man. He searched his hazy memory. "It's been so long. As I recall, one led to the caretaker's shack at the edge of the property, and one may have went to the

Hancock land, just the other side of ours. And then . . . oh, let me see now—''

The unexpected peal of the doorbell echoed through the house. It rung a second time and then a third, impatiently. The three men looked at each other, but there was no need for words. Their expressions conveyed their panic. With no more thought, Bean and Stiles were through the dining room, heading down the hallway. They could already hear voices up ahead.

Mrs. Atchison. ''Well, I never. It's like Grand Central Station around here.''

The squeak of a wheelchair. Uncle Jim's croaking Hoosier twang. ''Don't worry, Viney. Ah'll git it.''

The door unlatched.

Bean and Stiles broke into a run.

Cold and hollow, a lifeless belch of a voice. ''Our car broke down. Can we use your phone?''

. . . almost to the entry hall . . .

The old man's laugh. ''Sure. Y'all come on in.''

Y'all. You all. Every one of you.

No!

Stiles burst into the lobbylike entry just as a woman's scream rang out, shrill and piercing straight to the spine. Avina Atchison was on the floor, struggling with a young man clad in dirty pajamas. A crimson stream was already jetting from the open punctures in her throat, and the vampire scrambled to get his mouth back over the rampant fountain. Stiles's boot abruptly sank into the side of his skull and tore him from her. The creature recovered quickly, but received a second blow for its trouble, this one a side kick to the sternum that nearly knocked it through the only window in the hall. Stiles's shotgun rectified the matter, blasting the fiend through in a shower of tinkling glass.

Charlie brushed past him and went straight for the door, which was standing wide open. Facing it was Uncle Jim's wheelchair, and perched on top of him was an older female in a slip that let ample amounts of white flesh peak out in all directions. Her face was buried in the old man's neck, and the sucking sounds were enough to chill the deputy to the marrow. He raised the Mossberg to within inches of her side and fired. The silver buckshot knocked her from the wheelchair to the floor, where she lay convulsing on the threshold. Bean checked Uncle Jim. Saliva seeped from the corner of his mouth, and his eyes were glazed and unseeing. The attack itself had not killed him, but the resulting coronary had.

Bean kicked the dying vampire out onto the porch and pulled the door shut, but not before glimpsing the scene outside. There were three or four more coming across the front lawn, their faces lit with rapacious hunger. But that wasn't what caught his attention. There were more figures coming up Moffit Trail, barely silhouetted against the few lights of the town. Charlie's jaw dropped. There was a horde of them, at least twenty, maybe more.

Y'all come on in.

Every one of you.

"Christ," he muttered. "Stiles! They're coming!"

"Who's coming?" asked Hubert Ranall as Bean hurried back across the entry hall. The lanky black man was leaning over the shocked and muttering Mrs. Atchison while Jessie Shively tried to stem the flow of blood from the landlady's throat. Ida Moore was just coming through the parlor door on her walker, nervously fingering the small crucifix from her housecoat pocket. Hubert was persistent. "Deputy, who is this guy?" he motioned to Stiles. "What the hell is going on here?"

The soldier was a blur of motion as he moved from room to room, overturning tables, piling them on top of one another in front of the windows of the parlor. "Lend us a hand," he said. "Block the doors, the windows, with anything you can find—"

"What is it!" Ida was frantic. "What's out there?!" When neither of the men answered, the seniors went to the shattered window themselves. There they saw the army of shadows coming up the hill. "Oh, my lord," Mrs. Fleming squeaked breathlessly, clutching at her heart. "Who is that out there? What do they want?"

"Vampires," said George Bailey from behind them.

"Look, mister!" Hubert barked back at him. "This ain't no time for your bullshit. What're you trying to do, scare these ladies?" He peered back out the window. "What the hell is going on out there?"

A head popped up into the window, a negative image of Hubert, pale white to his black, mad to his sane. The three of them were too shocked to move, not just by the sudden appearance of the face, but by the familiarity of it. It looked a bit like Pooch Harrison from the hardware store. But it was a caricature of him, a cartoon figure with a bear trap in his mouth and a long white arm that snaked in through the window. It reached for Hubert's throat but suddenly the old man wasn't there, suddenly it was Stiles brushing past them and pinning the arm to the window frame with his boot. "Suck on this," he said and fired point-blank. Pooch grunted from the impact and disappeared from view.

"It's okay now," Stiles called to them. "Help me block this window, and . . ." He turned to find his allies retreating in every direction. Jessie Shively disappeared down the hallway and lanky old Hubert went lumbering up the stairs, taking them two at a time. Ida Fleming hobbled only as far as the stairs before collapsing, unable to even climb into her chair lift. She sat there on the steps, gasping, clutching the cross to her breast. George Bailey still cowered in the corner, his expression slack, his sanity questionable. "Just great," Stiles muttered as he shouldered a bureau into place against the window. "Looks like it's just you and me, Charlie."

"Can't blame 'em, can you?" the deputy called from inside the parlor. He dumped a coffee table and shoved it toward the nearest uncovered window, just as a crash came from the rear of the house. Stiles must have heard it too, for he started in that direction but Bean waved him off. "I've got it," he called, then stalked into the dining room, Mossberg first. Nothing. The room was empty, inviolate, the small accent windows high on the wall as yet unbroken. His eyes moved to the saloon doors to the kitchen, just as the sound of breaking glass reached his ears.

He burst through the doors with his shotgun ready and found a slight form squeezing through the small window over the sink. It was a young woman. Her jeans and blouse were earth-stained, and her long black hair was matted into a thicket before her face. She growled with anticipation as one leg cleared the window and stepped down into the dirty dishes. The other came through and she fell butt first into the sink and scrambled for balance.

"Stay the hell out!" Bean barked, swinging the Mossberg. The heavy buttstock made a sickening sound when it struck, like an ax hitting soft wood, and the vampire flopped back across the counter and spilled to the kitchen floor in a limp pile. With a round already chambered, the deputy leveled his gun at the hip.

The girl looked up.

And he froze. "Oh, my Lord," he muttered, unable to keep the tears from welling. "Oh, goddamn it, no!"

Susie's face was not feral. Not for the moment. She looked frightened and hurt, and tears filled her eyes as well. Empty, soulless eyes. "You hurt me, Charlie," she stammered, fingering the divot his buttstock had left in her forehead. "How can you hurt me like that? I've always loved you, Charlie, but you shit on me. You left me out there. With them."

"Susie, I didn't know, I swear . . ."

She smiled on him with pity. "It's all right now, honey," she soothed, but her tone betrayed any heartfelt words or expression. "I still love you, baby. I still want you. Ooh, do I want you!" She stood and held out her arms to him. "Baby'll make it all better."

"Just stay back, Susie," he stammered. "Please . . . for the love of God, just stay back!" When she took a step he reluctantly raised the shotgun. "Please . . ." His finger tensed on the trigger.

Susie took the barrel of the gun and placed it directly between her heaving breasts. "Then do it," she told him. "I said do it, Charlie." And then, almost under her breath, she whispered, "Please." But Bean's finger was locked on the trigger. It wouldn't bend. His big frame was racked with sobs, and her smile came back in response. She took the gun from his numb, shaking hands. "I know you too well, lover," she said and pulled him to her. And in that moment he saw her, really saw her as she now was. Her empty eyes were suddenly afire and her panting was hot and noxious on his face and neck, and her lips, those full pouting lips he'd always loved so, were thinned to translucence over the multitude of teeth behind them. It was a mockery of her, a Gahan Wilson portrait of his beloved Susan. And it was going to kill him.

He caught her by the throat and tried to hold her back. She growled and wrenched his arm aside so viciously that both bones of his forearm snapped clear through. He did not even have time to cry out; she slammed him backward into the refrigerator and they both slid to the floor, Susie on top. He found his voice only when her teeth sank into his throat

The saloon doors swung open in answer to the garbled cries. "You let him go right now!" Jessie Shively yelled. She slapped at the young woman atop Charlie, pulled at her and grabbed whole handfuls of hair to try wrenching her aside. But the creature wouldn't budge from her prey. In desperation Mrs. Shively grabbed for the closest thing within reach, a revolving spice rack on the counter, and slammed it down on the vampire's head. Several of the jars burst from the impact, showering herbs over the three of them.

Susie jerked upright, suddenly rigid, spitting flecks of Charlie's blood across the refrigerator's white enamel. She turned toward the old woman with a hiss, but then her eyes rolled back into her head, and Jessie realized that the hissing she heard was actually the sizzle of burning flesh. Acrid smoke rose from the creature's scalp and shoulders as she rolled away from Bean and began to convulse on the kitchen floor, spewing what little blood she'd had time to ingest. Jessie turned away, and for the first time she noticed Bean's shotgun on the floor. She bent with trouble, but managed to pick up the Mossberg and fired from the hip, just as her husband had shown her years ago on the farm. The silver hit home. Susie finally died.

Charlie was moaning on the floor, cradling his arm while blood squirted out onto his collar and down his front. He recoiled and tried to scoot away when Jessie touched him, but her soft, motherly voice was soothing. "There, there, you'll be all right now." She pulled a dishtowel from the counter, wadded it, and stuck it between his collar and the wound, then tilted his head over against it. "Charlie, can you hear me?"

He blinked his eyes and finally looked at her. "Go on," he whispered. "Go help Stiles."

She drew the revolver from his belt and put it in his good hand, then used the shotgun as a cane to help her stand. "I'll find your friend," she assured him as she started for the door. But she kicked something in passing. Part of the Durkee's garlic powder jar lay at her feet, shattered but with a small amount of the herb intact. So that was what did it! She picked it up and sprinkled the powder all along the windowsill. "That should slow them down," she said before hurrying back into the hall.

There was a great racket up ahead. The thunder of Stiles's shotgun echoed through the house two, three more times. She moved as fast as her stiff legs could carry her and found the door torn from its hinges and several men and women, at least six or seven, gathered around the base of the stairs, hissing like a den of vipers. Ida was still on those stairs, gasping and clutching her chest, but they did not move toward her. The cross in her hand held them at bay. Instead, their attention was centered on the man in their midst, Stiles, who used his empty shotgun like a club and threw blurring kicks just like in those kung-fu movies she'd watched with Ida on channel four late at night. But for all his efforts, nothing seemed to stop them. They were closing in.

The one nearest her was a workman—at least his uniform was gray and sported the name SPENCE over his left breast—and when his head swiveled toward her and his eyes flashed silver, she almost jumped out of her skin. The shotgun went off before she realized her finger was on the trigger, and it sprayed Spence's legs with silver and the woman next to him as well. They both fell to the floor and cried out, clawing at the fire in their own flesh. The rest of the vampires turned, saw her and what she had wrought, and the struggle between hunger and caution was evident in their faces.

Stiles dropped to one knee and fumbled for the spare shells in his coat pocket, cursing himself for leaving the other Remington out in the van. He thumbed two into the chamber and groped for a third when a hand caught his shoulder and spun him around, and another closed on his throat. The man holding him was big and looked nearly as bad as Dutch Larson had the previous night. Much of his face and torso had been peppered with gunfire, but it obviously had failed to stop him. "Yer dead, bo-ah," he said in the dialect of all Hoosier vampires, and opened his mouth extra wide to show a collection of gold fillings along with his tapered incisors. He drew the soldier in and bit down. But his jaws did not close on the soft throat he had expected. They clamped on something hard: the twin barrels of an old Japanese Very pistol that had been thrust over Stiles's shoulder. Before he could back off, Hubert pulled both triggers. One round fizzled from age, but the other ignited on cue and sent twenty-eight millimeters of phosphorous rocketing down the creature's gullet. He gagged and staggered back, but then his chest lit up from the inside like a Chinese lantern and he ran through the doorway and out into the night. His screams hung in the air behind him.

The big black man granted himself a nervous smile as he broke open the flare gun and loaded it from the old canvas bag over his shoulder. "Banzai!" he called. He was wearing the same helmet he'd worn on Okinawa in '45, and in the belt of his housecoat was another trophy from the war, a sheathed samurai sword. "Reload that shotgun fast, son," he told the other soldier. "I don't think this'll stop 'em for long."

"It won't have to," said Ida Fleming. She was forcing herself up from the steps, still wheezing and obviously unsteady. But there was a steely resolve in her eyes, a purpose. She held out her crucifix, and the undead, to a man and woman, stopped in their tracks. They turned away quickly, and even the wounded ones on the floor started dragging themselves toward the door. Hubert went to help her and the two of them advanced on the invaders, pushing them back, forcing them to retreat. When the vampires were herded together near the door, Stiles and Jessie opened fire. The creatures screamed and dropped and clawed one another to get across the threshold. Only one of them made it.

Ida slumped in Hubert's arms. She looked pale, and was twisting her robe just over her heart. "Somebody help me get her into the parlor," he called, but Stiles caught his shoulder.

"Get her to the door," he whispered.

They carried her there. The front door was standing propped against the wall, torn completely from its hinges by the weight of all those surging bodies. "There ain't no way we'll ever get this back up," Hubert told him, "let alone lock it."

"We may not have to," the soldier replied. He shoved the dead bodies back onto the porch and out of the way, then lifted the door and scooted it back into place. When he finished, he pointed to Ida's crucifix and motioned for her to put it in the small portal window of the door, in plain view from the outside. The diminutive old woman strained to reach it, but did as he asked. "That will keep them out," she whispered, more a question than anything else.

"This door at least," Stiles told her. He peeked through the window. The horde was still coming up the hill, a block or two away. ''Grandma,'' he said to Ida, ''you have other things like this cross? Other religious items?''

''Yes . . . up in my room.''

He stooped to look into her eyes. ''Then you have to help us now. We need to use those things to seal the doors and windows. We need your faith. Are you up to it?''

The old woman managed a weak smile. ''You 'uns just get me around. I'll manage.''

The two men all but picked up Mrs. Fleming off the floor and started up the staircase. Stiles glanced back over his shoulder at Jessie. ''Find Charlie, see if he's—''

''I'm okay,'' Deputy Bean said as he staggered down the main hallway, looking like hell. He was still pinching the bloody towel between his neck and shoulder, and his left forearm was bent at a crazy angle. He tried to smile in the face of it all, but his eyes betrayed his pain, both physical and otherwise. He sagged against the wall and slid onto his butt. ''Get going,'' he waved them on. ''I'll be all right.'' Stiles nodded and they continued their climb.

Jessie went over to help Charlie up. ''How are we doing?'' he asked, looking around. ''Where's the landlady? She was right here by the stairs earlier—''

''She's dead,'' said a weak voice from across the hall. George Bailey was hunched down behind the only real furniture in the room, a tall-backed sitting chair, and only now did he dare to come out. He still clutched his cross to his chest. ''They took her while you 'uns were fighting. Dragged her right out the door. I saw it.''

Bean stared at him, waiting for an excuse. ''And why didn't you stop them?''

The old man's gaze fell to his slippers. The cross hung limp in his hand. There was no answer. None that would explain.

Mrs. Shively helped the deputy up and into the parlor, where he collapsed on the couch. Then she fetched a first-aid kit and a half-full bottle of whisky from Mrs. Atchison's cupboard. She gave Bean a few stiff belts and took one herself, then splashed a little on the wounds in his neck. He stiffened, but didn't make a sound as she put gauze over them and taped it into place. He just reached for the bottle again.

There were sounds outside now, growing louder as they approached the house. Voices.

Stiles and Hubert finally came into the parlor, still carrying Mrs. Fleming between them. "They're almost here," Stiles reported. They went to both windows and moved the furniture aside just enough for the old woman to hang a picture of Jesus painted on velvet in one window and a "One Set of Footprints" commemorative plaque in the other. Then, finished, they sat her gently in her recliner near the television. She looked as if she might pass out at any minute. Hubert got her a glass of water and the bottle of medicine from the pocket of her housecoat. Then he motioned for Stiles to follow him out into the hall. Bean roused from the couch and staggered after them.

"Mister," the old black man confessed in a whisper, "I don't know a hell of a lot about what's going on here, and I ain't even sure of what those things are out there. But you two look like you know the score. So I'm asking you. How long do you think Ida's little things, her knickknacks, are gonna hold 'em out?"

The soldier shrugged. "That I don't know. Her faith appears to be pretty strong, but physically . . . You saw her, friend. She looks like she might slip at any time. And when that happens, we'd better be prepared for another fight." He held up his shotgun. "Charlie, where'd you put the other bandoliers?"

Bean's face drained of color. "Uh oh," he groaned. "I thought you had them. They must be—"

"Still in the van," Stiles sighed. He rubbed his face tiredly as he listened to the sounds outside, the muffled, lifeless voices of the night. "Dammit, we need that silver!"

"What do we do now?"

"Well," he sighed, forcing Charlie back into the parlor, "first, you're going to yell like hell while I set your arm. And then," he glanced over his shoulder at the window, "I suppose I'll be taking a little walk."

"I just can't take this any longer," the woman was saying, or ranting, since it was the fifth time in fifteen minutes that she'd said it. Everyone was scared, naturally, but she gave her hysteria a voice, a wheedling, irritating voice that had tempers in the basement flaring. Billie did not know who she was but had seen her a time or two in the IGA and once at the Laundromat. Her last name was Helton, and she always seemed a nice, quiet woman on the surface. Billie tried to remember that every time her present incarnation started to blabber, and it kept her from knocking Mrs. Helton on her ass.

"I tell you, I just can't take much more of this. . . ."

Ted Cooper must have been on much the same wavelength. "Hey, lady," he finally snapped. "Why don't you just sit down and shut the fuck up. You're not the only one in this, okay?" Some of the others grunted their agreement. Mrs. Helton looked indignant (obviously she wasn't frightened enough to forget her pride) but she did sit down and stay quiet. For a few minutes at least.

The silence came back for a time, and Billie wondered which was worse, it or the bitching. Because when it grew quiet they could hear the other sounds from outside. The barely audible cry of a baby—probably from the other basement, where most of the children had been put. The distant pop of gunfire. Running feet. Nails clicking against the small access window in the rear wall. The wiggling of the door handle. The voices, man and child alike. They spoke in furtive whispers, wondering who might be in there, occasionally being right. And they would plead to be let in. The door muffled some of it but not enough. Still, no one moved to answer them. Not even Ted, when Doreen Moody's sultry voice begged him. The knuckles whitened on the shotgun across his lap and his eyes moistened in the dim glow of the overhead bulbs, but he did not respond. And finally the voices went away.

There was more gunfire in the distance, like firecrackers on the Fourth, and each flayed Billie's nerves a little more. *Oh, Chris.* "Bart," she said softly.

"Yeah, Mom."

"Didn't you bring a radio?"

"Yeah, in my backpack."

"I think we need something to listen to." He looked questioningly toward the door, but she just shrugged. "They already know we're here. It can't hurt."

The teenager lifted the flap of the backpack beside him and eased out a miniature boom box, then extended the antenna and turned it on. The speaker crackled and then broke in on the fading lyrics of "In the Air Tonight." The announcer for the FM station out of Bloomington came on, a soft deep voice suitably laid back for the time of night. "And that was, of course, Phil Collins, a man who can do no wrong in my book . . . well, other than "Sussudio," right? It's one-twenty-five in the A.M. here at the Power, and the temperature's bottomed out at a chilly forty-nine degrees, but it's just a beautiful night out there, isn't it? Just a wisp of fog and that big, bright moon up there, big as a basketball. This is the kinda night you just want to throw a blanket 'round your shoulders and go out on the porch with a hot cup of coffee and breath in that crisp, clean air. But hey, don't forget to take the radio, huh? You wouldn't want to forget us. The extended forecast says that nights will continue to be a little nippy on into the weekend, so if you have to be out after dark . . . take a jacket, okay? Now, from the request line, let's jump back a few years with the Doobie Brothers. . . ."

The door handle jiggled again. Someone said something outside. But most of them listened to the music and were able to ignore it.

Del scooted over by his big brother and wasn't ashamed to scrunch up against him. Bart put an arm about his shoulders. "Cold?"

"Scared."

"Join the club."

The younger boy searched his drugstore sack for a moment, came up with a Mounds bar. He handed a piece to Bart. "What if, you know?"

"What if what?"

"What if they get in here? Could we hold them off?"

Bart jerked a thumb toward the shotgun propped beside him, then motioned to the one Ted held and their mom's as well. "We can take 'em. Don't worry about it, Cap."

"But I am worried. What if there's too many of them or something like that? What if we can't win?"

"And what if the Ruskies attack before morning? Then nothing'll matter anyway, will it? C'mon, Cap. Stop borrowing trouble."

The boy sniffed. "I just don't want to die. Not like that."

Bart squeezed his shoulders. "Don't worry. If it comes down to it, none of us'll go out that way." He lifted his backpack gently onto his lap, carefully so nothing clattered, and opened it. Inside were six or seven Little Kings bottles, corked, the stoppers threaded with a length of rag. The stench of gasoline was heavy in the pack.

Del sat back against the wall. It hadn't made him feel any better. He wagered that roasting would hurt just about as bad.

Chapter Nineteen

Charlie tried to argue but the pain kept getting in the way. He was still on the couch, his neck still stinging, his arm splinted with a broken broomstick and heavy strips of gauze. He fidgeted not only from discomfort, but from disgust—he wanted to go with Stiles, and not being able to rankled him. "Well, at least take one of the guns," he said. "You can't go out unarmed. That'd be suicide."

Stiles folded his overcoat and placed it atop the console television next to his shoulder rig and twin Smith & Wesson semi-autos. His shotgun was there as well. Between it and the Mossberg that Jessie nestled in the crook of her arm, there were exactly three silver shells left. "Let's be logical, Charlie. If I get caught out there, whatever guns I'm carrying will be useless to you people. Keep them in here, where they'll do the most good. Besides," he pulled his black knit cap down around his ears, "my other shotgun's in the van. If I can get to it."

"That's a big if," Bean grumbled.

"Mr. Stiles?" Ida Fleming called weakly from her recliner. She looked no better than before, maybe even a little worse. But there was a dreamy look to her eyes—not one of distance or senility, not by a long shot. She was very alert, and her gaze was lit with a personal satisfaction, a sense of victory. Her faith had finally been put to the test. Vindicated. Now, if only she could hold on . . . She reached up a trembling hand and took one of his, placed a small cross in his palm. "This will protect you," she said, smiling.

He looked at it and nodded, returning her smile. He also gave her back the symbol. "Keep it with you, Grandma. It only has its power when it's with you."

"But don't you believe by now? After all you've seen tonight?"

"I've seen it all before," he answered, "some even wilder than this. And I do believe, really. In goodness. Truth. In people like you. But I just don't have what it takes, I guess. Faith, true faith, isn't something you can give to someone like a library book, and you can't just decide it would be nice to have. It doesn't work like that—believe me, I've tried." He touched his chest. "It has to come from in here. You have it." He leaned closer. "If you can stay with us and stay strong, you can watch over all of us. All of them. I know you're tired, but you have to hold out. For them. Can you do that, Grandma?"

She sank back into the chair, grimacing and clutching her heart, but once the pain eased she managed a wink. "I'll be here, sonny boy. Don't you worry."

Just then Hubert came back into the parlor, having been the last of the residents to change their pajamas for warmer things to combat the new chill in the house. He was now in dungarees and a jacket, complete with combat medals from the Pacific. His helmet was still in place, and the Very pistol and sword as well. Stiles's eyes centered on the latter. "Is that the real thing?"

"You bet," he said, drawing the wooden scabbard from his belt and handing it over. "Took that off a Nip officer during my second month at Okinawa." He watched Stiles draw the three-foot blade and beamed like a proud father. "Now watch that edge—I keep 'er pretty sharp."

Stiles stepped back and took a few practice slashes in the air. It was obvious to all present that he'd had some experience with similar blades. Then he returned it to its sheath. "Do you mind if I borrow this for a few minutes?"

Hubert shrugged. "Go ahead, if it'll help you get through. You are going for help, aren't you?"

"He already explained that, Hubert," Jessie scolded him. "There ain't anyone left in town to call, and we can't bring anybody else here or they'll just become . . . well, like those things out there. We just gotta stay put, wait for morning. Mr. Stiles is just going for more of them silver shells."

"Oh. Well, maybe I'd better go with you. . . ."

"I don't think so," Stiles said, patting the man's shoulder. "One might get through, but not two. Besides, with the deputy laid up, it's up to you and Jessie to keep them out, okay?"

Hubert grinned and saluted. "Yessir. Don't you worry about a thing. This station will stay secure. You bet." He glanced toward the window. "I've got a question, though. Just how're you gonna get out without them seeing you?"

"That's what I've been asking myself. I'd say they'll be watching the doors and the windows down here. My better bet is upstairs." He loosened the braid wound ceremoniously around the scabbard and used it to strap the sword across his back.

Deputy Bean propped himself on his good arm and called to Chris. "I still think it's a damn fool plan," he said, "and the whole thing leaves a dark brown taste in my mouth. But there ain't much I can do to stop you. So what I can do is wish you luck. And if you come back in here with teeth to your knees, I promise to kill you proper."

Stiles nodded and gave a thumbs-up, then left the parlor.

His mind was working, hatching a plan as he climbed the stairs to the darkened second floor. He'd surveyed the house while taking Mrs. Fleming around, and now used that knowledge to gauge his best avenue of escape. He couldn't simply drop from a window, not in the open—it would be suicide. So that narrowed his choices to only two rooms, one in the front of the house and one in the back. Both had stout tree limbs within reach, and each had its advantages. The front window would be the riskier of the two, since the front yard was so well lit by the security lamp by the road. But it would put him out that much closer to the van. Perhaps it was worth the risk. He went there first.

The bedroom door opened to pitch darkness, thanks to the curtains that were still closed. But somehow Stiles sensed movement in there—the vibration in the air, or the whispery rustle of blanket and sheet. The bed. He turned and swept on the wall switch even as his other hand caught the hilt of the sword over his shoulder and drew it halfway from the scabbard. But the dim light of the overhead bulb showed the figure on the bed to be not some pasty cadaver but George Bailey. He was huddled back into the pillows and holding out a mason jar full of pee-colored liquid. In his other hand was a disposable lighter. The aroma of gasoline was heavy in the air and mixed with the stench of the garlic lining the window. The old man finally recognized Stiles and set the jar back on the nightstand, trying to slow his hyperventilating. The soldier just ignored him, went instead to the windows, and peaked past the curtains.

Through the limbs of the big elm out front, he could see the figures below, wandering around in the yard, calling out to the people in the house and mimicking what their dead minds recalled as enticing. A drunk offered a bottle he no longer drank from. A child held out his candy bar. A woman he recognized as Georgetta Stovall did a bump-and-grind just below the window in her jet black leather, rubbing her breasts and her crotch and moaning in monotone. Stiles found the scene distasteful and turned his attention to the van at the edge of the road, measuring the distance and the number of steps he would need, and the time. But then he noticed what he hadn't before. Bailey's window had been nailed shut. There was no way to break it loose without attracting attention. "Scratch one escape route," he whispered to himself. "Only one left." He started for the door.

"Mr. Stiles?" the old man on the bed croaked.

"Yes?"

"I just . . . well, I just wanted to say how sorry I am. About Mrs. Atchison. I liked her, you know. We weren't best friends, but she could be sweet when she wanted. She shouldn't have had to die like that."

"She didn't have to. You could have stopped it."

"I couldn't!" The veins in his neck stood out. "It was just like with Nathan. I couldn't move, I was rooted to the spot. All I could do was stand there and watch. I was so afraid . . . I'm afraid, dammit! Is that so hard to understand?!"

"I suppose not," Stiles said. "But then, you've been at it longer than the rest of us. You know, I feel sorry for you, Mr. Danner, I really do. You've been running for so long and dreading your nightmares for so many years that you've forgotten about anyone's life but your own. You're twice damned, Sebastian. Once by your brother. And once by yourself." He flipped off the lightswitch and closed the door behind him, leaving the old man alone in his own personal darkness.

Stiles went straight to the room farthest back. It was dark back there, even with the drapes open, and he didn't bother turning on the light. He went stealthily through Ida's room, past the autographed photos of Swaggart and Falwell and the holy bric-a-brac that covered the walls, and peeked through the window. It was dark out there, like the umbra of a distant planet. The big spruce that stood just a few feet beyond obscured the moonlight even more and left a zebra-stripe of shadows and dim light on the grass below. This was the place to leave from. But Stiles was still ill at ease. They could be out there, like sharks, circling, gliding just beneath the surface. Unseen until it's too late. He flipped the latch as quietly as possible and eased the window open and waited for nearly a minute for a response, but nothing came. He still couldn't see anyone out there. So he swung a leg up onto the outer sill and eased himself outside. The branch that reached closest to the window was part of the main trunk and half-again as thick as his thigh. He reached out and grabbed it and swung himself into space, and his throat caught when the branch began to sag. But then it stopped and held firm. He pulled his weight up onto it and slid along to the bough of the tree, one hand supporting his weight and keeping his balance, the other resting on the sword hilt over his shoulder. Still no one was in sight. So, little by little, he worked his way down, branch by branch, then dropped silently to the grass.

He moved to the corner of the house and peaked around. There was a female standing fifteen feet along, trying to work up the courage to approach one of the protected windows, and past her in a swirl of gathering fog were two more trying at another window and cursing their inability. *Now*, he wondered, *what's the best way to play this*?

The most obvious, of course.

He stepped around the corner into plain view, but he didn't run. He staggered along, imitating their own ambling gait as best he could, heading directly for the female and not around her. She glanced at him once but paid him little attention, not until he was much closer. But by then it was too late. The sword was drawn and already slicing toward her. By the time she reached up for her own throat, there was nothing to find but a stump.

The other two turned to look just as the female slumped to the ground. Stiles sprinted for them and slashed low as he passed the first, taking the vampire off at the knees. As it fell, he whirled on the second and took its head as cleanly as the girl and left its body staggering about as he rounded the next corner and headed across the front lawn.

His eyes scanned the yard, hoping to gauge the situation even as he acted on it. Six of them, maybe seven. At least the ones he could see. They turned casually as he ran past, surprise etched into the alabaster faces. It bought him a few extra seconds. A few more steps.

You're gonna make it, you're gonna make it . . .

A teenage boy and girl scrambled across the yard in a parallel path to his own, but as they approached the front gate they turned in and tried to intercept him. He held the sword against his side until the last minute, and as the boy groped at him he brought it up in a measured slash and sheared both arms off halfway to the elbow, then drove a kick into the boy's face to remove him from the path. The girl saw this and tried to slow her momentum but it was too late; it took her right into the arc of the blade. Her body slid to a stop, but her head kept going. And as her cadaver fell from Stiles's view, he found himself directly in front of the small wooden-slat gate to the property. No more than a few feet away, at the shoulder of the road, was rust-plagued salvation—the van.

The sound of many feet caused a realization to explode in his gut. The boy and girl hadn't thought to stop him. They were meant only to slow him down.

He started to turn. That was when they hit him.

He went down in a tangle of bodies, right through the gate and fence, splintering both. Stiles landed with two on top of him, but he quickly bridged and threw them over his head before their momentum was spent. He rolled with them and came up on top, clutching one of the jagged fence slats he'd landed on, and driving it through the top vampire with such force that it transfixed the one beneath him as well. Then two or more caught the soldier from behind and slammed him into the side door of the van with a jarring force that made his vision swim. Strong hands latched onto his throat and began to choke the fight from him even as others piled on top, man, woman, and child, all tugging and grabbing at him. One woman crawled over the rest and bit at his throat but her teeth found only the cold hands that held him.

Stiles reached, strained for the door latch.

The hands left his throat, and two mouths took their place.

He caught hold of the pull handle.

I hope you didn't lock it, Charlie. . . .

The sliding mechanism activated and the door panel moved beneath their weight, throwing the lot of them off balance and spilling Stiles and his immediate captors into the carpeted interior of the van. He twisted away from them for just an instant, and his hands found the spare Remington between the front seats, right where he'd left it. He drove the sawed-off handle into the nearest face he could find, then brought it across the jaw of the other female that had tumbled in with him. He shoved them back toward the door, then turned the yawning bore of the 12-gauge on them and blew them back onto the gravel and kept firing on the whole group. The vampires fell over one another trying to get away, and the shoulder of the road was littered with bodies by the time he hit an empty chamber. He jumped to the door and kicked a corpse aside so he could get it shut, then locked it and all the others too.

But the vampires were persistent. They were already pounding on the sides of the van.

He took the time right then to reload the shotgun, then drooped the extra bandoliers over his shoulders and, as an afterthought, picked up the Uzi from the counter and the H & K carbine from the bunk compartment. They didn't shoot silver, but they could still do their share of damage. He could never be overarmed.

The rest of the windshield shattered and a young boy tried crawling across the dash. A single blast sent him reeling back outside. Then the pounding on the vehicle increased, and it began to rock from side to side. *They're trying to turn it over!* He dumped his gear into the passenger seat and climbed in behind the wheel. The engine revved with the first turn of the key, so he slipped it into reverse and stomped on the gas and backed over a few of his attackers. And when he'd reached the middle of the road, he shifted into drive and steered the squealing vehicle straight at the front yard, plowing through what was left of the fence like a stampeding elephant, the van's wheels cutting furrows all the way across the lawn. He stopped it a few feet from the walk and swung out the door, weapons hanging from him like apples on the tree.

"Cocksucker," someone said from up close. He spun with the shotgun leveled, expecting attack, but the vampires were just coming back from the road and were wary of him now. The voice had to come again before he could trace it to its source, an older man on the ground by his feet who struggled and cussed but couldn't lift the van's front tire off his chest. The soldier just ignored him and went around the vehicle toward the porch.

They were gathering again—*Lord*, he thought, *how many of them are there!*—but they didn't charge him, now that he was armed. He'd left bodies all over the yard, and the gaping muzzle of the shotgun kept them at bay. Stiles backed up the walk, keeping all of them in sight.

Thud.

The weighty blow came out of nowhere and caught him in the middle of the back. It knocked the air from Stiles's lungs and drove him to his knees, and a second blow sent him farther down, onto his side and grimacing from the pain. The dark world spun madly and he could barely focus on the swaying figures looming above him, one face so scarred and bullet-ridden he could barely recognize it as Dutch Larson. Both he and his mousy wife were there, Dutch as animate as ever since Ladonna had climbed from her hiding place and pulled the silver cake knife from her husband's chest.

Dutch was leering down at him, saying, "Remember me, boy?" and then, just as suddenly, he was gone from Stiles's view. The soldier's ears were still ringing from Larson's blows, so he didn't hear the shotgun blast that dispatched him, nor the second that snatched poor Ladonna from her feet and pitched her atop her thrice-dead husband. Stiles didn't see anything but night sky until an even darker face leaned over him. "C'mon, Mr. Stiles," Hubert Ranall said as he pulled him to his feet. "I don't know how long we can keep them back."

"You just get moving," Jessie said, brandishing the deputy's smoking Mossberg. She picked up the weapons Stiles had dropped and followed them up the steps, keeping a wary eye on her neighbors until they were inside and the door shouldered back into place behind them.

Stiles all but collapsed onto the couch that Bean had vacated for him. It was as if that last beating had finally convinced his stubborn mind how injured he really was. His head pounded and his groin as well, and his arms and legs were leaden. Jessie immediately began dressing his newest wounds.

"Mr. Stiles?" Hubert was looking over the back of the couch at him, cradling one of the Remingtons against his chest. "What do we do now, Mr.—"

"*Stiles*!"

The soldier started. It was a young, forceful voice, and it made Stiles's spine shrivel. He did not need anyone to tell him where it came from or who it was. He already knew.

He waved Mrs. Shively away and motioned for Hubert to help him to the window.

There were more of them than ever, even after Stiles's assault. And Nathan Danner was standing out in the lead, now dressed in a bright red Adidas sweat suit and coming up the walk. Stiles blinked twice in disbelief. This was not the same man he'd been chasing all night . . . it couldn't be! This one did have Danner's mocking face, but it was even younger and stronger than before and completely unmarked. He stood tall and straight on uncrippled legs, and he was no longer missing an arm. And his cheeks were flushed with color, with blood.

Stiles was dumbstruck. It *was* Danner—completely regenerated in less than a single night!

"Son of a bitch," the soldier whispered. He was too far for the scatterguns to be effective, so he motioned for the H & K and flicked its setting to autofire and activated the laser sight. When he aimed, the dot danced along Danner's cheek, just as it had several nights past. But the vampire had obviously learned nothing from the experience. He just smiled. Even as the rifle burped to life. Even as the rounds ate up the side of his face.

He still smiled. Even as he healed himself.

No sooner had the excised tissue been blown away than new flesh began to form. It flowed into the wound channels like pale water until they were completely filled, until the face was as unblemished as before. "Do you see, Stiles?" he laughed.

"You've waited too long. I'm too powerful now. For you. For anyone."

He looked down at the bodies in front of him and with one hand lifted Dutch Larson's corpse by the back of the neck until the heavyset marshall's feet dangled above the walk. He stripped away Larson's shredded T-shirt and exposed the mangled flesh beneath. And with his free hand Danner began to dig into that fleshy chest, burrowing with his fingers until he found something, and then withdrawing it. His fingertips smoked as he held up the knot of silver for their inspection, and he refused to show any pain it caused him. His jaws were clenched as he methodically dug each piece from the marshall's chest, and in all that time the damning smile never left his face. When the last piece came out, Larson's eyes blinked open and he began to fidget in his master's grasp. Danner dropped him and turned to the parlor window as if to bow for his performance. "Come out, Stiles," he said. "We have unfinished business."

The four of them backed away from the window. All looked to Stiles for support, but they did not get it. It was the first time they had seen him visibly shaken. "What do we do now?" Hubert asked again.

Ida answered softly from her recliner, where she fingered the arms of her small cross. "We wait," she said. "And pray."

The voices were getting worse. Bart had turned up the radio three times already, but it still wouldn't drown them out. Mad, cackling laughter segued into pitiful moans and outright pleading. First a child's frightened voice, plaintive, cutting to the heart of all who listened. "Please, let me in," the girl said, "I can't find my mommy and there are bad men out here, please, let me in!" The occupants of the basement had looked from one to another, wondering how long they could hold out against such a pitiful plea. But then the child's wailing became a tantrum, the voice deepened, and whatever it was out there began spewing obscenities and hammering at the steel-reinforced door. *"Let me in, you fucking maggots, you pukes, let me in, you're dead anyway, all dead!"* But after a few minutes their assailant gave up, and the tirade stopped. Temporarily.

Billie was pouring a capful of coffee from her thermos to

soothe her jangled nerves when the next voice came. Unlike the others, it was barely a whisper, and hardly anyone heard it at first. Ted had to bring it to Billie's attention. "Mrs. Miller?" he motioned to her from his crate-seat by the door. "I hear another one out there."

She was irritable as were they all. "So what?" she snapped.

"This one's calling for you."

She started, spilling her coffee. The thought of it, the personalizing of it, sent shivers up her spine. But it also raised a macabre sort of curiosity in her. She picked up her shotgun and started for the door.

Del caught her pantleg. "Don't open it, Mom."

"I won't, honey. I'll be right back."

She went over, knelt by Ted Cooper, and listened. It was very slight, a hushed, urgent voice she could barely make out. But she did hear her name. "Billie," it said. "Billie Miller, you in there?"

"Bart, turn the radio down," she called, and the older boy complied. In the resulting silence, even through the door, the whisper was magnified. It was female, as far as Billie could determine. Oddly familiar.

"Billie? It's me, Carol Gastineau. I can't talk too loud, they'll find me. . . ."

"What do you want?" Billie said flatly. It felt wrong speaking back but it mattered little, since they obviously knew they were there.

"I've just come to tell you, Sharon Lou is in a lot of trouble. She needs your help."

"What's wrong with Sharon?"

The whisper grew perturbed. "Don't dillydally, girl, she really needs you."

"Where is she?"

"The drugstore. She's at the store, and she's trapped."

Billie looked at Ted. The store? "How long as she been there?"

A pause. "All night."

"Liar!" Billie screamed through the door. "I left her at her house just before dark. You haven't seen her at all, have you? Have you!"

There was no answer this time.

Ted snorted. "Way to go, Billie," he said with a frown. "You just told her where to find Mrs. Moore."

Billie's heart shriveled at his words. "Oh, Lord," she said, reaching for the door bolt but Ted got to it before her and held it firm. She hammered helplessly against the steel and yelled, "Carol! Don't you touch her! Don't you dare touch her!" Ted finally had to wrestle her away from the door and take her back across the basement. Del and Bart helped her to sit down. "What have I done?" was all she could sob. "What have I done?"

Thunder cracked suddenly, close by, just beyond the basement wall. It came again, three times. Gunfire. Then someone banged on the door from outside. "It's me!" Stiles yelled, out of breath. "Hurry up, get these doors open!" More shots fired. "We can't hold them off for long!"

"It's them!" Mrs. Helton exclaimed, jumping to her feet. "We've got to help them!" By the time Ted and Billie turned to look she was already at the door. Her hands were on the crossbolt.

"No!" Ted lunged across the room without a hope in hell of getting to her in time.

The bolt slid back. "You get in here, and hurry!" she said, swinging the door open. "They're all over the place!"

The doorway was dark, but not from the night. From the bodies. They were standing three deep there, clogging the solitary entrance, dark shadows with white clown faces and sardonic smiles. And at the lead was Rusty Sanders, now wearing his blood-streaked deputy's uniform and tarnished badge, his revolver in hand and the barrel still smoking. "You get in here and hurry!" he repeated, mocking a petrified Mrs. Helton with perfect mimicry of her own voice. Then he took her by the shoulders and put his leering death's face right down in hers and he laughed, "Was that an invitation?"

Something rigid bumped his sternum—the barrel of a shotgun sticking out from under the woman's arm. Ted looked over her shoulder at him and grinned. "Hey, Rusty. Whaddayasay?"

Boom.

The close proximity of the blast threw Sanders completely back through the doorway, his face frozen in a look of utter shock as he died. Again. The other creatures knocked him aside and started through the door themselves, but by then Bart and

Billie had joined Ted to form a skirmish line and they began firing into the doorway, firing at anything that moved, pumping two and three rounds into the same bodies until the damn things were completely and unquestionably dead.

"I'm out," Ted called when his trigger clicked on an empty chamber. "Cover me!" He went forward while skirting their direct line of fire and came up behind the door and tried to push it shut. But it would only swing halfway. There were too many corpses blocking the threshhold.

A wave of bodies surged against the half-closed door and knocked Ted Cooper to the ground. His shotgun went sliding away as a heavy weight landed astride his back and drove him to the floor. Hands snarled in his hair and pounded his head into the concrete once, twice, three times, till his skull made a soft sound and the teen stopped struggling altogether. Only then did Doreen Moody turn him onto his back and begin to feed.

Nightmares streamed into the basement like a dread and darkling tide, washing over the only line of defense, engulfing them all. Bart's shotgun went empty, but Billie's still roared defiantly. Its report mingled with the screaming, both men and women, rising in pitch until gender was no longer an issue. It was one long ululation, starting on one side of the room and then jumping to the other and back again. "You bastards!" Billie cursed and fired her last shots into the grinning horde and then drew the extra Magnum Charlie had given her and used that.

"Del, Bart, get behind me! Did you hear?" She turned to look for them in the dim light and confusion, and that was when someone grabbed her wrist and knocked the revolver from her grasp. They swept over her like a cold wind, arms enfolding her, dead mouths on her cheeks and chest and sliding over her until they could find her throat. The bare bulb hanging overhead swayed from the melee, splashing everything with a strobic split second of light but illuminating nothing. She couldn't even see who was going to kill her.

Teeth broke the skin of her neck. Her own screams joined the communal wailing.

A voice in the darkness, familiar to her. Frank Sipes. "Hold it."

The teeth sank no further. The mouths pulled away.

"Not her. She's Stiles's woman. The Master says he can use her. Take her to him."

She tried to twist away from them, pummeling at where she thought faces should be, kicking at them, struggling to get away, to get to her boys. "Delbert! Bart!" she called out in vain against the other screams of the basement-cum-dining room. But a fist split her lip and filled her mouth with blood, and a second blow stunned her, and a third left her limp as a rag doll. She felt herself thrown over a shoulder and jostled about, and then there was the sensation of motion and a chill to her skin and the screams began to fade. She realized she was outside in the cold night air, being carried away. And she couldn't even cry out. Not for her children. Not for herself.

She was gone almost ten minutes before the screaming in the basement finally stopped. But the other sounds didn't. The moans. The smack of lips.

The feeding.

Chapter Twenty

Del couldn't stop crying. He knew it wasn't doing him any good, and it sure as hell wasn't helping Bart or Mom. But he just couldn't stop. *C'mon. Tough it out. How long has it been since they dragged them out of here—fifteen minutes? Half an hour? What could have happened since then? Are they alive, or . . .*

They're alive! They've got to be alive!

Then you can still help them. You've got to try. But you can't do anything till you stop crying.

I will. I will.

He wiped his eyes, then removed his hand from his mouth, but only when he was sure he wouldn't sob or gag again. He'd almost given himself away last time, and he couldn't afford the mistake twice. He massaged his tingling thighs; the alcove behind the furnace and water heater was small and he'd had to scrunch himself into an uncomfortable fetal position to remain unseen. And every minute he stayed there, his muscles cramped a little worse. It took him forever just to inch himself around to where he could peek out through the crack between the heater tank and the wall. He couldn't make out much. The shadeless bulbs hung widely apart, and they were of low wattage. Their light barely reached to the floor, and that's where all the bodies were. From his low angle they were indistinct mounds of shadow, entwined in twos and threes to where he couldn't tell one body from another, the living from the dead from the undead. And with all the oohing and ahhing that reached his ears, the groaning and lip-smacking . . .

What if the plan doesn't work? What then?

Then everyone you love dies.

The answer was that obvious, and that sobering. He set his jaw and started to prepare himself.

He unrolled the top of the sack very slowly and slid the contents out onto his lap. Amidst the Zagnut bars and the Reese's Peanut-Butter Cups and the *Teen Titans* annual were the things he'd picked up as he stood in the aisle of the drugstore and surveyed the Halloween supplies and wondered, *What if?* They were the tools of his desperate doomsday plan: two sticks of clown-white facial paint, a pair of Vampire Teeth, and a thick tube of stage blood appropriately titled in dripping letters Tube O' Gore. He laid them out on his leg like surgical instruments. First the face paint. There wasn't enough light to read the instructions, but he remembered glancing at them in the store—the sticks needed to be moistened for application. He tried to spit into his hand but nothing would come out. His throat was too dry. He had to work at it, dredging it up with his tongue just like when he used to hocker out the window of the school bus onto passing cars. He finally got a drop or two into his palm, just enough to wet the stick. Then he ran it across the back of his hand. The grease came off thick and lumpy but was the right shade of death, and the lumps looked like the flesh was beginning to decompose. Neat. He covered his hands and then his face, all over, even up into his hairline and down his neck. Then he put the teeth in. If only he had a mirror . . . As a finishing touch, he used the Tube O' Gore to smear his lips red and dribbled the fake blood from the corners of his mouth, just like they always did in the Hammer films. The stuff had a pungent, plastic taste when he inadvertantly licked his lips. He was careful not to do it again.

He was hyperventilating by the time he finished. *It has to work*, he repeated. *It has to, it has to*. He took a deep breath and stood up.

No one turned to look at him. The vampires, which he could see more clearly now, were hunched over their prey and much too engrossed to notice him. *So far, so good. But how will you ever get past them?* It was like an obstacle course and an Indian gauntlet all rolled into one.

He stepped slowly, hesitantly around the furnace. Out into the open.

There was immediate movement to his right. He froze. His neck refused to turn; only his eyes would obey, sneaking to the corners to see.

One of those . . . things had been sitting on the other side of the furnace all the time, feeding contentedly only a few feet away. It was a large woman he had seen many times behind the cash register at the IGA, with her thick glasses and her hair in an ever-present bun. She still wore her smock and her "My Name Is Evie" badge, though both were speckled with red. Her mouth was wet and gleaming; Del knew it was not lipstick. She was sitting cross-legged and there was the limp form of a man draped across her lap but she was no longer looking at him. She was looking at Del.

Oh, God.

He turned on his heels and looked straight into Evie's face and into those empty, rimless eyes, magnified three times by the thickness of her glasses. His muscles began to quiver and his bladder control slipped and a warmth spread through the crotch of his pants. He started to mumble and in the process bared his plastic teeth. Evie's brow furrowed and she flashed her own fangs as she pulled her victim tight against her ample bosom. "Get your own," she snapped. Then she turned away from him and went back to the man across her lap, tilting his face aside so she could go at his neck once again.

Del was numb. *It worked*, he thought. *I can't believe it worked, she really . . .*

He caught himself. Shivered. Stepped closer so that he could look into the slack face of her unfortunate prey. In this dim light the features had looked familiar. The shape of the face. The red hair.

No, please . . .

His jaw began to quiver. The fake teeth fell to the floor. He had to jam a sleeve into his mouth to keep from screaming. It was Bart.

He felt the sting of tears again, rolling through the grease on his cheeks. They were tears of hate this time, of anger. It was the only way the shock could be assimilated, the only way it wouldn't make him faint or turn to a blubbering, helpless child. It triggered something in him, deep down, that transcended his own sense of self-preservation, stoked a rage that made him forget everything else, that made him search the floor for a stake, a pipe, anything he could use to shatter Evie's skull and beat to a pulp whatever foul tissue still pulsed beneath. All he could find within reach was the folding knife in his pocket, but that was okay. He'd just use it to stab at her throat and chop at it and saw through it until her head came off in his hands. He stepped toward her with his face twisted and his knife bared and he reached out for that bound-up bun because pulling that would bare the bitch's throat and he'd aim for between the second and third chin . . .

Bart looked up at him.

He halted. The rage was suddenly gone. It left him hollow, afraid, unsure of what to do next. Bart couldn't be turning already . . . could he? His skin was pale, drained, almost like Evie's. But the eyes told him no. They were barely open, just enough to show the dimming sparkle of life, and they spoke to Del. They told him the things that he didn't want to know, that he was surrounded, that it would be suicide to try to help him and that it was already too late. And when the tears came anew Bart's gaze stopped them, told him that there wasn't time for that. That he had a job to do.

But I can't leave you here, he wanted to say. *I can't leave you. Not like this.*

The older boy's gaze softened, and a solitary tear welled there in the corner. His eyes shifted toward his outstretched hand, which still groped limply for the backpack just beyond his reach. Del nodded. He understood. He picked up the pack, careful that the bottles didn't rattle, and he hugged it to his chest. When he looked back at his brother, the eyes were closed. They didn't reopen.

He backed up and slumped against the wall. He did not want to move again. He wanted only to curl into a ball and hide his head. He felt more alone than he'd ever been in his life, and yet—suddenly he didn't. There was Bart's voice inside his head, crystal clear, so real that he had to look at the body to be sure it hadn't moved or spoken. *Get moving, Cap,* it said. *Mom needs you. Get moving.*

He pushed off from the wall and walked straight, putting one foot in front of the other, stopping only to retrieve his plastic teeth, until he was past Evie and his brother and he didn't have to look at them again.

Watching the vampires dine was especially harrowing as he picked his way through the room. The manner of their feeding varied with each; some moaned passionately and stroked their victims like a lover, while others savaged the throats with animal glee and then lapped at the pooling blood or sipped from the ruptured artery like a water fountain. It made his stomach lurch. He fixed his eyes on the door and concentrated.

They'll sense your fear, he told himself, or maybe it was Bart, reminding him. *You can't let them see that you're afraid.*

He stepped over two bodies. The one on its back, beneath a snorting young man, looked like a wide-eyed Mrs. Helton.

Can't be afraid.

Ted's body was almost blocking his path ahead, along with the ample white flesh of his girlfriend sprawled atop him. She was holding his hand tenderly and playing with his fingers like always, even as she murdered him. Del stepped around them. That's when she grabbed the boy's ankle. She sat up straddling Ted's middle, her chest now in plain sight with its one full breast and the other partially collapsed where Charlie Bean's stake had left two gaping holes. She hissed at him, spitting flecks of blood onto his coat. Her leg muscles tensed for a reflexive spring.

There was little else Del could do. He hissed back. He got right back in her face and bared his dime-store fangs and summoned a cat's guttural warning from deep in his chest. Several heads bobbed up at his response, like cobras rearing. But they just as quickly dismissed him and the female and went back to their business. Even Doreen recoiled. Her snarling face softened and she looked almost apologetic. She let go of his ankle and went back to Ted with her head hung sheepishly.

Your luck won't hold forever, Cap. Move it. Now.

He picked his way through them at a faster pace, careful not to let momentum overcome his balance. The door loomed closer and closer, a goal that frightened him with its nearness. *I can't be making it, I can't be, they're bound to get me before I reach the threshold . . .* But then his feet found the hillock of bodies that clogged the doorway and he was climbing over them, stepping on Rusty Sanders, making his way into the fresh night air beyond.

But the job wasn't finished yet.

He sat the backpack down gently beside the door and lined up the Little Kings bottles, one by one. There were six in all, each sprouting a leaf of linen from its corked mouth.

"Boy," came a voice from the gloom of the basement. Del glanced inside and saw a figure standing just in front of the second hanging bulb. Only the silhouette was visible, though he could feel the eyes on him. He stood up with one of the Molotov cocktails in his hand . . . but where were the matches? He hadn't thought of that! He patted his coat pockets, his pants, all the places he knew they would not be.

"BOY!" There were several eyes trained on him now, several dark forms standing in the half-light of the basement. They were coming toward the door.

He grabbed the backpack and turned it inside out and envisioned a book of matches clutched in Bart's lifeless hand.

Don't be stupid. Unzip the front pocket.

Sure enough, there was a front pocket on the pack and he fumbled with the zipper and tore it open and his hand found Grandpa's old Zippo, the one he'd passed on to Bart on his fifteenth birthday (the year he got caught smoking). In triumph, he thumbed the flint wheel and birthed a flame and touched it to the rag fuse of the bottle in his hand. The fabric caught immediately.

When he stepped back into the doorway, he could see them

coming at him. They were so close now that the flickering flame played on their sinister faces. He held the firebomb out like a king's scepter and took grim satisfaction in their changing expressions. "Burn in hell!" he damned them as he threw the bottle at the first open patch of floor he saw, just inside the door. The green glass shattered and spewed flame in three directions, both blocking the doorway and unfurling into the gathering crowd itself. Screams reached his ears, glorious screams that fed a savage glee in his heart. He lit another and threw it into the thick of them, where it made a dull thud and clattered to the floor unbroken. Then the flames reached the gasoline. The bottle exploded in a bright flash, and Del heard glass ping off the walls like shrapnel. One of the monsters was caught in the plume of fire and set ablaze; it ran endlessly, bumping into its brethren and igniting them as well. Del threw the rest of the bombs as hard as he could, lobbing them over the heads of the trapped crowd so they might reach the rear of the basement where Evie and Bart had been. And then he stood back and watched it burn.

The fire spread upward, into the house itself, and he could see the orange glow through the upstairs windows. The roar of the flames was deafening now, drowning out the screams, and the heat forced him back.

The hate and anger bled away from him as he watched. The grief returned, but he would endure it. He had to. "Goodbye, Bart," he said, wiping the sting of ash from his eye. "Don't worry about Mom. I'll find her."

In his mind, Bart's voice was no longer there. But he imagined a nodded reply, and that was good enough.

He looked around him. The vampires would not go near the fire, but it might attract their attention. He had to move soon. He ran to the next yard, found the doorway to the basement there. He rapped on it with his fist. "Can you hear me in there?" There was no answer. He pressed an ear to the cold metal. There were sounds from within, though muffled. Someone sobbing fearfully. The cries of an infant, and someone trying to hush it. He could almost feel the fear that emanated from inside, and he knew that asking for their help was useless. They would never open that door. And he couldn't blame them.

You're on your own, he told himself. *Where to first?* He looked around the yard, hoping for one of those signs, like in the movies, a telltale hoofprint or a broken twig or tramped-down path in the grass that would tell him where they took his mother. But he knew it wouldn't be that simple. *So where to? Who can I get to help me? Or maybe that should be, who's left to help? Chris and Charlie are God-knows-where and Bart's gone and Ted too and everyone else is a vampire.*

Maybe not everyone . . .

Didn't Mom say that Mrs. Moore was holed up in her own basement? Maybe she can help . . . that is, if that real estate bimbo hasn't gotten to her already. Now, which street was it Mom said she lives on? Walnut? Oak? At least in that general direction. It's a start.

He began to run but that felt too conspicuous for a vampire. So he had to settle for walking very, very fast.

He harbored a slim hope that most of Isherwood's undead had been trapped in the inferno back there, but he soon learned otherwise. He had gone just a few blocks, not even to Vernal Avenue, when he saw them, fleeting shadows, skittering from house to house in search of a fix. His immediate impulse was to hide, before they could see through his childish disguise. But again, it would have been too conspicuous. So he kept his reflexes in check. He walked down the sidewalk, in plain view, waiting for them to get closer. And when they grew within fifteen feet and saw the cast of his flesh they would simply pass him by. Del held any sigh of relief; he was not out of this yet.

He crossed Main Street just up from the courthouse and his confidence began to grow. So much so, in fact, that he barely flinched when he turned the corner from Elm Street onto Walnut and found six of them coming toward him.

They were mostly older men, in their late fifties to early sixties, and wore faces that Del had seen only in passing in the drugstore or the town square. There was a girl there too, about Bart's age. Of the lot of them, it was she who spoke. "Aren't you coming to the hill?" Her eyes, like all the others he'd seen, were deep and empty and threatened to draw him in unless he averted his own gaze.

"The hill?"

There was genuine surprise in her dead face. "Of course. Haven't you heard him calling us? He's there," she motioned to the north, where the land swelled up and an old house he knew only as the Shady Rest stood. "He needs us. Come." She took his arm.

Del was panicky. What if she felt his warmth through the coat sleeve? He quickly pulled away. "Uh . . . I'm still hungry. I'll be there in a few minutes."

She stared at him and made an odd face. Del finally realized it was meant to be a smile. "You're a real pig," she said, reaching out to run a cold finger along his lip and dab at the artificial blood. She tasted it. The boy's breath caught. She rolled her tongue about, considering, and then grimaced. "No wonder you're still hungry. But hurry. You don't want to keep him waiting." The lot of them stepped around him and continued along Walnut Street, heading north.

"One last thing," Del blurted after them, even before he realized he was saying it. "What about the Miller woman? Was she taken to the hill?" *Oh, Lord, now you've done it, they'll figure you out and then your ass is grass . . .*

They looked at him in a dull, unreadable manner for a long time, and he did not dare to even breath. Then the girl simply replied, "Yes," and they resumed their trek to the hill.

Del stood there alone in the middle of the sidewalk and felt a shiver of dread wrack his small frame. Danner had his mother—it was his worst nightmare. And they would be surrounded by other vampires. What could he do alone?

Dammit, Stiles, where are you when I need you!

The night air split with the echoes of a gunshot that came rolling up the street. It awakened the boy, shook him from his fearful paralysis. A gunshot—that meant someone was fighting back. Someone was still alive! His mind raced as he ran south on Walnut, straining his ears to sort through the fading echoes, his eyes to make out the names on the mailboxes as he went. It could be anyone, he rationalized. Anyone who had held out that long. But on this street . . .

There it was just ahead. The side of the Conestoga mailbox was emblazoned with the name MOORE, and as he grew closer he could see that there was a body sprawled on the lawn, just to the side of the front porch. Del crept to the edge of the driveway, until he could see clearer. He'd been expecting to find Giggy Gastineau there, though not quite like this—splayed on her back with eyes staring glassily skyward, speechless for the first time in her life. She was still dressed in her best tweed suit and held her briefcase tighter in death than ever, clutching it to her chest. But it still hadn't been sufficient to stop a shotgun blast. The silver pellets had simply punched a fist-sized hole in the genuine imitation leather before moving on to more vital regions.

He turned, looked at the house, and saw the shotgun barrels retracting into the basement window. And he thought he heard Mrs. Moore sobbing before the window clamped shut.

The boy hesitantly crossed the ground to where the realtor lay and nudged her with his foot to make sure she was dead—he didn't want her jumping up while his back was turned. Then he approached the window and tapped the frosted glass with a knuckle. "Mrs. Moore? Don't shoot. It's me, Del Miller. I've got to talk to you." There was no sound from within. "Please, it's urgent." He could feel the tears returning. "Please. My brother's dead, and now they've got Mom!"

When Sharon spoke, the voice was right behind the glass. She'd been standing there all along. "Back away," she said warily. The boy complied, and only then would the window open, just a crack, same as before. But from this close Del could see Mrs. Moore's face, at least part of it. She looked haggard and spent, her expression spiderwebbed with lines of anxiety. The eyes behind her bifocals were puffed and red from crying and lack of sleep. She looked just on the edge, and her knuckles were already white on the trigger of the shotgun pointing his way. "Another trick," she muttered, aiming right for his chest. Del realized her intent with sudden clarity and his jaw went slack and the false teeth he'd almost forgotten about went tumbling from his mouth. The sight took the woman by surprise, enough that the double barrels lowered a bit. Her finger eased on the trigger.

"It's not real!" the boy was rattling as fast as he could, smearing the face paint and then showing her the pale smudge on his fingers. He kept at it, rubbing more and more away until his own facial pigment was more obvious. Obvious to him at least. Sharon's eyes still held that hard glint of mistrust, and the shotgun didn't lower any further than before. "It's me!" he said. "I'm alive!"

"It's another trick," she said. "You're trying to trick me."

"Then here . . . touch my hand."

"Stay back" The shotgun barrels looked deeply into his eyes.

"Dammit, how can I convince you? We're wasting time—they could be killing my mom!"

Sharon's face remained stony; her tears had all been cried out. "I'm sorry, Delbert," she said flatly, "if you are really Delbert. But I can't take the chance. I just can't." She kept the shotgun trained on him even as she backed away, and once the barrels cleared the window, she quickly closed and locked it.

"Wait! What do I do now? Where do I go . . ." but it was no use. She was gone. He sat back and started to cry. "I'm sorry, Mom," he whispered. "I'm sorry."

You can't give up on faith, sweetheart . . .

Her words from earlier in the day came back. But why? What had made him think of that now, unless . . . He looked around to confirm his location. The church wasn't far from there, just at the end of the next street, maybe two or three blocks. *But what good would that do*? he wondered. *The pastor's done gone cuckoo for Cocoa Puffs, so he won't be any help, and what's there for me anyway, I sleep through services and I couldn't even hold off Danner with a cross and Chris told me—*

Can't give up on faith.

He surrendered with a sigh. *All right, Mom. At least it's a place to go.*

He recovered his fake teeth, dusted them off, and put them in, then reached into his coat pocket for the stick of clown-white to fix his face again and . . . *oh, God*. It wasn't there, he realized coldly as he patted down all of his pockets. He could almost visualize laying it on the furnace before stepping out into the open basement. *Arrgh*, he groaned, slapping his own forehead. *What am I going to do now?* He looked around. There was no one else in sight. *No use complaining. Better git now, while the gittin's good.* He walked back out to the street, looked both ways, checking each house as well. And when he was sure the coast was clear, he pulled his collar up around his face, lowered his head, and ran.

He turned onto Oak at a dead run and saw the shape of the Little Bethlehem Congregational Church looming out of the fog from a block away, its steeple like a finger pointing skyward. As Del drew closer, his flight lost some of its momentum. Something wasn't right—it looked too . . . ordinary. It was the same backwater church he'd seen countless times, the same white board siding, the same long, thin windows with their dark shutters and frosted panes. It was a singularly plain cottagelike structure that differed from the rest of the neighborhood only in its modest size and needle-like spire. But where was the light, Del wanted to know. Where was the holy aura he'd almost talked himself into expecting, where was the light of God that would surround the place and guard it from the darkness and act as a beacon to all the lost ones out there, the ones who needed His protection? His heart sank as reality came washing in, and it brought with it the memory of his facing Danner, and his use of the cross. And the results. And he suddenly felt very stupid for even coming here. But he approached the church just the same.

Curiosity, perhaps. And where else did he have to go?

The church sat forward on the one-and-a-half acre plot, separated from the street by a semicircle of gravel for parking. Stone walkways led both to the front door and around the side of the building to the even smaller parsonage in the rear. He checked the latter as he approached and found the windows dark, but there was a light burning in the chapel. And there was something else . . . music playing, though not the monotonous groan of the pipe organ. Something familiar and strangely incongruous . . .

Sammy Hagar?

The strains of "Heavy Metal" grew louder as he neared the front door and found it standing open. He stood there on the walkway, staring into the darkness of the vestibule and beyond where the shadows receded and a light burned. A row of pews was in sight, and half the podium. Nothing else. No one.

He stepped into the darkened entryway and through the arch into the church proper. The overhead lights were off; only the track lamps above the pulpit shined, and they cast the lectern and its oversized Bible in a spotlight. The big, impressive crucifix on a pedestal to the rear was nearly as tall as Del and, since it was on the periphery of the light, its shadow was etched dimly on the back wall. The rest of the chapel was in darkness, and an adolescent imagination could easily have peopled those empty pews with twilight faces and parishioners of shadow. But Del's eyes were focused only on the pulpit as he walked slowly up the center aisle. He saw that Sammy Hagar's screeching guitar riffs were spilling from a dual-cassette machine sitting on the podium next to the lectern. He was concentrating on it so much that he didn't see the figure slouched in the first pew until he was right on top of it. Then he shrieked and tripped over his own feet and scrambled crablike across the floor, covering his head.

The figure did not move. Del realized that and jumped to his feet, and every shred of common sense told him to run. It told him that, even as he crept closer.

The position of the body and the circumstance of it were both so outright bizarre that Del could only stand there, gaping. It was male, no doubt about that. It wore a dark T-shirt but no pants or underwear. The legs were splayed wide and one hand was locked around its rigored member while the other clutched a bondage magazine with a big-breasted centerfold and lots of chains and straps. The boy couldn't identify him; the man's whole head was hidden beneath a big rubber mask, one which, in the gloom beyond the track lights, looked suspiciously like Tor Johnson. Del knew he would have to lift the mask to be sure. His stomach started doing flips as he crept still closer and looked. The head was tilted just enough to one side that he could see under the edge of the mask. The red puckered impression of a mouth could still be seen on the throat, surrounding two ragged punctures. And a trickle of blood, all that was left, had seeped down to defy the sanctity of the white collar. "Knutson."

The tape stopped. Midsong. He could hear something behind him. Pages turning. Chuckling. "Shame-y, shame-y. He was a real pee-vert, wasn't he?"

Del turned to Tommy Whitten, who sat on the edge of the podium platform. His sallow flesh all but glowed in the stark light of the overhead lamps. Behind him was "Fat Larry" Hovi, and Doug Baugh was there as well, cigarette grafted to his lip as always. They were dressed the same as when Del last saw them. Only their throats differed. Whitten had wrapped electrical tape around his neck, while Baugh's had been stitched shut with a shoestring. Hovi had simply stuffed the ragged tear with a piece of black plastic from a garbage bag. They crowded around while Tommy looked at one of the pastor's magazines with a smirking, gap-toothed grin, tsk-tsking as he flipped the pages. "Check this bitch," he said to them, then turned it over so Del could inspect the spread-eagled female. Then he laughed and spit a stream of Knutson's blood through his teeth.

"You can't be here," Del tried to sound firm. "This is a church. Holy ground."

"Holy ground," Fat Larry repeated, though in a dead teenager's mocking tone. He tore a picture of a naked girl from a magazine and dangled it in the air and made it dance and gave it a falsetto voice. "Beat me, whip me, tie me up. It's okay, we're on hallowed ground." He laughed. "You've gotta be kidding. You think beating the bishop's a sacred ritual or something? Look at that fucker. It wasn't holy to him. Why should it be to us?"

Del thought about making a run for the door but his eyes betrayed him. Before he could even convince himself to move, Doug Baugh jumped ahead of him into the central aisle. His teeth were showing now, a horrific set that made his jaws seem double-jointed. "It's funny," Tommy Whitten said, his own teeth bared and lips trembling. "No matter how much I take, person after person, it's never enough. You'd think you'd get full after a while, wouldn't you? But I don't. I just want more. Always more."

Del backed over to the podium and put the lectern between them. But Tommy growled, knocked it aside, and the three of them came forward, forcing him back even further. He turned, staggered into the pedestal behind the pulpit, heard the base crack under his weight, and the whole thing came loose in his hands. The solid wooden cross, fully four feet tall and three feet wide at the crossbar, was heavy and unwieldy but he still lifted it and held it out against his enemies.

Their response was like Danner's. They giggled.

"You've got to have faith for that to work, Mr. Vincent!" Tommy quoted dramatically. "Didn't you see *Fright Night* on HBO last week? Oh, I forgot. You hilljacks don't have cable. Too bad. Then you would've known. You gotta believe, you little dick."

"I believe."

"Yeah, sure." Larry's jaws unhinged like a feeding snake. The teeth grew larger. He took a step.

"Hold it," Del ordered. "Three against one isn't very fair. What the matter, Tommy? Afraid to face me alone?"

Whitten arched an eyebrow. "Say what?"

"C'mon, Tommy. Just you and me. What's the matter, you afraid?" The three snickered at that, but Delbert didn't bat an eye. "Well, you should be. Because you know what, Tommy? I do believe. I believe, 'cause there has to be more to this. What kept me going when there wasn't nowhere else to turn? What brought me in here, even when I knew something was wrong? There has to be more to it."

Doug rolled his eyes. "Hitch up them pantlegs, buckaroos. The shit's getting deep."

"C'mon, Tommy. Put your money where your god-awful mouth is. Touch the cross."

Whitten's smile thinned, grew cruel and serious. "I'm gonna make you suffer, punk—"

"Touch the fucking cross!"

Tommy came toward him until they stood an arm's length apart and only the wooden crucifix separated them. A seed of doubt sprouted in the pit of Del's stomach—*How is he standing so close to it? How?*—and he tried to override it by flushing his mind with prayers, any and all that he could dredge from memory. *Now I lay me down to sleep* . . .

Tommy's face split in two, and the fissure filled with teeth. "You're dead."

The Lord is my shepherd, I shall not want . . .

"Take him, Tommy. But save some for us, okay?"

Though I walk through the valley of the shadow of death . . .

Whitten moved with the abruptness of a viper. His hands snaked out and caught the crossbar of the symbol. Held firm. And nothing happened. Tommy's smile grew even larger. The others laughed.

A moment later, the screaming began.

Chapter Twenty-One

➢

"Time to come out, Mr. Stiles. We're waiting."

Charlie shivered. Nathan Danner's voice had a ghostly lilt and, beyond that, something more, something that his followers did not share. It was dead-sounding, but neither hollow nor monotone. Instead it was full and rich and masked a malignant core, a creeping malevolence. It was evil that Charlie felt, pure and tangible, and it chilled his flesh like a sharp wind and gnawed straight to the bone. He could imagine how it must have affected old man Danner upstairs—he must be certifiable by now. It was certainly having a like effect on the others. Since Danner had shown up, the five of them—Stiles, Hubert, Jessie, Ida, and himself—had each repaired to separate areas of the parlor and sat in impatient silence, saying nary a word and waiting for the time to creep by.

"Mr. Stiles?" Nathan called again. "We need to talk."

They all looked to Stiles for a response but there was nothing to read. He sat closest to the window, his back against the wall, but he did not look outside. He didn't acknowledge the voice at all, not even with a flinch or a turn of the head or a shift of the eyes. Not even when they had toppled over his van on the front lawn a few hours back. His gaze was blank and his mind was elsewhere, another time or place perhaps, far away from the pain that his battered body must have been enduring. Charlie could sympathize; he himself felt like death warmed over, and, except for the broken arm, Stiles was much worse off than he.

Jessie moved over to the couch where Bean reclined. She was looking at Stiles as well. "Do you think he's all right, Charlie?"

He shrugged. "Beats the hell out of me. I haven't known him very long, so I have nothing to judge his behavior against. He's got a right to hurt, though, I'll vouch for that. He's been through the mill a time or two."

"I sure hope he's okay," she said, looking at him with concern. "I figure that without him, we don't have a chance in hell." She looked at Charlie then, and gently touched the injured arm in a sling against his side. "How're you doing? Hurting too bad?"

The pain reaffirmed itself when his attention was brought back to it. "It's easing up," he lied. "The aspirin helped a lot, thanks. But I doubt I'll be playing the piano any time soon. What time is it, anyway?"

Hubert glanced at his watch again. "A quarter till five. Just a little bit longer. All we have to do is wait."

"Not quite." Bean placed one of the Remingtons across his lap. "Now we have to be more alert than ever. Time's running out and Danner's not about to let us out of here alive. I figure they'll storm the place, sooner or later. Before dawn."

"But how can they do that?" Jessie asked. "We've still got Ida's things in the windows to keep them out."

Charlie quietly motioned to the recliner near the television set. Ida was resting as best she could. Her eyes had rolled back behind nearly translucent lids and her face had drained of color. Indeed, she looked dead. Only the unsteady rise and fall of her chest told them otherwise. "Those pieces have power just as long as she believes," Charlie said in a soft, somber voice. "If she doesn't hold out, neither will they. We have to be ready, just in case."

"Mr. Stiles," Nathan called again.

Jessie snorted angrily. "Why doesn't he just shut up!"

"Mr. Stiles? Listen to this, will you? You may find it amusing." Then a woman screamed.

The soldier's eyes suddenly unclouded. He snapped upright, his once-blank face suddenly alive with emotion. Denial. Fear. He turned on the window with the Heckler & Koch at the ready. "Billie . . ."

Danner had her out there, surrounded by his horde, straight out from the parlor window so she would be in plain view. He held her arms behind her back with one hand and pulled her hair with the other, till she bent sideways at a torturous angle and cried out when he applied a little pressure. He was looking past her to the window, waiting for Stiles to appear. "They tell me you know this cow," he called, "that she means something to you." Then he smiled and lowered his head over that silken throat and bit into it. Not too hard—just enough to make her scream. Just enough to draw blood. It oozed from the punctures down the taut angle of her neck, down into the cleavage revealed by her open jacket. The vampires ooohed and aaahed, nearly swooning at the sight. And Nathan licked it up with exaggerated gusto, all the while keeping an eye on the window and watching the soldier's face tighten with rage. "Won't you come out now, Mr. Stiles?" he said, flicking his tongue at the wound. "I'm afraid I must insist."

Stiles turned to Charlie and the others. The look on his face was terrifying in its own right, a mask of barely controlled fury. "What do we do?" Jessie wanted to know.

He trembled as he said, "You people watch the doors and windows. Stay ready." He stood up. "I've got to go."

"What?" Hubert was incredulous, as were they all. "They'll kill you for sure."

"It's a chance I've got to take." He laid down the machine gun and turned toward the door. Bean and Hubert made a move to stop him. "No," he said, halting them with his harsh tone. "Don't try it. Not where Billie's concerned. You'll lose." He noticed that Ida's eyes were slightly open for the first time in hours and looking at him in concern. He went to her, kneeled by her chair, and took her hand. "How are you holding up, Grandma?"

"I'm a tough old bird," she barely managed. "But you . . . you be careful. You hear?" He nodded and kissed her, then headed toward the entry hall.

"Don't worry, Stiles," Charlie said as he passed. The deputy picked up the Heckler & Koch, extended the stock, and activated the laser sight. "If you can't get Billie out, or, well . . . I'll take care of you. Both of you."

The soldier said nothing as he left the parlor.

He scooted the leaning front door aside just enough for him to slip out onto the porch. The night air immediately wrapped him in a cold embrace, but he was too pumped with adrenaline to notice. What he did feel, however, were the eyes on him, unblinking, unrelenting, and he noted the increased number of undead gathered around the Shady Rest. There were at least thirty surrounding the porch, lining the front steps, and flanking the yard as well. He was the sole white man facing a tribe of late-show Indians, only these natives were long of tooth and glassy of eye. They became a gauntlet at the porch steps that he would have to pass. If only it were the late show, he wished. Tomahawks would be a welcome fate.

"Let the woman go," he called to Danner.

"Now, now," scolded the vampire. "This is my game. I make up the rules. Come here. Join us." When Stiles didn't move fast enough he tightened his hold on Billie and forced her to her knees. "Come here," he barked, "or I drain her here and now!"

Begrudgingly Stiles began his walk. He crossed the porch and started down the steps.

Jack-o'-lanterns lined the way, ghoulish grinning faces that could barely hold back their carnal need for sustenance. Despite their master's orders, some even grabbed for him, tearing his vest and shirt, raking his flesh with dirt-caked nails. One of them lunged too close and in reflex Stiles caught the groping arm and broke it. Then he swung at the accompanying leer and felt teeth shatter beneath his palm and then the whole mob seemed to fall on top of him. His only defense was to cover his head—blows rained down in torrents, hammering him to the ground, blinding him, filling his vision with starbursts and the shifting colors of pain. The mauling culminated quickly when he felt a singular body pin him to the ground and wrap cold arms around him. He could tell from the shape of the wriggling form that his attacker was female; from the scent of leather, that it was Georgetta Stovall. He felt her face burrow into his shoulder and keep moving, closer and closer and he tried to fight her off but he could not keep her teeth from finding his neck.

The pain of the bite itself was sharp but fleeting. It was the feelings and sensations it brought that repulsed him. There was nothing sensuous about the attack. It was an assault, pure and simple, same as a rat bite, only a rat doesn't hang on and nurse at the wound like a leech. At least she hadn't hit an artery—she was sucking too hard for that. It was the feel of that cold, soft-lipped mouth, kneading and working, that made him cry out. That, and the vertigo that immediately clutched at his mind.

Stiles felt his strength draining, his will gone, his very life being tugged and pulled, stolen away . . .

The cascade of horrific sensations ended abruptly, as did the attack itself. The hands of the mob were suddenly gone and so was the wet suction cup of a mouth, though he could still feel her hands on him and her squirming weight pinning him to the ground. He blinked his eyes into blurred but compliant sight. Georgetta's livid face hovered just above his own, mouth stained red and teeth bared, squirming to free her hair from Danner's iron grasp. He straddled the both of them and held her at bay with little effort. "Now now," he berated her gently. "I said no one touches our guest. Not yet."

"No!" she squealed, straining against his grasp even as she pulled the soldier up into her embrace once again. "He's mine! Mine!"

Nathan did not snarl at her, nor did he exhibit any anger at all. He simply reached out and cupped her chin with his palm and gave a sharp little twist, and Stiles suddenly found himself staring into the back of the woman's head. She rolled off of him, gagging and coughing, gazing at the stars even as she crawled away on her hands and knees. Danner smirked as he grabbed Stiles by his combat vest and jerked him into the air with one hand, dancing him about like a broken puppet. "Where are your guns now, my friend? Where is your ghostly guardian? Come, bring them all on. I'm too powerful for the lot of you!" He shook the man's limp form again but the response was the same. Stiles just hung there. "Aw, c'mon. Where's all that pluck and fight?" No response. He sighed, "You're no fun," and contemptuously tossed him away. A flick of the wrist sent him nearly ten feet. Stiles tried to hit and roll but his reflexes were as battered as the rest of him. He landed hard, bounced once, and came to rest in a crumpled heap. The rest of the undead all tensed at the sight of the downed man like jackals after a lion's kill, but they dared not advance. Not without their master's consent, and he did not give it. He wasn't through with this one. Not yet.

"Chris!"

Billie's cry cut through the miasma of his addled senses. He managed to get to his knees and saw her running toward him. But then she passed Danner. The vampire's hand snaked out and caught her by the hair, nearly jerking her off her feet and coaxing a painful scream from her lips. It was that scream that fed Stiles's anger. It drove him to his feet. "Danner! Let her go!"

Nathan pinned her flailing arms and looked her over hungrily. "I don't know, Mr. Stiles. She's a pretty one. What if I refuse?"

The soldier was succinct. "Then I'll tear you apart."

The vampires all laughed at the wounded man's audacity. All but Danner. He watched Stiles with a hard-learned wariness. "You've already tried that once tonight."

"Then I'll just have to try harder."

Nathan finally smiled and shook his head with wonderment. "What audacity, eh?" he called to the others. "You just can't help but like him." He raised his hands and released Billie, who ran to Stiles's side. She was sobbing incoherently, something about her sons, but Danner was still speaking to his throng. "Shall we tell them what we have planned?" he asked. "Or should it be a surprise? I don't know . . . perhaps we should put it to a vote—"

"Just get on with it," Stiles snapped.

"Yes, of course. I believe we should tell him. Then we can savor their reaction." He approached the two. There were fires dancing in his empty eyes that forced Billie to look away, but Stiles met his gaze and fought it. "Do you remember our conversation in your motel room last night? I wanted you to experience my reality, so to speak. Make you like me. Well, I intend to keep that promise, my friend."

Stiles did not blink or back down. "Then you must have forgotten what I told you. That I would use it to destroy you?"

"Oh, I remember. And I do believe you. That's why I won't stop there. No, I figure if you're deserving of my gift, you must also be worthy of my fate." He moved even closer, within whispering distance. "An immortal imprisoned is a tortured soul indeed. I thought about that quite a bit over the last three-quarters of a century. And so shall you. You'll take my place in that basement cell, my friend, walled in, and you'll feel yourself waste away, day by day by day, knowing that there will never be an end to your suffering, because you cannot die." He laughed triumphantly as he walked away, turning only on an afterthought. "But I was once a compassionate man. I know the loneliness of such an existence. So I will allow you company.'' He looked at Billie. ''She should last a little while. Till the hunger starts to burn.''

Stiles pulled Billie to his chest and turned her so that they both faced the parlor window. He hoped to find a red dot dancing on the back of her head, but there was nothing yet. ''Sounds like you've been a busy boy with all this thinking and planning,'' he replied. ''And I hate to disappoint you. But we won't be able to stick around for your games.'' He pulled Billie even closer, tensed himself for the impact, and hoped Bean was a good shot. ''Okay, Charlie . . . do it!''

There was no report. After a moment he opened his eyes and looked to the window. The lights were still on but, from this distance, he couldn't see anyone. ''Charlie!'' he called. ''Do us now!''

''The deputy can't help you. But maybe I can.'' It was Danner's voice, but not from where Nathan stood. It issued instead from the front porch of the house, and it had aged nearly a century in transit. Stiles had never realized until that moment how much the old man and his eternal twin sounded alike.

George Bailey was just slipping through the ruined doorway and out into the moonlight. He looked bad. His skin was as pale as Ida's, his features drawn, his posture slouched and unsteady. His limbs shook, either from infirmity or abject terror or both, and he must have been sweating fiercely since his hair was plastered to his forehead and his clothes were drenched and clung to his scarecrow frame. He leaned against one of the porch's pillars for support while the vampires just stared, not knowing quite what to make of him. He motioned to Stiles and Billie. ''Let them go.''

Nathan nodded imperceptibly, and in answer two of the vampires came slowly up onto the porch after Bailey. But when they drew within reach Bailey suddenly thrust out the big rosewood cross that had hung on his bedroom wall. The creatures immediately retreated, hissing and holding their eyes. ''There's still a little fight in me, Nathan,'' he said, buoyed by that small victory. ''You'll have to do better than that.''

Nathan's expression changed from one of mild annoyance to genuine curiosity. ''Do I know you, old man?''

Bailey held out the cross. All of the vampires took a step

back. Even Nathan flinched. "Don't you remember this, Nathan? It was my wife's. It had been her mother's."

The vampire leader gaped. "Sebastian . . ."

The old man's voice grew hot with anger. "And do you remember the last time you saw it? The night I put Lynn Anne to rest, again, after what you'd done to her? It's the same cross I used to track you down and burn that mark into your cheek that won't go away."

Nathan touched the black scar on his face. "Then it is you, brother? I thought you'd be dead by now. I told myself I imagined it when I was behind that wall and I heard the digging and felt . . . Ah, so I was right then. It wasn't those children who freed me. It was you. You came back—"

"To kill you," Bailey said icily. "To destroy you once and for all. It's something I should've done seventy-five years ago. This time I'll finish it."

The young man in the sweat suit smirked with confidence. "Will you now?" he said. "Don't be a fool. You were lucky last time. You caught me unaware, and you were young and strong then and you had a mad thirst for revenge to drive you. Do you have that now? No. You are just a bent, wizened old fool. Old. Ancient. Decrepid. I can hear your joints creak from across the yard, Bastian. I can hear your bones crumbling away, and the strain of your heart, laboring to maintain even an erratic beat. You're a shadow of your former self, Bastian. While I AM your former self."

"No, you're not," Bailey called back. He was sagging against the beam more and more. The cross lowered a bit. "You were never like me."

"No?" He was coming closer now, toward the steps, even though the cross was still before him. "Don't I have your body, brother? Your strength, your vitality? And even more—don't I look as you once did? Isn't this the face that Lynn Anne fell in love with? Your face?"

"Don't listen to him, Sebastian!" Stiles called, but the old man's gaze was caught and held by his advancing twin. Bailey's hand trembled and lowered still. Nathan no longer recoiled from the cross's presence.

"Join me, Bastian," he offered. "I can make you like me. I can give you everything you desire. I can give you your youth.

Can you imagine what it would be like to run again, to feel undreamed of strength in your arms instead of numbness or pain?'' His smile was seductive, devilish. ''You know you want it. Don't you?''

There was a moment of anxious silence. Then the crucifix clattered to the porch. ''Damn you, Nate,'' he sobbed in defeat.

Nathan opened his arms. ''All is forgiven, brother,'' he said. ''Come to me.''

The old man walked stiffly down the steps and into his brother's embrace. He even turned his head to bare his thin, wattled throat. But Nathan was suddenly hesitant. He was sniffing, looking about. There was a pungent aroma in the air around them. ''What is that?'' he muttered.

Sebastian tightened his arms around his brother's middle before snapping the deputy's pilfered handcuffs around his own wrists, locking the two of them in the embrace. Then he looked up into Nathan's face. The ruse was over. He was smiling. ''The smell, Nate? It's retribution.''

He thumbed the wheel of the Bic butane in his hand.

The flame all but leaped from the lighter and raced with glee up the old man's gas-soaked sleeves and across his shoulders, encircling the two of them in the blink of an eye. Sebastian Danner said nothing. He simply died. But his brother was another matter. He screamed as the fire licked around him and his thrashing made them look like an insane couple on the dance floor. He hammered at the dead man who held him until the arms came off at the sockets and he was free again. But it was already too late. The flames had spread too quickly, and pieces of Sebastian Danner's clothes and skin were still stuck to him and feeding the blaze. Nathan staggered backward, screaming and cursing as the fire enfolded him like an orange cocoon. He collapsed on the grass and continued to burn even after he stopped moving.

There was shocked silence. The pop and crack of the flames was the only sound. All eyes were on the fallen master. Except for Billie. She was trying to pull Stiles away. ''Chris,'' she whispered urgently, ''hurry, now's our chance—''

''No,'' he said. He was still hopelessly groggy, despite his bravado earlier, and her arms around him were mostly what kept him on his feet. ''I can't make it. Run yourself. I'll hold them.''

"Oh, no, you don't," she said, throwing one of his arms over her shoulder and pulling him along. "I'm not leaving without you!" They backed away toward the road. If they could get down the hill, maybe to another house . . .

She felt eyes on her. "Oh God, they see us—"

"Just keep moving," Stiles said firmly, gathering a momentum of his own now, turning and almost pulling her along. He chanced a look behind. The creatures had left their master and become a wall of white, yawning faces, their eyes intense and wanting as they came steadily forward. Danner was already forgotten, and without his coherence the communal whole was breaking up, and each cell had its own will and its own hunger, and about thirty other competitors for the same meal. It was that adversarial aspect that kept them from charging outright. They were watching each other as much as their prey, which worked to Stiles's and Billie's advantage. It gave them an extra few seconds of flight, got them that much closer to the open road.

Billie suddenly dug in her heels and dragged them both to a halt. She was looking ahead while he peered behind, so she was the first to see the movement out in the road. "Oh, God," she murmured, pointing. A shadow had extricated itself from the surrounding night and now wandered into the dim glow of the security light. She could make out a small figure against the light, a child, and as he approached he struggled with his unwieldy burden and held it up for all to see. The huge cross was an impressive sight to behold, even with the two lumps on the crossbar where Tommy Whitten's hands had melted. The boy braced the trunk of it against his hip like the flag-bearer in a marching band and came on ahead.

Billie was hesitant to let herself believe. "Del?" she barely whispered. Even Stiles didn't recognize the boy at first. He was ragged and dirty, his jacket stained with makeup, his face reddened from the fire he'd started, his eyebrows and bangs singed away. But that wasn't the difference in him. It was the way he held himself, straighter, taller, even with the weight of the cross. Perhaps it was his expression. There was a calm, yet steely resolve etched there that seemed out of place on an eleven-year-old. He held the crucifix out even further, directly at Stiles, until the soldier realized it was meant for the chalky wall of faces behind him.

The horde ceased its advance. The faces were pinched into sneers but they averted their eyes from the cross.

Mother ran to son and hugged him tight, though he struggled a bit to keep the massive symbol visible to all. "Thank God you're all right," she sobbed gratefully. "I was so worried! Where's your brother?"

Del avoided her gaze. "Please, Mom. Not now." He broke away from her to confront the vampires, but she was still left shaken. She had seen enough of his expression to know. She wouldn't let herself believe it. "Delbert!" she called after him, "Delbert, where is he? Where is your brother!" and she tried to get to him and shake it out of him, but Stiles caught her first and she all but collapsed in his arms.

"Stay close to me," Delbert called to the soldier. "I think I can get you back to the boardinghouse." He moved forward a step or two in the mob's direction, goading them into retreat. But they started pushing each other into his path like children on a playground. Those who jumped or were pushed too close got a searing jab from Del's holy weapon but their wounds did not stop them. The boy's advance was blocked. He looked over his shoulder at Stiles, frustrated. "Stalemate."

"Retreat then," Stiles told him. "Maybe we can get to a house down the hill and—"

The gunshots rang out almost in unison, taking Stiles and his allies by surprise, and at least six of the huddled undead fell in reply, their torsos perforated with fatal doses of silver. But the gunmen were still unseen; no one could tell where they had fired from, and a wave of confusion and panic swept through the rest of the creatures. They turned on each other in a mad scramble to get away without knowing which way to go. The mystery guns barked again, and this time Stiles could see the two cones of muzzle flame in the darkness. Charlie and the others—it had to be them! They had outflanked the vampires and hemmed them in on two sides, firing from a distance so the spread patterns were larger and encompassed a greater target area. After even a short barrage the mob was halved in number. The remainder pawed and trampled one another in blind panic as the rain of silver forced them back toward the Shady Rest, up onto the porch where they broke down the door and rushed inside . . .

The house! Stiles's jaw dropped. How could they get past the cross on the door and Ida's . . . Oh, Lord. "Ida!" he yelled, starting after them.

"Stiles, wait!" Bean's voice managed to slow him. The deputy hurried out of the shadows at the yard's edge, the Remington under his injured arm while he reloaded with his one good hand. He called out, "Hubert, they're coming your way!" before turning back to the soldier. "Ida's gone," he said. "Right after you went outside. Just gave out all of a sudden. It was only a matter of time after that. We decided to make our move while they were preoccupied." He started toward the house but then caught sight of the two bodies near the front porch, one a smoking piece of charcoal and the other still burning. "Bailey . . . Danner was still upstairs when we snuck out the back. I didn't know that he had this in mind." He looked apologetic for a moment, then gestured furiously to the other side of the lawn and continued the pursuit. Jessie answered his call and followed along as fast as she could, the Mossberg still smoking in her hands and the Uzi pistol slung over one shoulder. Bean yelled back to Delbert, "Watch the front, boy!" before he and the woman disappeared around either side of the house. Almost immediately there was more gunfire.

Del looked at Stiles. "Well? Aren't you going to help them?"

"In a minute," Stiles said. "I've got to be sure first." Supporting Billie, he headed across the yard to where Nathan Danner had finally collapsed.

The body was still burning long after Sebastian Danner's had gone out. Indeed, the gasoline that fueled it initially had already been consumed, along with his clothing and hair and flesh until he looked like an anatomist's mannequin of the muscular system. But still he burned, hotter and brighter than ever, and Stiles couldn't get too close for the heat. It reminded him of hydrogen peroxide poured into an infected wound; the chemical would react with any corruption present and bubble and fizz angrily as it purified. It was exactly what the fire was doing now. Reacting to the corruption. Purifying. Growing hotter and brighter as it burned away the layers that housed his demonic core. "Is it over then?" Billie whispered, hugging herself close to him. "Is it really over?"

"Yes," he soothed, kissing her lightly, "it's really—"

The fire flared suddenly, whether from a sudden breeze or a

bubble of gas in the entrails. It licked out and seared his vision and left it imprinted with a ghostly orange haze. He stumbled and grabbed at his stinging eyes, blinded, and felt a wave of intense heat rush past him.

And he heard Billie scream.

Stiles chased the spots from his gaze, only to find her cowering on the ground a few yards away, shielding her face to the fiery abomination that loomed over her. Nathan Danner was still the same apparition as a moment ago, still sheathed in angry flames, but now he stood upright, defying every natural law. He no longer appeared human; the face was skeletal, covered only in a thick gauze of blackening muscle, and the eyes bulged without benefit of lids to hide them. When they abruptly popped and melted from the heat, even the empty sockets seemed to stare with evil intent. The lipless smile was much too large for any human mouth, and the teeth clicked and worked as if attempting words, but all in vain. It emitted only harsh exhalations as its lungs dried up and turned to ash. The monstrosity took a shambling step toward her and a gaunt hand reached out, a charred skeleton's hand with a flap of loose muscle hanging like moss from the wrist, and it caught Billie by the shoulder. She squealed and tears filled her eyes as it burned through the jacket to the flesh beneath. That angry gust of air came again as it pulled her closer, and this time it somehow formed the word *blood*.

Stiles loosed a maniacal cry that echoed through the night, taking the both of them by surprise, and when he launched himself at the undying creature it was with a wide-eyed, slobbering rage. His own pain and limitations were forgotten as he pistoned a vicious kick into the Danner-thing's side and knocked it away from her. "Fight me!" the soldier roared, crouched and snarling like a wild animal.

The fiery creature drew back, its eyes sockets trained cautiously on both of them. It was wary of the man; it needed to feed desperately, for only blood could put out the flame, only blood could bring back the power as it had twice before. But the man would fight too much, too long. It needed the girl, needed her now . . .

It moved for Billie again, lunging, but Stiles drove it back with ferocious abandon, pummeling it madly, filling the air with the sharp crack of bone on bone. He ignored the heat and the pain, even when the creature's jaw muscles came loose and stuck to his fist like melted plastic, still aflame. He continued to fight. And the Danner-thing continued to burn.

The flames were brighter now, especially within the rib cage and in the very skull itself. The sockets were no longer dark; they now blazed with soul-eating fire. And it drove what was left of Nathan Danner berserk. From somewhere, perhaps from the blackened core of his very being, Danner finally found a voice, and it screamed with an indefinable rage as it charged Stiles in desperation, catching him by the throat and hauling him into the air.

Stiles knocked the hand away, tearing the thing's forearm loose at the elbow, and then dropped back to the ground. Immediately he torqued his body into a hard spin and his leg lashed out and dug a heel into the Danner-thing's head and, like a cigarette flung against a wall, the skull exploded in a shower of sparks. The body remained standing. It crouched and shifted its weight, even took a step toward them. But then the flames suddenly flared up and consumed it, and the resulting blaze lit the hilltop for miles around.

Stiles didn't know how long he stood there, watching the fire, waiting for it to die so he could scatter the ashes. The rage gradually spent itself; it left him dazed, disoriented, barely on his feet. He wasn't sure where he had been or what he'd done, and the returning waves of pain would not permit him to remember. He was shocked to realize that the sun was already peeking over the Indiana horizon. Daylight . . . he'd thought he would never see it again. He squinted at its brightness, reveled in its warmth.

"Chris?" Billie asked softly, touching his shoulder.

He turned to her and smiled. But he wasn't conscious when he hit the ground.

Chapter Twenty-Two

➢

Stiles awoke in pain, but that was no surprise. He was getting used to it by now. What did surprise him was that it was actually less severe than he'd come to expect. The newest injuries, the burns and contusions, all nagged him to be sure. But they were tolerable at least, and the older hurts seemed to be improving. The broken fingers and rib didn't ache quite so much now, and the throbbing in his crotch had been replaced with the simple agony of a torn muscle. *Lucky again*, he sighed. *Looks like you'll pull through after all.*

He stretched his sore frame beneath the covers—he was in bed, though not sure whose or how he got there—and in response the mound of warmth curled atop his chest stretched as well and gave him a raspy lick on the nose. He looked up into the slitted eyes of an orange tabby that cooed at him and rubbed against his chin. "Well, hello, puss. Who's cat are you?" He looked around the room for an answer and found his surroundings vaguely familiar. Then it dawned on him: it was the landlady's bedroom, the first Ida had "sealed" on their frantic tour of the Shady Rest the night before. He even recalled a passing glimpse of the cat, huddled in the covers, waiting for a mistress who wouldn't return. "Miss her already, don't you?" he said, scratching the feline's ear. She purred and gave him another affectionate lick.

How long have I been here? he wondered. A glance at the window told him it was noon or thereabouts. And that bothered him. There was still too much work to be done—even with Danner gone, there were the others to be tracked down and exterminated, and he'd wasted precious hours. Even if he did need the rest.

He eased back the covers, slowly swung his legs over the

edge of the bed, and sat there until the queasy feeling subsided. He felt like one big puffy wound and certainly looked the part; he was wrapped like a reject from a grade-B mummy movie, and what flesh wasn't covered in bandages seemed bruised to a splotchy shade of blue. But he didn't let that stop him. He stood with a groan, found his clothes on the foot of the bed beneath his cast-off covers, and dressed as quickly as his creaking body would allow. Then he sat back down and rested for a while, and waited until the urge to puke had left him before getting up again. His guns were nowhere in sight, but Hubert's sheathed sword had been left standing against the bedstand. He leaned on it for support as he draped the fat tabby around his neck like a warm and complacent scarf, then hobbled out into the hall.

There were sounds drifting up from the first floor . . . The television. "*Ding! Boink!* Ooh, I hate meeces to pieces!" Chris smiled. At least he knew Del was all right. The cartoons grew more distinct as he descended the stairs and turned into the parlor. "Hey, Cap, how're you . . . doing?"

The children around the television whirled and stared at him like frightened bunnies. These were smaller tykes, tousle-haired and wide-eyed, many still dressed in their pajamas. There were eight of them that he could see. A few he recognized from the day before at the basements, but . . .

The basements. Bart had died there last night, hadn't he? That much he remembered. Had both places been broken into? Were these all that survived? They huddled close as they silently appraised him, and he could see uncertainty in their eyes. Even fear. But then the children saw the tabby stretched languidly across his shoulders and their apprehension was forgotten. They approached, smiling and cooing at the feline, and he had to kneel so they could reach it. The cat, on the other hand, showed its opinion of the throng by sinking its claws into his shoulder. Stiles quickly got the message. He stood to end the petting session and save his deltoid, and the children reluctantly returned to the cartoon.

"I see you've already met." Billie came through the dining room, her arms lined with plates as only a true waitress could manage. "Who wants peanut butter and jelly?" She dealt the plates onto the coffee table with the dexterity of a cardshark, much to the children's delight. They grabbed up the sandwiches as Billie brushed up close to Stiles and pecked him on the lips. "You're looking better," she said.

"How can you tell?"

"It's in your eyes." She scratched the purring orange head that peeked around his neck. "Who's your friend?"

"Just someone I woke up with." He reached out to touch her swollen cheek and split lip, the bandage on her neck, the shoulder where she was burned. "How are you doing?"

"Mrs. Miller?" interrupted the smallest girl, "Billy took the last pena-butter sandwich. Are there any more?"

"Sure, hon," Billie said, heading for the kitchen. She glanced back over her shoulder at Stiles. "Cup of coffee, sailor?"

He followed her through the dining room and into the kitchen, which she had straightened a great deal after Bean's altercation last night. She pulled a bowl from the dish drainer and filled it with milk, then took the cat from his shoulder and sat them together on the floor. "There's a pot of coffee on the stove," she said over her shoulder as she raided the peanut butter again, then pushed a half-full cup across the counter. "Warm mine up a bit, okay?"

"Those kids," he said as he poured. "They're not the only ones left, are they?"

"Oh, no. Those things only broke into ours," she said rather matter-of-factly, as if she'd just heard about it rather than experienced it firsthand. "The ones in the other basement were all okay. That's the first place we checked this morning, and we've found more people since. Most stayed out to help Charlie, but they brought the younger kids back here."

"Help Charlie do what?"

"What you said had to be done—tracking down the rest of them. I'll be going out on the next run. I only stayed behind this long to keep an eye on you."

He came up behind her, put his hands around her waist. "I appreciate that, but I'm fine, honest. How's Del doing?"

"Oh, he's a real trooper. Never bats an eye, though I don't think it's really sunk in on him. He and Bart were very close."

"And what about you?"

"I'm okay, I guess. My shoulder hurts like hell, but other than that . . ." For a moment she let her guard down, and leaned back against him and enveloped herself in his arms. But then she pulled away on second thought and stood on her own. "I'm sorry, Chris. It's just that . . ."

He turned her around, hushed her with a finger to her lips and an understanding smile. "I'll be here," he said. "When you need me." He kissed her lightly and then stepped away. "I think I'll go out on the porch for a while. The sun should do me some good." He took his coffee cup and left the kitchen, with the cat following close behind.

The front yard had been cleaned up since he'd last seen it, the bodies swept away as if by a divine wind. But the effects of the battle were still prominent. Stray silver pellets pocked the siding and support columns and one of the metal porch chairs, and the front door still leaned drunkenly against the house a good three feet from its true moorings. The fence out front lay in splinters all along the sidewalk, and tire tracks were deeply carved into the well-tended lawn. And then, there was always the van itself, lying on its side like a beached whale a few feet from the walk. Stiles limped off the porch to inspect the damage, but he could see it was a lost cause already. The windshield was gone and the sides were crushed like a Coke can. The stink of leaking coolant and gasoline assailed his nostrils. But, surprisingly, he wasn't all that upset. This time he was happy just to be getting out alive.

The sun out there did feel good. Its rays were intense for that late in the year and burned some of the October crispness from the air. The cat must have enjoyed it too. He draped her across his shoulders and she made no move to climb down, instead preferring to stretch out and doze with her head resting on his collarbone. Stiles felt just as tired, and the porch chairs beckoned to him. *You can't do much till Charlie comes back*, they said, *so take a load off.*

He was almost to the steps when his eyes fell on the scorched sections of grass a few paces away. Especially the longer one where he'd stomped Nathan Danner's ashes into the soil. Suddenly the sun wasn't so warm after all. It left a cold place deep within him, down at his core where its rays could not reach, and that was where the bitterness and guilt roiled subconsciously. The questions centered there. *Was this my fault? Am I responsible? What if I'd been a little more decisive, a little quicker to act?*

He reproached himself. *Not that shit again. It wasn't even your fight. This town is lucky—if you hadn't stepped in, the virus would have spread everywhere. At least you stopped it.*

He nodded. But it was little consolation. If he had been a little more thorough that first night . . .

He looked down the hill toward town. There was a good view of Isherwood from here, but there wasn't much to be seen. The town was comatose. Nothing moved down there to his eye, no cars on the street, no people. It had simply gone to sleep the night before and never awakened. And he wondered if it ever would. Had the cancer been excised in time, or had it spread too far, infected too much tissue? He looked at the black patch of burned earth and he knew what his own answer would be. *Let it die. Let it go peacefully and then bury it. Doze it over. Indiana doesn't have enough parking lots.*

The sounds of engines intruded on his brooding silence. Two pickup trucks motored up Moffit Trail and pulled to the shoulder out front, and behind them a newer model Chevy van. People began to pour from the beds and cabs, probably twenty to twenty-five in all, men and women, teenagers to adults. They looked like a day-weary road crew coming in from the job: they carried picks and mallets and sharpened dowel rods along with their shotguns, and their faces were sullen from what they had seen. It was certainly not a job any of them wanted. But they had accepted the responsibility and hardened themselves to the task. Some of them unloaded groceries from the truck, but he wagered few would be in the mood to eat. He couldn't blame them. He was never completely used to it himself.

Charlie Bean climbed out of the van. He looked tired and favored his injured arm and grimaced when he had to move very fast, but he didn't let any of it stop him. Hubert and Jessie were among them too, still carrying his automatic weapons. And then there was Delbert. He slid out of the van as well, having traded his Magnum-caliber cross for one of more manageable size. It hadn't been the soldier's imagination last night—there was definitely a change about him. He'd grown up a lot in one night. Stiles just hoped it wasn't too fast.

"Well well," Bean smiled as he came up onto the porch. "It's nice to see you up and around." He motioned to the van by the road. "How do you like it?"

"Very nice. Yours?"

"Nope." The deputy dropped the keys in Stiles's lap. "Yours is pretty much scrap. It's the least we could do."

Stiles looked at them all in surprise and stammered, "You shouldn't . . . but . . . aw, hell. I don't know what to say."

"Nothing to say," Charlie said with a grin. "So, how're you doing?"

"Fair to middlin'. How about you—keeping busy?"

"You could say that. I think we got most of them. We've covered the whole town once. Another quick swath should pick up the ones we missed. Then we'll start fanning out to the farms and outlying homes." He grabbed Delbert as the boy passed and put an arm around his shoulder. "My buddy here is real good. He knows where they'll be hiding without even looking."

The boy's face was impassive. That worried Stiles. "How're you doing, Cap?"

"You mean about Bart?" Del replied. "I miss him, naturally. But it's okay, because I know he's at peace. That's what matters, right?" His expression changed all of a sudden; the exuberance of an eleven-year-old suddenly returned. He'd seen the cat on Chris's shoulder. "Hey, where'd you get the neat cat?" He came over, picked it up, and draped it over his own shoulder like burping a baby. To Stiles's surprise, the feline didn't react as it had with the children earlier. She cuddled against the boy's neck, her motor running in high gear.

"She's not mine," Stiles shrugged. "In fact, I think she's up for adoption. Interested?"

The boy's face lit up. "Are you serious?" He held her up and rubbed noses with her, and Stiles delighted in the sound of his laughter. "Wait till Mom sees this!" He hurried inside with his purring cargo, followed by most of the others present.

Hubert, Jessie, and the deputy were left on the porch with Stiles, and each pulled up a chair. Charlie dropped into his like a pile of bricks, but the seniors showed little of his weariness. Indeed, they were still moving even at rest, checking their guns, rechecking them, fidgeting uneasily with years and years of pent-up nervous energy. Stiles wagered that when the trucks rolled again, they would be the first ones back on board.

"So," he said, "what have you been doing with the bodies?"

Bean pointed just beyond the corner of the house. A thin ribbon of smoke curled into the sky above the treetops. "The city dump," he said. "We've burned 'em all. We aren't taking any chances."

Stiles nodded solemnly. "You know," he said, "sooner or later somebody's going to check this place out, like the county sheriff or the state police."

Bean sighed. "I know. I thought I'd beat them to the punch and call 'em first, right after the next hunt."

"What will you say?"

He shrugged. "Ain't decided. I'm too tired to think about it right now. Who knows, maybe the truth."

"Well, one thing's for sure," Stiles sighed. "I can't be here when they arrive. I'll help you make another pass through the town, and then I'll have to disappear for a—"

"You're leaving?" It was Billie, standing in the doorway. Del and the cat were right behind her, peeking around. She had a strange look on her face. Disappointment, perhaps. Maybe a little fear.

"I have to, Bill. They can't find me here."

"Why the rush?" Charlie asked. "You aren't wanted for anything." He added with a sheepish grin, "I had you checked out when you came to town. You're clean."

"But I am conspicuous. I'm a stranger, and when I came to town people started dying. You think they'll just let me go? Or will they grill the hell out of me, ask a lot of questions I can't answer?"

Billie took Del by the shoulders and walked with him out onto the porch. "Then we'll go with you."

He shook his head. "You can't, Billie. Not now." She looked away. "Don't you see? They'll want to talk to you, all of you. They'll want to know what you did, what you saw, about Bart . . . Especially about Bart. You can't run now. You'd be just as suspicious as me."

She wouldn't look at him. "So, you go and we stay, huh? Well, I guess that's that. Maybe we'll see you around sometime. C'mon, Del, back inside—"

"Wait a minute."

She looked back at him hopefully.

It would be easiest, he thought. *Let her go. Sever the ties here and now and go your own way, because you know what's hap-*

pened in the past. The Enemy's still out there, somewhere, and one morning you'll wake up and there'll be that premonition gnawing at the back of your neck and you'll have to go. No questions, no excuses, you'll just go.

It would be easiest . . .

He went to her and took her face in his hands and kissed her. Not a goodbye kiss—she sensed that right off. Her moist eyes brightened as he asked, "Where was it your parents live?"

"Ellettsville."

He considered it. "You know, I've always wanted to see that town. Uh . . . where the hell is it?" She laughed and threw her arms around his middle and hugged him tight. Stiles just wheezed uncomfortably and didn't remind her of his ribs. Hell, even the pain felt good for once.

"Now that that's settled," Hubert said, hoisting a shotgun in one hand and the Heckler & Koch in the other, "don't you think we've got work to be done? We may've got most of 'em that last trip, but I'm antsy to make sure."

"I'm with Hubert," Jessie said, tying a scarf on her head so her hair wouldn't blow. She slipped her purse off her shoulder and poked around inside until she found another full magazine, and she slammed it into the Uzi pistol and chambered a round. "Let's go kick some ass." She giggled and elbowed the big black man in the ribs as they went down the porch steps. "You know, I've always wanted to say that."

Epilogue

➢

It was early Friday morning in Bedford, just past 2:30 A.M., but few were sleeping. How could they, what with Death Town, USA located just so many miles down Highway 50? There had been little to allay their fears of the past week: the news agencies couldn't wring a story from the state police or even the FBI for that matter, and that left only the rumor mills to quench the public thirst. Some said a satanic cult had taken over the neighboring town, sacrificing the citizens in ways too hideous for mass consumption on the evening news. Or maybe it was a chemical spill that caused it, or a leak of biological weapons from Crane Naval Base, or maybe a hundred other doomsday scenarios. Before long Isherwood would be a dumping ground for PCBs and nuclear waste and crashed alien ships and God knows what else.

There was one man in Bedford who knew the truth. He stood in front of the new all-night convenience store on the main turnoff from SR37, holding the pay phone to his ear but calling no one. He waited. And he watched. He was bundled in an overcoat he had stolen from a car earlier, though not because he was cold, and the knit cap he wore was less to warm his ears than to cover the bullet holes in his forehead and keep that ornery flap of scalp from coming loose and blowing away in the breeze. Every few minutes Dutch Larson would creep over and peek through the big bay windows of the convenience store like a child at a candy shop, and his mouth would water at the sight.

There was someone in there. A human—alive, warm, luscious . . . full. He felt a knot of excitement in his gut. It had been days since he'd fed well, since he'd tasted human blood. Cows and hogs were loathsome to him but had sustained him for the past two nights. He'd been on the run constantly since he'd left Isherwood and bypassed the cordon of crosses. Hounded by that bastard Charlie Bean and his stake-wielding posse. It was all he could do to stay hidden, let alone find prey. But tonight . . . it finally appeared to be blowing over. He hadn't felt anyone on his trail since rising, and it was a good thing. The hunger within was now a raging need, all-encompassing. It would have brought him out this night, regardless.

He looked around him and made sure the area was deserted, the parking lot, the street. Then he sauntered along the big display windows of the convenience store and peered longingly inside.

There was a boy perched on a high stool behind the checkout counter, nursing a Cherry Coke and lost in a comic book he'd borrowed from the rack a few aisles over. He was a tall, skinny kid barely out of his teens, his face still plagued by a complexion he could've grated cheese on. To make matters worse, he celebrated his rebellious lifestyle by wearing a shirt that read, SHUT UP AND SUCK THIS, and by shaving the sides of his head and letting the rest grow long and wild like a horse's mane. Freedom of appearance was one of the few perks of the graveyard shift.

Larson considered waiting. It was logically the best strategy. Sooner or later someone would come along, a carload of teenagers cruising the town or an addled housewife who'd forgotten the cat food and a quart of milk at the Kroger store earlier in the day. If he was patient, someone would come, and he could take them out there on the sidewalk and he wouldn't have to worry about being invited in. But like all of his thoughts these days, the idea just came and went. He did not retain much; memories and ideas and emotions all eddied through his brain as they never had in life, unimpeded now as they had been by acculturation and his own close-mindedness. But the gray matter that his thoughts passed through was dead now, no more than a gravel bed for his stream of consciousness. Some things were retained and acted on from time to time, but only if triggered by that feral cell that ruled him. The hunger was all-important. The hunger was what drove him. As it always would. And right now it saw the young cashier and it said it must have him. Period.

He walked to the door and rapped on the glass with a dirty fist several times before the boy glanced up from his comic. "What is it?"

"Let me in."

"The door's open."

He hit the glass harder. "I said let me in, prick."

The cashier sneered and shook his head. "Goddamn drunk," he grumbled under his breath and turned his back to the door.

Larson shook with frustration. He could shatter the window if he wanted, but that still wouldn't gain him entrance. Not unless invited. But how could he be asked in looking like he did, shot up, torn, leaking—a barely disguised nightmare. He sagged against the door, trembling like an addict . . . and the door swung inward with him. The small bell above it dinged, and he was partway across the threshold before he realized it. But how? he wondered. Then he saw the big orange sign taped to the glass just above waist level. WELCOME, it read. COME ON IN.

Larson grinned. He pushed the door open all the way.

The young man at the register saw him enter from the corner of his eye. *Oh, great*, he thought, *just what I needed, another slobbering, shit-faced drunk*. "The beer's at the far end, pal," he gestured without looking up. *Maybe he'll just get a twelve-pack and go*, he hoped. But the man came to the counter instead. The boy sighed and looked up from *The Incredible Hulk*. "What's the problem? I said the beer's at the . . ."

The face was fish white. Part of a puckered bullet wound was evident beneath the edge of the cap and the nose was mashed flat and the smile showed a mouthful of teeth, some broken at the gum, others impossibly long. "I don't drink . . . beer," Dutch wheezed. Then he grabbed the boy by the hair and jerked him up onto the counter and slammed a hammy fist into the side of the cashier's head once, twice until he slumped there, moaning, barely able to move. Dutch hit him a few more times just for spite.

The hunger welled up immediately. Larson's head swam and he wanted to take the boy on the countertop right there and then—that neck was so long, so soft, and he could almost see the blood coarsing even through the skin, and the sound of it thundered in his ears—but he fought it, if only for a few moments more. He had the presence of mind to remove himself from the view of the world and those damn big windows. He went behind the counter out of sight and crouched down there, then dragged the boy off into his lap. No one would see them now, he thought. He brushed the hair from that ripe throat . . .

A car door slammed. It sounded very close, just outside even. Larson flinched, his fangs bared territorially, but then it occurred to him. Customers—his meals were coming to him now. He smacked his lips with glee and waited for the bell above the door to ring.

It didn't. He waited a little longer. Still nothing. They must have been using the phone, yeah, that was it. And if he moved quickly enough, he could catch them, too. He laid the cashier aside and raised up from behind the counter.

The front door was just swinging shut, though the bell still had yet to sound. And parked just outside the store, in plain view, was a new model van he hadn't seen before. But a van nonetheless.

No . . . it couldn't be . . .

There was a sound to his right. A conspicuous clearing of the throat. He turned as if in slow motion, catching a silvery flash as the overhead lights reflected off moving steel. Then he saw the soldier's face, the lips pursed but still half-smirking, and Dutch tried to curse the son of a bitch but found his vocal chords suddenly no longer connected. Neither was his larynx or esophagus or even his spinal column for that matter. The sword blade had passed cleanly through, separating all. His head kept on turning and slid forward off its base as if never truly attached, bounced once, and rolled into the open. The body joined it a moment later.

Stiles wiped the katana blade on Larson's scroungy coat and resheathed it, then went back to the counter and checked the almost-victim. The young man was just trying to sit up, and his eyes were spinning like pinwheels. "Are you okay?"

The kid blinked his eyes painfully, spat a tooth onto his lap. "I think so." He grabbed for the counter for support and pulled himself up. "Jeez, what was . . ." and that was when he saw the body. He looked to Stiles and back, his mouth moving but unable to form words, then made a gagging sound in his throat and turned just in time to fill the trash basket behind the counter. "Oh, man, this ain't happening . . ." he muttered, panting. He took another peek at the body and the retching continued.

"You sure you're okay, kid?"

The boy looked up at him, trembling. "Wha . . . what are you gonna do?"

The soldier looked around. "Oh, I don't know. I thought I might pick up a few things while I'm here. Do you mind?"

The boy laid a grocery sack on the counter and backed away. "Knock yourself out."

Stiles wandered down one or two aisles, humming to himself and filling his bag with canned goods and candy bars. When he came back toward the register, he stopped for a moment at the tobacco display. "What the hell," he said, signaling the end to another hunt by picking up two cartons of Vantage menthols. He took the time there to open a pack and light one up. "Nasty habit, huh?" he said, savoring the taste just the same. Then he sat the bag on the counter. "How much do I owe you?"

The boy backed away from the register. "Nothing, mister, nothing. It's on the house."

Stiles grinned. "Thanks a lot." He picked up his groceries, stepped over Larson's carcass, and went to the door. But he paused there a last time and turned to look at the boy. "You know what he was, don't you?"

The kid gulped, nodded. "I think so." He looked at the headless corpse again, stifling his nausea. "What should I do with him?"

The soldier shrugged. "I don't think he'll bother you. But then again, you can't be too careful." He motioned to the tobacco section, where the Red Devil lighter fluid lined the top shelf. Then he gave a smile and a wink. "Have a nice night." And then he was gone, the door chime tinkling behind him.

He went to the van and got in, propping his sword against the console. He silently thanked Hubert again; his gift had been perfect for "doing" Dutch. Decapitation made sure he wouldn't be coming back yet again, and it was swift and silent and didn't attract attention like a gunshot. Besides, it wasn't nearly as conspicuous. He could hang it on the wall of his van in plain view with little worry, unlike the two Remington scatterguns

Charlie had insisted he take. They were bundled in the back with his other guns and supplies, and he would have to devise hiding places for them all very soon. Until then, he would have to keep his speed well below the limit. He couldn't afford to attract attention.

He sat there in the driver's seat with the key in his hand and smiled without realizing it. He was thinking of Billie. It had been only two days, and yet he missed her and Del already. He wondered if they were still being detained in Isherwood, or if they would be waiting on him when he pulled into Ellettsville.

"Stop dreaming and put the key in. We don't have all night."

The voice actually took Stiles by surprise. He jolted in his seat and fumbled for his shoulder holster but by then the familiar monotone had sunk in. Alex was crouched in the back of the van, clothed in his normal wardrobe of shadow. "You know, Hoss, you were pretty good with the sword in there. I'm impressed. Now, can we get going before the cops come?"

Chris sighed with resignation. "I didn't know you were coming this time. No premonition or anything."

Alex came to the front of the van and climbed into the passenger seat. The lights of the storefront showed more of him than Chris had seen for some time. Thankfully it was his better side. "I didn't know I was coming either. I just thought, what the hell, you know? We don't talk much anymore." He gestured to the ignition. "You know, if you turn the key, the motor will go vroom, vroom."

"You could have at least given me time to rest, Alex," Chris snapped, irritated. So the hunt was back on already, destination unknown. In his mind, he could see Billie and Del getting farther and farther away. He wondered what they would think when he didn't show up at her parents.

Maybe it's for the best.

He started the van. "So? Where's the Enemy this time?"

Alex shrugged. "The hell if I know."

Chris looked at him suspiciously. "What? Are you saying you don't have a job for me?"

"Not yet. The trail's pretty cold at the moment. It might be a while till something turns up."

"Then what are you doing here?"

The phantom turned toward him, and the light played on the

mutilated countenance with its torn muscle and glaring bone. But that's not what Chris saw. To him, it was Alex for a change, really Alex. His brother. "Didn't you hear what I said, Hoss? I came to talk. We haven't done that for a while, and I thought . . . Now what are you grinning about?"

"Nothing," Chris said, his expression broadening into a smile. He popped John Prine into the cassette deck as he steered the van out onto the road and headed toward the highway. It would take them to Bloomington. Ellettsville wasn't much further than that.

Behind them, the store windows lit up with a dancing orange glow.

INCARNATE

Ramsey Campbell

The horror began when an experiment in prophetic dreaming got wildly out of control. It was instantly shut down – but not before some dark door a shadow-world of nightmare had been opened . . . and left ajar.

INCARNATE

Eleven years later, as bitter winter holds the country in its steely grip, a monstrous presence starts to invade the lives of the original participants. Creatures glimpsed fleetingly in the group dream are drawing them into a dreadful vortex of hallucination, insanity – and worse. And one by one the dreamers succumb to the diabolical force that threatens more than their mere lives . . .

INCARNATE

'An important, scary, involving novel . . . I had to fight with myself every time circumstances forced me to put it down'
Peter Straub

'Insidiously clever . . . far more disturbing than mere blood and guts . . . It leaves you with the feeling of having woken from a deliciously creepy nightmare'
Time Out

'A tour de force of shifting perspectives . . . A profoundly disturbing, intellectually stimulating book'
The Penguin Encyclopaedia of Horror and the Supernatural

FUTURA PUBLICATIONS
FICTION
0 7088 4359 6

INTERVIEW WITH THE VAMPIRE

Anne Rice

In a darkened room a young man sits telling the macabre and eerie story of his life . . . the story of a vampire, gifted with eternal life, cursed with an exquisite craving for human blood.

'The most seductive evocation of evil I have ever read. It is enthralling'
Detroit Free Press

'A supernatural thriller raised to the level of literature'
Philadelphia Inquirer

'A spine-chilling nightmare . . . highly accomplished . . . an impressive feat of imagination'
Sunday Times

'A voluptuous dream'
Boston Globe

'Compulsively readable . . . From the beginning we are hypnotised . . . The reader feels he has glimpsed experiences no mortal ever has'
Chicago Tribune

'Thrilling . . . A strikingly original work of the imagination . . . Sometimes horrible, sometimes beautiful, always unforgettable'
Washington Post

FUTURA PUBLICATIONS
FICTION
0 8600 7539 7

THE VIOLET CLOSET

Gary Gottesfeld

A terrified young voice cries out from the dark.

"Da hurt . . . Da kill . . . Help me!"

These are the panic-stricken words of a little girl phoning in to Dr Rena Halbrook's radio show. But who is little Alice – and where is she?

As Charles Halleran, veteran reporter, hears the child's plea over his car radio, he recalls another little girl named Alice who died in New York 18 years before. Can there possibly be a connection?

As the anniversary of that shocking death approaches, Charles teams up with Rena in a desperate search to uncover dark secrets from the past and prevent almost certain tragedy from striking again.

Their race against time will lead them on a spine-tingling chase from the placid streets of Beverly Hills to the burnt-out tenements of the South Bronx. And the more they discover, the surer they become that what they still don't know could definitely hurt them . . .

FUTURA PUBLICATIONS
FICTION
0 7088 4550 1